The Silver Lake

Also by
FIONA PATTON

The Novels of the Branion Realm:

THE STONE PRINCE
THE PAINTER KNIGHT
THE GRANITE SHIELD
THE GOLDEN SWORD

The
Silver Lake

Book One of
The Warriors of Estavia

FIONA PATTON

DAW BOOKS, INC.

DONALD A. WOLLHEIM, FOUNDER
375 Hudson Street, New York, NY 10014
ELIZABETH R. WOLLHEIM
SHEILA E. GILBERT
PUBLISHERS
http://www.dawbooks.com

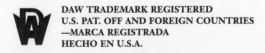

For my sister Isabelle, for the years together.

Acknowledgments

The author would like to thank Ozan Yigit and Ihsan Pala for sharing their wonderful stories and memories of Turkey which helped Anavatan come alive, and Shihan Kenzo Dozono of the Belleville Karate School for his wisdom and training.

ANAVATAN AND THE LAKE OF POWER
IN THE AGE OF CREATION AND DESTRUCTION

VOLINSK

DENIZ-SIYAH SEA

BARACHOIS

GOL-BARDAK

BOGAZI-ISIK STRAIT

HALIC-
SALMANAK

CALMAK-KOY

ANAVATAN

THE
BERBAT-DUNYA
WILDLANDS

THE
DEGISKEN
MOUNTAINS

GOL-BEYAZ
LAKE

YILDIZ-KOY

ADASI-KOY

SERIN-KOY

ORZIN-HISAR

CAMUS-KOY

THE
GURNEY-DAG
MOUNTAINS

KAPI-HISAR
CALISKAN-KOY

N

ANAHTAR-HISAR
SATOS-KOY

ITHOS

THASOS

DENIZ-HADI SEA

SKIROS

AMATUS

AHM/05

I

Anavatan

To come upon Anavatan, City of the Gods, from the south is to make a peaceful and leisurely journey up the shining Gol-Beyaz Lake, past its twelve prosperous villages, to the bustling wharves of the city's Temple Precinct. To come upon Anavatan from the north, however, is to make the more dramatic voyage. The dark and narrow Bogazi-Isik Strait with its three massive watchtowers gives over to the bare cliffs of the Degisken-Dag Mountains to the east and to the high walls of the city proper to the west. Statues of Anavatan's six Immortal Patrons, formed from multicolored marbles drawn up from the lake bed, stand sentinel along the wall, marking the position of each of its great temples. Estavia, crimson-eyed midnight God of Battles, points Her silver swords both north and west, blue-painted Usara, God of Healing, reaches out to any who might need His skills while icy-pale Incasa, God of Prophecy, oldest and most mysterious of all the Gods, holds a pair of opalescent dice in one hand as if He were about to hurl them into the waters of Gol-Beyaz for good or for ill. Oristo, ruddy-brown, bi-gender God of Hearth and Home, carried a flaming torch in one hand and a loaf of bread in the other, while many-colored Ystazia, God of the Arts, holds a fine reed pipe to Her lips, and finally, leaf-green and earth-brown Havo, bi-gender God of Seasonal Bounty, looks out upon the fields and orchards along the western shores of Gol-Beyaz.

It's said that to feel the Gods' touch is to be blessed beyond words, but to earn Their love is to be cursed for They're both fickle and dangerous.

—Anise Rostov, 11th Duc of Volinsk

"The life of a God is inexplicable even to Its most intimate followers. Its birth however, is more easily definable and by its very nature, violent. Its midwives would do well to remember this."

—The Chronicles of Anavatan: City of the Gods.
Book twenty-eight: The Age of Creation and Destruction.
By: Ihsan, First Scribe to Ystazia, God of the Arts

"Gods are big, and They'll do you if you let Them."

—Found scrawled on a Western Trisect pier,
author unknown

THE singing began just before dawn. From the hundred lofty minarets which graced the skyline of the capital city to the nine village towers which guarded Gol-Beyaz, the priests of Havo gathered to call forth the sun for another day. As their joined voices rose, the shadows which had been building in every corner like heavy spiderwebbing grudgingly withdrew. But they did not vanish. The rising wind and the heavy, concealing bank of storm clouds which had brought them from the western wild lands of the Berbat-Dunya plains whispered to them of power and potential and they stirred hungrily, impatient for the coming of night.

The strength of their desire sent ripples of disquiet through Gol-Beyaz, disturbing the vision-filled slumber of Incasa, pale-haired God of Prophecy and Probability. A frown marring the smooth perfection of His features, He opened His snow-white eyes to stare into the depths. Something was happening. Raising one delicate, fine-boned hand, He blew a line of icy breath across the pair of opalescent dice nestled in His palm, then flung them into the waters.

A dozen rippling streams formed in their wake, each one leading to a single, familiar destination and Incasa bared His silvery-white teeth in displeasure. Three times before, the shadowy spirits of the Berbat-Dunya had risen to challenge the supremacy of the Gods, and three times before they'd been defeated so utterly that their shattered potential had been re-formed to Incasa's own desire without a flicker of resistance. And so it would be again. The great wall of stone and power erected about Gol-Beyaz when its twelve villages had been in their infancy was still strong and the champions who kept it so had been in place for more than a millennium. The spirits could not win through, not now, not ever.

As if in agreement, a cold breath of wind scored the surface of the lake and Incasa smiled. It was the final day of Low Spring, the final day before Usara, God of Healing, gave dominion over the land to Havo who heralded the coming of High Spring with three nights of violent wind, rain, and hailstorms, known as Havo's Dance. Nothing stirred when the God of Wind and Rain wreaked havoc above the world; nothing the spirits of the wild lands could lay claim to or draw strength from. With a flick of His hand, Incasa swept the streams aside, then returned to His slumber in the depths of Gol-Beyaz, secure in His power and in His defenses.

✦

Once free from His regard, the spirits crept forward to gather about a single, fragile stream sparkling like a line of tiny raindrops on the dark streets of Anavatan; a line so small it had been missed by the God of Prophecy; a line that relied upon a single, desperate decision, yet unmade, to take form. Rustling excitedly in their nest of shadows, the spirits peered up at the ones who might make that decision, knowing, as Incasa did, that such things could not be forced, they could only be manipulated. But during Havo's violent Dance above the capital a great many manipulations might be possible and a great many decisions made by those who held the true power in the City of the Gods.

✦

Above them, two boys, one dark-haired, the other blond, crouched on a dilapidated rooftop in Anavatan's western dockyards, unaware of the battle about to be fought on the streets of their city, watching as the sun struggled to breach the heavy bank of clouds on the horizon. As a single shaft of light broke free to bathe their faces in a pale saffron glow, the younger of the two boys dropped his gaze to the dark drifts of shadow clinging to the buildings like moss. They seemed to stare back at him. He shivered and the older boy's head snapped around at once.

"You all right, Spar?"

He gave a distracted nod.

"You sure?"

"I'm just cold, Brax," he answered vaguely, his blue eyes unusually pale.

The older boy frowned. "You need a new jacket; the winter really did that one in. Hey, maybe if you look really sick today Usara's lot'll give you a new one." Spar shot him a cynical glance and he snickered. "Right, the God Himself's as likely to give you a golden cloak as His priests are to give you anything more useful than a packet of moldy powder today. Piss-heads." He spat, then made himself smile reassuringly. "But don't worry, all right? We'll get you one." After Spar nodded, he returned his gaze to the horizon, taking in a deep breath of the chilly, predawn air. "Looks like the rain's gonna keep on," he observed. "You might figure that'd keep people inside, but a hailstorm of snakes and lizards wouldn't stop half the city from jamming into Usara's temples today, would it? Not with all that free . . ." he paused dramatically, ". . . *medicine* just lying around for the taking."

He laughed at his own joke as Spar gave a very unchildlike snort in reply. On the last morning of Low Spring, the priests of Usara traditionally doled out free advice and medicines to the poor. Or rather, emptied their cabinets and trunks of all the leftover stale herbs and rancid salves that were no longer worth the exorbitant prices they charged. But even knowing that, Usara's temple courtyards would be bursting with people today, the poor and the not so poor alike, all pushing and shoving and fighting for their share of the Healer God's charity.

And none of them paying enough attention to their own pockets.

"Still, you gotta watch it," Brax continued, the predatory gleam in his eyes replaced by an expression of caution. "Greedy people are careless, but they're also really ugly if they catch you lifting their shine, so you gotta be careful and you gotta be fast. Use the crowds; keep hidden."

Spar nodded absently.

"An' Cindar'll want us at the dockside Usara-Cami this morning," Brax continued. "That'll help. The pickings won't be so rich as at the bigger temples but there'll be a lot more people and a lot fewer guards." Cocking his head to catch the faint sounds of snoring coming through the broken shutters behind them, he grimaced. "If Cindar *ever* wakes up," he added with a sneer.

Spar rolled his eyes in agreement. Cindar was their abayos, a lake-side village word that had come to mean either parent, employer, or one who acted as guardian in exchange for service as delinkon—apprentices—in this case two undersized children able to maneuver through the city's crowded marketplaces without being detected. Cindar had taken Spar in five years ago when Brax had grown too big to squeeze through the narrow windows and openings their profession demanded. Slight, quiet, and small, he usually distracted their potential victims while Brax and Cindar cut their purses or robbed their stalls by day, and acted as a lookout while they plundered local businesses and warehouses by night. They were a team, a family, and as long as each one of them did his part, a successful one.

Now Brax interrupted his reverie with an inquisitive noise. "So, what do you figure?" he asked. "Is it safe to go, or will the Battle God's arse-pickers be out nosing for a quick snatch today?"

Spar considered the question seriously despite the older boy's scornful remarks. The city garrisons that patrolled Anavatan's streets were the traditional soldiers of Estavia, God of Battles, and although the best and the brightest of them served at Her main temple, those that were left were still a force to be reckoned with. Brax knew this, whatever he might say, but what he didn't know was whether they'd be a force to be reckoned with *today*. And Spar would. Although five years younger than the fourteen-year-old Brax, the older boy always asked him what he thought—what he *felt*—before making any decision because Spar *knew* things. He could sense a patrol coming within half a mile and he often dreamed of dangers that came true later. And although Cindar would be sure to ask him, too, Cindar drank, and so every morning Brax and Spar came up here to watch the dawn sun paint the city streets with orange fire and get a feel for the day's trade. It wouldn't be the first time Brax had refused to follow some raki-addled plan of Cindar's because of what Spar had said up here and it likely wouldn't be the last time either.

But not today. Spar shrugged in response to Brax's impatient cough. Despite his earlier disquiet, he couldn't sense any immediate danger around the morning's trade other than the usual hazards in picking pockets inside a God's temple courtyard, but the risks there were actually pretty small. They were unsworn, among the very few—mostly poorer—citizens in the City of the Gods who refused to worship any of its six divine patrons and so the three of them could plunder an entire temple and it would be the fault of the sworn for not guarding it properly. If Brax and Cindar wanted to rob Usara's prayer niches this morning; Spar would help them unhook the wall lamps; it was all the same to him. As long as it felt safe. And it did. Mostly. There was something happening on the very edge of his senses, something dark and frightening, but it was not happening today. When it did, he'd be ready for it.

A crash behind him interrupted his thoughts and a familiar voice slurred by sleep and drink shouted out a string of incoherent curses before finally making sense.

"Brax! Spar! Where the . . . get in here!"

Shaking his head, Brax stood. "The way he was pourin' it down his throat last night, I figured he'd be out for at least another half an hour," he said in disgust as he pushed open the dilapidated shutters. "Good thing we lifted the last of his shine early, yeah?" With a grin, he tossed Spar one of the two copper aspers he'd taken from Cindar's purse before throwing a leg over the windowsill. "We're done here anyway, right?"

Spar nodded slowly.

"Good, then. C'mon, before he shouts himself into a fit."

Together, they returned inside as, across the city, Havo's Invocation song ended and Oristo's began.

✦

By the time they reached the small, second-floor room they shared with their abayos, Cindar was up and trying with little success to scrape the last four days' worth of stubble off his face, his hands shaking visibly. He was not a tall man, but he still towered over the two boys. He had Brax's dark hair and eyes, a pockmarked, dissipated face, and a twisted, poorly healed scar that ran along one corner of his mouth where a garrison guard's spear had caught him last summer as he'd come out of a silver smithy late one night. His eyes were red-rimmed and deeply suspicious, but when Brax held out his hand for the knife, he grudgingly gave it up.

"Don't think this means squat," he growled as he dropped heavily on the lumpy pallet behind him. "I can still outlift either one of you any buggerin' day of any buggerin' God's month you can name."

"Not if you slit your own throat first," Brax sneered back at him as he began to carefully scrape the coarse, curly hair from the man's cheeks. "Why're you botherin' with this anyway?" he asked.

Cindar spat a gob of spittle at the wall. "We gotta look respectable, don't we?" he growled in reply. "Poor but respectable, so those second-rate butchers at Usara-Cami'll give us what we want and don't go reporting me to the buggerin' priests of Oristo just because you two ain't eating offa golden plates."

Seated by the room's tiny, dirt-encrusted window, Spar rolled his eyes. The priests of Oristo were the self-appointed guardians of the young in Anavatan and the priests of the Dockside Precinct where they made their home were particularly aggressive in their duty. They knew about Cindar's profession and they disapproved of it, and although they'd never been able to gather up enough proof to send the Battle God's garrisons after him, that didn't stop them from making daily attempts to convince him to surrender his delinkon into their keeping. But Cindar had been brought up by Oristo's abayos-priests himself and had raised Brax and Spar to despise the yellow-clad Protectorates that huddled in the Hearth God's temple, trading menial labor for flatbread and boza, a thick, brownish drink made of fermented wheat. He'd raised them to hate the priests they served as well.

"There's no greater pack of hypocrites in Anavatan than Oristo's bloody lot," he snarled, warming up to his topic. "Sure, they may talk high and fine, but they don't give a rat's arse for the poor; they only care for what they can squeeze out of them." He glowered at Brax. "No self-respecting thief would ever serve a priest, and don't you forget it. You wouldn't be in their tender care for five minutes before you'd be breaking your back for them. And as for Spar, they'd sell him to the God of Prophecy's white-eyed lunatics at Incasa-Sarayi in a heartbeat if they ever found out what he could do for them. They'd addle his brains with their seeking so fast he'd go mad from the strain before he was old enough for you to shave *him*, if they even let you near him. So you keep your mouths shut today, both of you, 'cause Usara's so-called physicians are no better; charlatans and thieves every last one of them. They're only giving away free medicines so they can spy on us."

He shook a finger at Spar who was, as usual, ignoring him. Cindar could rave for hours about his opinion of the Gods and their temples and had done it so many times before that Spar was bored by it.

"Well, piss on them if they are," Brax retorted, allowing the effect of Cindar's words to drive him to angry bravado despite Spar's warning glance. "The day we can't outrun those fat farts is the day you deserve to be reported." He frowned suddenly. "An' I'll report you myself if we don't eat soon."

He moved to work on Cindar's other cheek as the man answered his threat with a sideways scowl from beneath his heavy, black brows, but then jerked his head at a small, cloth-wrapped bundle by the side of the pallet, ignoring Brax's curse as he almost took off an eyebrow. "So eat," he snarled.

Spar pounced on the bundle at once.

"Havo's Dance tonight," Cindar continued grimly as the younger boy tossed Brax half the day-old flat bread inside. "Don't hog it all! That's for the three of us!"

"You sure your stomach's up to it?" Brax asked pointedly and, as Cindar's face paled in remembered nausea, he wolfed down his share of the bread with a smirk.

"Like I said," Cindar continued darkly. "Havo's Dance starts tonight, and it looks to be a messy one this year, so we'd best finish our business up early and get under cover before those filthy little life-sucking shadows show up. You know what they do to the unsworn."

Spar stilled a sudden shudder and Cindar shot him a hard-eyed look.

"What?" he demanded.

He shook his head, but Cindar caught him by the arm, giving him a penetrating stare.

"You sure? You look like you just tramped over your own grave. Or mine." He shook him. "Well, did you?"

"He's just cold," Brax interrupted, his voice suddenly low and dangerous. "He needs a new jacket."

"So do I," Cindar retorted, shooting the older boy a withering glance, despite the knife perilously close to his throat. "Do your job today and we might both get one; otherwise you'll just have to give him yours."

The two of them glared at each other for a long moment and then

Brax gave a stiff nod before he returned to his task. "Fair enough," he answered.

Mollified, Cindar allowed a sour smile to cross his ravaged features as he released Spar's arm. "Whatever happens, Usara's powders oughta get us enough for one decent meal tonight if nothing else, eh, youngling? He ruffled Spar's hair in a gruff apology for his rough handling. "Then it's three nights off to sleep warm and sleep late." He turned, risking the other eyebrow. "Aren't you done yet?" he demanded querulously.

"Just." Brax returned the knife to him and Cindar ran a hand along his cheeks with an appreciative expression, his mood lightening as quickly as it had darkened. "You get caught someday, Delin," he said making use of the rarely spoken endearment, "and you can always beg off time by becoming the prison barber." He stood, then grinned wickedly as he saw that his hands had stopped shaking "Like I said," he repeated, aiming a fake punch at Brax's head, "I can still outlift either one of you any buggerin' day of any buggerin' God's month you can name. Now c'mon, before the crowds thin out."

He headed for the door. Glancing at Spar, Brax made an obscene gesture behind Cindar's back, then, as the younger boy snickered, followed him out with a mock swagger. Alone, Spar's eyes paled slightly as he scanned the room, then fished a copper asper out from beneath the pallet, schooling his expression as Brax turned back with an inquisitive look.

"You coming?"

The younger boy nodded. "I am now."

✦

The air was still cold and the cobblestones laced with uncharacteristic frost as they made their way along the wide dockside market streets already crowded with people despite the early hour. Cindar strode on ahead, seemingly oblivious to the two boys doing their best to keep up with him, but every now and then, he shot a glance back at Spar to make sure he hadn't vanished. Spar smiled slyly. Brax had once accused him of taking the piss on their abayos, but even he kept an eye on him. If the younger boy went to ground, whatever the reason, Brax went with him. For the moment, however, Spar was content to trot along behind Cindar with an even expression. The sense of unease, or rather, uncertainty, he amended, was still with him, but now he could feel that it had nothing to do with the morning's plan. It was more like a vague sense of . . . maybe-ness, he thought for want of a better word, hovering off behind the clouds. Probably nothing more than a warning that the rains would come early like Brax had said they would and they'd get soaked before the day was done. It had been an unusually cold Low Spring, and High Spring looked to start just as miserably.

Passing Oristo-Cami with its high, wrought-iron fence, vast sweeping cinar trees, and tall, ruddy-brown painted statues of the bi-gender Hearth God, Cindar favored the abayos-priest frowning down at them from the top step with a scowl of his own and the sense of unease suddenly returned. Spar's chest tightened, afraid that Cindar would start into his usual tirade—this close to any temple it was never a good idea—but instead he just turned the corner, leaving the woman unengaged, and Spar breathed a sigh of relief as the unease passed.

Beside him, he felt Brax relax as well. When a heavyset brush merchant arguing with his own delinkos, a thin, gangly youth overladen with packages, pushed past them, the older boy gave them a speculative glance, but allowed them to pass unmolested. Spar nodded his approval. Brax was a good thief—Cindar said he could lift the nectar from a hummingbird's beak without it feeling his fingers when he put his mind to it—but he was also reckless and impatient. There'd be plenty of pickings at Usara-Cami later; there was no point in running any risks before that. Spar was relieved that both Brax and Cindar seemed to agree with him this morning. It wasn't their trade that put them in danger of being snatched by either the priests of Oristo or the garrisons of Estavia; he thought, it was Cindar's temper and Brax's overconfident bravado. Without him to watch their backs, they probably would have been either snatched or stiffed a long time ago.

A chill breeze drove its fingers through his threadbare jacket and he acknowledged the random admonishment with a silent nod. Without *them*, he probably would have starved, he admitted. Maybe. Remembering the extra asper in his pocket, he gave a faint snort. And then again, maybe not. With a smirk, he hurried to catch up with the others as they headed for the dozen blue-and-white banners that fluttered above the treetops at Usara-Cami.

They reached the God of Healing's Dockside subtemple a few moments later. In keeping with tradition, it was no more than a single story high and built around a central, hexagonal courtyard lined with great cinar trees, but its fine twisting minarets were as tall as those at the main temple of Usara-Sarayi and its high stone walls, carved to resemble a delicate latticework of ivy and climbing rose vines, rivaled anything even the Art God's people could display.

A dozen junior physicians were already hard at work pushing several hundred people into lines based on obvious or not-so-obvious need when they arrived. After pausing to catch Spar up in his arms, Cindar took his place, exchanging mock pleasantries with a family of tinsmiths behind him while Spar leaned his head on his abayos' shoulder to watch, through half-lidded eyes, as Brax vanished into the crowd.

The sense of unease returned then, and he cast about worriedly, checking out those of Estavia's garrison that he could see. The Battle God's people knew full well why many of them were there and maintained a minimum of two troops in and around Usara's temples for that very reason. But each one of the leather-clad soldiers looked bored and disgruntled so, as a light misting of rain began to dampen his cheeks, he shook off the feeling. It was just the weather after all, he told himself firmly. Havo's Dance was scary enough without adding priests or Gods or garrison guards to the mix. Brax was good, so was Cindar; they'd make enough shine for a decent supper tonight—a shrimp pilaf or maybe even a lamb and walnut curry—then they'd all hole up until Havo's Dance blew the last shreds of Low Spring into the sea; the streets would fill up with the High Spring trade and the pickings would ripen; he'd get a new jacket, Cindar'd get a new jug of raki, and Brax would get . . . he frowned, well, Brax would get whatever it was that Brax wanted. Everything was going to go smoothly; he'd seen it; he'd done his job; now it was time for him to trust Brax to do his. Head pillowed against Cindar's ear, Spar closed his eyes, ignoring the unease that refused to be banished despite his reasoning, and made himself relax.

✦

Halfway across the courtyard already, Brax gave Spar and Cindar one last half glance before losing himself in the jostling crowds. He was glad to see that Spar was trying to get some sleep. He looked tired and pale this morning; the winter and Low Spring had taken as huge a toll on him as it had on his jacket. Frowning, Brax made a cursory inspection of the people around him even though he knew that particular task would have to wait. No one was going to lay a coat aside in this weather. If Spar was going to get a new one, Brax would either have to lift one off a clothier's stall for him—always a risk—or buy him one—always expensive—because he had no illusions that Cindar would do anything about it, the stinking tosspot.

"So get to work," he told himself sternly. Setting his features into an innocent expression of boredom, he began to weave a seemingly random pattern through the crowds, yet by the time he broke free a few minutes later, he'd already cut three purses. Grinning, he made his way up the temple's wide, marble steps. Cindar said he was one of the best young lifters along the docks. Brax knew better. He was only good; but part of being good was in knowing when to quit, or at least when to take a break so, once he reached the top, he paused, standing up on tiptoe as if searching the crowds for his companions, but really to check out the marble tributary statue of Usara that stood sentinel beside one of the city's largest and oldest cinar trees just before the entrance.

The great blue-painted figure of the male God of Healing had been carved holding a flowering staff in one hand while the other was held out at hip level. The number of coins lying in His deep, open palm was always a good indication of the prosperity of the day's crowd. Several glittered temptingly at him, but Brax was not so stupid as to try and lift any of them. There was always a delinkos hovering about to empty it as soon as it grew too full and he had no intention of getting snatched for lifting a God's tribute, no matter how little the God or His temple really needed it. Brax spotted the girl standing just inside the shadowy doorway easily enough but didn't bother to look her way, merely sat down beside the God's great feet and, ignoring her frown of disapproval, returned to the increasing problem of their abayos' neglect.

Brax had been with Cindar for as long as he could remember. He had no idea if the man had sired him any more than he knew who'd birthed him, but it didn't matter. Cindar kept them safe. More or less. And Brax was grateful. More or less.

Leaning his back against the statue, he closed his eyes. More or less was the problem. He was tired of living from lift to lift, never having enough clothes to keep him warm or enough food to fill his belly. The worst of it was that they should have had plenty of both, but ever since Cindar had nearly been snatched outside that silver smithy, he'd been drinking more and more of their shine away. He'd blamed Spar who'd been too sick to act as lookout that night. (Too sick because Cindar had refused to pay one of Usara's physician-priests to see him when he'd fallen and cut himself two days before. He'd nearly lost his leg and still favored it whenever he was tired or cold.) Brax's eyes narrowed as he remembered having to protect the feverish boy from their angry, blood-covered abayos. It was the closest Brax had ever come to knifing the man and Cindar'd known it. He'd backed off, but the next day he'd lost his temper at Brax outside a sandal maker's stall, and then again at Spar the day after right in front of a priest of Oristo. He was picking fights and take stupid risks. If he wasn't careful, he was going to get snatched, and Brax and Spar right along with him.

The boy ground his teeth in frustration. In two years' time he'd be a man and he and Spar could go out on their own, maybe cross the strait for the more lucrative pickings in the new foreign docks in the Northern Trisect, or even head south to the richly ornate commercial and religious wharves that serviced the Temple Precinct; both areas that Cindar's temper had denied them. They might even be able to buy themselves into legitimate apprenticeships as cutlers maybe or even vintners, and make enough shine to run a tavern or buy shares in a merchant ship going south to Thasos to trade for wine and oil or north across the sea to Volinsk for furs and gold. Anavatan was the largest and most prosperous city in the known world; there were hundreds of opportunities beyond those that a drunken lifter from the Western Dockside Precinct could give them.

But it was still risky, he cautioned himself. Spar would only be eleven years old, and Cindar would never willingly let Brax take him away. He'd come after them, and Brax wasn't sure he could protect them both if Cindar really lost his temper.

So just wait until the sodden arse-pick's falling down drunk, his mind supplied savagely. *Which these days is nearly all the time, anyway. If he comes after you then, you can just knock him on the head and pitch his body into the strait, and it would serve him right besides.*

Stop it.

Forcing himself to loosen fists suddenly clenched, Brax shook off the burst of anger. It didn't matter what they could do in two years' time; it only mattered what they could and couldn't do right now. And right now they couldn't leave because Spar, no matter how old he acted sometimes, wasn't ready.

Are you? his mind prodded.

He didn't know, he allowed, but he was ready for something. Lately he'd begun to feel restless and impatient, itchy even, and it wasn't head lice, he'd checked. Last week Cindar had said it was *urges* and suggested with a leer that he go give his virginity up to one of Ystazia's bawds—the Arts God's people were the most learned of all those involved in the sex trade—far better than Oristo's who had a habit of preaching afterward—but they also expected the greatest offering and, since Cindar hadn't *offered* to put up any shine to pay for it, Brax had approached another street thief, a fifteen-year-old girl named Tamas, and she'd taken it for free.

It hadn't helped. Well, not for long, he amended. He'd gone looking for her a few days later but found out she'd been snatched by the local garrison and had been given a choice: prison or the temple of Oristo. She'd chosen the temple, which had upset him more than he thought it should have. He'd have chosen prison.

If you don't get back to work, you won't even have that choice, his mind supplied again. *You'll end up at the temple because you'll all starve.*

Which was only the truth. Standing, he made a show of searching the crowds for his companions again, but really to see if any trade he was in the mood to exploit presented itself. He found what he was looking for fairly quickly: a well-dressed, well-fed apothecary's family pointedly haranguing a junior priest to hurry up and deal with the "riffraff" in front of them so that they might have their turn. With a hard smile, Brax jumped down from the dais and vanished into the crowds again, heading their way.

✦

He returned to Spar and Cindar just as they reached the head of the line. The physician-priest making a brief examination of the younger boy, listened with half her attention as Cindar outlined his ailments: rickets and scurvy this year—last year it had been consumption and strangulary. Harried skepticism was evident on her face but she spoke briefly to the young delinkos at her side who handed their abayos a small, cloth-wrapped package with the instructions to make an infusion of the contents twice daily.

Then Cindar caught him by the back of the jacket and it was his turn to be examined. Simple-minded, prone to fits, Cindar declared. Brax tried to look vacant-eyed and twitchy and their abayos was rewarded with a hard look but also another very small cloth bundle and the suggestion that they visit the Hearth God's temple if he was unable to keep his delon healthy. Cindar thanked the woman with a show of earnest helplessness, but as they made their way toward the gate, he spat at the wall.

"Bloody spies," he snarled. Then his mood lightened. Setting Spar back on his feet, he lifted the two packages to his nose. "Not a bad haul, though," he observed, taking a deep sniff of each. "Dried lime slices and old ginger powder, milk thistle and chamomile, I'd wager." He glanced at Brax. "How'd you do?" he asked under his breath.

"One pretty tight, two about half, and one nothing but crap," Brax answered carelessly. Cindar tried to look equally unimpressed, but Brax could see the corner of his lip twitch upward. Four without alerting anyone to his presence was a very good morning's work.

As long as you get out safely, Brax reminded himself cautiously. Plenty of lifters were snatched *outside* Usara-Cami on the last day of Low Spring. But they made it past the gate guards without incident and the three of them relaxed. As they headed back toward the market street and a proper breakfast, Cindar began to whistle.

✦

They stopped at a small, moldy-smelling fishmonger's stall built against Oristo-Cami's outer wall to barter the lime slices and ginger for a large helping of fresh tchiros—the first of the season as hundreds of the small, silvery fish had come through Gol-Beyaz the day before on their way to the northern Deniz-Siyah Sea. After a pointless argument with the fishmonger, Cindar gave the bulk of the food to Spar after Brax had glared at him. Then, once his oldest delinkos had quietly slipped him the purses, he handed them each a few copper aspers. "Go eat," he ordered, "then get back to work and meet me at Uzum-Dukkan after the noon song. Don't go near that bastard ironmonger's shop; he thinks I owe him money for a lock pick, and keep away from the bookbinders or I'll skin you both. I'll not have them filling your heads with romantic garbage." Before the boys could even acknowledge his words, he was heading for his favorite and most disreputable raki shop in Dockside. Shaking his head, Brax turned back to the fishmonger who handed them an extra piece of tchiros with a neutral expression.

✦

They passed it between them as they made their way through the crowded market streets. Brax haggled with a fruitier while Spar managed to hook two dried apricots off her counter, then they both ducked under an awning when the younger boy sensed a troop of Estavia's guards approaching. With Spar tucked protectively behind him, Brax watched as the six armored soldiers passed them by, tall spears gleaming as brightly as the red painted eyes of Estavia on their leather breastplates, then led the way down a narrow close. Slipping into the deep, boarded-up doorway of an empty warehouse, he crouched and emptied the fifth purse he hadn't mentioned to Cindar onto the wooden threshold between them while Spar kept watch.

"Five—no, piss on it—four aspers," he said, peering at the smooth bit of metal in his hand. "One pretty good slug, and a half decent purse to barter with later; not bad." Returning two of the coins to the purse, he handed it to Spar before his share and the slug went into a small cloth bag held around his neck by a frayed length of twine. "Not enough for a jacket," he admitted, "but enough for tea with bread and honey before we meet up with Cindar later, yeah?" Pressing his back against the door, he tested its strength absently, before glancing up at the younger boy. "So, how're you feeling now?" he asked.

Spar stuffed his apricot into his mouth before giving a careless, half-nod, half-shrug in reply.

"Great." Brax stood. "So, where do you wanna go, the bookbinders just 'cause Cindar told us not to?' he asked with a laugh, then sobered at Spar's hopeful expression. Spar had a thing for beautiful books and Cindar was always afraid that some binder would fall for his wide blue eyes and wistful expression. If truth be told, Brax was a little afraid of that too, but unlike Cindar, he wouldn't deny it to him if it happened. He didn't think he would anyway. "We'll go this afternoon," he promised. "But we have to make some shine this morning and we can't do that with you gawking at books all day." At Spar's reluctant nod, he leaned against the building. "So where'll it be? You wanna head over to the docks, maybe? The wharves'll be full of ships tied up for Havo's Dance, and their sailors'll be out and about with the shine burning holes in their pockets. We could . . . you know, catch it as it falls out?" he said with an air of such exaggerated innocence that the younger boy gave a snorting laugh. His answering grin of pure avarice brought an equally greedy smile to Brax's face and, throwing one arm over the younger boy's shoulder, he drew him back onto the street. "Well, c'mon, then," he said in gruff imitation of Cindar's voice, "before the crowds thin out." Together they made for the high, flag-decked masts just visible to the north.

✦

The territorial shrieking of the gulls and terns perched on the docks' many stone piers announced their arrival long before the cold, glistening waters of the Halic-Salmanak Strait came into view. As Brax had said they'd be, the wharves were tightly packed with ships of every size, shape, and description, sails wrapped and cargo safely stowed away before the coming of Havo's Dance. The wooden walkways were crowded with people: sailors from northern Volinsk and Rostov, glaring at each other from under their distinctively honey-brown and sun-bleached brows; Yuruk nomads of the Berbat-Dunya, looking both romantic and dangerous with their ornately carved horse bows and tall animal-tail standards, wild-haired Petchan hill fighters, looking half mad from the unaccustomed crowds even though most people gave them a wide berth, southern traders from the far off islands of Thasos and Ithos, and even a few farmers from the Northern Trisect come to barter the last of their dried fruit and beans for spices, clothing, and metalwork, all surrounded by dozens of local porters, donkey drivers, translators, salap sellers, money changers, scribes, and priests eager to accept their coin and their goods. Beside them carters and street vendors selling everything from raki, tea, and cider, to kindling, candles, and oil, lined up before every hostel, inn, and tavern on the docks. One harried looking youth in a leather apron passed a bag of flaxseed, two small white cats, and a broom through a doorway from one seller before accepting a large jar of honey perched precariously on top of a huge wheel of cheese and a joint of mutton from another, all the while arguing furiously with a local rat-catcher who was insulted by the purchase of the cats. Every establishment with room to lay a spare blanket in would be filled to bursting tonight as half the city crowded together to sit out Havo's Dance in comfort and company, and all the city's merchants were scrambling to take advantage of it before dusk. Including the ratcatchers.

Brax's dark mood returned at the thought of the festivities they'd be missing. Cindar'd been thrown out of every half decent public house on the docks. If it wasn't for him they could have spent Havo's Dance by a warm taproom fire listening to songs and stories from across the sea, drinking rize chai and being fussed over by the more maternal servers, instead of crouching in their cold little room listening to him snore. Growling to himself, Brax made for a knot of inebriated Volinski sailors, determined to steal his way into a better mood.

Behind him, Spar followed, his own expression cautious. In this mood Brax was motivated but combative, much like Cindar, and needed extra watching.

✦

An hour later they shared a boka stuffed with lufer fish at a food stall tucked under the shadow of a large fishing vessel from Rostov. The trade had been good, and Brax's mood was considerably lighter. As the noon song began, he ignored Spar's pointed glance with casual élan. He was probably just reminding him of Cindar's order, and Brax had no intention of obeying him right then. They had a chance to make some real shine today and Cindar was probably so drunk by now he'd have forgotten his own name, never mind what time they were supposed to meet him.

So piss on him, he thought truculently. *Maybe we'll even go to Spar's bookbinders just to spite him.*

The younger boy dug him in the ribs.

"What?"

Spar jerked his head past the ship's great prow and Brax froze.

Across the quay, two boys around his own age were just leaving Kedi-Meyhane, one of the better dockside inns. They were well-dressed in warm hide jackets and sandals that looked almost new, and the younger of the two was wearing a woolen cap that came down over his ears, protecting them from the cold. Brax felt a sudden stab of jealousy as his fingers dropped to the pommel of his knife.

"Graize," he spat. "And Drove."

Beside him Spar's face had twisted into an uncharacteristic mask of hatred. Like Spar, Graize had latent, almost instinctive prophetic abilities, but unlike Spar he was able to use that ability to lift the ripest pickings in Dockside without causing so much as a ripple from the authorities; an ability their abayos often reminded both Brax and Spar of when pickings were slim. But Graize and Drove had also robbed Cindar himself as he'd lain passed out before a raki stall last autumn. Brax had sworn he would kill him for that one day.

Now, as the other boys passed them by, ignoring them with studied contempt, Spar glanced over at Brax worriedly, but the older boy just gave a sharp shake of his head.

" 'Sall right," he growled darkly. "There's too many people around."

"We'll get him one day," Spar assured him gravely, the danger inherent in the situation driving away his usual silence. When Spar spoke, Brax listened. "Graize's just a cheap trickster," he added. "He'll slip up. Then we'll get him."

Nodding, Brax jerked his head in the direction of the marketplace. "Yeah, besides, we need to get Cindar before he can drink away all our shine." He allowed the younger boy to draw him away but, just before they turned the corner, he glanced back to see Graize sneering triumphantly at him, an expression of sarcastic invitation in his cold gray eyes. His face flushed in sudden anger, Brax took a single step back the way they'd come, but as Spar grabbed his arm, he made himself think clearly and, breathing heavily, allowed the younger boy to pull him down the close. Not now, but one day, he promised himself, one day they'd get him, just like Spar said they would. And even if that wasn't one of Spar's prophecies, Brax would make it one, but for now they had other, more important, business to deal with. As they made their way back toward Uzum-Dukkan, he forced himself to put the other boy out of his mind.

✦

Leaning against a stack of eastern timber, thirteen-year-old Graize grinned triumphantly as he watched his fellow lifters retreat. Seeing

Brax and Spar was always good for a laugh, he thought, especially on a dark and grubby day like today. Fishing through his pockets, he pulled out a bag of dried figs, popping one into his mouth, before turning to his companion.

"I guess they remember last autumn," he said with a wicked chuckle, tossing a fig into the air. It was snatched up by a passing gull and he tipped his head in acknowledgment of its skill. "I wonder if their abayos does," he wondered idly.

Beside him, Drove snickered. "Him? Not likely, he could hardly see straight, he was so drunk."

"He could hardly even see crooked," Graize added. "He was face-down in the dust." He snickered at the memory. The sight of Cindar lying, snoring, on the street had been too good an opportunity to ignore. Brax and Spar had come running a few moments later but not before he and Drove had striped the man of his purse, his belt, and his knife. They'd have had his sandals off as well if a troop of garrison guards hadn't appeared around the corner, forcing them to make a run for it. Brax had sworn he'd get even with them, but Graize had just laughed at him from the safety of a winding close. Brax was no threat to either of them and Spar was only a child.

He began to laugh again, his gray eyes paling until the pupils stood out like jet-black dots, giving him an unfocused, otherworldly gaze as he remembered the look on Brax's face just now. A passing butcher's delinkos whistled appreciatively at him and he smiled back at her with an easy grace, used to the attention. Light brown hair was unusual among the Anavatanon; gray eyes even more so. The priests of Oristo who'd raised him until he'd run away at the age of eight had believed he had Volinski blood and had treated him kindly but distantly. The leader of the pack of young lifters he'd made a place for himself in had believed Incasa was sending him visions that were slowly leaching the color from his eyes, and had treated him like a respected seer.

Graize didn't care which, if either, were true. He believed in himself and his ability to get whatever he wanted from people. If their beliefs helped him to do that, then they could think whatever they liked. He knew he would be rich one day. And powerful. He'd seen it. He'd *dreamed* it, and he always got what he wanted in his dreams.

He bared his teeth in the direction Brax and Spar had retreated.

What he wanted from most people was their shine, but what he wanted from Spar was the acknowledgment that he was the stronger seer; from Brax . . . he paused. He wasn't sure what he wanted from Brax, submission certainly—the cocky little bastard always acted as if he were better than everyone else—but whether he wanted submission in friendship or in enmity he was never quite sure. The conflict confused him and confusion made him angry, so he usually chose enmity. He knew that Brax and he would make a powerful team; he'd dreamed that, too. He'd even told the ungrateful little jerk that last summer when Spar lay dying from an infected injury and Cindar was too drunk to do anything about it, but Brax had been too scared to leave them. If Spar had died, he might have pried him away, but Spar had recovered and Brax had turned his back on Graize's offer. He thought he didn't need him, but that was going to change soon enough; Graize could feel it.

Maybe, he thought spitefully, he should change it for him. If he knifed Cindar the next time the drunken old fart fell down in the street, Brax would have no choice but to come crawling to him. And he needed him to come, crawling or not. Brax was key, somehow, to either his own prosperity or his obscurity. Graize hated to admit it, but he'd dreamed that as well. Brax was key.

Something flickered past his vision and he glanced about suspiciously, but when nothing untoward presented itself, he shook it off. Probably nothing more than a passing harbinger of rain, he decided.

Or a passing harbinger of Cindar's own passing, his mind supplied.

Graize nodded, his lighter mood returning like the sun after a rainstorm.

"They're gonna lose Cindar to the raki or the garrisons one day soon enough," he noted out loud. "Then both of them'll have to either come crawling to us or starve."

Beside him, Drove nodded in silent agreement. Two years older than Graize, he'd survived on the streets his whole life and knew just how harsh it could be without protection. As a small child, he'd begged for food with his crippled mother in the Tannery Precinct, the poorest section of Anavatan. When she'd died, he'd joined the same gang of lifters as Graize had, using his size and strength to help them hold their territory until they'd come to the attention of the dockside factor—a kind of thief's procurer—who'd carved out his territory by threatening any lifter who wasn't already protected by an abayos. He'd objected to them plying their trade without paying for it and had set the garrison guards on them. Only he and Graize had managed to avoid capture. Now they worked together running dice and shell games to fleece the dockside delinkon. With his quick mind and sharp prophetic abilities, Graize formulated the plans while Drove provided the solidifying strength needed to carry them out. Together, they made twice as much shine as they had with the lifters and, so far, they'd managed to avoid the local factor, rival gangs, Estavia's guards, Oristo's abayos-priests, and any divine attention—no mean trick in the City of the Gods. Graize was concerned, no, more like obsessed, Drove amended, with Brax and Spar, but he couldn't see why. Half starved dockside rats were as common-place as the actual rodents they were named for in Anavatan.

He said as much to Graize now and the other boy turned, his pale eyes sparkling wickedly.

"So, do you feel like being rat-catchers today and chasing them down?" he asked, fingers drumming excitedly against the pommel of his knife.

Drove just shrugged. "If you want to, but I kinda hoped we could go to Usara-Cami today," he answered.

Graize gave a sneering laugh. "What for? The pickings are far better here."

"Well, I have these . . . um, things on my neck." He pulled his fleece-lined collar down to show the other boy a scattering of red spots beneath the patina of dirt. "Terv thought it might be the smallpox," he said quoting the ash collector's delinkos from the Kedi-Meyhane, the only person he knew with any kind of an education other than Graize.

"Terv doesn't know his arse from the moon," Graize answered scornfully. "They're flea bites."

"You sure?"

"Completely."

Drove looked disappointed. "Still, I could get some, you know, salve for them."

"Soak your clothes in lye. That'll get rid of them."

"The bites?"

"The fleas, stupid." Bored with the conversation, Graize moved off toward a group of delinkon gathered around two porters gesticulating wildly, a pile of bundles lying on the ground between them. "C'mon, there's gonna be a fight," he said over his shoulder. "Time to work." Sidling up behind the crowd, he leaned toward the ear of the best dressed youth, a jeweler's or goldsmith's delinkos by the look of him.

"A silver asper says the scrawny one throws the first punch," he whispered.

Watching the larger of the two porters bunch his hands into fists, the youth nodded eagerly. "It's a bet."

Behind them, Drove grinned to himself. No one ever won a bet against Graize; he always knew who was going to throw the first punch.

As if to prove him right, the smaller of the two porters aimed a wild swing at the larger man's head, but before the crestfallen delinkos could even reach for his purse, Graize had proposed another bet. And so it would go, Drove knew, until the youth had run out of shine or the dockyard guards had come to restore the peace. But, by then, Graize would have discovered another opportunity, anyway. Drove chuckled to himself. It was going to be a very profitable Havo's Dance this year, he thought happily; nothing was going to go wrong.

✦

Tucked between the planking at his feet, the host of gathering shadows felt the prophetic bond between all four boys tighten like a noose and agreed.

✦

Three streets away, Brax and Spar had almost reached Oristo-Cami before the older boy stopped shaking with rage. Seeing Graize and Drove had brought up all his old feelings of resentment and frustration, and seeing them prosper without an abayos just made it worse. He was so distracted by his anger that he almost didn't notice when Spar misread a step on the uneven cobblestones and stumbled. He threw out a hand reflexively, catching the younger boy before he realized what had happened—Spar never stumbled, not even when he was tired. Turning, he saw the younger boy's eyes widen in fear and felt a shiver run up his spine. He glanced about quickly but couldn't see anything that might have alerted Spar to danger.

"What?" he asked in a harsh whisper.

His gaze riveted on some inward peril, Spar could only shake his head, but when Brax caught him by the chin and snapped his fingers in front of his face, his blue eyes jerked back to focus on him.

"Is it us?" Brax demanded.

The younger boy managed to choke out a half strangled "No," and Brax felt a sinking feeling grow in the pit of his stomach.

"Cindar."

Without bothering to confirm his guess, Spar turned and ran for the marketplace.

✦

Brax caught up with him just before he pelted into the open street and, grabbing him by the back of the jacket, yanked him behind a confectionary shop wall.

"Wait," he ordered.

Gulping air like a stranded fish, Spar obeyed, his eyes wide and staring, as Brax craned his neck around the corner.

He saw Cindar almost at once, coming out of Uzum-Dukkan. He was already drunk and reeling, an earthenware jug cradled in the crook of one arm, and Brax's lip curled in disgust. Beside him, Spar gave a jerk of renewed fear and Brax scanned the street, catching sight of a senior priest of Oristo, his richly brocaded robes stretching over a vast belly, chatting amiably with a troop of garrison guards about fifty yards away.

"Oh, crap," he breathed and suddenly he could see what was going to happen as clearly as if he were the one with the prophetic sight and not Spar. If they moved now, *right now*, they could still intercept their abayos, distract him with whispered promises of shine and alcohol, and get him out of harm's way. If they didn't . . .

Spar made to dart around him and, almost as if he was acting in a dream, Brax reached out and swung him back, pressing him against his body with one arm wrapped tightly around his chest to hold him back.

"No," he said with almost preternatural calm. "It's too late."

He felt Spar tense in wordless protest, and then it truly was too late as priest and thief spotted each other at the same moment. Brax saw Cindar's shoulders tense, saw his fists rise, and then he couldn't believe his eyes as their abayos turned and, with a hateful sneer, snatched a jug from another customer just leaving the shop behind him. He flung the protesting man into the street, then turned to the priest and, raising the jug to his lips in belligerent defiance, took a deep drink as if daring him to do anything about it.

His eyes narrowed, the priest made a terse gesture and the garrison guards moved forward.

Cindar's answering roar of fury echoed through the narrow streets. He flung both jugs toward them and, as the guards closed in, spears raised, Brax turned away to bury his face in Spar's tangled hair, feeling rather than hearing the sounds of fighting through the younger boy's slight frame as Spar jerked at the sound of every blow and shouted curse. Each time Spar tried to pull away and each time Brax held him back. When they finally heard a loud crack, he jumped and would have fallen if Brax hadn't maintained his grip across his chest. He slumped then, his face white and, holding him up with one arm, Brax craned his neck around the corner again.

The guards were heading their way, dragging Cindar's limp figure behind them. Two more carried one of their own and another supported the priest who had an ugly red mark across his face. There was blood on their weapons and blood on the suddenly misty ground.

His strength deserted him and, as the guards passed their hiding spot, Spar forced his head under Brax's arm and came face-to-face with Cindar's staring eyes, partially concealed by a mat of shadowy gore-soaked hair. He shuddered once then collapsed, and as he caught Spar instinctively, Brax knew. Cindar was dead. Back against the building, he slid to the ground, supporting Spar in his arms, suddenly unsure if his decision had been the right one but knowing now that it didn't matter. For good or for ill, they were finally on their own and Cindar would never be able to come after them.

✦

Two guards and an abayos-priest were waiting for them at the door to their room when they returned, not knowing where else to go. The priest took one look at Spar's ashen features and guessed what had happened at once. Catching him around the waist, she thrust him, unresisting, into the arms of the older guard, then took Brax by the shoulder.

His first instinct was to fight like Cindar had done, but then his sense of self-preservation took hold and he forced himself to calm. Now was not the time, he told himself urgently. They had Spar and Spar couldn't run. He needed to wait, to stay calm and to wait.

Making himself appear small and frightened, he shrank against the woman's side in studied relief, allowing her to lead him down the dust-covered stairs and away from the only home he'd ever known, away toward Oristo-Cami and all the horrors Cindar had warned them of all their lives. As the Hearth God's wrought-iron gates appeared before them, his heart began to pound overloud in his chest, but again he forced himself to wait.

✦

By the time they reached the inner temple, he was almost shaking with the effort not to break and run. Spar had recovered enough to be set down, and the priest dismissed the guards, then led them along a wide, hushed antechamber to a wooden bench seated before a tall, mahogany statue of Oristo, hands held out in a position of, to Brax's eyes, menacing welcome. Brax scowled at it, but said nothing as the priest ordered them each a cup of boza from an ancient protectorate hovering nearby.

As the priest turned, he suddenly recognized the woman who'd traded glares with Cindar from the temple steps not five hours before. The shock must have shown on his face because she attempted a stiff smile of reassurance.

"Don't be afraid," she said. "You're not in trouble. Just sit here quietly until I return."

He nodded weakly as she headed down the hall in a swish of heavy brown robes then, after accepting the cup held out to him, he waited until the protectorate shuffled away before turning to Spar. The younger boy was sitting on the bench clutching his own cup, his face still dazed and blank, and his eyes glassy. Brax knelt in front of him.

"Spar?"

He blinked but did not look up.

"Spar, I have to go see if I can hear what they're gonna do with us, all right? I'll be just down the hall. Just there, yeah?" He pointed but Spar did not move his head. "You can see me there if you look, and I'll be right back. All right? Spar?"

The younger boy finally gave the faintest of nods and, after pushing his cup under the bench, Brax rose and tiptoed to the open door of the room the priest had disappeared through, leaning as far forward as he dared.

"He attacked Mavin, Sayin," he heard the priest explain to an unseen superior, her voice hinting at a barely controlled anger she hadn't allowed the boys to see. "Estavia's garrison attempted to restrain him and he was killed in the ensuing struggle. His delon must have witnessed the event, for the younger of the two is still quite prostrate."

Brax frowned, unsure of the meaning of the word. He glanced at Spar who'd laid his head against the back of the bench and closed his eyes again. He looked gaunt and sickly and Brax guessed that whatever prostrate meant it was probably a pretty good description. He turned back to the door.

"How old would you say the delon are?" a voice of privilege and rank that made Brax's teeth clench asked from deeper inside the room.

"The older looks to be no more than eleven or twelve," the priest answered, and Brax smirked. "The younger may be six, possibly seven. I can petition Oristo for more accuracy tonight if you wish it."

"Do that. In the meantime, however, I see no need to involve Estavia's people any further due to their obvious youth," the voice said.

"Yes, Sayin."

Brax released a breath he hadn't known he was holding, thankful as always that the two of them were so much smaller than others their age.

"I should imagine that the younger of the two has very little understanding of the life he's led up until now," the first priest continued. "We should be able to find him abayon willing to raise him without the fear that thievery has already twisted his nature. If not, I'm told that Duwan has been accepted at Oristo-Sarayi, so there's room for another delinkos at Oristo-Cami in the Tannery Precinct."

Brax stiffened.

"As for the older," she continued, "if he can be placed in an honest, hard-working trade, he should be able to overcome his upbringing— with extremely close supervision of course."

"Did you have a trade in mind?"

"Porter, perhaps, or cleaner, something like that, I should think. Their abayos left nothing behind to aid them in securing anything better."

"Neglectful fool." Brax heard the sound of a chair squeaking and knew the senior priest had stood. "Very well. Have the kitchens fix them something to eat, then have Evrin take the younger one to the Tannery Precinct Cami at once. The older can stay with the protectorates for the duration of Havo's Dance and then . . ."

Brax didn't wait to hear the rest. Making his way back to the bench as swiftly and as quietly as possible, he crouched before the younger boy, touching him lightly on the arm to rouse him.

"Spar?" he whispered.

The other boy opened eyes still dull and lifeless.

"They're gonna split us up, Spar," he said urgently. "So if we're gonna run, we gotta run now."

Spar blinked, his face twisted in uncertainty.

"I'm not asking you if it's safe," Brax continued, " 'cause it probably isn't. In fact, it's probably the dumbest thing we've ever done." He took the younger boy's hand, looking earnestly into his face. "And it's all right if you want to stay. You'll be safe and fed, and they'll give you a warm place to sleep. It'll be at the Tannery Precinct Cami for now, but they're gonna try and find you abayon." He swallowed. "*Real* abayon, not like Cindar or me. They might even teach you to read and write more than just a few words." He paused, glancing down the hall with a nervous expression, then turned back. "I won't make you come with me," he said quietly. "Not now, not after . . . what happened. But I can't stay here." He squared his shoulders. "I *won't* stay here. And if I'm gonna find a place to hole up before Havo's Dance, I gotta go now." He took a deep breath. "So, will you come with me?"

Spar looked up. His blue eyes were shadowy and blank, but there was an intensity in his face that Brax had never seen before.

"Did you let Cindar die?" he asked bluntly.

The older boy took a deep breath. "Yes."

He made no excuses and no apologies and after a moment, Spar nodded almost to himself, then stood.

Together, they broke for the main doors just as the priest came around the corner with a heavyset delinkos in tow. She gave a shout of alarm, but by that time they were already pelting down the steps and across the courtyard. Brax flung himself to the left away from the reaching arms of one gate guard while Spar dove under the legs of the other and then they were past the gates and disappearing into the crowded market street beyond. Ignoring the sprinkles of rain that were beginning to fall all around them, Brax allowed himself a sigh of relief as they slowed. For good or for ill, they were on their own now, but at least they were together.

✦

In the city's growing shadows, the spirits stirred in gleeful anticipation. The decision had been made. They had fed from the big man's death, just a little, but enough to grow stronger. It was almost time.

✦

Deep within Gol-Beyaz, Incasa flung His prophetic dice into the current, reading the streams of possibility as they fell. The spirits were naive if they thought He had no knowledge of their little spark. Like them, He'd watched it grow, flashing back and forth between four boys, each one with a different talent for creation and destruction. The next few hours would tell which would be the most useful to the spirits and to the Gods.

Kemal

THE FIRST MORNING of Havo's Dance dawned wet and gray. The rain and hail that had begun in earnest just before dusk had beaten down on the city with such a fury that even the bravest of the sworn had fled indoors before the priest of Havo had finished singing the Evening Invocation. Not daring to return home in case the priests of Oristo had set a guard to wait for them, Brax and Spar had broken into a dilapidated rope maker's stall in the western market, huddling together under the counter for warmth. It had been damp and cold, but it had been enough shelter to protect them throughout the night.

Now, as a dry, rustling sound caused Spar to stir uneasily in his sleep, Brax's eyes snapped open. The stall's owner was a drunkard, unlikely to return until well past dawn, and no shadowy immortal danger could reach them here, but there were wharf rats on the docks that ran in packs of a hundred, feral dogs, and even people driven mad by the storm beating on their shutters all night who might choose this spot for their own refuge.

Tucking Spar more firmly behind him, Brax worked his knife free as he stared into the darkness, but nothing moved. As the younger boy whimpered in his sleep, Brax worked one arm around him, his mind returning to their situation as it had for most of the night. They had no shine, no food, nowhere to live, and no one to protect them.

Should have thought of that before you let Cindar die, his mind supplied coldly.

He ignored it. What's done was done and if the know-it-all hindsight part of his brain couldn't come up with a solution on its own, it could just shut up and get over it.

Scratching absently at a tiny, red bite on his ankle, he brought his mind back to the problem at hand. He could petition the local factor to allow them to work, but the factor had hated Cindar because their larger and far more dangerous abayos had always sneered at his demands. He'd be expensive and they had nothing to bargain with. He would want the bulk of their take and they would still be vulnerable to anyone stronger than themselves.

"Which is everyone," Brax muttered. Hissing at a pair of tiny eyes glowing in the faint dawn light, he drew Spar closer.

You could always go to Graize, his mind suggested.

No.

He's successful.

He's an arrogant little shit.

He offered you a place beside him once; remember that time when Spar was so sick?

He offered me *a place, not us. He doesn't want Spar. Spar knows he blows smoke through his arse most of the time. He doesn't want anyone knowing that.*

You could talk him into taking Spar. He'd do it for you.

Brax gave an audible sneer. *I'd rather go back to Oristo-Cami.*

No self-respecting thief would ever serve a priest.

Brax scowled as Cindar's voice sounded overloud in his memory.

No self-respecting abayos would get himself killed by one either, he shot back, ignoring the lump in his throat. *What are we supposed to do now, starve?*

There was no answer and Brax hadn't expected one. Cindar was dead. Even if he could have spoken with his delinkon, he wouldn't have bothered. They were on their own.

And whose fault is that? his mind demanded again.

Shut up.

Outside the stall, the winds died down as the first, wavering notes of Havo's Morning Invocation song filled the air. The sun had risen. Brax squared his shoulders. Whatever else he did, he had to find them someplace more secure than this to sleep; the Second Night was more dangerous than the First and Brax would rather indenture them both to the docks' shine-grubbing factor than face the shadows that came out in the rain and hail to suck the life from the unsworn on Havo's Dance; the shadows that were growing stronger with each passing year. No, he would find them a place, whatever it took, a place where they would be safe, protected, and never have to fear the streets again, that he *would* swear, but for now he had to find them something to eat. As the dawn sun cast a dimpling of light across the stall's wooden sides, he reached over and gently shook the younger boy awake.

✦

Far to the south, the waters of Gol-Beyaz stirred as Incasa rose from the depths, drawn to the future formed about the young thief's peril. The spirits had found a way to coalesce about the boy's desperation. They would feed on it and grow until they could take on some murky, physical form like half-curdled milk, and with that form they would be able to reach the waters of Gol-Beyaz and the shining power that gave the Gods Their strength. Incasa did not doubt that they would do it any more than He doubted that it would be His hand that drew them in and fashioned them to a form that most suited His desires when they did.

Narrowing His snow-white eyes, the God of All Possible Futures considered the most important element necessary to bring this into being: the lake dwellers, mortal creatures of flesh and unclaimed power who had come to the shores of Gol-Beyaz so many centuries ago. The lake dwellers whose dreams and prayers had pattered down upon the waves like a constantly falling rain. As they'd built their homes, tilled their fields, and lifted the fish from the waters into their boats, the lake dwellers had prayed for knowledge that their crops would grow and that their children would flourish. From those prayers Incasa, the God of Probability, had been born, forming Havo, the God of Crops, and Oristo, the God of Children, in His wake.

More centuries had passed and, as the lives of the lake dwellers had grown more sophisticated, so had their prayers. Medicine, Learning, and Martial Prowess had soon joined Prophecy, Food, and Family in their pantheon and now it was time to bring yet another aspect of those prayers into being: Conquest and Expansion would join Prosperity, Culture, and Protection in the lake of power, but only under Prophecy's very tight control.

Rising from the waters like a shining star, Incasa drew Estavia and Oristo up beside Him. As They broke the surface without so much as a ripple to mark their passage, He gestured, and the image of Anavatan appeared around them like a ghostly mirage. The three Deities danced along the dawn-lit streets, Incasa's long white hair swirling half a heartbeat beyond Estavia's flashing swords, and Oristo twirling along behind Them.

Standing poised above the golden dome of Anavatan's Derneke-Mahalle Citadel, the seat of the lake dweller's physical power, the God of Prophecy held His dice high above His head. The new deity needed a champion and a sacrifice to come into being, and Incasa Himself needed an agent of His will, a single loaded die, in case this new deity somehow managed to slip from the net of His control. It was time to see which one this boy was most likely to become. With a snap of His wrist, Incasa flung the dice into the air and Brax's future rose up before Them.

The young thief stood in the center of a broiling sea of blood-flecked mist, the body of another lying dead at his feet. As he fought to keep his balance, the waves crashed against him, trying to drive him down into the clutches of a hundred sharp-clawed creatures of power and need hovering just below the surface. Finally, they knocked him off his feet. As the creatures closed over his head, he managed one choked-off cry for help. His call shot through the mist like a blazing arrow and, drawn by the violence of his desperation, Estavia leaped forward as Incasa'd known She would, only to have him disappear before She could reach him.

The streets of Anavatan grew still.

Her red eyes glowing hotly, Estavia sheathed Her swords, then turned toward Her temple-fortress just visible in the dawn light. As the sun crested the Degisken-Dag Mountains to the east, She reached out.

Behind Her, Incasa cast a mantle of obscuring mist across the darkened streets so fine that even the Battle God did not notice it, directing Her touch toward the mind of one of Her favorites, a mind receptive enough to help build the future Incasa Himself desired. Then, catching His dice back up in His fist, He, too, reached out for one of His favorites, Freyiz, First Oracle of Incasa-Sarayi, and fashioned His desire in the form of a cryptic and subtle prophecy. It wouldn't do to give His seers too much knowledge all at once any more than it would do to give the other Gods knowledge of Their own birthing. Knowledge was power, and the God of Chance did not like to share power; even with His own temple.

Behind Him, Oristo frowned, distracted by the spray of blood which marred the perfection of the city streets. Oristo did not like violence; it interfered with the order and tranquillity of the Home. Eyes narrowed, the bi-gender Hearth God too reached out for Neclan, Senior Abayos-Priest of Oristo-Sarayi, just as the God of Battles made contact with Her own.

✦

At Estavia-Sarayi, Ghazi-Priest Kemal of Her Most Loyal Cyan Infantry Company stirred restlessly in his sleep. His dreams merged and flowed, became the dark, rain, and hail-drenched cobblestones of Anavatan on Havo's Dance. He saw the shadowy outline of a child, saw it fall, then jerked awake with the knowledge that something was happening; something dangerous. Estavia's presence thrummed through his mind like a distant drum, beating out a message he could barely hear and, rubbing at the short growth of beard along the side of his face, he frowned.

Something was happening or something was *going* to happen? Something he was supposed to prevent or something he was supposed to aid?

The darkened room made no reply. Beside him, his arkados, Yashar, slept on undisturbed, his snoring vying with that of Kemal's dog Jaq, sprawled across their legs. Both had taken up far more than their fair share of the pallet as usual and, as Kemal worked one hand free of what little blanket they'd left him, both grumbled in sleepy annoyance but did not awaken. Reaching for his knife, he gripped the familiar wire-bound handle and tried to clear his mind enough to understand Her message.

He didn't hold out much hope.

Kemal had served as a warrior and priest at the Battle God's main temple for eight years now, chosen from the ranks of the Serin-Koy village militia to command one of Her fighting units. Like most of Her field officers he was not known for any particularly strong metaphysical ability, and when Estavia chose to touch his sleeping mind, Her messages were generally clear, simple warnings of danger on the battlefield; Her more cryptic and important pronouncements were usually saved for Her battle-seers who had the talent for prophetic dreaming.

As soon as he formed the thought, he felt the sense of Her reaction, his mind insisting on giving words to what was always a feeling rather than a dialogue.

NOT THIS TIME.

He closed his eyes, reaching out through his bond with the God, seeking clarity. There was no response except the faintest tingle of impatience. Clearly, She felt She'd given him all the information he needed. He concentrated, forming his confusion into a prayer. He was rewarded with a single image.

ELIF.

He nodded. Slowly removing Yashar's arm from across his chest, he pressed one foot against Jaq's side and shoved him off the pallet. The dog rolled onto the floor, then rose and shook himself with a reproachful grunt. After using the pot, Kemal pulled a short tunic over his head, then he and Jaq slipped from the room.

✦

The long, inlaid marble corridor which separated the Cyan quarters from those of Estavia's seven other temple companies was chilly this early in the morning, the high latticed windows still dark. Kemal walked quickly, following Jaq's shadowy form and listening to the tick, tick of his toenails on the floor. Few of Estavia's warriors would be up this early on Havo's First Morning. Few except Elif, he amended. Elif would rise early during a hurricane. Reaching the far end of the hall, he silently acknowledged the salute of the dormitory guard before heading outside into the temple's innermost courtyard.

The air smelled of mulberry and magnolia trees, rain-soaked earth and stone. Kemal breathed in the sharp, spicy odor with pleasure, then followed Jaq as he took the ornately carved stone steps three at a time. Bounding across the graveled path, the dog shoved his nose under the hand of an old woman seated on an iron divan beneath a sweeping cinar tree. As he turned his ministering tongue to her face, one chestnut-colored hand emerged from the depths of a heavy, woolen blanket to grab his muzzle. Kemal chuckled.

Elif, late of Sable Company, had served Estavia-Sarayi as the temple's most powerful battle-seer for over sixty years until age and encroaching blindness had forced her to retire. Refusing the offer of a comfortable bed at Calmak-Koy—the nearby convalescent garden and hospital village—she'd chosen instead to spend her last days seated in the temple's inner courtyards, speaking prophecy and being waited on by the many warriors she'd trained over the years. To one side, politely out of earshot, her ever-present attendant met Kemal's gaze with the silent request not to tire her. Kemal nodded. As he approached, Elif turned her mist-shrouded, brown eyes in his direction.

"Good morning, Ghazi."

"Good morning, Elif-Sayin." Crouching beside her, he kissed her fingers, noting how thin and translucent they'd become since last autumn.

"And why are you abroad so early?" she queried, her voice still strong despite her age. "Not even the most dedicated priest could tell the white thread from the black just yet."

"Except for the priests of Havo," he allowed.

"The priests of Havo are awakened by their God."

Kemal glanced over at the broken bits of multicolored tile scattered about the courtyard. "From the sound of last night's storm, their God nearly tore the roof off," he noted. "It's a wonder Estavia didn't rise in response."

The old woman gave a cackling laugh. "Now that would be a sight to see, yes? Estavia and Havo doing battle across the rooftops of Anavatan. Who do you think would win, eh?"

"I know who would lose: anyone caught in the crossfire."

"You don't believe Estavia would protect Her warriors?"

Her voice was teasing, but Kemal could hear the steel beneath it. As she bent her head to accept one of Jaq's increasingly boisterous kisses, he could see the glow of the Battle God's painted protections across her cheeks. Only the most beloved of Estavia's chosen were guided to draw Her wards where they could be seen. Elif had earned that privilege many times over.

"I believe Estavia would allow anyone foolish enough to stand gawking at a God-Battle to reap the harvest of their own folly," he answered piously.

"Spoken like a true farmer."

He chuckled. "Perhaps."

"So, tell me, why are you here keeping the company of a mad, old seer instead of remaining in the warm arms of your arkados on this cold Havo's Morning? Jaq, sit!" Pushing the dog's head away, she straightened. "It can't be for his sake," she added, jerking her head toward the dog who gazed up at her reproachfully. "Nandeen told me she caught him pissing in the west wing conservatory not five hours ago."

"So that's where he goes. No, I had a dream."

"A dream of encroaching danger?"

He started. "Yes. Why, did you have it, too?"

"No, but what else could it have been?"

"It could have been a little more clear."

Deep in his mind, he felt Estavia's response as a tingling warmth through his thoughts; a loving stroke mixed with a mental smack.

"Serves you right," Elif admonished absently, sensing the God's answer as she always could. "Estavia has a lot of nerve making such a powerful ghazi as yourself use his brain instead of his arm, does She?"

"Actually, She sent me to you."

"Figures." The old woman hunkered more deeply into her blankets. "Well, She hasn't seen fit to discuss anything but the weather with me this morning," she sniffed, "and you're right, She's disgruntled about Her roofs, so you'll just have to wait. Will you be representing us at Assembly this morning?"

"Most likely. The duty will get passed down until there's no one left to pass it down to."

"You could pass it down yourself."

"I don't like to, it's . . ." He shrugged.

"A duty?"

"Yes."

"A *civic* duty."

"Still . . ."

"Yes, still." She chuckled. "Be careful, Kemin-Delin. Marshals have been appointed for less and the paperwork would kill you. However, come and see me afterward. Estavia may have gotten over Her pique about broken chimney pots and scattered roof tiles by then. Yes, Murad," she added loudly as the last of Havo's Invocation sounded in the distance. We'll be going inside for breakfast now. Delon," she added, "no stamina." As her attendant came forward to lift her, blankets and all, she gave Jaq one last pat on the head. "Get the rabbit, Delin!"

The dog took off straight through the burlap-wrapped rose gardens, scattering fallen hail as he went and, with a chuckle at his master's disapproving expression, Elif allowed herself to be carried back inside. After he managed to drag Jaq away from his imaginary prey, Kemal followed.

✦

Yashar had already risen and gone when they returned; the shutters were thrown open with pale sunlight filtering in through the haze of morning incense. As Jaq clambered onto the rolled-up pallet, Kemal pulled off his tunic and crossed, naked, to the wall altar, his eyes watering. He preferred a lighter scent in the mornings, lily or lotus, but Yashar liked to use a heavy eastern sandalwood. He believed it cleared his mind so that he might more fully communicate with Estavia. Kemal believed it accomplished that by burning a scorching path up through the nose and into the brain. With a sigh, he lit a new sandalwood stick off the small devotion lamp, resisting the urge to sneeze as a fine trickle of smoke made for one nostril, then reached for a goat's-hair brush.

Staring into the tiny red eyes of Estavia's altar statue, he sank quickly into a receptive state, then, opening the nearby dye pot with one hand, dipped the brush inside by memory, feeling Her touch sizzle through his fingers. As usual, the tip touched his skin before he realized his hand had moved, painting the God's daily protections over his body in a series of quick, simple strokes. Those for Anavatan and Serin-Koy traced themselves along his shield arm, with Estavia-Sarayi's wrapped about Cyan Company's on his sword arm. Another dip and his hand moved to his chest above his heart, adding his own symbol, Yashar's, his family's, and one small, four-legged stick figure that made him smile. Estavia was particularly fond of dogs.

Jaq woofed as if he could sense his master's thoughts, leaping down to stuff his head under his hand as he came out of trance, and Kemal ruffled the dog's huge, flopping ears with a smile.

"Who knows why, eh?" he asked him fondly. "Come on, it's time for breakfast."

✦

The huge main refectory wing was filled to bursting when they arrived. Estavia's warriors numbered nearly ten thousand at full strength, and although most were stationed at the nine village towers around Gol-Beyaz or at Anavatan's many gates, there were usually upward of seven or eight hundred people taking meals at Estavia-Sarayi at any given time. The kitchens, staffed by dozens of Oristo's stewards, were enormous.

Lining up before the long, central table, Kemal tossed Jaq a slab of tripe before helping himself to a piece of flat bread liberally spread with quince jam, a slice of sheep's cheese, and a handful of dried figs. Weaving his way through the crowds to the blue-and-gold-tiled Cyan dining hall, he glanced around for Yashar but didn't see him. Kaptin Julide, however, saw Kemal, and pointed at an empty cushion across from her.

"Good morning, Ghazi."

He took the seat with a resigned expression. "Kaptin."

"Tea?"

"Thank you."

"Bazmin, tea." She gestured and her delinkos caught up the large, silver urn from the center of the low table and poured Kemal a cup. Allowing him to take a single sip, she then caught him in a firm stare.

"You're to attend Assembly this morning."

He sighed. "Yes, Kaptin."

"There shouldn't be much more than damage reports from across the city; Lazim-Hisar reports no signal from the lake towers, the walls are secure, and the city garrisons survived the night intact, so you'll have no more to say than anyone else. You should be out of there in less than an hour."

"No movement from the north, Kaptin?"

"The northern watchtowers report the strait's empty of all movement—friend, foe, and fish alike. Which makes sense on Havo's First Morning. We'll know more about the smaller harbors when we hear from the coastal garrison later today, but it would take some pretty powerful magics to sail across the northern sea during Havo's Dance.

These first spring storms are always the worst once they push past the strait into open water. Relax and enjoy the boredom for a few more days, Ghazi. Cyan Company is being deployed south to Anahtar-Hisar next week, and there'll be plenty there to keep you occupied."

"Yes, Kaptin." Draining his cup, Kemal picked up his bread and jam with a distracted frown. Last season they'd driven several suspicious-acting ships away from the Bogazi-Isik Strait to the north—Estavia's naval kaptins had been certain they were scout ships. Betting was three to one in the temple that the northern powers of Rostov and Volinsk were taking an interest in Anavatan and its profitable hold on the southern route through the walled-off and guarded silvery Gol-Beyaz Lake once again, but Elif and the temple-seers disagreed; Rostov and Volinsk had been at war for over two decades and showed no signs of mending their earlier alliance. The towers of Anahtar, Kapi and Kenor-Hisar, however, had reported increased activity on the Deniz-Hadi Sea to the south, and their traditional trading partners and sometime allies of Thasos and Ithos Islands had been distinctively nervous all winter. If a new power were rising to the south, they had to be ready to meet it. The bulk of the Battle God's fighting companies would be stationed at the southernmost towers this season especially since their ancient enemies, the Yuruk nomads of the Berbat-Dunya wild lands to the northwest and the Petchan hill fighters of the Gurney-Dag Mountains to the southwest had been defeated so thoroughly in the last decade that they were now at a fraction of their earlier numbers. But, like most of the rank and file drawn from the western villages, Kemal believed they were making a mistake in ignoring these regions.

"But no one asks us, do they, Delin?" he asked Jaq, ruffling his ears.

"Ghazi?"

"Nothing, Kaptin."

"Then we'll see you at the Invocation." With a nod, Kaptin Julide withdrew, her delinkos in tow. Kemal was left to stare into his empty cup as if the few remaining tea leaves could show him the future. As he reached for the urn, the hazy form of a child outlined against the city's dark, cobblestone streets rose up before his eyes again, then winked out in a spray of mist. He nodded. Something *was* happening, it just wasn't happening to the south.

Nor to the north either, his mind supplied.

No, he agreed, it was happening here. He just wished he knew what it was and what he was supposed to do about it. Suddenly no longer hungry, he tossed the rest of his breakfast to Jaq, then followed the kaptin from the hall.

✦

Across the city, as the rising sun painted the many battlements and minarets of Anavatan with broad streaks of fire, Brax and Spar scrambled onto a stone pier overlooking the Halic-Salmanak, the freshwater strait that separated the Northern from the Western Trisect. As a new set of priests began to sing, calling the sworn to the Morning Invocations, Brax handed the younger boy a piece of bread they'd managed to barter for yesterday's purse.

"The streets'll be bare in a moment," he observed, watching a school of mercan fish swim by. "Anyone not singing at Gods'll be at breakfast." Squinting up at the cloudy sky, his expression grew thoughtful. "We could sniff around the market and see what Havo left us." He shot Spar a quick glance. The younger boy had been quiet and withdrawn all morning, but the dark circles under his eyes were fading and he'd attacked his breakfast with his usual appetite. "Or maybe slip in through some hostel's back door and check out their kitchens? What do you think?" he continued.

Spar stared out across the water, then nodded slowly.

Satisfied, Brax stood, dusting invisible crumbs off his tunic before leaping from the pier to the soft, white sand below. "Meyhane-Kopek's the closest," he observed. "We could see if anything's been left lying around and if not, we could always beg some work at Ystazia-Cami. All those outdoor stalls in the main courtyard must have gotten tossed around pretty well last night. They might need help putting them back together, yeah?"

Spar nodded. Work wasn't as profitable as lifting, but it was safer. He was glad Brax was keeping their options open. As the singing ended, he clambered down and followed the older boy through the deserted streets toward Meyhane-Kopek, his eyes darting this way and that, alert for any sign of danger. As Anavatan began to shimmer with a faint silvery-yellow glow as the sworn evoked the power of their Gods, he shivered. Gods were a frightening unknown and the unknown was always a danger.

✦

In Estavia-Sarayi's huge central parade ground, Kemal, now fully dressed in deep blue tunic, sandals, and leather armor, stood beside Yashar, the fingers of his right hand resting easily against the pommel of his sword. Around him, the Battle God's warriors stood as still as statues, each company occupying the position it would hold on the battlefield: archers from Verdant and Turquoise Companies on the flanks, Sable Company, with its many powerful seers, to the rear protecting the long line of delinkon behind them, the lines of mounted Bronze Company cavalry on their huge warhorses at the vanguard, and the four infantry companies of Azure, Cyan, Sapphire, and Indigo in the center. Those who no longer actively served the God through age or infirmity rested on long, marble benches beneath the encircling line of cinar and poplar trees to one side. Kemal could just make out Elif seated with her hands resting on Jaq's broad shoulders, but she too, like the rest, remained motionless, waiting.

The muted notes of Usara's Invocation filtered out to them from different parts of the temple complex. Both the Hearth and Healing Gods maintained contingents of followers at Estavia-Sarayi to support the warriors in their protection of the city. The Battle God's song would not begin until first one and then the other had ended. But it would be soon. As the last note faded, a single mounted figure crossed the courtyard. The waiting companies tensed.

Marshal Brayazi had served as the temple's supreme commander for over a decade and as kaptin and ghazi-priest in Bronze Company for thirty years before that. Her long black hair, bound in several thick braids, was streaked with gray, and her face, nearly as dark as the Battle God's own, was deeply lined, but she still carried herself as stiff and straight as an arrow. Her black eyes swept across the assembled companies, then, in one swift motion, she drew her sword, standing up in the saddle to call out the first, loud note of Estavia's Invocation. A moment later they heard the answering call from far out on the Bogazi-Isik Strait as the admiral of Her Battle Fleet joined in. Across the city and from every tower along the shores of Gol-Beyaz, each kaptin took up the call, adding the strength of their voices to their marshal's.

Estavia's power rippled through the assembled warriors. Another call, another thread of power, and Kemal felt a chill run up his spine. His sword arm tensed. She was near; he could feel Her hovering just beneath the surface of his awareness. Another note, this time deeper and richer than the two before it, and he saw Yashar's head tip back, the tendons in his neck standing out with the strain, his teeth shining brightly through the dark thickness of his beard. His own chin began to lift. Around him, the warriors shifted and moved as their God's presence began to flow through them. A third note, a fourth, and his muscles began to shake with the steady buildup of power. As always, he felt his own will begin to wash away under the overwhelming need to do Her bidding as a blood-red fog washed across his vision, and his fists clenched with the sudden fierce desire to do battle, to kill and maim the bodies of Her enemies in Her name. Finally, the power grew too strong to be contained, and he and every other warrior in the courtyard jerked their weapons free as Estavia burst into being above them with a crack of displaced air.

Red eyes blazing, She spun Her swords above their heads and, as one, Her people raised their own weapons to meet them, bolts of deep-red energy crackling down the blades like gouts of fire. Kemal jerked as his own sword sent a rush of power shooting through his arm and it was all he could do not to turn his blade on the others. Instead, he rode the sensation, feeling his entire body stiffen in response to Her power. He felt invulnerable, unstoppable, and drunk on the power of Her touch. The feeling grew, became almost unbearable. Then, as fast as She'd come, Estavia's presence exploded into the morning sun and vanished. Around him, the others staggered about the courtyard before discipline brought them back into formation. But Kemal was left reeling from the violence of Her passing, unable to speak, his vision spinning with the knowledge that something hovered just beyond his understanding, something he was supposed to know, something he was supposed to do. Before he could reach out for it, Marshal Brayazi held her sword aloft for one more heartbeat, then shot it back into its scabbard. The Invocation was over.

Breathing hard, Yashar threw one arm over Kemal's shoulders to support himself as the assembled broke into a hundred ragged groups, many of then heading for a private corner. "That was better than sex," he panted. "I hope we get to kill something soon, I don't think I can take many more of these peacetime Invocations."

Kemal could only hold his head groggily as Jaq bounded across the courtyard to swipe his tongue across his face.

"She's angry about something, anyway," his arkados continued. "Get down, Jaq. I swear She nearly blew my head off. That's a good sign."

"Your head?"

"Both heads," the older man chuckled. "And on that note . . ." He waggled his eyebrows suggestively.

Kemal shook his head, his eyes still glassy and unfocused. "I can't . . . I have to do something." He frowned. "I have to . . . go to Assembly?"

Yashar's dark eyes showed a flash of annoyance, then he shrugged. "Well, better you than me. Find me later—Cyan's on the east wall today—and you know they fixed the lock on the second sentinel box door." His hand caressed the back of Kemal's neck. "So if that bloodless lot at the Citadel doesn't suck all the vitality out of you," he whispered, "I soon will." After kissing him fiercely on the palm, the older man then strode off with a jaunty whistle, pleased by the growing flush of desire on his arkados' face. Breathing hard, Kemal bent his head to his knees, his sense of confusion fading before the familiar ache in his groin caused by Estavia and exploited by Yashar. He wasn't too sure he could survive many more peacetime Invocations either, he admitted. The afterimage of Her presence still burning brightly behind his eyes, he made himself straighten, then headed for the west gate stables at as fast a pace as he was able, Jaq at his heels. If Kaptin Julide was right, he'd be back from Assembly before he lost his erection. After that, he would worry about whatever else he was supposed to do.

✦

In the very center of the capital, Anavatan's governing assembly met once a week in the ancient and ornate Derneke-Mahalle Citadel. Built by the Gods, its latticed stone walls encompassed five acres of lush, cinar-tree-shaded rose and rhododendron gardens, sparkling fountains, and rows of sweet-smelling apple, cherry, peach, and pear trees. The building itself formed a series of spiraling halls eventually leading to the massive central assembly chamber. Its swirling white marble floors and deep blue, green, and silver painted walls represented of Gol-Beyaz, with the huge vaulted blue-and-golden-tiled dome, wrapped by white marble viewing galleries, acting as the sky above. Richly embroidered divans sat against the south wall while long tables laden with bowls of nuts and dried fruit and great silver carafes of both tea and imported coffee stood to the east and west and a huge mosaic-tiled map of Gol-Beyaz, bordered by two seas, twelve villages, and one great city dominated the north. A dozen golden candelabra chased away the gloom of Havo's First Day, while in the center, a low, inlaid mahogany table made up of six separate, interlocking pieces, legs carved to resemble lion paws and fish tails, stood on a thick, azure carpet surrounded by crimson-colored cushions. It was a fitting place from which to govern the richest nation in the known world.

On Open Assembly Days, the room would be bursting with people. Twenty-one beys made up the Senior Council: six for the Gods' main temples, twelve for the villages, and one for each of Anavatan's three main Trisects. With the addition of junior beys, aides, delinkon, scribes, stewards, visiting dignitaries, and anyone who had business with the Assembly that day or just wanted to watch, the hall was often crowded with as many as a hundred and fifty people below and up to a thousand in the galleries above. This morning, however, there were only ten: an ancient steward filling teacups by the side table, three clerks clutching the city's damage reports, a single scribe already seated to one side, and five of the six temple representatives. Kemal tossed Jaq a candied date before glancing around to see who the others were today.

The temples of Usara, God of Healing, and Ystazia, God of the Arts, were each represented by proxy-beys of equal rank to Kemal himself, and, not surprisingly, Havo's temple had sent a junior bey's delinkos. Only Oristo was represented by a true bey: Neclan, Senior Abayos-Priest at Oristo-Sarayi—the Hearth God's people took all Assemblies very seriously. A gaunt woman, whose features generally lent themselves to expressions of disapproval, Bey Neclan's face seemed particularly lined this morning, her stiff posture revealing both annoyance and suspicion. As Jaq padded over to stuff his nose under the scribe's arm and Kemal took his own seat, she looked down her long, thin nose at him.

"You're late," she noted coldly. "Even Havo's temple has seen fit to send someone on time."

"Havo's temple is indeed most devout in their civic duty, Sayin," Kemal agreed, ignoring the reproof. "Yusef, isn't it?"

His hands wrapped tightly about a porcelain teacup, Havo's delinkos smiled painfully back at him.

"My seniors send their regrets, Sayin. They are . . . indisposed this morning."

"You mean hung over," Neclan sniffed.

"Yes, Sayin. This First Night was a wild one within Havo-Sarayi as well as without." Starting slightly, he reached down as Jaq, finished with the scribe, thrust his nose into his lap. "Um, good dog, please move."

Aurad, one of Ystazia's master musicians, leaned his heavily muscled forearms on the table. "Shall I send some drummers over to keep time with the beating in their skulls?" he asked with an evil grin.

Yusef laughed carefully. "If it were up to me, I would say, yes, please. I was drafted to help Tahir-Sayin up a rickety flight of minaret stairs this morning and she puked on my shoes."

"Then she deserves drummers; I'll see to it."

"No, you won't." Jemil, Usara's representative turned a firm stare on both of them. Of medium height and build with thinning light brown hair and smooth, fluidly androgynous features, the bi-gender physician to the God of Healing was not an imposing figure, but nonetheless, Ystazia's proxy-bey shrugged sheepishly.

"I was only joking . . ."

Jemil raised one arched eyebrow.

"Mostly. Physicians, no sense of humor," Aurad muttered, winking at Neclan.

"Musicians, no sense of propriety," she retorted.

Jemil raised a hand to forestall further argument. "Dorn, more tea for everyone please. No, Jaq, I do not have anything for you. Please remove your head from my knee."

As the dog shuffled away, Kemal glanced at the empty place at the head of the table. "Don't tell me Incasa's people are hung over as well," he asked, accepting a cup from the steward. "Their festival was months ago."

"Maybe they couldn't wait," Aurad chuckled. "Get your nose out of there, Jaq."

"I imagine their representative is merely late as well. The streets are treacherous this morning," Jemil surmised.

The musician leaned across the table. "Ten aspers says it's Bessic," he offered Kemal in a loud stage whisper. "He wouldn't miss the chance to attend Assembly."

"Done. He hates being out in poor weather."

"But he's ambitious and what other day could we expect Freyiz-Sayin to be absent?"

"Point."

"An unseemly point," Neclan snapped peevishly. "Incasa-Sarayi will send whoever is appropriate to their God's desire. Down, Jaq." She shoved the dog's head away. "Kemal, control your animal or leave him outside."

"Jaq, come."

The dog sighed deeply and, having ascertained that no one at the table would feed him, obeyed, slumping against Kemal's leg with a disconsolate expression.

Aurad grinned. Opening his mouth to say something else guaranteed to annoy Neclan again, he was interrupted as Freyiz, Incasa's First Oracle and Anavatan's most senior bey entered the room on the arm of a delinkos. As one, the Assembly rose in surprise.

No one knew how long Freyiz had served at Incasa's temple; she'd been the God of Prophecy's most favored seer for as long as anyone there could remember. Slight and frail, her body bent, and her hair as well as her eyes long ago turned white from the strength of Incasa's vision-gifts, she was bundled in layer upon layer of heavy woolens to keep out the damp. Even so, she gave off an air of earthly fragility combined with immense unearthly power. It was said that she ruled Incasa's temple with an iron fist and even the God trod lightly when she was angered. No one at that table would have dared to disagree. After allowing her delinkos to help her onto her cushion, she swept her inward gaze across the table, taking in the gathered representatives despite her outer blindness. She gestured.

"Please sit."

When everyone had returned to their seats, she turned her milky-white gaze on Kemal. "Something is happening," she said firmly.

He started.

"Incasa has sent this image to me in a dream," she continued, turning her head slightly to address the entire council, "a child of great potential still unformed standing on the streets of Anavatan. The twin dogs of creation and destruction crouch at its feet. The child is ringed by silver swords and golden knives and its eyes are filled with fire. It draws strength from Anavatan's unsworn and will be born tonight under the cover of Havo's Dance."

There was silence across the assembly table. When she did not elaborate further, Jemil stirred.

"What does it mean, Sayin?"

She gave an eloquent shrug. "The God is being . . . cryptic," she replied with a grimace. "But the simplest answer would be that something of great potential for either good or ill will begin tonight."

"Some thing or some one?"

"The image of the child could be either literal or symbolic. Incasa has not seen fit to enlighten me regarding which it may be. Yet."

Her tone was one of annoyance and Kemal stifled a smile. Remembering his own dream, he made to speak and suddenly felt himself silenced as if a cloud of mist had taken hold of his tongue. Startled, he closed his mouth.

"Did Incasa indicate what He wishes done about this . . . delon?" Jemil continued, using the more urban word for child.

"No."

"Then why . . . ?"

"I have no idea."

"What could we do, anyway?" Aurad interjected with an impatient wave of his teacup. "We can't go out looking for it, whether it's real or symbolic, not on Havo's Second Night. We'd all be swept into the strait."

"Perhaps Incasa has left the decision up to each one of us whether to risk that or not," Neclan countered stiffly.

Freyiz inclined her head toward him. "Possibly."

"Or perhaps we're simply to recognize that it's happening and act at a later date," Jemil offered.

"Again, possibly."

Aurad frowned. "Well, that's all fine and good, but if the choice is mine I choose to remain indoors tonight."

Jemil took a sip of tea before nodding in agreement. "I'm concerned about the these images of swords and knives, however, as well as the . . . what was it?"

"Twin dogs of creation and destruction," Aurad supplied, watching as Jaq padded around the table to lie beside Freyiz, his head resting gently against one white-clad knee. She reached down to stroke his ears absently.

"Yes. I like the former well enough, just not the latter, and I don't like that it's happening on the streets of Anavatan," Jemil continued.

"It's bad for trade," Aurad agreed.

"It's bad for the security of Anavatan's citizens," Neclan snapped. "Oristo's and Usara's temples are responsible for the well-being of the city and Estavia's for its safety," she added, giving a stiff jerk of a nod in Kemal's direction. "If nothing else, we should at least petition our own Gods for answers to this riddle."

Freyiz inclined her head. "Yes, that would be the wisest course of action at this time, Neclan-Delin, even if these weapons are merely symbolic of something else entirely."

"Nice to see that's sorted out, then," Aurad noted. "Now what's all this nonsense about the unsworn; what's that symbolic of?"

"Perhaps it's just as it seems," Jemil answered mildly.

"Bollocks. There are no unsworn in Anavatan. It's the City of the Gods; everyone follows one Deity or another here."

Jemil raised an eyebrow at him.

"Well, apart from the odd foreigner . . ."

"Apart from all foreigners," the physician retorted. "Of whom there are a great many, even in springtime. The docks are teeming with Rostovics, Volinski, Petchans, Thasosians, and many others, not to mention the Yuruk; all of whom have no relationship with the Gods of Gol-Beyaz."

"No, but they must have a relationship with some God or another. Besides, on Havo's Dance there isn't so much as a rat's arse to be seen on the streets of Anavatan. The citizens are all locked safely behind their own shutters and the foreigners are all holed up in hostels or taverns."

"What about the poor?" Jemil prodded.

"What *about* the poor? Don't they have shutters of their own?"

"Do they?"

"How should I know? Bey Neclan?"

"Anyone in need of shelter during Havo's Dance is welcome at Oristo's temples," she answered stiffly. "Whether they be rich, poor, Anavatanon or foreigner. This is known throughout the city."

"Yes, but for a price, Sayin," Jemil noted gently.

"Of course for a price, but no price higher than is possible to be paid," she snapped back angrily. "Those who do not have money may offer service. *All* are protected on Havo's Dance. Period."

"So, what does it mean, then?" Aurad repeated.

"I don't know, *I'm* not a seer."

"Enough." Freyiz frowned at all three of them. "Yusef?"

The delinkos started.

"Yes, Sayin?"

"You've been trying to speak for some time now, what is it that you wish to add?"

"Um, nothing of any real importance, Sayin, it's just that Havo would not respond tonight anyway . . ."

"I'm sure," Neclan sniffed.

The delinkos flushed and Freyiz cast Oristo's bey a reproving glance.

"Please, go on, Yusef."

"Um . . . it's just that our God will be out in force tonight, and if anything is stirring on the streets of Anavatan, Havo will know of it. We can always petition for answers in the morning."

"An excellent idea," Aurad declared. "So, we inform our temples' leaders—those leaders that aren't already here today, of course," he added, winking at Neclan who ignored him. "They petition the Gods, and we wait and see. Unless, of course, Bey Freyiz, there's more?"

"No more at the moment."

"Good. Then it's settled." Rubbing his hands together vigorously, he made to rise, but Neclan frowned him back into his seat.

"We still have the damage reports from across the city, Aurad-*Delin*," she reminded him.

"Oh, right." As the clerks came forward hesitantly, he made a re-signed gesture at the steward to refill his cup.

Across from him, Kemal rubbed Jaq's belly with one foot while he mulled over Incasa's prophecy. The child in his own dream had been standing on the streets of Anavatan, but he hadn't seen any dogs or weapons and Aurad was right, there were no unsworn, whether citizen or foreigner, vulnerable on Havo's Dance. Were there? He frowned. What if the child were to be born during Havo's Dance, but draw strength later? That would fit. Sort of. But again Aurad was right; everyone in Anavatan was sworn to one of the six Deities of Gol-Beyaz. Weren't they? He rubbed his forehead as a faint throbbing began to make itself felt across his temples. He was no battle-seer and interpreting prophecy always gave him a headache. Knowing this, the Battle God rarely asked it of him.

A whisper of intimate power caressed his cheek, and with relief, he let it go. Something *was* happening, but Estavia would tell him when and where he should do something about it. In the meantime, he had other, less confusing things to concentrate on. Straightening his back, he tried to look interested in the damage reports.

Murad was waiting at the west wall gate when he returned.

"Elif-Sayin wants you, Ghazi. So does Marshal Brayazi."

Estavia-Sarayi's official audience-chamber-come-armory had been built against the imposing central gatehouse tower which separated the temple's living quarters from the long, outer courtyard. Built to echo the city's three great watchtowers of Lazim, Gerek, and Dovek-Hisar, which loomed over the northern strait, it presented a plain, blank facade for three stories, after which each wall was pierced by half a dozen thin, defensible windows. The shadowy interior walls were decorated with weapons and armor and devoid of furniture save for six daises which held various battle trophies. It was lit by several hanging lamps which, however, did nothing to alleviate the air of brooding menace. Murad led Kemal and Jaq through it quickly to the marshal's private audience chamber beyond.

By comparison this much smaller structure was both bright and airy, made to resemble an outdoor kiosk or pavilion rather than a fortress. Built against the gatehouse's eastern face, it was possible to open it to the elements on three sides—the walls made of slatted screens that could be moved to accommodate the weather—and filled with plants and small potted trees of every description. When they entered, Marshal Brayazi was standing before a brass mangel, speaking quietly with Elif who was seated on a nearby divan. The marshal acknowledged Kemal's salute with a distracted gesture and, as Jaq bounded over to shove his head under the seer's elbow, she came straight to the point.

"We already know what you discussed in Assembly," she said bluntly. "The God's commanded a full Invocation for the duration of

Havo's Dance tonight. Messenger birds have already been sent to each of the village towers. We begin at dusk with a fully coordinated ritual which you will command from here."

Kemal blinked. "Me, Marshal?"

Elif chuckled. "She came to you first, Ghazi. Officially, that makes this your God-quest."

"But I'm not even a battle-seer."

"You wield Her power through your company in the field," the marshal countered. "This will be no different."

"But . . ."

"Estavia wills it, Kemal," Elif said firmly. "She came to me mere moments after the Invocation. Something is happening and She requires all the strength and power of Her people to meet it. You are intimately involved, and although She did not see fit to tell me why or how, She was clear in Her orders that you were to command the ritual."

The echo of Her touch at the Morning Invocation tingling through his groin, Kemal nodded in resignation.

"What do I do?"

"Sable Company will familiarize you with the command rituals," the marshal answered. "They're waiting for you in their shrine."

"And you'd better get over there right away. It'll likely take you all afternoon to get it right," Elif added.

"Stop by the kitchens and have them wrap you up something to eat. And, Kemal?"

"Yes, Marshal?"

"Leave Jaq behind."

Wistfully thinking of Yashar's now to be broken promise, Kemal gave both women a glum salute before heading from the room, the dog in tow. Elif sent Murad for a hot salap and when they were alone again, the Marshal turned a concerned frown on her retired seer.

"Are you sure he can do this?"

Elif shrugged. "He has a strong physique and, as you said, he's not unfamiliar with Her Power in the field. She loves him and will, *probably*, remember to be gentle with his mind. He should survive it with little more than a headache."

"Still, this is Havo's time," the marshal reminded her. "The power drain will be enormous."

Elif shrugged. "It really doesn't matter, Brayazi-Delin. *She* wants him, and so She will have him."

Watching Kemal cross the parade ground, the marshal nodded tightly. "Yes, She will."

✦

As Elif had predicted, it did indeed take the rest of the day for Kemal to gain a basic enough understanding of the command rituals to satisfy Her seers that his head wouldn't explode that night. Kaptin Liel of Sable Company then reluctantly turned their shrine over to Kaptin Julide—as one of its officers, Kemal had the right to Cyan Company's presence during the Invocation—with strict orders not to touch *anything*. Having already been excused duty for an early supper, the hundred-odd warriors began to file in with a buoyant air, most staring unabashedly around at the seers' inner sanctum and grinning proudly at their ghazi-priest. As they took their places—each one pointedly touching whatever they could reach—Kemal looked up at the eight-foot-tall onyx statue of Estavia, twin swords gleaming in the lamplight, and began to clear his mind for the Invocation.

✦

To the south, in her private bathing room at Oristo-Sarayi, Senior Abayos-Priest Neclan leaned back in a wide porcelain tub as her delinkos poured a vial of lavender oil into the water. The scent wafted up to her, smoothing the deep lines across her forehead, and bringing a small amount of calm in its wake. The day had been disturbing, more for what it had not revealed than for what it had, and she was feeling uncharacteristically drained by it.

Outside, the wind began to whistle past, fluttering the lamplight despite the tightly closed shutters, while the faint sounds of the temple's temporary guests filtered in to her, reminded her that she had less than an hour's respite before the evening's duties demanded her presence.

She sighed wearily. She had the monthy Anavatanon Cami Reception as well as the weekly Temple Luncheon tomorrow. She barely had time for Havo's disruption to her schedule never mind Incasa's, but Oristo was also feeling skittish and disturbed and had filled her dreams just before dawn with a vague sense of disorder and chaos, much more so than what Havo's Dance usually stirred up. Neclan had hoped to gain some understanding of this disturbance at Assembly—all Oristo could send her was the traditional imagery of the Hearth God's disquiet: stained linen and overcooked mutton—but Bey-Freyiz's revelation had left her feeling more unsettled than when she'd arrived. She did not like cryptic visions at the best of times—they disturbed the city's orderly flow—and despite her opinion of Aurad and his so-called sense of humor, she had to admit that the musician was right. It was bad for trade, and trade was the single most stabilizing influence on the city and its people.

As her delinkos began to wash her hair, she sank a little lower into the water. If truth be told, she admitted, it wasn't cryptic visions she disliked so much as Incasa and His temple becoming involved in any aspect of the city's day-to-day life at all. It was her experience that prophecies and prophets complicated things rather than clarifying them. Few of Oristo's people had any kind of prophetic ability; they preferred to rely on the five simple physical senses and their accompanying needs. Take care of those and the metaphysical ones would take care of themselves.

And on that note . . . Opening her eyes, she raised herself up slightly. "Yorin."

The scribe hovering just outside the bathing room door entered promptly. "Yes, Sayin?"

"Have messages sent to each temple chamberlain at once. I wish them to attend me in private consultation tomorrow in midafternoon. Stress the word private, no delinkon or servers to accompany them. They can expect this to occupy approximately one hour of their time and should readjust their daily schedules as necessary." She paused. "Tea and confectionaries will be provided. They needn't bring anything."

"Yes, Sayin.

The scribe withdrew and Neclan leaned back again. Seers and warriors were all very well for dealing with creation and destruction, she sniffed, but when it came right down to it, the only thing that really mattered was that the people of her city needed to be fed and sheltered every day, and nothing, certainly not cryptic prophecies, was going to interfere with that.

Deep within her mind, she felt Oristo's satisfaction sweep away her sense of unease—with the comfortingly normal image of a large broom—and, invigorated once again, she closed her eyes, allowing the last moments of warm water to relax her muscles.

✦

Outside, the sky began to darken as the God of the Seasons slowly rose to begin the Second Night of Havo's Dance. A light spattering of rain began to fall upon the cobblestones of Anavatan, while the rising wind whistled through the streets, rattling the already closed shutters. In the Western Trisect dockyards, Brax and Spar sprinted for the protection of a temporary safe house, while in the depths of Gol-Beyaz the God of Prophecy watched the possibilities of their future unfold and nodded in satisfaction. They would do.

Out on the plains, the spirits of the Berbat-Dunya began to flock together like great, silvery birds, called by their smaller brethren who crouched before the newly bubbling stream of possibility on the streets of Anavatan, waiting impatiently for the coming of night and their opportunity for power.

3

Graize

ON THE BERBAT-DUNYA the air was thick with unrealized potential. As the sun began to set behind its mask of heavy storm clouds and the shining lake's Deity of wind and rain began to stir, the spirits of the western wild lands drifted slowly from the hollows and crevices that made up their own places of power. Stretching themselves upon the winds, they passed over the Yuruk encampments along the small northern lake of Gol-Bardak, running feather-light fingers of need across the flocks of sheep and herds of goats until they were turned aside by a firm but gentle command from a nearby hilltop. Swirling about the head of the man who'd checked their progress, they accepted a small seed of his power to assuage their hunger, then sped off toward the central plains.

Wyrdin-Kazak Kurskili Ranisev of the Rus-Yuruk waited until they were out of range, then signaled the herders that all was safe with a single, shrill whistle. In the distance, his fourth child, fourteen-year-old Raynziern, waved the family's white yak's tail standard in response and Kursk smiled indulgently.

Traditionally the white standard was used only in battle—herders used red—but ever since she'd been made standard-bearer two years before, Rayne had refused to use anything else. She would be a powerful wyrdin and a dangerous raider one day if she learned to control her wayward nature. With a fond expression, Kursk watched her wheel her pony about with effortless grace to join her kardon—siblings—in gathering the few straggling sheep that had failed to keep up when the kazakin had brought the rest from their more sheltered winter pastures, then returned his gaze to the evening sky. These first spring storms were dangerous ones. The spirits were drawn by the chaos in the air, and although not usually a threat to adult livestock, they could still suck the life from a newborn lamb or kid in a heartbeat if the herders dropped their guard.

Closing his eyes, he tasted the warm scents of new life and growth on the wind, then frowned.

Something was happening.

Opening his eyes, he stared out at the distant horizon. The land was still, but there was a dark and heavy portent behind the clouds. Choosing a hawk fetish from the hide bag at his belt, he held it up. The three tied tail feathers wavered in the breeze. He added a plains fetish, four stalks of last year's grasses still smelling sweetly of meadow flowers. They, too, began to tremble. He nodded, then took out a fine piece of hide with several knots tied at one end. Whistling quietly between his teeth, he slowly sliced through the smallest of them with the tip of his kinjal knife.

The spirit he'd summoned replied immediately, snatching the plains fetish from his fingers and flinging it away. It then made a grab for the hawk fetish. Kursk gave a sharp, commanding whistle and it settled for knocking the plains fetish farther down the hill before calling up a small whirlwind to whip about Kursk's head. Reading the fine strands of prophecy that feathered out from the spirit's wake, he nodded, then thanked it with another tiny seed of power. It sucked it from his fingertips, then sped away over the hills while Kursk retrieved his fetish with a thoughtful expression. Something would be born over the Berbat-Dunya tonight. He could not respond until morning, but at dawn he would take his kazakin out to see what the spirits had written on the land and try to divine what it foretold. Mounting up, he turning his pony toward the encampment, allowing it to find its own path, his mind still unsettled by the portents on the breeze.

✦

Rayne met him at the bottom of the hill. Commanding her pony to a series of sidesteps with only the faintest pressure of her knees, she turned her head slyly to see if he was impressed, then, at his smile, fell into step beside him. Noting the plains fetish still held loosely in one hand, she gave him an eager, wide-eyed look.

"What did you see, Aba? Will the storm be worse than you foretold?"

Kursk gave a noncommittal shrug. "The strength of the storm hasn't changed," he allowed. "But there's something else on the wind that could be many things." He swept his hand before him. "Tell me what you think it might be, child. What do *you* see?"

Shaking off her deep hide and woolen hood at once, she quickly scanned the horizon.

"The clouds are densely packed," she observed, her voice taking on a lecturing tone. "And I can see the wild lands shivering in anticipation of the coming rains. The storm will be nurturing, but cold, and the force of it may shred the younger, more delicate grasses.

"*Timur* would say it was an omen of flooding, pestilence, and starvation," she added, rolling her eyes.

"Yes. But Timur is . . ." Kursk searched for as respectful a word as possible, knowing that it was likely to be repeated to the Rus-Yuruk's most venerable wyrdin. "An elder," he said finally. "And a dense packing of years often sees different omens in a dense packing of clouds. What does *youth* see?"

"*Not* flooding," she replied forcefully. "Strong rains maybe, but nothing the plains haven't seen before and nothing they can't recover from. Abia taught me that."

"Your Abia's very wise. So, no pestilence?"

Rayne snorted. "Nor starvation."

"What, then?"

Turning her attention to the west, Rayne's gaze clouded over as she reached out for a sense of the vast world of power and potential that lay just below the surface of the physical plains. "The spirits are rising from the hollows in the earth, drawn by the awakening power of spring," she answered, her voice taking on a singsong tone. "But they do that every year," she added impatiently, her eyes clearing. "Still . . ."

"Still?" Kursk prodded.

"They're . . . agitated," she decided after a moment. "Like they're waiting for something to happen; something besides the storm." She tugged thoughtfully at her yak's tail standard. "Danjel says the spirits are made up of raw prophecy and that they sing songs of power to each other as they rise. If you can capture their words, you'll gain the power to see the future, but if you capture too many, the song will drive you mad and you'll chase after the rest of it forever." She glanced over at him, a tinge of worry darkening her features. "Have you ever heard them sing, Aba?"

Kursk nodded. "Once, just before I became wyrdin. Your tayin, Ozan, dared me to walk out into the storm. The spirits swirled all around me like a thick fog and I heard them singing of hunger and of rage. They wanted my life, my power." He smiled reassuringly down at her. "But they couldn't take it. I'm too wily." He turned his attention to the shimmering plains in the distance. "They frightened me that night, but they also taught me that they're no different than any other wild creature, regardless of what they're made of; when hungry, they'll attack the weak but flee the strong. And sometimes they can be tamed just enough to give up a little of their prophecy in exchange for the power they crave." He smiled. "But that prophecy's hardly ever given in song, and even less often in words. Usually it's more like a vague sense of anticipation, much like what you're sensing now. And the responding emotion it evokes: dread, or caution, or joy, speaks more to the future than the anticipation itself."

"What emotion did it evoke for you today?"

"Caution, but then, I'm an elder, too," he said with a chuckle, "and riding toward flooding and pestilence at a gallop. Why don't you call a spirit up yourself and tell me what it evokes for you."

With a pleased smile, Rayne rose up in the saddle and, putting two fingers into her mouth, gave a piercingly high whistle.

The spirit that shot up from the ground beneath her pony's hooves caused the animal to jump back nervously, and as the tiny, protective bells woven into its mane jangled with the movement, the spirit spun into Rayne's hair in agitation.

She flicked it away with an impatient shake of her head. "Serves you right for trying to spook her," she admonished. "Behave!"

The spirit froze a hand's width from her face and she stared at it, watching it shimmer with a translucent, silvery light. Held by the force of her directive, it twisted in the breeze, growing first substantial and then insubstantial until she released it, tossing it a seed of power as Kursk had taught her to do. As it rose straight up into the air like a tiny shooting star, Rayne tucked a loose strand of hair back into her braid.

"They're a lot more nippy than usual," she noted with a disapproving frown. "And less playful."

"How did that make you feel?" Kursk asked.

"Tense and . . . annoyed," she said after a moment. "But mostly . . ."

"Mostly?"

"Excited." She turned. "Something's going to happen, Aba, something big."

He nodded his agreement. "And you see the difference between age and youth? Where one sees caution, the other sees excitement."

"So what are we supposed to do?"

"Go and find out why we should be cautious about something exciting. But not tonight," he added as she made to turn her pony toward the wild lands at once. "Tomorrow we go chasing after prophecy; tonight we bring in the flocks, and it seems that your kardon may have missed a sheep to the east."

Her head snapped around instantly. "That was Caleb's fault," she huffed angrily. "He was supposed to have cleared that whole area by now. He's so lazy!"

"He has a broken arm, Raynziern," Kursk admonished gently.

She snorted unsympathetically back at him.

"Well, why don't you go show him how it's done, then," he suggested.

"Don't think I won't." With a wrathful expression, she urged her pony into a gallop, making for the distant figure of her youngest sibling already heading back toward the encampment.

Shaking his head, Kursk watched her go, then after a final glance toward the darkening plains to the west, he followed her.

✦

Beyond the hills, the spirits slowly drew together as the sun continued its downward trek toward the horizon. They came from the wild lands of the west, rising from the pockets of power which dappled the Berbat Ridge, from the small Gol-Bardak Lake with its scattering of Yuruk encampments to the north, and from the southern range of the Gurney-Dag Mountains where the Petchan hill fighters still sprinkled their hair with goat's blood to protect their people and their herds from the spirits' touch as they had for over a thousand years. Merging and flowing like a huge flock of misty migrating birds, they slowly made their way east toward the great silvery lake of power, as they had every spring since the world was formed.

And every spring since the Lake Deities had risen from the depths and joined with their human worshipers to surround the source of Their strength with walls of stone and power, the spirits came up short against an impassable barrier. They pressed forward once again, and once again they were denied. Swirling in frustration, they began to hammer against the barrier, spreading themselves thinner and thinner along the miles of guarded shoreline seeking entry, but as always, the barrier held. Thwarted, the spirits withdrew, some to the south, some to the west, but most to the north—making for the great shining place the Deities had built at the mouth of the sea.

The barrier was at its weakest there—so far from the lake of power—and in the past a few tiny spirits had managed to thrust their way inside just long enough to snatch up the life of some tiny, incautious creature, especially on the nights when the Wind Deity screamed and gyrated in time with the High Spring storms, spinning their energy into ribbons of rain and balls of jagged hail. Yesterday the smallest of their number had managed to squeeze through the cracks in the wall of power just long enough to taste the fluttering life of a dying man unclaimed by any God. It had strengthened them as nothing had before and they wanted more. Tonight. As the cloud-obscured sun touched the distant horizon, a growing army of spirits began to press against the barrier around Anavatan.

✦

Deep in the depths of Gol-Beyaz, the God of Prophecy sensed the spirits' hunger and knew it was time. Calling up His newly fashioned prophecy, He reached out for the boys whose futures He had marked: one to feed the spirits so that they might have strength enough to breach the barrier about Gol-Beyaz, one to give them form and substance enough to take their place among the Gods, and one of two candidates chosen to possibly destroy them should Incasa deem that necessary. This latter choice was the most important and, as He cast a fine white mist over their thoughts and intentions, the easier to manipulate them to His will alone, the God of Probability reached out for His first candidate, the one with the greatest potential for both creation and destruction with a mind sharp but fragile and prophetic gifts both powerful and unrealized.

Tossing his dice into the depths, Incasa spoke his name like a whisper of wind on the waves.

"GRAIZE."

Unaware of the God's attention, Graize crouched beside two large stag beetles battling in a ring of sand on the Western Trisect dockyards. Around him, half a dozen youths watched silently, each one intent on the combat, until a sudden gust of wind caused the largest of them to glance up uneasily.

Drove frowned at the cloudy sky, sensing the approaching storm's growing nexus of power above his head. Fourteen years of experiencing Havo's Dance on the streets as one of the unsworn had made him acutely aware of the passage of time, but now it seemed that they'd somehow, inexplicably, lost track of the hour. Chewing uncertainly on a ragged hangnail, he tried to remember the afternoon's events.

They'd dined at Kedi-Meyhane, then made their way along docks still crowded with people finishing up the afternoon's trade until they'd met up with a party of vintners' and brewers' delinkon. With plenty of time, Graize had directed him to build the sand ring. That had been less than an hour ago. He narrowed his eyes. Hadn't it been?

A faint crack of thunder in the distance made him jump, but as a tinker's cart trundled past them, he relaxed, feeling foolish. It would be all right, he told himself firmly. Graize knew what he was doing; he *always* knew when to cut and run. Always.

A skip of lightning across the skies made him flinch.

Always until now.

He glanced nervously up at the darkening sky again, then down at the other boy. He coughed gruffly. Graize ignored him. He coughed again, and finally Graize glanced up with a studied frown, his eyes as pale as mirrored glass.

✦

Graize had calculated the afternoon's game precisely, so much time for so many gamblers to add so many coins to the pile neatly stacked to one side before Havo's Second Night called the game. The combatants' weariness and Drove's nervousness was right on schedule. Now, narrowing his eyes, he fixed the larger boy with an appropriately impatient glare.

"What?" he demanded.

Drove bit his lower lip. "Um . . ." He jerked his head at the sky.

As one, the other youths looked up, suddenly realizing how late it had become. They glanced at Graize who showed no sign of calling the game, then to the owner of the other beetle, who began to gnaw uncertainly at her lower lip, her eyes straying longingly to the pile of coins. Torn between their own greed and their fear of Havo's Dance, they hesitated for one moment longer, then, as the sky suddenly crackled with thunder again, they scattered. The rising wind whipping through his ragged, light brown hair, Graize turned a challenging stare on the other combatant, who finally caught up her beetle and made off as well. Graize smiled coldly, tucking his own insect into a pouch at his side, then began to pick up the money with a satisfied air.

Drove fidgeted impatiently as rain began to splatter against the docks.

"We should go, Graize," he urged, his voice tinged with panic.

"Yeah, in a moment."

Across the city, the priests of Havo began the first notes of the day's farewell.

"No, really, we should go *now*."

Graize glanced up with an annoyed expression, then frowned. The sky had grown unrepentantly dark in the last few moments and, for the first time the pale-eyed boy felt a thrill of uncertainty. Was it really as late as it seemed? It couldn't be. Could it? He stood.

"All right, come on," he decided. "We can just make the Sakin Hostel."

Together, they took off running through a faint snow-white mist that began to swirl almost imperceptibly about their feet.

✦

In Gol-Beyaz, Incasa nodded, then reached out for his second candidate, the one more likely to choose creation perhaps, but the one more likely to wield destruction nonetheless.

"SPAR."

Two streets down, Brax and Spar were also running for shelter. They'd spent the afternoon hovering about the docks as well, and had made enough shine to feed themselves but not enough to buy a place to sleep and, like Graize and Drove, the dusk had somehow come upon them more quickly than they'd expected. Realizing with a start that they'd also strayed too far to reach any dockyard safe house, Brax glanced about uncertainly, clenching and unclenching his fists as it began to rain.

"All right. He took a deep breath. "All right, you remember that place under the docks where we saw that really big, dead rat?" he asked.

His eyes wide with fear, Spar nodded.

"Well, just past it, you know where that street, what's it called . . . Liman-Caddesi starts up, there's an old, upturned fishing boat. It's small, but it should hide both of us if we can get underneath it. We can make it if we run. You game?"

Spar nodded again.

"All right, then, c'mon."

Together, the two boys pelted down the docks. At the end of the final wharf, they hesitated for just an instant, then jumped. Spar hit the sand hard, but Brax caught him up by the jacket and half dragged, half carried him beneath the pier. The light was already gone when they reached the first broken cobblestones of Liman-Caddesi.

✦

"We'll never make it!"

Shouting to be heard above the rising wind, Drove's panic-filled voice rocked Graize to a halt. He glanced about wildly. The buildings around them were already locked tight and he snapped his head back and forth in frustration, feeling more and more like a cornered rat.

"Shit, shit, shit." Banging his knuckles against his teeth, he racked his mind for the memory for some, for any, bolt-hole. "C'mon, Graize, c'mon, you wanna die tonight? Think, think, think," he chanted to himself, using the words to try and clear him mind gone suddenly, frighteningly, cloudy. "Where you gonna go? Find somewhere, find *anywhere*." His eyes wide and unfocused, he raked his gaze across the docks, then gave a sharp nod as a sudden breath of icy wind cleared his mind. "All right, I know a place. It's not much, but it'll be safe. C'mon."

Together they raced down the pier.

✦

Across the city, four of the Gods' six main temples were preparing to meet the Second Night of Havo's Dance in the same manner as the rest of Anavatan, with fastened shutters and bolted doors, while at Havo-Sarayi the festivities were already in full swing, the revelry invoking their God as surely as any ritual, and at Estavia-Sarayi the Battle God's warriors prepared to obey Her command.

In the seer's shrine, Cyan Company held its collective breath as Kemal drew his sword. Dropping to one knee, he held the weapon out across his palms, offering his worship and his service to the God of Battles. As the rest of his company followed his lead a heartbeat later, he felt Estavia's presence within him begin to stir. At his signal, Bazmin tolled the shrine's wide, bronze bell once.

The sound echoed across the temple's empty courtyards. To the east, the great bell of Lazim-Hisar responded, then one by one, each stronghold from the smallest of the city gates to the largest of the village watchtowers, signaled their readiness. With a deep breath taken to still the sudden pounding in his chest, Kemal began the Invocation.

"God of Battles, I pledge you my strength!"

On Liman-Caddesi, Incasa's four boys reached the fishing boat at the same time. Brax immediately pushed Spar behind him and drew his knife. With a snarl, Drove did the same and, as the rain turned to hail, he attacked.

✦

"God of Battles, I pledge you my blood!"

The waters of Gol-Beyaz began to swirl as each company, each garrison, and each tower took up the call, channeling their power through Kemal to their God struggling to break the constraints of another Deity's territorial hold on the physical realm. His body shaking with the force of their combined strength, he gripped his weapon by the hilt, sweeping it upward to point toward the domed ceiling high above his head.

"God of Battles, I pledge you my worship!"

✦

"Spar, get under there!"

Swinging his own knife in a tight arc, Brax kept Drove at bay as Spar threw himself against the boat. It shifted slightly, but then he was tugging his own knife free as Graize darted around Brax's flank.

Shifting his blade from one hand to another, the pale-eyed boy smiled coldly.

"Hey, Spar, you wanna move or you wanna die?" he asked conversationally.

Spar's own eyes narrowed, but he said nothing as Graize leaped forward, only to come face-to-face with Brax as the other boy jumped between them. Graize showed his teeth at him as Drove edged closer.

"You can't hold us both off forever, Brax. Better run now while you still can," he sneered.

Squinting into the growing darkness, Brax snapped his head from side to side, trying to keep both opponents in view. A spattering of hail scored across his cheek and, as he flinched back, Drove swept in under his guard to slice through his sleeve, leaving a thin, red line along his arm.

Beyond the ancient wall of stone and power the spirits reared up, alert to the sudden call of blood and pain. As Brax took a staggered step backward, they threw themselves at the barrier and, as Drove brought his knife slashing down again, they broke through en masse for the first time in a millennium.

The streets of Anavatan filled with a broiling, blood-flecked mist. Within it, driven along by the wind, the spirits sucked up whatever power they could snatch from the tiny creatures in their path, then turned toward the dockyards.

✦

"God of Battles I pledge you my will!"

In Estavia's shrine, the power of ten thousand warriors surging through him flung Kemal to his feet. He felt as if he'd been thrust onto a great wheel, arms and legs stretched out along the spokes and held immobile by the force of their worship. As his sense of self slowly shredded under the onslaught, Estavia rent Havo's prerogative and burst from the waters of Gol-Beyaz.

Kemal's vision went red. Jerking like a puppet, his teeth scored across his lower lip and, as the Battle God's presence flowed into his mouth to catch up each and every tiny drop of blood for Her own, he found his voice again.

"God of Battles I pledge you my service for as long as I have breath in my body!"

As the force of Her power took control of his mind, Kemal felt Estavia shoot into the air like a behemoth, then, twirling Her flashing blades in the air, She turned and streaked toward the western streets of Anavatan.

✦

Lightning skipped across the sky as Drove leaped forward, jabbing his blade at Brax's face. Brax fell back, then swept his own knife up, slicing through Drove's jacket but missing the arm. Behind him, Spar caught up a rock and threw it at Graize with all his strength. Graize avoided it easily. Waggling his knife at the smaller boy, he stepped forward, then froze.

A fine, white mist had gathered around them while they fought, clinging to their feet and legs like strands of sticky spider webbing. As Graize looked down, he saw the faint outline of a thousand wraithlike creatures racing toward them. He opened his mouth to shout a warning to Drove, but as the thunder cracked above their heads, the spirits attacked.

They lunged forward, knifelike teeth and claws outstretched in raging hunger. Graize stumbled backward, screaming in terror and, as Drove turned, the spirits caught him up in a deadly enveloping shroud. Flinging him about like a rag doll, more and more of them leaping upon his back and neck with every turn, they sucked greedily at his body like huge, misty lampreys, then flung his corpse into the street. Strengthened now to a terrible degree, they swept toward the other boys, nearly corporeal hands reaching out with blood-covered claws, while hundreds more poured into the street behind them. Dozens clamped themselves onto Brax's injured arm, the rest made for Graize and Spar.

Almost hysterical with fear, Graize stumbled back against the younger boy, then catching him by the back of the jacket, spun him into the street. Spar skidded on the slippery cobblestones and fell and, as the spirits raced toward him, Graize jerked the boat upright.

Spar screamed.

The world seemed to slow as Brax turned toward the sound. He saw Spar snap into a fetal position, arms wrapped about his head to protect his face from the hundreds of horrible creatures tearing at his hair and clothes, saw Graize duck under the upturned boat, and then he was running, his own face drawn into a grimace of rage and denial. Catching the pale-eyed boy around the middle, he lifted him into the air and, with a strength he didn't know he possessed, he flung him headfirst into the arms of the attacking spirits. Graize's knife scored across his cheek before he was snatched up, struggling and screaming, and then he was gone. Brax had barely enough time to react before the remaining spirits swarmed toward him.

Dozens made for the blood pouring down his face while a hundred more streaked toward Spar. Throwing himself over the younger boy, he wrapped his arms around him, trying to shield him with his own body. The spirits latched onto his back, driving their razor-sharp teeth into his head and neck. A numbing pain swept over him. He cried out, and as his body slowly grew cold, he thought he saw a reddish glow build all around them. Something silver flashed above his head; the midnight silhouette of a huge, ruby-eyed figure wavered in and out of the darkness and, as it reached for him, he realized what it must be. Almost incoherent with pain and fear, he threw one arm out toward it.

"Help us!"

✦

In the shrine, Kemal lurched forward as Estavia suddenly sucked in a great gout of power. His chin cracked against the altar and, as the room flipped sideways, his sword went flying to clatter off the far wall. The Battle God slammed against the unfinished Invocation, knocking Kemal off his feet, and sending sprays of power shooting through the room like a thousand wicked little knives. As one, Cyan Company dove for cover.

✦

The figure disappeared in a gust of wind, and Brax cried out in frustration. Holding Spar tightly against his chest, he struggled to his knees, his mouth and nose already coated with spirits. Calling up every ounce of strength he possessed, he flung his own words into the night like a challenge.

"I know who you are! I know what you want! Save us and you can have it!"

✦

Blood pouring from a dozen tiny cuts on his face and neck, Kemal scrambled to find his weapon as Estavia fought to manifest in the physical world. She sucked in another great gout of power and Kemal nearly blacked out from the force of it, then his sword was stuffed into his hand and a pair of strong arms locked about his chest, hauling him to his feet. Yashar's familiar voice shouted in his ear.

"Finish the Invocation, Kem!"

Raising the blade with both hands, Kemal spat a gob of blood from his mouth and gasped out the final words.

"God of Battles, I pledge you my life! Come into this world and use me as you will!"

✦

The words slapped against Brax's mind like a cyclone. Forcing himself to stand, he snarled at the surrounding spirits, then flung his knife hand, already slick with blood from the wound on his arm, toward the now familiar Deity, shouting out his promise as it spilled into his mind.

"Save us, God of Battles, and I will pledge you my life, my worship, AND MY LAST DROP OF BLOOD, FOREVER!"

✦

The resulting explosion of manifested power flung both Kemal and Yashar against the far wall as Estavia burst fully into the physical world. Whirling Her great swords above Her head, She fell upon the attacking spirits. The nearest were shredded instantly, their fleeting energy devoured by the raging Battle God or taken by Havo manifesting above the city walls; the farthest fled into the sky, transformed by the blood and power they'd feasted upon and by the subtle will of Incasa. The God of Battles howled in triumph, then caught up Brax's pledge in a savage, gluttonous embrace. He felt his spirit lifted into the air, felt it sucked dry and then filled up again as Her lien burned a new kind of life through his veins. Then he was slammed back into his body. His injuries blazing from Her touch, he dragged Spar under the fishing boat and blacked out.

High above the city, Estavia carved a great arch of protection around their hiding place then, as even the storm itself retreated before Her wards, She vanished as violently as She'd come.

There was silence across the dockyards.

✦

In Her shrine, Yashar dabbed the blood from Kemal's face as he shuddered in the throes of Estavia's passing. Finally, he stilled. As Cyan Company began to pick themselves up, he opened his eyes and stared blearily about. Yashar smiled down at him.

"How do you feel?"

Kemal coughed weakly.

"I hurt . . . everywhere," he whispered.

"I'm not surprised."

"Did it . . . work?"

"I imagine. She seemed . . ." Yashar searched for the right words to describe the God's response. ". . . pleased with the result, whatever it was. You, uh, didn't happen to *see* anything about that while She was throwing you around the room, did you?"

"No."

"Well, maybe someone in Sable Company did."

"Maybe. Remind me . . ." Kemal's eyelids fluttered. "Remind me to thank them."

"For what?"

"For not being one of them."

Yashar chuckled. "All right, now you're babbling. Time to stand up, Kemin," he said, using the diminutive in a gentle, but patronizing voice. "That is, if you can."

"I'm not standing?"

"No, you're lying on the floor."

"Oh."

Tucking one arm around Kemal's waist, Yashar drew him to his feet. "Come on. There's a nice, clean bed in the infirmary waiting for you."

"I don't need . . . the infirmary."

"Yes, you do."

"I'm fine. I just . . . need sleep . . ." Kemal made a weak grab for one of the half a dozen Yashars spinning in front of his eyes. "And . . . sex."

"Not tonight. You'd get blood all over the blankets."

"Oh. Point."

"Yes, point," Kaptin Julide agreed in a dry voice from behind them. "Enas, help him."

The other warrior caught Kemal up and, together, he and Yashar half-supported, half-carried him from the shrine. The rest of Cyan Company stumbled out behind them. As the last delinkos took down the hanging lamp, she glanced over at the great onyx statue of Estavia, noting the sated gleam in Her ruby eyes. She grinned back at it. Ghazi-Priest Kemal wasn't the only one wanting sex tonight. Calling out to another delinkos to wait for her, she hurried after the rest of her company.

✦

In his bed of future possibilities, Incasa stared into the depths of Gol-Beyaz, watching the new streams of possibility snake off into the darkness. The spirits of the wild lands had chosen their champion and their sacrifice this night. Creation had been seen to, only destruction remained unquickened before they might become trade and expansion, prosperity and power, as the lake dwellers prayed they would. But the choice was a delicate one; each candidate brought a host of unpredictable possibility streams with him that might destroy the future if left to their own devices. It required a delicate touch to sort out the odds on which one of these candidates was the most valuable without being the most dangerous. And Gods were not known for delicacy.

Closing His fist around His ever present pair of mystical dice, the Patron Deity of Anavatan's gamblers reached out for His First Oracle again.

✦

At Incasa-Sarayi, Freyiz sat unmoving on a small woolen carpet in the center of her meditation room. She'd been there all night, feeling the

shifting currents of the future's many streams washing over her and waiting for the new vision she knew Incasa would send to her. The single
lamp flame illuminating a square foot of polished walnut floor around it
was nearly spent, but her outwardly blinded eyes continued to stare into
the depths of the small bowl of water before her, regardless. She was patient. She had waited many nights in the past and would wait a few more
before her time was done. Taking in a deep breath, she tasted the faintest
hint of incense in the room. The burner had long since dried out, but
the years of divination smoke had pervaded the air with the permanent
taste of oil, acacia, marigold, and wormwood. It was a comfortable, familiar scent, and she let it weave about her, calming her mind and soothing her stiffening joints. When the God's icy presence finally touched
her mind, she was ready to receive His vision-gift.

A hundred future streams bubbled up before her, each with its most
critical moment fanning out from the events of that night. Some ended
in blood, others in flowers, but most snaked off into a watery void, trailing reactions like fine strands of sea grass drifting in the ocean. She
reached out, seeking clarity, but the futures slipped through her mind,
refusing to be restrained. She bore down and finally, bit by bit, they
steadied. Four hazy figures made of fire, features still unformed, appeared over the streets of Anavatan. They wavered in and out of being,
first united and then apart, creating and destroying a hundred new
streams with every turn, each one growing more tangled and more
volatile with every passing moment. As she watched, one vanished into
death while another transformed into a shaft of silver light, but the two
who remained still battled across the currents, causing ripples of chaos
in their wake.

Deep within her mind, she felt Incasa's growing agitation, and
reaching out, she ran her thoughts over each figure until she found the
single moment of weakness that undermined their futures: a hitherto
unseen tower by the sea that one day would force a choice from both of
them. She flicked it aside impatiently, and once free of its influence the
first figure became a frightened, injured child, held safe in the arms of
the Battle God's newest Champion. But as she reached for the other,
the storm-tossed wild lands of the Berbat-Dunya appeared before her.
She tasted madness, pain, and fear, and saw a thousand blood-splattered
creatures of mist and power tearing at a boy-child of flesh and bone.

Beyond his death, the futures lay like withered seaweed across the tower's western face; beyond its life, they writhed like water snakes along the south.

"*Not much of a choice,*" she noted silently, offering the image and its fate to Incasa. "But either way, the odds favor this one. His future is more malleable."

She felt the God of Prophecy raise one snow-white fist then, after a heartbeat's pause, He nodded and flung the dice toward the second boy and his tormentors above the Berbat-Dunya. The newly created stream surged toward His chosen candidate and the unmasked tower vanished into the unfashioned future once again, delayed but undefeated.

✦

Above the wild lands, Graize screamed out his defiance at his attackers. Engulfed by thousands of ravaging teeth and claws, he no longer knew where he ended and they began, he only knew that their savagery fueled his own rage and he clung to that, striking out at them as they tore at him. But he was growing weaker, his body drawing closer and closer to death with each attack. Just as he felt the final darkness poised to sweep over him, a crack of power, as icy as the Deniz-Siyah Sea in winter, slammed into his thoughts; some half formed wall of both protection and restraint deep inside his mind cracked under the onslaught, releasing a surge of energy that flung him forward and, without thinking, he sucked it back into his body. It tore its way through his mind, filling him with an overpowering sense of invincibility and, with a scream of renewed hatred, he caught up the largest of the spirits and drove his own teeth into its misty face. The ice-cold power of pure prophecy shot down his throat, freezing a path through his entire body even as he snatched up another.

His latent prophetic gifts merged with the spirits' life force, creating a powerful, new future that shone in his mind like a beacon. It grew until it encompassed all the world, then shattered into a kaleidoscope of brilliant white lights, each with its own tiny shred of emerging consciousness. Images flew past his eyes: a vast legion of riders thundering across the plains, a tall tower on the sea perched above a stone cell that echoed with pain and despair, and a face both familiar and unknown that filled him with a conflicting sense of hatred and desire, all directed by an emerging consciousness that hammered at his own sense of self.

Sucking it into his body, Graize renewed his attack on the spirits with a savage concentration he'd never known before. As the night wore on, they fought, both now equally matched in strength and fury, until the eastern sky grew pale with the rising sun. The spirits made one last assault, then flung him aside and melted into the dawn as Graize fell heavily to the ground, cold and still, but alive.

✦

At Incasa-Sarayi, the figures became three frightened and bloodied children, and in her meditation chamber, Freyiz blinked as the lamplight finally guttered out. The future streams had dug themselves a more stabilized channel to flow through for now with Incasa's choice, but the passageway was still uncertain. One false move and that destabilizing tower would rise up again and they would silt up into chaos once more. They must be carefully watched and she was too old to maintain that kind of vigil for long, especially so far from the God's source of power. Rising with a groan, she crossed to the southernmost window, frowning as the rising sun turned the distant power of Gol-Beyaz to rippling silvery orange and yellow satin in her prophetic gaze. It had been years since she'd been back to her childhood village of Adasi-Koy on the eastern shore, but only there, where the lake cupped about the jut of land on three sides, could she hope to call up enough strength to hold the futures intact against the tower's influence.

"*Gods,*" she snorted inwardly, ignoring Incasa's responding caress as a twinge of pain feathered up her right knee. "*Can't ever leave well enough alone. Or let an old woman retire in peace, for that matter.*"

Both Incasa and Estavia had interfered with Havo's Dance this night, she noted, choosing their champions in blood and in power—whether for good or ill, it was too early to tell—but one thing was certain, when one God stepped into the territory of another, the repercussions always touched the lives of their worshipers. With a resentful grumble, she crossed to her delinkos slumbering in the corner, and shook the bi-gender fifteen-year-old awake. It was time to choose a new First Oracle and then journey to Gol-Beyaz to try and save the future from two boys who slept, exhausted, beneath a decrepit fishing vessel and another who lay near death on the rocky plains of the

Berbat-Dunya, surrounded by a swarm of shining, silvery lights that might lead them all to either creation or destruction.

As Freyiz hobbled painfully toward the small bedchamber off her meditation room, the image of the tower rose up in her mind again, suddenly strengthened by a new figure whose power shone like a golden beacon in the night, but she thrust it aside. One thing at a time, she snorted to herself, first sleep, then travel, then battle with towers, golden figures, or whatever else might rise up against her.

"I am *far* too old for this nonsense, you know," she growled in the direction of the small white marble statue of Incasa, standing in its wall niche by the door.

The statue made no reply, and Freyiz acknowledged the wisdom of its silence with a sharp nod of her head; she was in no mood for lip from anyone, least of all a God that should know better. As she accepted the arm of her delinkos, the image of the golden figure winked into being once more. She narrowed her eyes.

"I said, from *anyone*," she warned. With a burst of musical light, it disappeared again.

✦

Far to the south on the island of Amatus, a golden-haired young woman smiled in her sleep. Lying in an open-air pavilion bedecked with early spring flowers and hung with fine curtains of green-and-yellow silk, she breathed in the warm, salty air of the Deniz-Hadi Sea, allowing it to color her dreams with prophecy.

An old woman stood in the center of a shining silver lake, barring passage to all but those who'd accepted her authority. Beyond her a tall stone tower beckoned, offering pleasures and power. Between them lay a swirling, chaotic mass of soldiers, riders, Gods, and priests.

She opened her eyes.

The rising sun shone down on the still turquoise waters of the southern sea like a balm. Rising, she stepped lightly across the beach, enjoying the feel of the early morning breeze rippling through her shift and the cool sand spraying across her feet. They spoke to her of so many subtle variations in the future that she felt almost giddy with possibility, but when the water lapped against her toes with the cool reminder that the physical world was as important as the metaphysical, she brought herself back to the present.

Taking one careful step backward, she glanced over at the old man who stood a respectful distance away, a spear cradled easily in the crook of his arm.

"It was a long night for you, Hares," she noted, a smile lighting up her unusually black eyes.

"It was, Panos," he agreed, carefully avoiding her gaze—her mental powers were considerable even at so young an age. "But it was also a quiet and peaceful night. I drew maps in my mind while I waited for the dawn."

She nodded, watching as the lines and colors of his artistry played across her mind like so many harp strings.

"So, you don't resent accompanying me, then?"

"When the Oracle of Amatus asked for you personally, how could you feel anything but honored?"

"Quite easily," she laughed. "Drawing imaginary maps on a beach can't be half so pleasant as drawing real maps in the royal gardens of Skiros."

He gave an eloquent shrug. "Perhaps not, but when the child of your oldest and dearest friend asks that you guard her sleep while she journeys in the realm of prophecy, you're only too pleased to do so. However, I am tired," he admitted. "It's been a long time since I carried anything bigger than an ink brush in offense or defense. Military service is for the young."

"We'll take in a large breakfast very soon and then you can return me to my mother and sleep the day away in her best guest suite," she promised.

"You got your answer, then?"

"Most of it." Crouching down, Panos watched a tiny turtle make its struggling way toward the water, trailing its past and its present along behind it in a series of sparkling, musical notes that seemed to bounce off her skin. The notes became drops of water breaking across a broken marble surface and she frowned thoughtfully. "Have you ever drawn a map of Gol-Beyaz?" she asked.

"I have."

"Have you ever been there?"

"When I was young. I traveled with King Pyrros to the mighty city of Anavatan and beyond."

"It's said they have no king," she observed.

"That's true. They follow the directives of their Gods only."

"But someone must lead them?"

He shrugged. "Priests, for the most part."

"I should think that the lack of a centralized authority would be a weakness."

"They have a very great army."

"They'd have to." Making a swift decision, she lifted the turtle, and ignoring its indignant attempts to bite her, carried it the last few paces to the water.

Her mother would not have approved, she mused. She would have admonished her in words that fell like purple grapes on the ground, that creatures, like people, must make their own way in this world, but Panos saw no reason to refuse aid when doing so gave her such a pleasant tactile experience. The turtle's belly had been smooth and soft and sounded like cork trees whispering in the night. She never would have expected that. She watched as it disappeared into the waves with a splash of color and music, then stood.

"I will travel to Anavatan and beyond myself this season," she stated. "And you will come with me."

"Oh?"

His lack of enthusiasm pattered against her thoughts like tiny footsteps and she laughed.

"Don't worry, you'll be able to bring your inks and parchments with you." Her expression grew serious. "Something's happening in the midst of Gol-Beyaz, Hares, and the king will want an oracle nearby to determine whether it will be advantageous for the south, and the oracle will need a friend to help draw its deciphering.

"Besides," she added, pressing her hands to her cheeks grown suddenly warm and scented like flowers. "There's a tall stone tower in my dreams that keeps calling to me. I think I should like to see what it wants."

Hares gave her a look of amusement and alarm equally mixed. "It probably wants what all towers want," he said in a warning tone of voice. "Be careful you don't give it more than *you* want."

"Oh, don't be silly," she scoffed. "I'm not talking about sex. Sex is a pleasant . . . tactile diversion, nothing more. I'm talking about power, the kind that plays deep and sinuous music in my head."

"Mm-hm. It's obvious why I'm going now. Once your mother finds out about this, she'll likely send me herself." He glanced up at the great mansion perched on the hill above them. "And on that note, perhaps we should return to her."

"If you like." Following him toward a small barge tied up beside the beach, she smiled secretly to herself. Power was as pleasantly diverting as sex, the more so if they were experienced together, and it was very likely they would be, whatever the combative, old woman in her dreams might be planning. Together, the tower and the Oracle would prevail. She didn't need a dream to tell her that.

4

Brax

Havo's SECOND MORNING was as peaceful as Havo's Second Night had been violent. Drove's corpse lay where it had been flung, one desiccated hand reaching out, the other clutching at his throat. Brax stared down at him for a long time, then swiftly searched through what was left of his clothing, finding five copper aspers in the remains of a shredded leather purse. Nothing else was salvageable. He turned away.

He and Spar had crept out from beneath the fishing boat as soon as dawn had brought an end to the storm. Both had taken a dozen deep scratches to the back and neck and the wounds across Brax's arm and face felt numb and tight.

"But at least they're not infected," he muttered.

Yet.

Beneath the now constant buzz of Estavia's lien he could feel the heat tickling at the edges of his injuries. Apparently, instant healing was not part of the Battle God's bag of tricks.

The buzz grew stronger, and he acknowledged the point with an exaggerated shrug. She'd provided the means to buy healing, and that was great, but . . . He jiggled the money in his hand pointedly. Five aspers would buy them the necessary salve to doctor their injuries or feed them, but not both.

The buzz became an impatient itch and suddenly something glinted just under the corpse's right arm. Crouching, Brax pulled up Drove's knife. It was heavier than his, and better made, with a smooth wooden handle and a carved jewel worked into the top. Worth a couple dozen aspers at least. He should have remembered it. With a nod, he tucked it through his belt.

"Thanks."

The responding caress made him flush. It was going to take a while to remember that now when he talked about the Gods, one of them would be talking back—and loudly, too. Still—he glanced down at the knife with a grin—if he'd known that worshiping a God was going to be this profitable, he'd have joined him and Spar up a long time ago whatever Cindar had wanted.

His smile faded as he glanced over at the younger boy.

Spar had taken one brief look at Drove—the second corpse he'd seen in as many days—then turned away with a shudder. Now he stood, staring out at the cold waters of the Halic-Salmanak, thin shoulders hunched under what was left of his jacket, waiting, as always, for the older boy to decide on their next move, for good fortune or bad.

Brax joined him.

"C'mon," he said gently. "We don't wanna be anywhere near this place when the Watch finds Drove, and besides, we've got a long walk ahead of us."

Spar turned, a questioning frown on his face.

"We have to get to Estavia-Sarayi," Brax explained, feeling the imperative in the unfamiliar shifting pressure of the God's touch. "And it's a long way over . . . there someplace." He waved one hand toward the tall minarets of the Temple Precinct just visible to the southeast.

Spar's expression grew cynical.

"Don't worry," Brax assured him. "They have to take us in. She rescued us, and it's Her that's sending us there. It won't be like what Oristo's temple does. They won't try to put us to any menial work. We'll be city guards, or maybe even ghazis or something."

Spar gave a very unchildlike snort.

"Sure we will," Brax insisted. "That's what they do there. It doesn't matter who we are, *were*," he amended. "We're Hers now, and She's a Battle God so we'll go into battle—with weapons and armor and everything. It'll be great, you'll see." Draping one arm across the younger boy's shoulders, Brax drew him past Drove's body and up Liman-Caddesi. "I heard that when they're not out killing people," he began in a conspiratorial tone, "they eat huge mounds of lamb and fish and curried rice off golden plates. And those olives that you like so much, they eat them every day, sometimes two or three times a day if they want to."

Spar gave him a faint, disbelieving smile.

"No, really," Brax continued. "They're rich, all of them. Nothing's too good for the Warriors of Estavia 'cause they risk their lives to protect the city from the Yuruk and all our other enemies—whoever they are," he added. "So when they're not out killing people, they sleep on beds made of goose down covered with silk sheets, and they wear leather sandals on the street and satin slippers inside the temple. There's rooms piled ten foot high with gold and jewels and, in the courtyards, the trees throw so much fruit that they can't keep up with it and it falls into piles all over the place. They have special gardeners whose only job is to pick it up. I even heard a garrison guard once say that the kitchens alone were as big as Oristo-Cami. They could feed the entire city if they wanted to, so, don't worry about anything, all right? We're never gonna go hungry again. This is gonna be the best thing that's ever happened to us. I promise."

Turning them toward the dockside market, Brax glanced up at the overcast sky. *As long as you make it there in time*, his mind observed darkly. *So don't mess around today or you'll fail him again. He won't survive another night of Havo's Dance on the streets and neither will you.*

Brax clenched his teeth. *We won't have to*, he retorted. *We're Estavia's now and She won't let those things touch us ever again. We're not gonna end up like Drove and Graize, or even like Cindar either. We're safe now, safe forever. So shut up and think about food.*

Leading them to the nearest stall, Brax pushed away the memory of Graize fighting off a dozen ravaging spirits as they dragged him into the air. *I said, we aren't going to end up that way*, he repeated. "Not ever."

Spar gave him an inquiring glance and Brax shook his head.

"Nothing. C'mon, let's eat."

✦

Far away, crouched on the edge of a small rise on the Berbat-Dunya, Graize blinked at the strange thought that someone was thinking about him before staring out at wild lands, his pale eyes misty and unfocused, one pupil distinctly larger than the other, and a dazed expression on his face. His newly expanded abilities scrabbled to make some sense of the chaotic swirl of images called up by the vast expanse of power and possibility stretching out before him, but quickly became overwhelmed once more.

"It's like piles of yellow-and-green carpets," he murmured. "But where're the carpet sellers, hm? It's long past dawn. They should be up and opening their stalls for the morning trade."

Looking down at the dead beetle clamped in his fist, he brought it up to his ear, then nodded.

"Ah, the market's closed today," he said gravely. "There's been a death in the family."

The beetle said no more and he closed his hand, pressing it to his chest. It was the only possession he had left and he didn't want it to leave him, too. Everything had left him, even the buildings. His eyes narrowed as he tried to remember how that had happened. The night before was a confusing jumble of images and sensations; in fact everything before that morning was a confusing jumble of images and sensations. Everything except the spirits, he amended; he remembered the spirits. They had . . . fed him? No, something had *made* them feed him, something cold, like ice water with a terrible consciousness behind it, something just beyond remembering. As he strained to bring the memory into focus, a dull ache began to throb behind his left temple and he abandoned the attempt. It didn't matter anyway.

Catching up one of the wispy creatures that still clung to his cheek; he pressed it against his teeth. Its tiny allotment of power and prophecy trickled down his throat and his eyes cleared for just an instant. Yes, they had . . . fed him with their own shining, ice-cold life force. That morning. Slowly, his sense of time and space began to return.

He'd come back to consciousness some time after dawn, lying facedown in a gully, knife gone, money gone, and his clothes hanging off him in bloody rags. The gout of power that had saved his life was long since used up and the path it had torn through his body spasmed every time he'd tried to move or even think. The pain had threatened to overwhelm his mind with a flood of cold, silvery shards that almost seemed to be alive they were so bright. He shivered. They were alive, he'd realized. Alive and hungry, but so very tasty, like silvery sweetmeats on a confectioner's tray.

"They're tasty, but they're deadly," he warned himself, feeling the truth of his words in the ebb and flow of the spirits' power within his veins. "You can't eat too many of them or you'll go mad. You can't even look at them for long or you'll freeze to death. But, maybe, you could look for just a little while."

He stared at them until the silvery shards became the kaleidoscope of brilliant white lights he'd seen above the wild lands and he nodded triumphantly. He'd *thought* they'd been hiding back there.

He bared his teeth at them experimentally, but they just twinkled back at him and he remembered. The silvery lights and the powerful new future he'd tasted had kept the spirits at bay until the dawn. Somehow weakened by the sunlight, the spirits could no longer attack him, but they still clung to him, unwilling to let go, covering his mouth and nose in a sticky, white mass. He breathed them in and felt their now familiar power flowing down his throat to warm his chest and limbs with potential. He'd begun to scoop them up from the pools of power all around him then, cramming them into his mouth and, after only a few minutes, he grew strong enough to scramble from the gully and clamber up the rise.

But once there, there was nothing to see but miles of empty landscape and the vast, cloudy sky. Anavatan had disappeared. He was alone.

He cocked his head to one side. Hadn't he always been alone?

The image of a dark-haired boy, watching as he was carried into the air on a tide of agony hovered before his eyes and he swiped at it impatiently. He didn't know who that was. Scratching angrily at a dirt-smeared scab on his chin, he frowned. Or maybe he did know, but he didn't care; it could be either.

The dark-haired boy became an older, larger youth and Graize shook his fist at it.

"No, no, no," he whispered as he stared into its empty eye sockets. "Fly away, Drove. They ate you. You lost the game and you're dead now. Fly away."

The image vanished in a puff of silver dust and Graize swayed dizzily in its wake. Sucking at a tiny spirit entwined around his fingers, he tasted moisture, then turned. There was a tall tower in the distance. He squinted. No, in the future, he amended, standing on a rocky ledge overlooking a storm-tossed sea. He licked his lips. The sea. Water. He needed water. He was so thirsty. But he couldn't get water from the tower. Not yet. Nor from the sea. He had to find it somewhere else. With the allotment of prophecy he'd gained from the tiny spirit, he knew that water lay to the north and he began to make his way down the rise, his mind consumed with the need to drink.

✦

He wandered aimlessly until the cloud-obscured sun began its downward journey to the west, drinking from the rapidly shrinking puddles on the plains, then moving on to search for food, guided this way and that by the silvery lights and the new knowledge in his mind. The spirits swirled about him, whispering to each other in their own sibilant language, and every now and then, if he listened hard enough, he could almost understand them. But the concentration made his head ache so, after a while, he stopped trying. Then their world flowed over him like the tide, transforming the wild lands into a vast sea of darkly shaded dunes that looked like islands in the distance; islands dappled with pools of silvery-orange-and-yellow light. He tasted the cast-off power of insects, birds, and burrowing creatures, felt the spirits' insatiable hunger for the deeper, richer power growing stronger with every passing season behind its distant barriers of steel and stone, and knew their frustration as that power was denied to them over and over again by shepherds, warriors, and Gods. By the time the black dots on the horizon caught his attention, he'd forgotten that anything except the hunger had ever existed.

The dots became a host of riders and, as his accompanying spirits fled, Graize stared fixedly down at them, feeling the growing interest of the silvery lights. The dots wavered in and out of his sight like distant waves sparkling in the sunlight, first near and then far away, many becoming few, than breaking up into many again. As they drew closer, he was able to discern ten figures dressed in black boots and pantaloons, brown sheepskin jackets under boiled leather cuirasses, with iron-strengthened leather helmets on their heads and curved swords at their backs. They carried bone-and-wood bows with quivers of black-and-brown arrows at their hips, lances tipped with horsehair and nasty-looking iron hooks, and their shaggy little mounts wore braided feathers and tiny bells in their manes. A single memory came to him from the Anavatanon docks: Yuruk riders from the Berbat-Dunya, powerful, dangerous, and unpredictable, people to be feared and avoided; the greatest of all challenges to the game, but a challenge he'd never taken up. Until now.

As he watched, one figure, riding before the others, carrying a tall stick with a white animal's tail attached, became as familiar and yet as unknowable as tomorrow's dawn, but it was the one who rode in the very center that drew his attention like a moth to a flame. His new vision saw strands of pale, multicolored power emanating from his chest like the spokes of a misty wagon wheel, ending at the chest of each of the other riders. The shining lights whispered his name: Kursk, their leader, their wyrdin—the word flowed over his tongue as if he had spoken it a hundred times—their seer. Captivated by the strength of his abilities, Graize reached out.

✦

The kazakin been riding all day, following the path of a small whirlwind that Kursk had called up just after daybreak. The spirits of the wild lands were unsettled and distracted, unable to say more than that something portentous was still happening to the southeast. Alert to the signs from the night before, Kursk had sent several of his people fanning out ahead as they tracked the wake of the disturbance.

It was Rayne who spotted the figure standing all alone in the middle of the plain. She gave the short, low whistle that meant unknown danger in the distance and, signaling the others to wait, Kursk joined her on a small hillock overlooking the strange creature. It stood as still as stone, giving no indication that it knew they were there, even after they began their approach, but Kursk could sense the chaotic swirls of power spinning about it like a cloud of spring flies. Whatever it was, this was the center of the disturbance on the plains.

He halted the kazakin several hundred yards away. He was still uncertain whether the figure was human or spirit, but now, as it raised one hand toward them, he could feel it reaching greedily for his life's power.

Frowning, he brought up his own hand to deflect its attack, and it swayed weakly in response.

Spirit, then.

"Wait here."

Removing a ward fetish from his belt, he dismounted. As the company fingered their own protections nervously, he approached the creature as cautiously as one might approach a wild animal, holding the fetish up before him.

Behind him, Rayne stirred with impatience, unwilling to make use of her own wards until the creature proved to be other than physical.

On closer inspection, the figure seemed to be a slight, brown-haired boy of eleven or twelve, his sunburned face a mask of bruises and ugly red scratches, his eyes squeezed tightly shut. His clothes were little more than tattered and bloody rags and, as Kursk drew near, he saw him shiver with cold. Keeping his movements slow and careful, he held one hand out toward him.

"Child," he said gently, "what do you do here?"

The boy turned gray eyes streaked with wisps of bright white power on Kursk's face and the Yuruk leader felt a chill run up his spine.

Not spirit, but not truly human either.

"I'm watching for the dawn," the boy whispered, his voice low and rasping. "The dawn is creation." He frowned. "Or destruction, I'm not sure which yet. But the dawn will help me *see* which one it is."

"But the dawn is long past, child."

"No, it's a prisoner in a tall tower. But I'll get it out. One day. *If* I feel like it," he snarled, his gaze suddenly turned inward.

Kursk stilled the urge to back away. The spirits had told him something strange and powerful would be born on the wild lands, but he hadn't expected it to look like a half dead, half mad boy-child. That limited his responses. Forcing himself to take another step forward, he froze as the boy suddenly tensed.

"It's all right. I won't hurt you. But what are you, human or spirit?"

The boy cocked his head to one side as if the question gave him some pause. "I don't remember," he said finally.

"You're bleeding. Who harmed you?"

"Others."

"Others? Others like yourself?"

"Maybe."

"Where do you come from?"

The boy's eerily bright eyes narrowed. "The shining city," he answered after a moment.

"Shining?"

The boy gestured toward the southeast. "The city . . ." he repeated, then paused with a frown as if he wasn't sure what to say next. "The city of lights and power," he added finally. "The city of steel and stone."

"The city of . . . ? Do you mean Anavatan?"

The boy nodded.

"But that's miles away. How did you come to be here? Where are your abayon?"

The faintest of smiles crossed the boy's face. He raised his fist to his ear and Kursk could see something black clutched in his fingers. "Dead," he answered flatly. "Everyone's dead, even . . ."

He held his hand out to show Kursk a large stag beetle, its carapace badly cracked, lying in his palm. The boy closed his fist over it again.

"It's dead, but it still talks to me, helps me think. It didn't leave." He glanced around blankly. "It's the only thing that didn't leave. Even the spirits left."

"The spirits?"

The boy nodded, his face paling to a sickly shade of gray. "They ran away when they saw you coming and I'm so thirsty . . ." His eyes grew pinched. "I want them to come back."

A tinkling of bells swept a few of the wisps of power from his eyes and Kursk glanced over to see Rayne sliding down from her mount. He gestured.

"Bring water."

"Yes, Aba."

Making her way to his side, she handed him her waterskin, then stared frankly at the boy, taking in his injuries and dazed demeanor with a flick of her eyes. As he snatched the waterskin from Kursk's fingers, she tilted her head to one side.

"Who is he, Aba?" she asked.

"I don't know."

She turned. "Who are you? What's your name?"

He blinked uncomprehendingly at her as water dribbled down his chin, then shrugged. "Graize," he said finally as if he'd had to pull the word from some far distant place, then returned his attention to the waterskin.

Kursk frowned. Graize was a Volinski name, meaning lonely mountain if he remembered correctly. The boy had the look of the people across the northern sea, but it still didn't explain how he'd gotten there.

"Aren't you cold?" Rayne continued.

The boy—Graize—brought the beetle up to stare intently at it for a moment, then nodded.

"Yes."

Kursk pulled off his sheepskin jacket.

"If you come with us, you'll be warm and fed, Graize. Will you come with us?"

"Come . . . ?" He tipped his head to one side as if the question made no sense to him, then brought his unfocused gaze to bear on Kursk's face. "Will you let the spirits come back?" he asked.

Now it was the wyrdin's turn to pause. The spirits could be very dangerous if they weren't handled properly, but for all his physical appearance, this boy might still be only human seeming himself. To refuse the spirits might be to refuse the boy, and the portents had led them to the boy.

"As long as the spirits do us no harm," he answered finally.

"They won't; they're mine."

"Then they may come with us."

Graize's eyes cleared for a moment. "Then I'll come with you, too."

"Good."

Stepping forward, Kursk draped his jacket very gently over the boy's blood-encrusted shoulders, but as soon as it touched his skin, he collapsed. Kursk caught him before he hit the ground and, noting with some relief that Graize felt as human as any one of his own children, lifted him into his arms and jerked his chin toward Rayne.

"Well, it looks as if we've got what we came to the wild lands to find. Fetch my pony."

"Yes, Aba."

As she passed by, she bent and picked up the beetle that had fallen from Graize's limp fingers. Kursk glanced over at it.

"Keep it for him. I think it's his birth fetish."

Her lip drawn up in a faint sneer, she nodded and, after tucking it into the small hide bag at her belt, headed for her mount.

✦

Lost in his sea of silver lights, Graize gave himself over to the encompassing safety of the older man's arms as a host of comfortingly physical sensations washed over him. Kursk smelled like exotic plants and animal hides, and felt like clear, clean water. The tinkle of his pony's bells sounded like raindrops on the water and seemed to keep the power of the spirits from overwhelming his mind. He felt calm and quiet with no need for thoughts or words. No one had ever made him feel like that before.

For a brief moment, a distant memory of a man's face looking down at him, his own gray eyes smiling, flitted by and then was lost again as the image of another man, black hair falling into dark, fathomless eyes, rose up again. But once again he swept it aside. He still didn't know who that was. He didn't know who anyone was, but for the first time since he'd woken up with dirt in his mouth and a host of spirits swimming through his veins, he didn't care. He was safe and he was warm, his battle on the streets of Anavatan the night before already fading to no more than a distant nightmare. As Kursk lifted him onto his own mount, Graize released all memory of the shining city and the life he'd once lived there and embraced the shimmering power of the Yuruk leader and his people.

✦

Miles away, Brax was giving up his old life with a lot more difficulty, wincing as the growing pressure of Estavia's presence pushed him down the street toward Her temple.

He and Spar had been walking all day after Drove's knife had bought them a jar of comfrey salve for their injuries and his five aspers a breakfast of bread and honey with two cups of extra-sweet tea and a handful of dried apricots. Spar was looking better already, especially after Brax had hooked a new jacket for him off a clothier's cart while the merchant argued with a customer about the meaning of Estavia's bells the night before. The God had given him a sharp, mental smack for that, but after Brax had patiently explained that the younger boy could not possibly walk through the damp and chilly streets all day without it, She'd relented. With the resigned belief that this was only going to get worse once they reached the temple, he glanced over at Spar. Despite the jacket, he was starting to flag; his eyes as shocky as they'd been that morning and he was beginning to favor his bad leg. Never a good sign.

"Who'd of thought the city was so big, huh?" Brax joked. "But that tea seller said the temple was close. Breathe deep; you can smell the fruit trees, can't you?"

Spar nodded wearily.

"So we're nearly there. Come on."

He quickened their pace as drops of rain began to hit the cobblestones all around them. Nightfall was nearly an hour away, but it wouldn't do them any good to get caught in the rain. He could feel Spar's growing agitation and, as the thunder cracked above their heads, both boys broke into a run.

✦

They reached the temple's public parade square a few moments later. A hundred yards away, across the vast, open expanse of flagstones, two sentries, looking a hundred times more dangerous than any garrison guard in their black enameled armor, stood as still as onyx statues before the huge cylindrical front gatehouse towers of Estavia-Sarayi. Their tall, hook-bladed halberds gleamed in the dull light and their sharp eyes tracked immediately to the two boys as they stepped onto the square. Spar froze.

"It's them or that," Brax said simply, jerking his head toward the glowering sky.

Spar glanced longingly back toward the city and Brax shook his head.

"We'd never make it. Not now. Look," he said, his voice taking on an urgent tone as a streak of lightning rippled across the sky. "You're feeling the storm, not the temple, but if you don't like it, we can always leave in the morning, all right? She won't make us stay if we're not happy. And I won't make us stay if *you're* not happy. I trust your feelings, but just give it one night's try, all right? Just one?"

His eyes wide and fearful, Spar nodded reluctantly.

"All right. C'mon, then. Like Cindar taught us, yeah? Confident and like we're meant to be here, 'cause we are."

They started walking. Rain began to fall all around them and Brax fought the urge to run. One wrong move and Spar would bolt; he could feel it. As they came abreast of the sentries, he felt Estavia pushing him forward and used the feeling to square his shoulders. They *were* meant to be there. *She* had sent them. Bunching his fists into the back of Spar's jacket, he shoved him past. Through his new bond with the Battle God, he felt Her touch the minds of the sentries, commanding passage, but the skin between his shoulder blades still crawled with the knowledge that they could've killed them both in a heartbeat. Breathing carefully through his mouth, he propelled Spar under the bristling teeth of the raised portcullis and into the dark entrance tunnel beyond.

The patch of dim light at the end seemed a hundred miles away.

✦

When they finally stepped out into a shadowy, rain-slicked courtyard, bigger than any they'd ever seen, Spar sagged and would have fallen if Brax hadn't caught him by the arm.

"Almost there."

Behind them, the gate closed with a heavy boom and Spar jumped. Brax forced himself to laugh.

"That was close, huh?" he asked lightly. "Well, we're through the first part, anyway. Which way do we go now, do you think?" He glanced around at the huge empty courtyard. High-walled buildings, their shuttered windows dark save for the occasional flicker of lamplight through the slats, surrounded them on all sides, shielded by tall, dark trees and wrapped about by four long, pillared galleries. Something he couldn't name drew his gaze to the far southern corner, but as he took a step in that direction, the God's presence impelled him to the east, past the smell of cooking. He shook his head at Spar's imploring glance.

"We can't go to the kitchens just yet," he explained, feeling the truth of his words as a God-wrought image of warmth and safety grew in his head. "We'll eat soon, I promise." *Right? Eat really soon?* he asked silently. "But right now we've got to get to where we're going and that's that big, blocky tower up ahead. Someone's going to meet us there."

Spar didn't bother to glance past Brax's pointing finger. His face pinched and hungry, he just hunkered down inside his new jacket, following the older boy as he started along the shadowy gallery and shivering as lightning lit up the sky. They reached a small wooden door at the far end just as a slight fall of hail began to patter against the courtyard. Pushing at the door experimentally, Brax shot the other boy a confident smile as it creaked open.

"See, soon we'll be safe inside and Havo's Dance can howl for us all it wants to. C'mon." He slipped through the door and, after only a heartbeat's hesitation, Spar followed.

They found themselves in a long dark corridor, high latticed windows throwing just enough light to see the length of marble wall to the left and rows of closed doors to the right. It was empty of people, just like the courtyard.

"Everyone must be at prayers or something," Brax noted. "This way."

Their bare feet slapping against the floor, they followed the corridor along until it opened into a wide central atrium, flanked by two sets of heavy, brass double doors. Brax indicated the left ones with his chin.

"They lead back outside, I'd guess," he said quietly, the large, echoing space making him want to whisper.

Spar jerked his own chin at the opposite corridor with a questioning expression and the older boy shook his head.

"No. She wants us to go this way."

He made for the right-hand doors. Easing one open a crack, he gaped as a shaft of lamplight spilled into the atrium.

"Look at this."

Beyond the door, they saw a huge room, lit by a number of hanging lamps, their fine chains disappearing toward the dark, unseen ceiling above. Rows of weapons and strange-looking pieces of armor lined the walls beside huge round plates of beaten silver and gold. Half a dozen carved marble daises sat in the center of the room, one under each lamp. As they approached, the gleam of precious metals and fine gems sparkled invitingly at them.

"I told you so," Brax mouthed, running his fingers along the smooth, golden handle of what looked like—but probably wasn't—a beautifully wrought oyster shucking knife on the central dais.

Nearby, Spar nodded in mute amazement, going up on his toes to peer at a jewel-encrusted book set on a silver base. His brows drew down.

"Yeah," Brax agreed. "Ugly, isn't it?" He turned a wide grin on the other boy. "But even the smallest of those little rocks'd keep us for a month. They sure are a trusting lot here." He glanced over at an equally jewel-encrusted sword lying across a black-and-gold-damask cloth on the next dais. It tingled under his fingertips and he rubbed them absently against his tunic. "I guess they can afford to be, though," he finished. "I mean, who'd steal from the Battle God's temple?"

"The same thieves who'd steal from the Healer God's temple," his thoughts supplied.

The tingle in the back of his mind grew more intense.

"We wouldn't," he thought back absently, then laughed. *"Especially not tonight; we'd never get away during Havo's Dance, would we? And besides, we didn't steal from the Healer God's temple; we stole in front of the Healer God's temple. There's a big difference."*

A thread of amusement at this practical irreverence trickled through his mind before Her presence directed his gaze toward a small, open door in the far wall. Warm lamplight spilled across the floor and he could smell plants and incense. And food. Spar was already heading that way and Brax hurried after him. If there was anyone inside, they were probably the ones who were supposed to meet them, but it didn't hurt to be cautious. Catching the younger boy by the jacket, he jerked him behind him before peering through the door. The room was empty of people. Surprised, Brax allowed Spar to duck under his arm. He was sure they were supposed to meet someone before now. Shaking his head, he followed Spar inside.

✦

To the south, in the temple's plant-filled infirmary atrium, Yashar leaned against the gold-tiled central pillar and frowned at Kemal. His arkados had been pacing the length of the room like a caged tiger, Jaq tight on his heels, for the better part of an hour and the constant slap of sandals and tick of toenails on the marble floor was starting to annoy him.

"Will you please stop doing that and sit down?" he asked bluntly. "Samlin says you're supposed to rest."

Taking him by the shoulders, he forced the other man onto a long, velvet divan. "Jaq, sit on his feet. Good dog.

"Now, do you want to be discharged in time for supper or do you want to take broth and unsweetened yogurt for yet another meal?" he growled at him.

Kemal shot the older man a sour expression, but leaned back pointedly.

"Thank you."

Kemal didn't bother to respond.

He'd awakened remarkably fit and energized after a long, drugged night's sleep, and although the cuts and scratches he'd taken during the ritual felt tight and itchy, he himself felt fine. He'd been ready to return to duty at once, but Samlin, the temple's chief physician of Usara, had refused to allow it. He'd swept in early that morning, fussed over the salve and bandages his delinkon had applied, promised to return and discharge Kemal that afternoon, then vanished. As the sun had made its slow journey westward, there'd been no sign of him.

"Typical healer," he muttered irritably.

"Practice patience."

"*You* practice it."

"I *am* practicing it."

Kemal glared at Yashar, but dropped the subject. "You'd think She might at least push the old fart along a little," he grumbled after a moment.

His arkados just shrugged. "Physicians serve Usara, God of Healing," he answered piously, bringing his clasped hands up to rest against the wall behind his head. "So that those who serve Estavia, God of Battles, will return to those battles when they're actually ready and not when they think they're ready."

"I was actually ready nine hours ago."

"As I said."

With a gesture of frustration, Kemal made to rise, then stopped as Yashar laid his arm across his chest.

"Be calm."

"I can't. I need to move. I need to go," he added.

"You just went."

"That's not what I meant." He banged the back of his head lightly against the mosaic-tiled wall until Yashar caught him by the ear.

"Stop that."

Kemal grimaced at him. "Something's happening, Yash," he insisted. "And I need to be there. I can feel it."

"What?"

"I don't know."

"Ask the God."

"I did. She won't answer me. She hasn't answered me all day."

"She's probably angry at you for disobeying Samlin's orders to stay in bed this morning."

Kemal shrugged. "Point," he allowed.

"Then you need to meditate and ask Her forgiveness for believing that you know more about healing than a healer. Start now."

"Fine, you're probably right, but the least *you* could do is go and see if he's coming."

"No, the least I could do is catch up on some sleep right here, and the most I could do is go and eat without you. I swear, Kem, you're the worst patient in the temple. Face the truth, you can't leave until Samlin returns and he'll return in his own good time, so follow your very sensible orders, *Ghazi*. Get some rest, and shut up."

Kemal subsided, muttering. It wasn't a case of following orders, sensible or otherwise, he thought resentfully. A very real sense of urgency had grown as the long, boring day had progressed; he had to do something, he had to *be* somewhere. Letting out an explosive breath, he began to bang the back of his head against the wall again.

Yashar sighed. "Are you meditating on the God's forgiveness?" he asked pointedly.

"No. She'll just have to punish me."

"Well, it's too late now. Here comes Samlin."

"About time."

Both warriors stood as the chief physician appeared in the doorway, flanked by half a dozen assistants. Yashar nudged Kemal in the side.

"Why don't you go tell him that?"

Kemal shot the other man a withering glance. "Why don't you go wait for me in the conservatory?"

"Why don't I do that." Leaning down, Yashar gave him a light kiss on the mouth. "Be respectful and obedient, Kem. I won't take supper with you here if you annoy him into making you stay. I don't deserve broth and unsweetened yogurt even if you do."

"Just go."

With a grin, Yashar ambled from the room and, as lightning flashed beyond the shuttered windows, Kemal turned to face Samlin with a strained expression. It was nearly dusk, nearly the Third Night of Havo's Dance, and nearly too late, he could feel it. Something was happening; he needed to be there, he didn't know why or even where, but he did know that it wasn't happening in the infirmary.

✦

"It's beautiful."

In Marshal Brayazi's private audience chamber, Brax held up a clear-cut wine glass, marveling at its design.

"It's so thin and so perfect. It must have cost a fortune."

Beside him, Spar shrugged. Stuffing a large piece of breaded zucchini into his mouth, he reached for a nearby bowl of olives.

The two boys had crossed the small, plant-filled room at a run past a glowing mangel, toward three comfortable divans arranged about a low table heaped with food. Oblivious to anything else, Spar had flung himself to his knees before a silver platter of steaming lamb, rice, and vegetables. Brax had made for the crystal carafe of perfectly clear raki. Now, with the remains of their meal strewn about the table, they sat with their backs against the largest divan, polishing off cups of something creamy and sweet they couldn't identify.

"See, what'd I tell you," Brax said, stuffing a couple of silk cushions behind them. "Good food and a safe place to spend the night." He glanced about at the three outside walls. "Still, it's kind of a strange room," he mused. "You'd hardly think it would hold up in a storm like Havo's Dance."

As if on cue, the wind picked up, rattling the screens. Something flickered past the lamps and Spar's blue eyes widened. His hand strayed to his knife.

"It's just the wind through the slats," Brax told him firmly. "It's still daylight, and even if it wasn't, the spirits can't get in here, it's a temple. The danger's outside, and it's gonna stay outside, yeah?"

His eyes riveted on the largest of the lamps, Spar nodded uncertainly.

"Good." Reaching for the carafe again, Brax poured himself another glass of raki as Spar gestured at the door. The older boy shook his head. "No. Like I said we're meant to be here, *right here*." Suddenly very tired, he yawned. "After whoever's supposed to meet us here gets here we can go . . . wherever we're supposed to go, but for now, have some more of this. It's really good. See," he added, holding the glass up to show Spar the clarity of the liquid within it. "Not a drop of water to cloudy it up."

Still staring at the lamp, Spar nodded, holding his glass out so Brax could refill it. The older boy then pulled a heavily embroidered lap blanket off the divan and draped it over them.

"I told you, everything's gonna be all right now," he said, emptying his own glass in one swallow. "So get some sleep. She'll wake us when She wants us."

Spar nodded again, but continued to stare at the lamp as Brax's head fell back against the divan. The light cast a weaving pattern across the inner stone wall, reflecting in his eyes like a troupe of fiery dancers, and he frowned as he finished his raki. All his life the images and feelings whispering through his mind'd had very simple meanings: safety or danger. But now everything was new and strange and he had no idea what was dangerous and what wasn't.

The memory of a thousand misty creatures of hate and need tearing at his mind and body made him shudder, and he pushed it away almost frantically. He would *not* remember that, he told himself. Brax had said they were safe. He would believe him.

But the memory refused to be banished.

What if it happened again?

The lamplight flickered, sketching the shape of a tall tower across the walls, offering answers, promising safety. All he had to do was reach out to it and he would know . . . everything.

He frowned.

And then what? he demanded in his head. *Nothing's free. Everyone always wants something back. What do* you *want?*

The shadowy tower made no reply and he snorted cynically. He'd thought so. After carefully setting his glass onto the table, he curled up under the lap blanket beside Brax and, after tucking his head under the other boy's arm, closed his eyes, deliberately blocking out the sight of the flickering image. He might not be able to tell the difference between danger and safety in this new place, *yet*, but he could still spot a lifter from a thousand yards and he was no mark. Until the tower could give him a proper answer, it could piss off.

✦

"I missed it."

Cutting swiftly through the crowded infirmary kitchens, Kemal shook his head in frustration. After an absurdly long examination, Samlin had finally discharged him just before nightfall, and he'd practically run from the room. Now, as the God's presence returned, directing him deeper into the temple proper, he pushed through the south wing door and into the central corridor, Yashar and Jaq at his heels.

"I missed it," he repeated.

Yashar glanced over at him. "How can you know that, Kem?" he asked. "You've never been trained as a seer."

"I don't know; I just feel it."

"Is it something dangerous?"

"Probably."

"But you don't know what it is?

"No."

"And the God won't say?"

"Again, no."

"I don't like that."

"Neither do I." Heading for the main wing, Kem gestured. "This way."

He barely broke stride as they reached the central gatehouse tower, hurrying through the armory toward the marshal's private audience hall. The lamps were lit inside and the two men exchanged a surprised glance. The room was rarely used in the evening and certainly not during Havo's Dance. Striding forward, Kemal rocked to a halt in the doorway, catching Jaq by the collar, as he saw who occupied the room.

Two young boys slept propped against Elif's divan, her best lap blanket pulled up to their chins, the remains of a large meal and an empty carafe spread out on the table before them. As he stepped forward, Yashar shot Kemal a questioning look and his arkados just shook his head. All his instincts were telling him that these were the ones he'd been sent to find, but something wasn't right.

You mean besides the fact that they're delon? his mind asked sarcastically. *Yes, besides that.*

The sense of urgency faded as he studied the two boys. The younger had the look of the southern villages, ragged blond hair falling over a thin face, the older looked more like a native Anavatanon with thick black hair, darker skin, and wider cheekbones.

"But . . . delon?" he asked in confusion.

Yashar elbowed him in the ribs, interrupting his thoughts. "Look at their faces, Kem."

Both had a number of nasty-looking red scratches across their cheeks and foreheads, identical to Kemal's own.

"They must have taken them during last night's ritual."

"But how?"

"I don't know. Jaq, sit," Kemal hissed as the dog headed for the divan. "Maybe they just got caught in the cross fire."

"I hope that's not true, I'd hate to think we caused that."

"So would I, but it would explain why they're here, for reparations."

"That or they were involved somehow. Didn't you tell me that Incasa sent Bey Freyiz a vision of a child?"

"Yes, but one child, not two."

"Still, it's a pretty obvious coincidence. We should inform the marshal."

"You go. I'll wait here in case they wake up. No, Jaq, sit." Kemal stuck his foot in front of the dog who reluctantly dropped his hindquarters.

"What about supper?"

"Bring me back something stuffed in a pita."

Yashar grinned at him. "Are you sure you can handle these two alone? After all, you know how dangerous child inebriates can be, especially prophetic child inebriates."

"Just go."

As his arkados left the room, Kemal crouched down beside Jaq. The God's presence within him felt both fiercely possessive and remotely disinterested in the two delon, which confused him even further. Either they were here by Her command or they weren't.

Jaq squirmed closer to the divan and Kemal wove his fingers through his braided collar and pulled him gently back. "Whatever they are, the last thing they need is to wake up staring into your great slobbering muzzle," he said fondly. "Lie down."

As Jaq settled unwillingly, Kemal glanced about the room. It looked as if their two unexpected guests had touched nothing except the food. Which was hardly surprising given their pinched expressions and ragged clothes.

"But where did you come from?" he whispered. "And what are you doing here?"

The wind suddenly whistled through the screen, ruffling the fur on Jaq's back, and he half rose with a whine.

"What is it?"

The dog strained toward the far wall. Kemal sent a questioning prayer toward the God, but Estavia simply returned the sense that all was as it should be in Her temple courtyards.

"There's nothing there, Jaq."

The dog whined again and Kemal frowned. He'd had Jaq for two years, ever since the God had directed him to a bloody bundle clutched in a dead farmer's arms after a battle at Kepek-Koy. The bundle had turned out to be a frightened, five-month-old russet-colored puppy with a powerful protective streak toward children and an uncanny sense of danger. Kemal had never doubted either before.

"So I won't doubt you now, then. But go gently."

He released the dog's collar, and keeping low, Jaq crept forward until he was between the boys and the far screen, then he stilled. Kemal shook his head.

"Now if that isn't the strangest thing you've ever done."

The dog's ears flicked, but he otherwise remained motionless.

"All right, stay there, then. That's a good dog." Kemal sat back on his heels. As the wind continued to whistle through the screens with an almost musical tone, he watched the flickering lamplight, his mind mulling over his earlier concern. Something had happened, and he'd missed it; he was as sure of that as Jaq was of his intangible threat. But he still had no more idea of what it had been than what had gotten Jaq so edgy.

"And were they the same thing?" he asked the dog rhetorically. "And why am I asking you anyway when I should be asking the God?"

As the first notes of the day's evening Invocations echoed in the distance, Kemal reached out with his thoughts, seeking clarity. As the Third and final Night of Havo's Dance began, he saw once again the shadowy image of a child standing on the rain-slicked streets of Anavatan but nothing else. He glanced over at the boys again.

"But which child is it?" he asked. "Or is it neither of them?"

Deep within him, the God gave back no response and, standing with a sigh, he dropped into parade rest and waited for them to awaken.

✦

Out on the wild lands, the setting sun sent fingers of orange light feathering through the grasses. Kursk halted the kazakin for the night under the first rocky tor they reached and, while Rayne and the other youths took the ponies and the water bags to a nearby stream and the adults made camp, he passed Graize gently down to his younger kardos, Ozan.

"Watch his head. He's dazed."

Ozan frowned. "Are you sure he's even alive?"

"He lives; whether or not he's alive remains to be seen."

Dismounting, he accepted the boy back into his arms.

"I'll hold him now. You pitch the tent."

✦

As Kursk laid Graize gently down on a sheepskin in his own tent, he opened his eyes, staring past him to the open flap in Ozan's hand. He'd not stirred from his stupor of bright lights once during the afternoon's ride, not even after the first drops of rain had begun to sprinkle against his face.

"Drops of blood and gold," he whispered, his eyes white and wispy again.

Kursk glanced behind him as his kardos made a warding gesture.

"It's the setting sun shining through the rain," he replied.

"No. It's the future."

The Yuruk leader shrugged as he rummaged through his saddlebags. "Is it, now? Well, that's a good sign, then. Blood and gold feed the people."

Ozan sidled away, the strings of the small kopuz at his back strumming faintly.

"I . . . um . . . should see to our defenses, Kardos."

Kursk nodded. "Send Rayne in with some water."

"I will."

The younger man withdrew quickly as Kursk very carefully helped Graize out of his tattered jacket.

"You make him nervous," he said bluntly, setting the bloody cloth to one side.

Graize shrugged. "He makes me think of hooves tearing up the ground and metal flashing in the moonlight."

"He's a fine rider and a good fighter."

"I see him playing music in the blood and in the gold."

"He'll like that."

Graize turned his luminescent gaze on Kursk's face. "I see you in the blood, too, but not in the gold," he said almost defiantly.

Kursk just shrugged. "Pity." Easing off the boy's bloody tunic, he tossed it onto the pile, his sandals beside it. "I'll just have to rely on my children to keep me in my old age, then."

Graize said nothing and Kursk smiled down at him. "What, no old age either?"

For the first time the boy looked uncertain.

"I . . . don't know. I can't see that."

"Well, that's for the best. Too much of that kind of knowledge can drive a person mad." He looked quizzically down at him. "And you're about halfway along that path already, aren't you, child?"

Graize just shrugged. "Maybe. *Danjel says the spirits are made up of raw prophecy and that they sing songs of power to each other as they rise. If you can capture their words, you'll gain the power to see the future, but if you capture too many, the song will drive you mad and you'll chase after the rest of it forever.*"

The breath hissing between his teeth as he recognized Rayne's words from the day before, Kursk made himself smile easily.

"Well, we'll have to see what we can do to slow its progress, won't we?" The Yuruk leader turned. "Ah, Rayne, there you are. Come and help me," he said, as she pushed open the tent flap with a questioning frown.

✦

While Kursk washed and doctored Graize's wounds, Rayne hovering nearby to help. No single part of the boy's body was free from injury, and her eyes narrowed as she studied the long, red scratches with a dark expression.

"Did the spirits do that to you?" she asked bluntly.

Graize nodded.

"Last night?"

"Yes."

"Why?"

"They wanted to kill me." He stared out at the sunlight reflecting in the rain for a long moment. "They wanted to suck my life away."

"But they failed."

He nodded. Breathing in the few tiny spirits that had returned to hover about his lips, he gave her a toothy smile. "I sucked theirs away instead."

"So you're strong, then, that's good. The Yuruk can't afford to coddle weakness."

Kursk gave her a deep frown at this discourtesy.

"Well, we can't," she protested. "Abia said so."

He sighed. "Your abia's from the west. They live a harsher life."

"My abia came east to find new blood to breed with," she told Graize proudly. "She picked my aba because he was the strongest and fastest kazak on the Berbat-Dunya."

"She told me she liked my tent," Kursk said mildly.

Rayne ignored him. "Where's your abia?" she demanded.

For a moment Graize thought he could remember soft arms and an expression of pain and love, before it, too, vanished like the image of the gray-eyed man.

"I never had one," he said, the defensive tone back in his voice, but Rayne just gave him a sympathetic look.

"I'm sorry."

He shrugged. "You don't miss what you never had," he said carelessly.

She touched him on the hand, her expression gently disbelieving. "Yes, you do." She straightened before he could answer. "When I'm ready to have children, I'll do the same as my abia," she continued. "I'll be the most powerful wyrdin in the Rus-Yuruk and I'll go out and find the strongest, fastest kazak there is and make him mine. He'll have to be strong in mind and in body," she added, "strong enough to control the spirits and make them talk to him, and strong enough to ride all night long and raid a fat and lazy village in the morning." She studied him speculatively. "You seem strong," she noted, "but are you fast?"

Graize felt his cheek go unaccountably red. "I . . . uh . . ."

"Raynziern, go and ask Ozan to heat up some kimiz," Kursk interrupted sternly.

"Yes, Aba. Oh, here," she dropped Graize's beetle into his hand before skipping from the tent. Clutching it tightly, he watched her go with a dazed, but equally speculative expression, ignoring Kursk's frown of disapproval.

She returned with the cup a few moments later. While Graize drank the unfamiliar fermented drink, Kursk washed each of his wounds with a comfrey-and-rosemary tincture, then eased a clean tunic over his head. Graize allowed the ministrations in silence, gathering his scattered sense of self and watching the sun beyond the tent flap pour through the gathering clouds like a spill of fire. Behind it, the spirits merged and flowed, waiting for nightfall to breach the walls of. . . He shook his head as the thought slipped from his mind.

Kursk followed his gaze. "It's a fire sun tonight," he noted conversationally as he handed Rayne the blood-soaked clothes. "Here, burn these.

"A harbinger of your blood and gold and a fine morning ahead," he continued.

Graize blinked as a dozen tiny spirits whispered their prophecies in his ears. He sucked up the largest of them, feeling its energy flowing down his throat in a gush of warm potential. "It'll be a cold morning," he answered in a distant tone, passing on its words. "But it won't snow."

"It rarely does on the plains." Tucking the tincture into his saddlebag, Kursk straightened. "Have you ever seen the snow, child?"

Graize's mist-filled eyes grew very wide, the left pupil opening significantly farther than the right. "I see it now," he answered. "It's snowing on the southern mountains' sides where the spirits can't feed. The people are too strong for them there. Just like here." He smiled. "So they'll go to the shining city."

"Anavatan."

"Yes. They broke through last night and they'll try again tonight while Havo's Dance still hides their movements." Lifting his hand up to his face, he stared at the spirit entwined around his fingers. "You won't get in, though; not now," he told it gravely. "The Gods are watching now." He shook the spirit free and it feathered about his ears until it came to rest entangled in a lock of hair. "But they'll try, anyway," he said, returning his attention to Kursk. " 'Cause there's so much there to feed on. It calls to them all the time. It drives them mad for it. But they can't feed, not until we open the gates for them," he added. "Then they'll feed." Watching as a half formed future blossomed in his mind, he nodded. "And so will we."

Kursk's gaze moved with deliberate casualness to the boy's face. "We?" he asked.

"Yes." Graize stared out at the setting sun again, watching as his lights took up the future, fleshing it out like a street poet might for a handful of coins. "But not now," he explained, "not yet, but one day very soon. We'll attack the shining city and feed the spirits . . . *and the lights*," he added silently.

"Oh, and why would we do that?" the Yuruk leader asked, carefully masking his sudden interest.

"Because the city and its villages walled off the lake of power." Smiling, Graize watched as the events of centuries past played out before his eyes like misty shadow puppets. "They've grown fat just like their Gods while others have grown thin. And hungry." His eyes cleared. "The Yuruk have attacked the villages every year to try and break through the God-Wall around the lake of power. Everyone knows that. This shouldn't surprise you," he added reproachfully.

Kursk shrugged. "We've never gotten away with more than a small flock or two," he answered in an even voice. "We're always driven back by the Warriors of Estavia. Their seers always know when we're coming."

Graize smiled coldly. "Not this time," he whispered almost to himself as he watched the future unfold. "This time the lights will guide us and the spirits of the wild lands will hide us. We'll flow over the God-Wall like a river, and the spirits will flow with us. I can see it." He raised one hand to caress the image playing out before him, then yawned suddenly. "But not tonight. Tonight the Gods are awake and expecting a fight. They'll protect the city tonight. They'll eat all the spirits. But then They'll think They've won and They'll go back to sleep in Their silvery beds of broken marble and shimmering lake water and the people will get fatter and fatter and then we'll attack."

"Well, that's wise," Kursk allowed. "You never arrive when your enemies are expecting you and have had time to lay out a meal of their choosing." He smiled as Graize's eyelids began to droop. "So for now, come and eat a little something of my choosing before you go to sleep. There's cheese and flat bread, even a bit of mutton to make you strong."

"I am strong."

"Stronger, then."

Graize nodded, his gaze trailing back to the setting sun. "And fast?"

Kursk frowned. "That remains to be seen."

Graize smiled slyly. "Fast." He closed his eyes. "One day we'll attack the shining city, but we'll attack . . . another place sooner," he murmured as the lights supplied him with the name of a shadowy village that wavered in and out of sight. "We'll attack . . . Yildiz-Koy this season before the ewes have finished lambing."

"Will we now?"

"Yes."

"And the Warriors of Estavia?"

"Will be busy protecting the villages to the south. I can see them, standing tall and strong and alert. But the threat there is a feint." He frowned as the lights showed him a fleet of oddly shaped ships sailing up the southern strait toward Gol-Beyaz. They fluttered like the flame from a half empty lamp before guttering out before the image of a tall red tower and a golden sun. "This season anyway," he added.

"A feint?"

"Yes; a false trail laid by a tower on the sea."

"To draw them away from Yildiz-Koy?"

Graize gave his sly, sleepy smile again. "Oh, no. It had nothing to do with Yildiz-Koy at first, but now that's changed," he said as the lights fed him new images. "Now something special will come there and we'll get away with more than just a small flock or two."

Kursk shook his head in wonder. "How do you know all this, child?" he asked.

Graize opened his eyes, watching as the dark-haired boy from his earlier visions appeared then disappeared behind a silver storm cloud. "The lights told me," he answered truthfully.

"The lights?"

"The ones that came to me last night. They speak to me through the stream of prophecy they burned through my veins. They swim in that stream and so do I."

"And they told you we would attack Yildiz-Koy?"

Graize smiled coldly, his eyes perfectly clear for the first time. "That," he acknowledged. "And other things."

✦

Later, after Graize had eaten his fill and fallen asleep, Kursk and Ozan stood, staring at the last streaks of sunlight along the horizon and listening with half an ear to the sounds of the camp behind them. Far above their heads, the first stars were beginning to twinkle through the breaks in the darkening clouds and Ozan studied them intently as he strummed quietly on his kopuz.

"Is he mad?" he asked after a time.

Kursk shrugged. "Maybe."

"Is he human?"

Kursk watched as dozen spirits swirled around the tent flap. "Yes."

With a grin, he clapped his kardos on the back. "He's a wyrdin—a prophet," he said. "*Our* prophet. *One day we'll flow over the walls of Anavatan and the spirits will flow with us*," he added in Graize's strange, singsong accent.

Ozan's face brightened. "Did he say that, truly?"

"Yes, truly. Apparently we'll attack Yildiz-Koy this season while the Warriors of Estavia wait for a threat to the south which will never materialize."

"Will we, truly?"

"Perhaps. We have to weigh the possibilities and speak with Timur. Whatever the child may turn out to be, Timur's still our most senior-wyrdin, not me. It will ultimately be her decision."

Ozan nodded. "And I imagine Danjel will have a thing or two to say about it as well."

"No doubt." Kursk laughed suddenly. "Still, why not? Yildiz-Koy's as good a place as any to mount a raid against, is it not?"

"It is." Ozan showed his teeth in eager anticipation. "I'll tell the others. They'll be pleased."

Kursk nodded. "Yes, they will." As the last slip of sunlight faded from the sky, the Yuruk leader turned his gaze to the storm clouds gathering to the southwest through the boy's drops of fire and gold and nodded grimly to himself.

"They'll be very pleased."

5

Spar

"THEY CANNOT STAY HERE."

♦

Late that night, in one of the temple's huge guest wing apartments, Brax lay back against a pile of overly soft cushions and stared into the darkness, the words of the Battle God's command council echoing in his head. Beside him, Spar slept with his arms around the man Kemal's big red dog, too full of food and drink and too exhausted to care about the future. But Brax cared. They'd faced death, hunger, priests, life-sucking spirits, and halberd-wielding sentinels, indentured themselves to a God of warfare and bloodshed, and walked all day long at Her order to get here, and here was where they were going to stay. Standing in the center of the huge, vaulted, and windowless command chamber that looked more like a prison cell for rich merchants than a military council room, he'd spelled out the God's plans for the two of them, but even after Kemal had added his voice in support, the council had remained stubbornly unconvinced.

"Delon do not live at Estavia-Sarayi."

He snorted. Kaptin Omal of Indigo Infantry Company had been pretty adamant about that, as if it mattered. The Battle God had sent them to Estavia-Sarayi, so that was where they were meant to be. The dog had understood that right away—he hadn't left their side since they'd woken up. Kemal had taken a bit more convincing, but eventually he, too, had understood.

"She fed us; we didn't steal anything!"

He'd had been dreaming of wind and rain beating down on a silver mist-covered plain surrounded by lights when a small noise had jerked him awake to find a tall bearded man in a dark blue tunic watching them from the doorway. Cursing himself for letting his guard down so completely, he'd leaped up, thrust Spar behind him, and drawn his knife. His vehement denial of wrongdoing had been the first thing out of his mouth.

The man had reacted with a smile.

"I'm sure you didn't steal anything, Delin. No one steals from the temple of Estavia. But . . . what are you doing here?"

"I told you, She brought us here." Tucking his knife into his belt, Brax straightened with a scowl. "We're to be warriors, both of us. She said so."

The man grinned openly at that. "She did, did She? And did She also specify what company you were to join?"

Brax glared back at him. "No, but She would if I asked Her to. Should I?" His tone was challenging, but the man just chuckled.

"No need, Delin."

Brax bridled at the second diminutive. "It's Brax," he said stiffly.

"My apologies. Brax." The man turned to Spar who edged a step farther behind the older boy as Jaq began to sniff at him cautiously. "And you are?"

"He's called Spar."

"Can't he answer for himself?"

"He can, he just doesn't want to."

"Why not?"

"Because he doesn't know you."

"Fair enough. My name is Kemal. That's Jaq. He seems to like you, Spar," he added, as the younger boy began to hesitantly scratch the great, red head that had stuffed itself under his hand.

Brax narrowed his eyes. "You're a warrior?" he asked suspiciously, refusing to be lulled by the man's gentle tone.

"And a priest."

"A priest?"

Kemal smiled at his suspicious tone. "All Estavia's warriors are priests. Why, don't you like priests?"

"No. They're . . ." Brax hesitated, searching for a word that was accurate enough without being too insulting and settled on, "pushy and they think they know everything."

"Well, this priest doesn't." Kemal's expression grew sober. "What happened to your face, Brax?"

The softly asked question was as unexpected as the concern in the man's voice. Suddenly noticing the red welts and scratches on Kemal's own face and hands, Brax shrugged with studied indifference.

"Nothing really. Why, what happened to yours?"

"I took some injuries last night conducting a ritual to manifest the God of Battles."

"That's when we got ours, too."

Kemal's face twisted in distress. Coming forward, he knelt down and, taking Brax's hand in his, studied the wide red marks across the back of his knuckles, then up to the ugly red wound on his cheek. "Then I'm responsible for your injuries; for both of yours," he said.

Brax blinked. "Why? Did you call the spirits up, too?"

"Spirits?"

Brax exchanged a glance with Spar. "You know, *the spirits that attack the unsworn on Havo's Dance?*"

Kemal stiffened. "The unsworn? You're unsworn; both of you?"

"We were until last night. We got caught out on the streets and the spirits attacked us. If Estavia hadn't shown up and destroyed them all, they'd have sucked the life right out of us, like they did to Gr . . . to two others."

"And this happens frequently?"

"What's that?"

"A lot?"

"Sure. You know, that's why *nobody goes out on Havo's Dance.*" At Kemal's mystified expression, he continued. "The spirits used to just suck the life out of things like spiders and mice, sometimes a sick rat, but last year they started on the feral dogs and cats. That made them strong enough to go after people, but they can only get to the unsworn, so we keep under cover when they're out hunting." He frowned. "You really didn't know all this?"

Kemal sighed. "Delin, until yesterday I didn't even know there were unsworn, never mind that the spirits of the wild lands could enter Anavatan to prey on them."

Brax gave him an incredulous look but didn't reply as Kemal sat back on his heel.

"Clearly, there's a lot I don't know," he said with a sigh. "All right. Tell me exactly what happened last night."

✦

Brax had barely finished when Kemal's arkados, Yashar, had shown up with the head of the temple, Marshal Brayazi. After making Brax go over the events of last night for the second time, she immediately called a full command council. By the third explanation he was getting a little tired of talking. The council hadn't helped.

✦

"How many of these unsworn reside within the city walls?" Kaptin Liel of Sable Company asked bluntly, leaning forward to fix Brax with a seer's intense stare.

"I dunno. Lots."

Kaptin Omal gave a snort of disbelief. "In the City of the Gods? Impossible."

"Why? Not everyone wants some God telling them what to do every moment of every day," Brax shot back, fed up with trying to explain something that seemed to him to be an unimportant detail.

The kaptin bridled at both his words and his tone, but the old woman, Elif, raised one wizened hand to forestall an outburst.

"The youngster has lived in a different world, Omalin-Delin. Let it go. He's here now, sworn, as we are, to Estavia, and come to warn us that ethereal creatures of mist and unquenchable hunger—which we now know to be the spirits of the wild lands—have breached the walls of Anavatan during Havo's Dance. As, I might add, we have long feared they might do with the capital situated, as it is, so far from Gol-Beyaz. He's told us that the spirits draw strength from the unsworn and that the unsworn are numerous, so this leads us to one question, not how is this possible, but rather, how do we combat it?"

"So, how do we combat it, Elif-Sayin? How do we fight ethereal creatures of mist and hunger?" Omal demanded in as respectful a tone as he could muster. "In battle it is Estavia who combats the spirits of the wild lands, not Her warriors."

"Really?" she replied in a tone of steely sarcasm, "I'm so glad you reminded me of this fact; I was afraid my memory might have gone the way of my eyesight."

As the marshal laid a gently restraining hand on Elif's sleeve, Kaptin Nateen of Turquoise Archery Company leaned back. "As obvious as his words might have been, it's just as Kaptin Omal says, Sayin," she observed. "We do not traditionally bring these creatures to bear at all, so it's highly unlikely that we're being asked to do so now. The God commanded an Invocation that She might do battle against these creatures Herself last night. Therefore, lending our strength to Hers in the future may be our only expected course of action."

"Highly unlikely," Kaptin Liel responded. "The God was very specific in commanding that Ghazi-Priest *Kemal* lead Her Invocation . . ."

Standing behind Brax and Spar, Kemal started at the sound of his name and Brax smirked. He guessed he wasn't the only person growing bored with the entire argument. Beside him, Spar stifled a yawn.

". . . and then She led him directly to these delon. Yet he's no seer; he's not even a battle-seer, he's a ghazi. That suggests Her ghazis have a part to play in this."

"And what part might that be?" Kaptin Nateen asked stiffly.

"That remains unclear. We must petition the God."

"And the delon, what part do they play?"

"Again, we'll have to petition the God."

"Ask a seer the time and you'll get the weather," Kaptin Alesar of Azure Infantry Company observed dryly to Kaptin Iyril of Verdant Archery Company, "You can never get a straight answer from any of them."

Elif chuckled. "That's because where the Gods are concerned there are no straight answers, Alesarin-Delin, only a multitude of spiraling questions. However, in this case, I believe that together these individual elements may provide us with some clue, especially in light of the First Oracle's earlier vision. Remember, something momentous was to be born last night during Havo's Dance; something which would draw strength from the unsworn. Estavia has risen to do battle with creatures that attack the unsworn, and here we have two of their number brought to our temple by the God Herself to verify these events. The coincidences are piling up at a very suspicious rate. I suggest that we do indeed petition Estavia for a clarified answer while also preparing for the necessity of physical conflict."

"A wise plan," the marshal agreed before anyone else could speak. "As always, the seer and the ghazi will work together to ensure a victorious conclusion, as the God of Battles commanded when She accepted both into Her service so many centuries ago. The seers will petition the God for clarity regarding our role in this conflict and the ghazis will go out into the city and discover all they can about these spirits and how long they've been preying on the unsworn."

"We might well begin by asking the temple of Oristo why there are so many unsworn," Kaptin Omal added. "They have the closest ear to the ground, ministering to the poor as they do."

Brax snorted, but was ignored.

"And the delon?" Kaptin Daxin of Sapphire Infantry Company inquired, watching as Spar's head began to droop wearily. "What's to become of them?"

"Perhaps we could find them abayon in the city," Kaptin Nateen suggested.

"We don't need abayon," Brax broke in.

Kaptin Daxin studied him with a somber expression. "Don't you want to live with a proper family, Brax? Run and play without adult cares for a year or two longer as the young should?"

Brax studied the bi-gender kaptin with a frown. "No," he said finally. "It's too late for that. I'm an adult already."

"And Spar? Is he an adult, too? Don't you think he deserves a family?"

"I'm his family."

"Regardless," Kaptin Omal interrupted. "You have to live somewhere and you cannot live here. There are no delon at Estavia-Sarayi. Period."

Brax glared at him. "Why not?" he asked, trying to tone down the level of disrespect in his voice as Kemal gave him a cautionary glance.

"Because they live and train in the village militias and in the city garrisons," Kaptin Rabin of Bronze Cavalry Company answered, raising his gaze from the gouge he'd carved into the tabletop. "They come here only as delinkon."

"Then we'll be delinkon."

Kaptin Daxin smiled. "Temple delinkon are chosen by the militia commanders once they've shown superior skill and ability, Brax, and they serve at sixteen, not at . . . ?"

The question was pointed. Brax made to answer sixteen but found himself unable to speak the words. Resentfully, he shrugged.

"Fourteen, I think."

"And Spar?"

"He's about nine. But we have shown superior skill and ability already," he added hotly. "We survived Havo's Dance. We're tougher than we look."

"I don't doubt it, but this isn't about toughness, Brax."

"So, what's it about, then?"

Kaptin Daxin shrugged. "Tradition mostly."

"Bollocks," Kaptin Rabin retorted. "It's about practicality. We haven't the facilities here to care for you or to train you. You'd never keep up, especially you, Brax, not with the sword or bow and certainly not on horseback."

"I can knife fight."

Kaptin Omal didn't bother to mask a sneer. "You'd be killed in your very first engagement."

"She wouldn't let that happen."

"She lets it happen every day, Delin," the marshal answered. "We're not invulnerable just because we serve the God of Battles. Without proper training, you would endanger both yourself and others in your company."

"I'd catch up," Brax insisted. "She'd make sure I did."

"Oh, She would, would She?" Elif chuckled.

Brax crossed his arms with an equal mix of confidence and bravado. "Yes, She would. I can feel it. I'd ask Her and She'd help me."

"Then She can help you in one of the city garrisons," Kaptin Omal answered firmly. "You don't belong here."

Kemal laid a restraining hand on Brax's arm as the boy took one, angry step forward. "Kaptins, perhaps we might consider billeting the delon here temporarily. Just until we receive further orders from the God," he added as Kaptin Omal glared at him. "After all, She did lead them to us."

"From what I've heard, Ghazi, it seems that Estavia didn't so much lead them to us as She led them to you," Kaptin Daxin noted with a faint smile.

"Then perhaps Ghazi-Priest Kemal should take charge of them and return to his own village to raise them properly," Kaptin Nateen suggested.

"Out of the question," Kaptin Julide answered at once. "Kemal's needed to command his troops at Anahtar-Hisar this season."

"Then send the delon south with him as far as Satos-Koy."

"It's much too dangerous," Kaptin Daxin protested. "They'd be killed."

"I'm not suggesting they join the garrison at Anahtar-Hisar," Kaptin Nateen growled back. "I said Satos-Koy. There are plenty of youngsters in the lake villages, you know that. It *is* where most of them come from, after all."

"Really?" Kaptin Daxin replied with equal sarcasm, "I thought they sprang, fully armored, from the mouths of the Gods."

"Enough," the marshal said sternly as Spar began to sway, despite one hand wrapped tightly around Jaq's collar. With a glare that took in the entire council, Brax threw an arm about his shoulders to steady him as the marshal raised a hand. "It's late and wherever the delon eventually end up, they do not need to wait on our decision for respite. They will remain with us as our guests until Estavia makes Her intentions for them clear. Kemal, you will escort them to Chamberlain Tanay and ask her to find them a bed in the guest quarters."

"Yes, marshal."

"And, Brax?" She fixed him with a penetrating stare. "Be careful what words you put in the God's mouth. She may not be so predisposed to your interpretation as you believe."

Eyes narrowed at the unfamiliar words, Brax, nonetheless, nodded stiffly, allowing Kemal to usher him and Spar from the room. Behind them, he heard Kaptin Omal take up the argument again.

✦

Now, much later, lying beside Spar in a room so big he couldn't feel the walls around them, he pulled the soft silk sheets up to his chin and reached inside for Estavia's presence, smiling sleepily as the God stirred in response.

"I know You want us to stay here," he thought, *"but You're going to have to tell them that as clearly as You can. They seem kind of . . ."* he paused, searching for a more polite word than stupid to describe what was, after all, Her command council, and settled on . . . *"thick."*

A ripple of amusement whispered across his thoughts.

"STUBBORN."

"Whatever. They are right in one way, though," he allowed reluctantly. *"We do need your help with training. We've got to prove to them we wouldn't be a danger to anyone. Except the enemy,"* he added almost as an afterthought. *"Whoever that is."*

The reassurance that filled his mind made him smile and he let go of the last of his worries about the future. The God would take care of them. He could feel Her promise sizzling through his veins. The command council would understand that eventually. Hunkering down under the sheets, he closed his eyes. As the bright lights and the mist-covered plain rose up in his mind again, he fell asleep to the sound of horses' hooves drowning out the last throes of Havo's Dance outside.

✦

In the bed beside him, Spar listened as Brax's breathing slowly deepened, then sat up carefully. He'd slept for a while himself, arms wrapped around Jaq, letting the dog's body heat warm him and feeling his heartbeat thump against his chest, but once Brax had stopped muttering to himself, he'd awakened to lie staring into the darkness as he'd done every night since they'd lost their home. He didn't like strange places no matter how safe they were supposed to be. There was always someone or something hiding in the shadows watching for weakness and waiting to take what little they had away, and he wasn't nearly as convinced as Brax that they would be allowed to stay here.

No guard had ever helped them out and, as fancy as these warriors might talk and dress, they were still guards. And guards had killed Cindar. Brax might have forgotten that in his enthusiasm for Estavia's love and comfort, but he hadn't. Brax had already angered Kaptin Omal, and Kaptin Liel seemed to be able to look right through them. Spar had made sure he hadn't met the frightening gaze of the bi-gender seer kaptin that made him feel so strange inside. In fact, everything about this place made him feel strange, ever since that tower in the lamplight had tried to tempt him into . . . whatever it was it wanted. It made his head ache. He wished Brax had never brought them here. He didn't like any of it.

Except Tanay, he amended reluctantly. He liked Tanay even if she was a priest of Oristo. Tanay had taken care of them.

✦

"What's a chamberlain?"

Brax had peppered Kemal with questions as he'd led the two of them down a long corridor that smelled of spices and cooking meat. Most of the answers had meant nothing to Spar, but now, as he rested one hand on Jaq's broad back, he cocked his head to hear the man's response.

"The chamberlain runs the temple," Kemal answered simply.

"I thought the marshal did that."

"The marshall commands the Warriors of Estavia. The chamberlain runs the temple; sees that everyone's fed and clothed, that sort of thing. Every Sarayi has one; usually a senior priest of Oristo."

"Figures."

Kemal glanced curiously down at Brax's sudden frown. "So, tell me, is it priests in general that you don't like, or priests of Oristo in particular?"

"Mostly priests of Oristo."

"Why? Do they think they know everything more than priests in general?"

Ignoring the teasing in Kemal's voice, Brax just shrugged and, making a quick decision, Spar jabbed Brax in the ribs with one elbow. The older boy started.

"What?"

Spar gave him a sharp, expectant look. They needed Kemal. Brax should have known that without his help.

"Not a good idea, Spar," the older boy countered.

He folded his arms, silently demanding that Brax take him seriously, and finally, Brax threw one hand into the air.

"Fine. The priests of Oristo ratted out our abayos to the Western Trisect dockyard garrison," he said bluntly, turning back to Kemal.

"Ratted out?"

"Yeah. They thought he wasn't a good enough abayos, so they ratted him out and the garrison guards killed him."

Kemal looked confused. "He was killed because he wasn't a good enough abayos?"

"No, he was killed because he was a thief," Brax answered, his voice dripping with condescension.

"But thieving doesn't carry a death sentence in Anavatan."

"Yeah, well," Brax glanced at Spar, then sighed. "It does when you resist arrest and crack a garrison guard—and a priest—in the head. They took him down. He died."

"Ah."

"Anyway, it was a priest of Oristo that set the guards on him in the first place," Brax continued, refusing to be mollified.

"But you said he was a thief."

"That's not the point," Brax snapped. "The priests didn't care that he was a thief. They set the guards on him because they didn't think a thief made a proper abayos."

"I'm inclined to agree with them."

"Maybe, but when Cindar died, we lost everything. Then we nearly died. Is that any better?"

"No, I suppose it isn't. Ah, here we are." Kemal pushed open a door at the end of the corridor with a relieved expression as Spar and Brax shared a cynical glance well beyond their years before following him and Jaq inside.

✦

The woman counting jars in the small, lamplit room off the huge, bustling kitchens was tall for an Anavatanos with paler skin than most and sandy hair the color of Spar's own. She didn't bother to turn around when the door opened.

"Is that you back already, Monee? I told you, the dried chick peas are on the top shelf of the cold cellar."

Kemal grinned. "Isn't Monee a little short to be rummaging about up there?"

The woman turned with a frown that changed to an indulgent smile as she realized who'd spoken.

"Hello, Kemal."

"Chamberlain Tanay."

Setting her counting board down on the long, worktable in the center of the room, her gray eyes warmed at the sight of the two boys, then darkened when she saw their injuries, but, smoothing her expression to one of professional welcome, she crossed the room to greet them. Spar stared unabashedly up at her.

"Who do you have there?" she asked with a smile that made his senses reel. "A couple of visiting kardon-delon?"

Kemal smiled in return. "No, a couple of honored guests, Tanay. This is Brax and Spar, newly sworn to Estavia. The God led them here this evening with a message for the council."

"Ah. You'd be the ones I was directed to make up that tray for, then. Down, Jaq! Bad dog!" She smacked the dog's head away from the table before turning back to them, smiling at Spar's indignant expression in Jaq's defense. "I was wondering," she continued, "the marshal usually eats with Bronze Company."

"The marshal asks that you find them a bed in the guest wing."

"Of course." She turned toward the kitchens. "Tyre?"

A tall, gangly delinkos looked up from the huge pot he was scrubbing. "Yes, Chamberlain?"

"Where's Hatem?"

"Finishing his supper."

"Have him make up the golden guest suite and bathing room when he's done." Turning back, she took in the boys' ragged clothes and pinched expressions with a swift, practical glance. "Are either of you still hungry?"

They looked at each other in surprise, then Spar nodded.

"We can always eat," Brax answered.

"Tyre, fetch some asure for our guests."

"Yes, Chamberlain."

"We'll see to bathing after you've eaten. Now then, clothes?" she asked, glancing at Kemal.

He nodded.

"What color?"

"Oh. Um . . ." He looked down and met Brax's firm, defiant gaze. "I suppose they'd better be blue."

"You suppose?"

"It's a long story. The council . . ."

Tanay snorted. "Enough said. Blue it is. I'm sure I can find something that used to be Bazmin's or Brin's; they've both grown a foot since last High Summer." She turned her warm gaze on the two boys again. "Do you mind castoffs for the time being?"

Spar frowned as Brax glanced up at her, his expression carefully neutral. "We don't have any shine," he answered.

"Shine?"

"Money."

"You're not buying them; you're borrowing them until I can get you measured up."

"The temple provides all who serve at the Sarayi with two new uniforms per year," Kemal added with a smile. "The council pays for them."

Both boys grinned. "Then castoffs'll do fine . . . until we can get measured up," Brax allowed.

Tanay nodded. "Good. And here's Tyre with your asure."

Brax accepted two ceramic bowls filled with the same sweet, paste-like dessert they'd had earlier, handing the larger one to Spar who continued to stare at Tanay in besotted wonder.

"You look like him," Brax explained. "We've never seen more than one or two Anavatanon who do."

Tanay nodded. "That's because I'm from Ekmir-Koy village in the south. Many of us are fair. It comes from our mountain blood."

"Cindar thought Spar might have mountain blood," he observed, taking a huge spoonful of asure.

"Cindar?"

"Our abayos."

"And where is he?"

"He's dead."

"I'm sorry to hear that."

" 'Sall right. We don't need him now."

"Hm." She glanced over at Kemal. "Will you be taking them to the infirmary next, Ghazi?" she asked pointedly.

"What for?"

Her eyes flashed. "To have their injuries tended to by a proper physician of Usara," she replied, her tone suddenly chilly.

"We're fine," Brax broke in at once as Spar took an involuntary step back. "We put some comfrey on the scratches this morning. They're healing."

Kemal smiled. "Don't you like the priests of Usara either, Brax?" he asked.

"They're expensive, and they're usually fakes."

"Not these ones."

Brax shrugged. "We're fine," he repeated.

"Well, would you mind if I had a quick look at your injuries, anyway," Tanay asked. "I have a bit of extra salve I keep for minor kitchen mishaps—it will only go bad if I don't use it up—and Spar seems to have at least one scratch that's become inflamed."

Brax's head snapped around and, mutely, the younger boy pushed up his left jacket sleeve to more fully expose the puffy red line that extended along his forearm.

"Why didn't you tell me?" Brax hissed.

Spar just looked away, the answer obvious. There'd been no point in telling him when they'd had no more shine for salve.

"You can doctor that?" Brax asked, returning his gaze to Tanay.

"Yes, if it's not too badly infected."

"All right, then, yes . . . um, please look at it."

She turned. "Tyre, fetch me some warm water and that jar of salve from my counting room trunk."

The young man looked up from his next pot with a faintly annoyed expression, but dutifully laid down his brush.

"The ceramic jar, Chamberlain?"

"No, the porcelain jar." Watching as Brax helped Spar out of his jacket, she narrowed her eyes at the torn and bloody state of the tunic underneath.

"Did you get these from fighting?" she asked, her tone disapproving.

"Spirit attack," Brax supplied for him.

"I see. You're dealing with this, Kemal?"

He nodded.

"Good. Here, take this." She handed Spar's jacket to Tyre as he passed her the jar. "Brax, if you will remove yours as well . . ."

The older boy hesitated for a moment, then stripped off his own jacket, handing it to Tyre who tried not to stare at the long welts down his neck and arms.

"Have it washed and see if it can be mended. Now . . ." she indicated to Spar, who held his arm out shyly. Cleaning around the injury first, she then expertly cracked open the jar's wax seal and Brax wrinkled his nose at the unfamiliar smell.

"What is that?"

"Frankincense."

His mouth dropped open as Spar immediately snatched his arm away.

"We can't pay for that," Brax said bluntly.

"Estavia's people don't pay for treatment in Her temple," Kemal replied.

"Still, we don't need anything that expensive. Comfrey'll do fine."

"The better the salve the more effective it is and the less you need," Tanay explained.

"I don't care. It's too much. We can't . . . it's too much." Brax broke off, unable to voice his sudden fear as Spar began to shake his head.

Tanay gave them both a thoughtful look. "Nothing comes without a price, does it, delon?" she said gently.

Spar looked away as Brax chewed uncertainly on his lip. "No," the older boy allowed finally.

"And that price is usually high," she added gently. "Even here." She smiled reassuringly at them. "Look at me," she offered, "I have to battle every day to keep an entire temple of mannerless, sword-wielding ruffians—and their dogs; Jaq, I'm warning you, get down *now*—from eating their way through my stores like a swarm of locusts."

Spar couldn't help but smirk as Kemal looked insulted.

"So, what do you get out of it?" Brax asked.

"She gets to push them around all day," Kemal answered.

Tanay chuckled at his sour tone. "Well, that's certainly a benefit," she allowed, then her expression grew serious. "But I also get to take care of people, which is something I've always been good at." She touched Brax's cheek just below the angry red cut left by Drove's knife. "Will you let me take care of you, Delin?"

Brax's face grew pinched. He made to say something flip, then just gave a quick shrug. "I guess so."

"And Spar?" She turned and he felt his face flush. "Will you let me take care of you also?"

He stared into her eyes for a long moment, then nodded. After stepping cautiously out from behind Brax, he very slowly put his hand in hers.

✦

Now, he pushed up the silken sleeve of the overlarge nightshirt he'd been given and sniffed at the strange aroma beneath the bandage. Most of his injuries felt better, but this one was starting to throb again. She'd said it was infected and had suggested the infirmary again but had dropped the subject when he'd vehemently shook his head. He didn't trust physicians any more than Brax did; he'd seen the effects of their work in the marketplaces and on the streets, and there was no proof that this temple's people were any better. Most only cared about their fee and the ten percent extra that went to their God. But Tanay had smiled reassuringly at him as if sensing his thoughts, then told him to come back if it started bothering him and she'd take care of it herself.

He nodded his head with a dreamy smile. It *was* bothering him, so he could go and see her and she would take care of it; she would take care of *him*.

Very slowly, so as not to disturb Brax, he eased himself off the enormous and overly soft bed pallet. When his bare feet touched the thick woolen carpet, Jaq raised his head, and Spar put a finger to his lips. He'd never liked dogs much, they barked when you wanted them to be quiet and were quiet when you wanted them to bark, but Jaq was different. For some reason he felt safer with the great red animal beside him. He indicated that the dog should follow him with a jerk of his head and, surprisingly, Jaq dropped the sheep shank he'd been chewing on and stepped down from the pallet both carefully and silently. Even so, Spar peered at Brax to make sure the gentle motion hadn't disturbed him.

The older boy looked five years younger in the dim light, his dark olive skin pale with exhaustion, his face gaunt under its cap of heavy black hair, clean and shining for the first time in days. His expression was peaceful, even trusting; the Battle God's protection had allowed him to fall into a truly deep sleep for the first time since Cindar'd been killed and for that Spar was grateful. She would look after him. With Jaq padding along behind him, he slipped silently through the door, the nightshirt bunched up in one fist to keep from tripping over it.

✦

Oil lamps attached to the walls at each junction cast just enough light to see by and, as he padded down the shadowy corridor—retracing their earlier walk from the kitchens—he breathed in the damp, scented air that spilled in from the latticed windows high above. The moonlight was obscured by the last of Havo's Dance, but it smelled very late. There shouldn't be anyone about at this hour. He'd be safe.

Pausing to peer around the corner to the central corridor, he was distressed to see a single green-clad guard standing duty by the doors to the armory tower. He almost turned back, but Jaq thrust his head under his hand, and gathering up his courage, he took him by the collar. He was supposed to be here, he told himself firmly. Brax had said so. And he could go to Tanay to have his injury taken care of any time he needed to. *She* had said so. Taking a deep breath, he allowed Jaq to pull him into the corridor.

The guard cast him a curious but nonthreatening glance as they approached.

"Taking Jaq for his nightly pee, are you, Spar?" she asked.

He nodded, masking his surprise that she knew his name. He guessed news traveled as fast inside a temple as out.

"Well, don't let him near the west wing conservatory," she warned. "The head gardener say's he'll become a wall trophy if he marks another herb bed. You can let him out into any of the central courtyards. He'll come back when he's done."

Spar's eyes widened.

"Oh, you needn't worry about Havo's Dance," she laughed. "For some reason the great scruffy mutt's beloved of the Gods. All of them. He just weaves in and out of the rain drops." Her voice hushed. "And those spirits you brought word of wouldn't dare touch him either. Not here behind Estavia's walls. He'll be fine."

Nodding dubiously, Spar allowed Jaq to pull him past the guard. His shoulder muscles tensed as he turned his back on her, but they made the small wooden door he and Brax had entered through earlier without incident and he took a deep, calming breath as he pulled it open a crack. The dog slipped through and he risked one, quick glance outside.

The courtyard beyond the gallery was pitch-dark, but his imagination added the hint of sharp-clawed mist pooling about on the ground ready to rise up and attack them. He stood frozen, suddenly unable to breathe except in short, shallow breaths. The image of a great tower rose up in his mind, then Jaq glanced back with a faint whine, and deliberately lifted his leg against the gallery wall. Both the mist and the tower disappeared, and Spar grinned in embarrassed relief. When the dog returned inside, looking smug, the two of them continued on in a lighter mood.

✦

The kitchens were quiet and still, empty of the bustling crowds of pot-banging cooks and scrubbers when they peered through the door a few moments later. For a instant he was afraid that Tanay had left as well, and then he saw her sitting by the brass counting room mangel, a steaming ceramic cup in one hand and her feet propped up on a cushion. When Jaq shoved his way through the door, she glanced over at the small bit of him she could see around the dog.

"Well, you cleaned up well," she noted. "Come in."

✦

The salve was as soothing as before, her touch as gentle. Seated on the largest cutting board he'd ever seen, he glanced around the empty kitchens with a questioning look as she resealed the jar.

"It's past midnight, Delin," she replied. "Everyone's gone to their beds." Dribbling a few drops of an aromatic oil he didn't recognize into a bowl of warm water, she began to bathe the scratches across his cheeks and neck with a soft cloth. "Ordinarily I'd be gone myself, but tomorrow's market day and it's the only time I have to sit and plan the week in peace. Oh, yes, and there's that meeting in midafternoon as well; I'll need to bring some seed cakes," she added to herself. "Jaq, sit!" Turning, she glared at the dog who'd been pacing around the table, whining, and pointed sternly at the mangel. He flopped down before it with a reproachful sigh and she chuckled. "He's become very protective of you," she noted.

Spar gave a half nod, half shrug of studied indifference, but the faintest of smiles worked its way past his usual reticent expression, pleased that she'd noticed.

"You can have him back in a moment," she said over her shoulder. "There, that should just about do it." Wringing out the cloth, she set it and the bowl aside. "Now, I'm going to finish my tea. If you'd like to join me, there's a cup on the shelf there and the pot's beside you."

Without hesitation, he nodded.

✦

The tea was warm, sweet, and smelled of cinnamon. It made him feel safe and sleepy. Seated where he could see both Tanay and the mangel, he leaned against Jaq's flank, feet tucked into the bottom of the nightshirt, and stared fuzzily into the fire. The crackle of bright flames on walnut wood chips spoke louder than the whisper of oil lamps but the words were the same; and just as unwelcome. Looking away, he found himself meeting Tanay's warm, gray eyes.

"You're awfully young to be thinking so deeply," she observed. "Age will bring about its share of decisions, you know; you don't have to make any of them now."

He frowned. Beside him, Jaq flicked an ear at a stray fly and he watched it buzz its way to the cutting board, seeking some tiny crumb left behind by the kitchen staff. When he turned back, Tanay was still gazing at him and he waved one hand about him impatiently.

"What of it?" she answered shrewdly. "You're nine years old. No one holds a nine-year-old to a decision made by a fourteen-year-old."

His eyes widened and now it was her turn to give him an impatient look.

"Kemal told me. Brax made his choice for his own reasons a full two years before the traditional age to do so. He may be old enough to know what that decision means, but you aren't. And it hardly matters," she added, ignoring his indignant expression. "Brax will be given the opportunity to take his final vows at sixteen, regardless of what he may have sworn two nights ago, and until then, he's free to change his mind without any argument from the Gods. And so are you." Her gaze softened. "Try to stay young for as long as you can, Spar. You'll never get another chance."

He rolled his eyes at her, but his cynical expression softened as he stood.

"Come back and see me again if you like," she offered as Jaq led him to the door.

He nodded briefly.

"Good night, Spar."

Pausing at the door, he glanced back at her, then smiled shyly. "Good night, Tanay." Fingers entwined in Jaq's collar, he slipped through the door, closing it quietly behind him.

✦

Across the city and beyond its walls, Havo's Third and final Night of storms raged on, but the God of the Seasons was already returning to Gol-Beyaz, smacking at a few chimney pots for good measure, just as the spirits of the Berbat-Dunya were returning to their rocks and crevices on the plains. By morning there would be nothing more than a few broken roof tiles and fallen tree limbs to mark the beginning of High Spring.

At Incasa-Sarayi, Bessic, the God of Prophecy's new First Oracle, received a fleeting glimpse of a tower perched above a dark, storm-tossed sea, illuminated by a figure of shining light and power, before it was shrouded in mist once more. At Oristo-Sarayi, Senior Abayos-Priest Neclan rose early to prepare a platter of seed cakes for her chamberlains— she liked to keep a hand in the kitchens now and then—while, at Estavia-Sarayi, those who'd brought the God of Battle forth slept deeply, including the two boys who might make or break their future.

✦

Meanwhile, deep beneath the waters of Gol-Beyaz, the God of Prophecy tossed his silvery dice from hand to hand with a thoughtful expression, then closed His own snow-white eyes. The spirits had been pressed into a new form that could be molded to His design as they had been five times before and two of the candidates who would safeguard

Its passage to maturity or to death had been safely tucked into Estavia's temple. All He had to do now was to wait patiently while the third nursed the new consciousness into a more physical awareness. Everything was in place.

✦

Far to the west, wrapped in a warm and heavy sheepskin beneath an escarpment on the plains, Graize lay surrounded by a multitude of cold, bright lights, sharing their dream of conquest and of death. To the north, a shadowy figure in a tall tower stood staring out at the waves of the Deniz-Siyah Sea and made his own plans while in the south, Panos of Amatus dreamed of a tall, brown-haired man, as interested in the vision of his broad shoulders and fine, narrow hips as she was in his prophetic abilities and political standing.

6

Abayon

"BRAX. AWAKEN."

His eyes snapped open. Beside him, Spar and Jaq slept on undisturbed and, for a moment he stared up at the gold-and-silver mosaic-tiled ceiling with a disoriented frown. Then, as the God's presence filled his mind, he smiled. With a contented yawn, he spent a moment enjoying the unfamiliar sensations of warmth and security before rising up on one elbow to glance around the room.

The temple's golden guest suite was even more opulent in daylight than it had been by candlelight. A wide latticed window dominated the east wall, a large sculpted white marble altar, the west; the north and south were draped with brilliantly woven tapestries, and the lush woolen carpet was so bright in the morning sun it made his eyes water. Wondering idly if gold threads were worth more than gold tiles, he turned and poked both Spar and Jaq in the ribs. Boy and dog opened their eyes at once to glare at him resentfully and he grinned as he untangled himself from the nest of silken sheets and made for the window.

"Well, this is sure different from yesterday morning," he noted taking in a deep breath of the spicy spring air. "A warm room and a full belly." Fixing the younger boy with an expression of mock seriousness, he cocked his head to one side. "Do you still wanna leave?" he asked.

Spar pointedly ignored him and, with a laugh, Brax crossed the suite to peer into the now empty bathing room. Last night it had blazed with light from half a dozen wall lamps, causing the inlaid metallic tiles to sparkle almost painfully around them. The porcelain tub, big enough to fit both of them, had been filled with hot, lavender-scented water and two of Oristo's servers had been there to help them bathe. Brax had laughed aloud as he watched them try to comb through Spar's tangled hair, but the constant tugging on his own head had nearly ruined the mood. However, when it was all over and they'd stood before the largest, gilt-framed mirror they'd ever seen, gawking at the two clean, linen-clad strangers staring back at them, he'd felt suddenly as if they'd stumbled into some kind of street poet's song.

The morning sun lighting up the tiles in streaks of golden brilliance did little to change that.

Rubbing his eyes, Brax moved on to the altar, running a wondering finger along the smooth surface of Estavia's ebony-and-silver statue before staring down at the unfamiliar objects laid out before it. Then, following the pressure of Her presence, he reached for a stick of incense, lit it off a small lamp he was sure hadn't been lit last night, and wrinkled his nose as the scent of lilac filtered up to him.

Spar padded up behind him with a curious expression and he shook his head. "I don't know, but it's what She wants."

Shrugging out of his nightshirt, he picked up a fine, bone-handled paint brush and, after running his finger along the soft bristles, popped the seal on a small jar sitting beside it. As Spar watched, transfixed, he dipped the end of the brush inside, wiped the extra off against the lip, then turned it so that it pointed toward him. Feeling Her hand wrap about his he watched as, together, they drew the outline of a high, wobbly minaret along his left arm. Its meaning became clear almost at once.

"That's Anavatan," he explained in a faraway voice, knowing that his certainty came from the God.

Taking the brush awkwardly in his left hand, he then traced a crescent moon cupped about two crossed swords along his right.

"And that's Her temple along with . . . Cyan Infantry Company. Told them so," he added.

He then exchanged hands again and moved on to his chest, drawing a stick figure with a small knife in one hand, "that's me," another shorter one, "that's you," and one with four legs and a long tail. "That's . . . the dog?" His eyes cleared. "You're not serious." The replying mental swat made him raise one hand in quick compliance. "All right, all right, You are serious. Here."

Spar shook his head as Brax made to hand him the brush, but after a moment, he dutifully narrowed his eyes, tracing the same symbols on his own body, before handing it back. Brax grinned as he wiped the brush clean on a piece of silk cloth lying nearby.

"See, I told you we were meant to be here. I can't wait till the council hears about *this*."

"I can't wait either."

The boys spun about to see both Yashar and Kemal leaning against the doorjamb. As the latter came forward, he glanced at their handiwork with an approving smile.

"Not too bad for your first protections. In time, the figures will be a little more detailed and a little less shaky."

Brax glanced up at him.

"So everyone does this?" he asked.

"Every one of Estavia's people do, yes. What the other Gods' worshipers do, I couldn't say." He raised his sleeve to show the painted figures along his own forearm. "The symbols are the physical representations of the God's protections."

"They itch."

"That's the dye drying," Yashar explained. "You get used to it."

"How often do you have to do it?"

"We reapply them every morning."

"Do they change?"

"Not usually."

"Then why do you have to do it *every* morning?"

"Because the dye washes off as you sweat."

"Doesn't that make a mess?"

Yashar just shrugged. "That's the laundry's problem."

Both boys exchanged a knowing glance. "Wouldn't it be better to use a dye that didn't wash off so fast?"

"No."

"We reapply the symbols every morning so that we're reminded of what we're fighting for," Kemal explained. "Home, Temple, the God, and our families."

"Even your *pets?*" Brax interrupted.

"Anything we love."

"I don't love Jaq," the boy countered, ignoring Spar's indignant expression. "He took up way too much of the bed last night and he has dog breath."

"I don't much love him either," Yashar agreed, "and for the very same reasons, but I have to add him every morning as well."

"Well, sometimes it's what the God loves," Kemal noted. "Why, are you questioning Her already?"

His tone was much the same as Brax had used when asking Spar if he wanted to leave, but he took the question seriously, closing his eyes as he felt the growing warmth of the God flowing inside him. The thought of returning to a life without it made his chest ache.

"No."

"There you are."

"But . . . what?" Brax paused as Spar elbowed him in the ribs. Following the younger boy's gaze to the line of hair above Yashar's collar, he rolled his eyes. "I'm not asking him that," he responded sharply, knowing at once what was bothering him.

Spar continued to stare and finally Brax threw up his hands.

"Fine. He wants to know if you're that hairy all the way down. It's a stupid question," he growled at the younger boy.

Kemal guffawed as Yashar nodded with an expression of mock seriousness.

"Even more so," he answered.

"*Everywhere?*"

"Everywhere. Arms, legs. And back," he added with an evil grin as Spar made a face.

"So, how does the dye get through all that to your skin?"

Yashar put his palms together. "The God commands." He opened them. "And the hair parts for the brush."

"You mean it moves?" Spar and Brax exchanged a sickly glance.

"He's lying," Kemal said mildly.

"I am not. The God loves hair on a man. She likes to run her fingers through it," Yashar retorted, stroking his much thicker beard than Kemal's with a superior expression. "It moves with Her touch like grain in the wind."

Spar gave him a disbelieving glance, but Brax unconsciously echoed the movement with a frown.

"You'll grow whiskers soon enough," Kemal assured him in an amused voice.

The boy shot him a sour look. "I haven't grown any yet," he groused.

"You're still a youngster." He held up one hand to cut off Brax's immediate protest. "You're an adult when Estavia says you are and not before. When that time comes, you'll have as much hair as you're meant to have and no more, *but* . . ." he gave Yashar a warning glance. "She'll love you regardless. *And*, in the meantime," he gestured at the two piles of neatly folded clothes on an inlaid mahogany trunk by the bed, "get dressed and we'll help you roll up the pallet; it's time for breakfast."

✦

The news of their arrival had swept through the temple and the eyes of everyone in the refectory hall followed them as they made their way to the long, central table. Tanay had managed to find two reasonably new delinkon tunics in deep blue and even though they'd no sandals just yet, and Spar's tunic was far too big for him, both of them made a point of carrying themselves as if they'd always worn uniforms. It was a gesture that was not lost on the gathered. Whispers followed in their wake and Jaq, padding along beside Spar close enough for him to rest one hand on his broad back as they walked, growled low in his throat at anyone who stared at them for too long. Finally, Kemal rapped him on the forehead with one knuckle.

"Stop that."

At the central table the long line of warriors parted for them and Spar gaped at the size of the serving platters heaped with food, but it was only after Brax pushed him forward with a whispered, "Eat," that he took up a huge piece of bread and began to pile olives, cheese, and stuffed vine leaves almost frantically on to it. Wordlessly, Kemal handed him a porcelain plate and he accepted it without breaking stride, adding another piece of bread liberally smeared with honey and four large chunks of mutton to the pile before turning his attention to the rows of ewers, jugs, and tall silver urns which lined one end of the table.

Beside him, his own plate heaped with smoked fish, bread, dates and dried apricots, Brax glared at a plain jug of boza then, ignoring a second jug of warm, milk-based salap, poured himself a cup of black tea instead. After a longing glance at the second jug, Spar also reached for the tea.

Over their heads, Yashar and Kemal exchanged a quick look. The older man reached for the jug and casually knocked Spar's hand away as if by accident.

"Oh, sorry, Delin," he said, "I was just getting myself some milk."

Spar stared at him as he filled a tall, crystal glass, watching the thick, white liquid froth over the sides and across his fingers. "What, you didn't think I got this big drinking tea every morning, did you?" Yashar paused. "Do you want some before I put the jug back?" He winked at him and, with a shy smile of understanding, Spar took up a cup and held it out.

"Tell you what, why don't you use a glass. It'll hold more." As the boy hesitated, he smiled. "Don't worry; I know you won't drop it."

Looking dubious, Spar glanced over at Brax and the older boy just shrugged.

"Go ahead. If you break it now, it's his fault for giving it to you."

With a satisfied nod, Spar accepted the glass as Yashar chuckled. After filling it to the brim, he then laid a hand on the younger boy's shoulder and guided him over to the cutlery table as Kemal glanced down at Brax.

"He follows your lead, you know," he said quietly, as he poured himself a small cup of thick, black coffee. "And he's not yet finished growing by a long way. He'll need milk and the like to make him strong, so you might think about having a glass or two from time to time, if only for his sake."

Brax glanced sideways at him, guessing at the unspoken words. "I wasn't trying to act any older than I am," he said defensively but in the same quiet tone of voice. "I drink milk sometimes. It's just that tea's cheaper."

"Not here."

"All right." Deliberately, Brax set the teacup down and caught up another of the large crystal glasses. "You'll need to pour it," he said stiffly. "I can't manage it one-handed."

With a deliberately casual nod, Kemal lifted the jug.

✦

Those gathered in the Cyan Company dining room were no less interested in them when they entered, but most greeted them casually, some raising their cups in salute, others just grinning at them as they passed. Once they were settled, with Jaq chewing noisily on yet another shank bone at their feet, Spar began to eat at once, but Brax glanced around with a frown.

"What's the matter, Delin?" Yashar chuckled. "Don't you like the decor?"

"What? No, it's not that." Brax turned his attention to his plate. "I just don't like it when people stare at us," he said tightly.

Kemal shrugged. "What do you expect? You're famous. You're messengers from the God."

"That's right," Yashar agreed. "She led you to us as you said. You're delinkon to ten thousand abayon now."

Spar choked on his bread.

"I thought delinkon didn't serve at the temple until they were sixteen," Brax retorted sarcastically as he thumped the younger boy on the back.

"Well, think of it less like delinkon and more like . . . mascots," Yashar suggested. "Or good luck charms."

"Delon will do," Kemal corrected. "And you've no more than a few hundred abayon, anyway. You're Cyan Company's now. Kaptin Julide will make sure the council understands that."

"That's right," Yashar agreed with a mischievous grin. "We helped to bring you into this world," he said, taking in the gathered with an expansive wave. "And the God has given you to *us*." He thumped his chest loudly.

Brax glared at the older man as the company murmured their approval, suspecting they were being mocked. "How do you mean, brought into this world?" he asked suspiciously.

"On the night the God of Battles manifested to save your lives, it was Cyan Company who offered up their strength to make it possible," Kemal replied before Yashar could offer up a more humorously offensive explanation.

Food halfway to their mouths, both boys gave him a confused look.

"Well, the Gods don't inhabit . . . don't live in the physical world, do They?" he continued. "It takes a lot of strength to enter it. Strength They gain from Their followers."

"How do you mean?"

"All that we are and all we do either strengthens or weakens the God we worship. If we live strong, the God is strong; if we live weak, the God is weak. And sometimes when the God requires it, we gift Them with that strength in the form of pure power."

Brax looked shocked.

"Haven't you had *any* religious instruction at all?" Yashar asked.

Lifting his head, Spar gave another of his unchildlike snorts as Brax rolled his eyes. "The poor don't need religious instruction," he retorted, spitting a date pit onto his plate. "They need bread."

"Well, there's plenty of bread here and you're not poor any longer. You've sworn your lives to Estavia's service. How do you expect to do that if you don't know how or even why?"

"So tell us why."

As both boys stared at them expectantly, Kemal gestured at his arkados. "Go ahead, Yash, it was your idea."

The older man sat back, turning his glass thoughtfully between his fingers.

"All right. Well, just so I don't repeat myself, what *do* you know about the Gods?"

Brax shrugged. "Just what Cindar told us."

"Which is?"

"That They're only interested in the sworn. And the *rich* sworn at that."

"Cindar was wrong. The Gods are always interested in all the people."

"So why don't they help the poor?"

"Oristo's temple helps the poor, don't they?"

"Sure, for a price."

"Which is?"

"Worship," Brax sneered.

"What's wrong with worship?"

After stuffing a piece of fish in his mouth, he shrugged again. "It shackles you."

"Shackles?"

"You know, it keeps you from doing the things you need to do, like leg irons would."

"You mean it keeps you from doing things you *shouldn't* do. Things like stealing?"

"That and other things." Brax took a long drink of milk, then carefully set the glass down. "It works well enough when you're rich," he continued, "but not when you're poor. The Gods don't make bread magically appear, do they?"

"No, but they do create the opportunities you need to work for bread."

"For some maybe, but not for everyone. Not for us. Cindar did that for us. We worked for him and he fed us, kept us safe. The Gods didn't do that."

"One might argue that it was the Gods who gave you to Cindar in the first place."

"Then the Gods can't have a problem with stealing because Cindar was a thief and he taught us to steal."

Kemal snickered. "Point, Yash."

The older man grimaced at him. "Maybe," he allowed. "I'm no theologian, I'm just a ghazi-priest. *My* point, however, is that if the Gods didn't care about the poor, then why did Estavia help *you*? Why did she come to your aid and lead you here as you keep insisting so vehemently."

"Because I asked Her to."

"That's right. You needed help, you called out, and the God responded. If you hadn't believed She might do that, you never would have tried in the first place."

"Sure I would of. She showed up before I called."

"Then She must have known you needed help before you did."

"So why didn't She help us before?"

"Maybe you didn't need help before."

Both boys gave him an impatient look, then Brax just shrugged. "All right, whatever. Why?"

"Why what?"

"Why did She help us?"

"I don't know. You'll have to ask Her."

Brax and Spar exchanged a cynical glance.

"The Gods have Their own agenda," Yashar continued. "Maybe the possibility of your worship was enough or maybe She just liked the look of you, I don't know. I do know that by accepting your worship, Estavia accepted your strength. That could be reason enough."

"But why would She need it? Why would She care about it? She's a *God*."

Yashar rubbed at his temples. "We told you, the Gods need the strength of Their worshipers to manifest in the physical world. They aren't physical creatures by nature, They're spirit. And They aren't all-powerful, Delin; even minor manifestations take a great deal of energy." He shook his head. "Didn't your abayon ever tell you the story about the birth of the Gods?"

"No, *I told you* Cindar didn't worship Gods. And he didn't tell stories, especially not about *Them*."

"And you never heard it in the marketplace? It's a very common tale."

"We had other things to do in the marketplace."

"And we won't follow that line of inquiry too closely," Kemal interrupted.

"Fair enough. Why don't *you* tell them the story," Yashar suggested, gesturing to a delinkos to bring him a cup of tea. "I'm worn out from all his arguing."

"All right." Kemal set his coffee cup to one side. "Once upon a time, a very long time ago," he began, smiling as both Brax and Spar rolled their eyes at the traditional beginning, "there was a shining, silver lake of power called Gol-Beyaz and deep beneath its surface dwelled six mysterious beings of vitality and potential, for in the beginning the Gods of Gol-Beyaz were spirits much the same as the ones who attacked you the night before last." At Brax's disbelieving sneer, he raised a hand in defense. "Honestly. Over time . . . over a very long time, they began to . . . interact with the people who settled along the lake shores. They had no more form than mist on the water then, but they had power, great reserves of raw unformed power, and as the centuries passed and their association with the shore dwellers grew, they slowly . . . association means to spend time together," he explained as both boys frowned at him.

Brax raised a cynical eyebrow at him but said nothing.

"As they spent more and more time together," Kemal continued, "a deeply symbiotic . . . I'm sorry, um, a mutual . . . no wait . . . a very strong bond grew up between them; the shore dwellers came to depend on the lake spirits for power to protect them from their enemies—raiders from the plains, mountains, and the northern and southern seas—and the lake spirits relied on the shore dwellers to give them access to the physical world and a form able to physically impact upon that world as a defense against their own enemies, other envious spirits of these very same plains, mountains, and seas, who wished to take the power of Gol-Beyaz for themselves.

"Now, as the centuries passed, this bond grew so strong that the Gods of Gol-Beyaz—as they came to be known—became intimately involved in the life of the shore dwellers, the Gol-Yearli—as *they* came to be known—and the form of each God came to represent and protect each of the six most important elements of that life: Hearth, Healing, the Arts, the Seasons, Prophecy . . ."

"And Battle," Yashar interjected.

"And Battle. Both Gods and Gol-Yearli grew stronger and stronger as their . . . association grew deeper and more intimate. But . . ." Kemal raised one hand dramatically. "As their strength increased, so did the strength of their enemies, envious of their prosperity . . . their riches, Brax."

"I know what prosperity means," Brax replied hotly.

"So why the frown?"

"I was just wondering why you haven't said anything about Anavatan yet. I thought it was the city and its garrisons that kept all our enemies away."

"The city in partnership with the villages."

"They're just a bunch of farmers."

"A bunch of farmers that keep the city folk from starving," Yashar pointed out coldly. "Where do you think your bread and meat comes from? Rooftop gardens?"

"I guess not."

"And where do you think the bulk of Estavia's warriors come from as well?" Kemal added. "From the twelve village militias. But don't fret, Brax. Anavatan's story starts very soon." He took a drink from Yashar's teacup. "Where was I? Oh, yes, enemies. As their strength increased, so did the strength of their enemies, envious of their prosperity," he repeated, "so together the Gods and the Gol-Yearli built a great wall of stone and power buttressed with nine strong towers that encircled the lake and its dozen villages. This wall kept them safe for many years, but eventually even that wasn't enough. Raiders from Volinsk and Rostov continued to pour in through the northern strait, so the God Incasa reached into the future to pull forth a mighty vision which sent Oristo and Ystazia to the north with a flood of followers. Guarded by Estavia and nurtured by Usara they cracked the western peninsula in two and Havo filled the rift with a great reservoir of fresh water, then together They walled off the three main promontories which now jutted into the northern strait and set three massive towers: Lazim, Dovek, and Gerek-Hisar to guard them, and so Anavatan, the most powerful city in the world, was born."

He fell silent. Around them, the gathered members of Cyan Company, who'd hushed during the telling of their story, slowly took a deep, collective breath then, one by one, returned to their breakfasts. Kemal smiled.

"It's a good tale," he finished.

"And one which illustrates the point that the Gods and their followers rely on each other for strength," Yashar added. "The Gods do care, Brax, but They'll only intervene in our lives if we ask Them to. Anything else brings Them no strength."

"But once you ask, you'd better be prepared for the response," Kemal added with a smile. "Gods are . . . well, They're big, and so are Their answers sometimes."

"Yeah, we figured that out two nights ago," Brax agreed. Within him, he felt the God chuckle.

Outside, the sound of a single note interrupted their conversation. Cyan Company began to rise and Kemal nodded his head.

"And speaking of responses, it's time for the Morning Invocation."

"And She's gonna show up there," Brax asked.

"Yes."

"How?"

"That depends on Her mood," Yashar answered. "Sometimes, dramatically, sometimes gently, sometimes with a great deal of outward power so that you almost feel She's as solid as a tower, sometimes with more of an internal sensation, like She's interacting with you alone. Every warrior experiences the God's manifestation differently every time."

Brax and Spar exchanged a glance.

"So, what do *we* do?" Brax insisted.

"For now, you'll sit with the noncombatants as guests of the temple," Kemal replied.

"For now?"

"Until the council decides what to do with you."

"And then what?"

"And then we'll see," Yashar added firmly as he gestured them to their feet.

"But you said Cyan Company . . ."

"Enough, Brax. You can argue with us all you like later, but for now you'll sit where we tell you to sit."

"Besides," Kemal added. "Someone has to keep track of Jaq."

Beneath the table, the dog thumped his tail at the sound of his name and Spar reached down to stroke his head nervously. As they joined the throng heading for the central courtyard, he wrapped his hands about the animal's collar to keep from bolting.

✦

Outside, although the last morning of Havo's Dance officially marked the beginning of High Spring, the air was cold and smelled heavy and damp. Taking a seat on the long, marble bench beside Elif, Brax looked out across the rows of warriors gathering before him and shivered as the sense of anticipation grew. To keep from fidgeting, he ran silently through the list of Morning Invocations—and possible trade opportunities—that Cindar had taught him years before. Speaking almost absently to Estavia's presence within him, he felt Her give a very un-Godlike snort as he began with the green-and-brown God of the Seasons.

Havo at dawn.

"The priests of Havo climb to the highest minarets at the very first hint of day," he began. *"They can see down on the entire city so it's not too smart to do business until after they've come back down."*

Another snort.

First Oristo, and then Usara after Havo.

"Their priests sing inside—the Hearth God's in the kitchens, the Healing God's in the infirmaries. It's pretty hard to sneak a meal at Oristo's and the

food at Usara's is usually pretty bland 'cause it's for sick people. I dunno why. Maybe sick people'd throw up if they ate better food."

A thread of amusement feathered through his mind, followed by a sudden spark of interest as She anticipated his words.

After Usara; Estavia.

"Your warriors worship outside—but I guess You knew that—in front of their garrisons and towers." A mental tweak made him shrug. *"All right, in front of* our *garrisons and towers,"* he amended. *"Anyway, this is the best time to make a quick snatch and grab when there's only merchants around to chase you, but you need to be long gone before they're done 'cause the city garrison patrols can come after you pretty fast."*

The warmth of the Battle God's pleasure blossomed in his chest, but ebbed again as he continued.

Next Ystazia.

"All the Art God's people sing—not just the priests—and mostly they do it inside their workshops and studios, although the potters like to sing beside their kilns. Again, it's a poor time to visit these places 'cause they're standing over their shine. Besides, musical instruments and books are too hard to sell off, anyway," he added thoughtfully.

An image of a blacksmith's shop filled his mind.

"Weapons and armor are even harder to sell," he explained. *"They're too big and too heavy to hide for long."*

He sensed Her satisfaction with his answer and continued.

Finally, Incasa.

"This is the worst time to do a job, plan it, or even think about planning it. The priests of Prophecy worship all over the place, sometimes in the temples, sometimes outside, sometimes in large groups, sometimes in small. And they can read your mind when they pray. Most lifters eat, or crap," he added, almost as an afterthought, *"when Incasa's people sing. It's safest."*

Estavia snickered, then returned Her attention to Her warriors as the last of them filed into place and, warmer now, Brax listened as the final notes of Usara's Invocation sounded in the distance. Beside him Spar shifted nervously and he squeezed his hand.

"Here it comes."

Before him, the warriors froze as still as statues as the hollow clank of iron-shod hooves against cobblestones heralded the arrival of

Marshal Brayazi on the biggest, blackest horse Brax had ever seen. Staring out at them for a single breath, she drew her sword. Then, rising up in the saddle, she sang the first clear, piercing note of the Battle God's Invocation. The echoing voice across the strait sounded as much within his head as without and, far away, he could feel Estavia shaking off the watery confines of Gol-Beyaz like a dog shaking off sleep.

The wind picked up. It ruffled through the hair of those infantry who stood helmetless and whipped through the cloaks of the riders behind. Brax saw Kemal's head tip back, then Yashar's, and unconsciously echoed the movement as the pressure of the God's response began to tighten his muscles. He found that he was holding his breath and forced himself to breathe deeply.

Soon. It'll be soon.

The marshal sang the second note, the third, and the fourth, and the hair on the back of his neck began to rise. The sky darkened. Convulsively clenching and unclenching his fists, he rubbed his knuckles against his knees, unable to sit still as the God's growing presence began to sizzle through his veins like a stream of tiny fire ants. Around him, the rest of the seated shifted impatiently, then, as a sudden tremor ran through those standing, the warriors swept their swords from their sheaths.

Now!

A single shout from the marshal and the God of Battles burst into being above their heads.

The power of Her manifested form hit Brax like a hurricane, slamming both in and out of his body at the same time and jerking him into the air as Estavia towered above him like a colossus, a thousand times more frightening and more powerful than She'd been on Liman-Caddesi. Streaks of red flame shot from Her twirling swords to etch a crimson path along the blades of her followers and he suddenly screamed in pain as a bolt of lightning shot down his right arm, across his chest, and out the fingers of his left hand. As it burned a path of flames through his body, a thousand stars exploded in his head.

Time twisted around him. He saw a man bathed in silver light commanding lines of warriors on a hundred battlefields; saw them calling to their God to come and fight with them and felt Her joyful, savage answer as She thundered down upon their enemies. He saw towers and battlements overlooking fields and villages, and a great, snaking wall of stone and power that wrapped about a silver lake so bright it burned his eyes to look at it. He saw a tiny, mounted host in the distance led by a figure surrounded by shining lights, saw the spirits of the wild lands forcing their way through the walls of Anavatan season after season until they burst through in a flood of murderous need and saw himself as a man, both armed and armored, taking the field against them. He saw a child of power hovering on the edge of being, but as he reached for it, he was snatched away and driven down into the frigid, mist-covered waters of Gol-Beyaz.

His breath froze in his lungs, his vision blurred, but just before everything went dark, he felt himself caught up in the embrace of a God. Warmth flooded back into his body. He looked up into Estavia's face and felt a peace and a stillness greater than even death could have delivered. She held him cradled in Her arms for what seemed like an eternity, then, Her red eyes glowing down at him with a possessive love so powerful it nearly shredded his mind, She slammed him back into his body so hard he felt his teeth drive through his lower lip. His back arched and, as blood sprayed from his mouth, he saw Cyan Company break ranks and rush toward him. Then everything went black.

✦

He awoke in an unfamiliar room looking up into the branches of a huge green tree. For a long moment he stared up at it, trying to remember what was wrong about trees growing inside, then he tried to speak. He managed a harsh croak.

"Wha . . ."

Faces swan into his vision, Spar, Kemal, Yashar, and . . . Jaq.

The dog swiped at his face with his tongue and Brax shoved him away with more strength then he expected.

"Get outta here, dog!"

Spar placed one protective hand around Jaq's neck as Yashar chuckled.

"Well, that answers one question: he's alive and none the worse for wear."

Kemal crouched down by the side of the bed.

"How do you feel, Delin?"

Brax closed his eyes. How did he feel?

A thousand stars exploded through his mind.

"All burned up," he answered.

"Are you in pain?

He blinked in surprise. He wasn't. Even the injuries on his face and arm felt better. "Not . . . really. Just . . . kinda scraped."

"Hm."

Kemal sat back on his heels as Brax ran one fingertip across where the gash on his lip should have been but wasn't.

"All right, not so scraped." He glanced around. "How long have I been here?"

"Over an hour."

"Kemal carried you here after your . . . experience in the courtyard," Yashar supplied.

"Experience?"

"You don't remember?"

A peace and stillness greater than even death could have delivered.

"I remember. She held me."

The two men exchanged a suddenly worried look.

"How did she hold you?" Kemal asked gently.

Brax shrugged. "I dunno . . . just . . . Why? Does it matter?"

"Sometimes. How did you feel when She held you?"

"Peaceful. Safe."

"Alive?" Yashar asked.

"What kinda question is that?"

"An important one, Brax," Kemal answered. "Estavia is the God of Battles . . ."

". . . Not known for nurturing behavior," Yashar added. "Unless you're dead. Or . . ." he glanced over at Kemal, then shrugged. ". . . about to die. Sometimes She'll send one of Her warriors—one of Her favorites usually—a premonition of death."

"Why?"

"Why what?"

"Why would She do that?"

The older man shrugged. "To prepare them, maybe, or to welcome them to Her embrace. I don't really know."

"Is that what it felt like, Brax?" Kemal asked again.

He made a dismissive gesture. "No. It was more like She was saving me."

"So you didn't see or smell anything unusual? Roses or maybe tulips?"

"What? No." He tipped his head to one side then gave a lopsided grin. "So, you think I'm one of Her favorites?"

Kemal stood as Yashar rolled his eyes. "I can't think why you might be," the older man said, his voice dripping with sarcasm. "You're already as argumentative, overconfident, and arrogant as any of them."

Brax frowned. "How many more are there?"

Kemal shook his head. "That's not the point . . ."

"Kem," Yashar gave a slight jerk of his head as Kaptin Julide entered the infirmary. As they straightened, she gave a sharp nod their way before glancing over at Brax.

"Ghazis."

"Kaptin."

"How is he?"

"Recovering," Kemal allowed cautiously.

"The God gave him quite a ride," Yashar added.

"Yes." She looked him up and down with an appraising expression. "What does the physician say?"

"He hasn't been in since he woke up, but he'll probably tell him to rest," Kemal replied dryly.

"No doubt," the kaptin agreed, ignoring his tone. "Well, he has a week."

"Kaptin?"

"The council's made their decision. Based on this morning's *events*, they've agreed the delon are favored by the God and should remain with us, and yes, before you ask, specifically with Cyan Company, and even more specifically with you as *your* delon. You'll begin their training at once and they'll accompany you when you leave for Anahtar-Hisar a week from today." She caught them both in a firm-eyed stare. "Congratulations, Ghazis. You're abayon. Raise your delon well and make your company proud. I'm sure they'll have a lot to say about how you do it."

As she turned to leave, Brax raised himself up painfully. "Kaptin?"

"Yes, Brax-Delin?"

Momentarily distracted by the casual endearment, Brax shook his head. "The spirits," he said after a moment. "The ones that are attacking the unsworn?"

"What about them?"

"What are we doing about them?"

She raised an eyebrow at him. "*We* are consulting with the other five temples in formulating a strategy against them."

"What can *they* do?" he muttered, sinking down under the sheets again, ignoring Kemal's frown.

"They can gather intelligence. A warrior that runs headlong against an enemy without it swiftly becomes a corpse," the kaptin admonished and Brax nodded reluctantly.

"I guess so."

"You need to learn both patience and cooperation," she added. "I'll leave that impossible task in the hands of your new abayon. Ghazis."

With one last glance at Kemal and Yashar, she turned and left the infirmary. The two men exchanged a slightly shocked look before turning to the boys. Spar's features were carefully neutral, but Brax's expression was already abstracted.

A thousand stars exploded in his mind.

He narrowed his eyes.

A tiny, mounted host in the distance led by a figure surrounded by shining lights.

Why did that seem so familiar?

A man bathed in light, commanding lines of warriors on a hundred battlefields.

A child of potential hovering on the edge of being.

His mind shied away from the images, afraid of the icy backlash that had come after, and he pushed the fear away with an impatient mental shove. She loved him; he was one of Her favorites, and no icy plunge into Gol-Beyaz or possible premonition of death was going to change that. Pushing himself into a sitting position, he looked up at Kemal.

"*Abayos?*" he asked, putting deliberate emphasis on the word.

Kemal started. "Yes, Brax?"

"I'm hungry."

As Yashar sent a junior physician scurrying off to find food, Spar snickered, but Brax lay back with a frown.

A figure surrounded by shining lights . . .

A man bathed in light commanding lines of warriors on a hundred battle-fields.

Different but similar.

He closed his eyes and the images faded away leaving nothing but the faintest memory of a boy lying dead on the cobblestones of Liman-Caddesi and another snatched into the air by a host of lights and spirits. He pushed the thought away.

It's over, he told himself firmly. *We're safe. It doesn't matter what anyone says or does now. We made it.*

✦

At Oristo-Sarayi, Tanay was discussing the boys' sudden arrival with Chamberlain Rakeed of Usara's temple as they entered the smallest of the five council rooms. Old friends, the two of them had walked over together, grumbling about the disruption to their schedules and speculating on what the other chamberlains were going to bring to eat. Together, they set down their individual platters of seed cakes beside a huge silver tea service, and Tanay gave a deep, drawn-out sigh as she glanced along the length of the long, linen-draped side table.

"And yet, if I'd decided to make halva, everyone else would have made that, too," she muttered huffily.

"Hm?" Rakeed glanced over as he lifted two cakes from each platter with an air of greedy anticipation.

"I was just saying that sometimes the Hearth God is a little too close to us all," she explained. "Next time I'm going to bring a bucket of asure."

"It won't help. But look, Farok's brought lokum and Kadar's made simit rings. I love simit rings." He added three to his plate with a flourish.

"Kadar made simit rings because the Senior Abayos-Priest made. . . . ?" Tanay lifted one, sarcastic hand to her ear. "Seed cakes," she finished for him. "And Farok probably made lokum because someone at Incasa-Sarayi saw too many seed cakes in a vision this morning."

"Well, pardon me for seeing the best of the situation," he said in an injured tone belied by the twinkle in his eye. "We could sample them all and see who made the best. Do we dare?"

Tanay laughed in spite of herself. "No, Rakeedin-Delin, everyone knows your seed cakes are the best."

"Why, thank you, ravishing one, it's too true." He leaned toward her with a conspiratorial air. "Speaking of visions, do you suppose that this all too inconveniently called last minute consultation is due to Bey Freyiz and her cryptic little vision?"

"Likely." Tanay glanced over as Senior Abayos-Priest Neclan entered the room, Chamberlain Kadar in tow. "I imagine we'll find out."

As one, the gathered joined them at the low council table, sinking quickly into its accompanying nest of silken cushions and Neclan glanced about until she was sure she had everyone's attention.

"Before we get to the meat of today's discussion, Chamberlain Farok has a piece of very pertinent information to share with us. Farok?"

The chamberlain of Incasa's temple finished off a piece of lokum before clearing his throat. "First Oracle Freyiz has stepped down, naming Seer-Priest Bessic as her successor. She's leaving for Adasi-Koy within the week."

Talk broke out around the table immediately, but eventually Chamberlain Isabet of Ystazia's temple gave her superior a shrewd glance.

"The timing is suspicious," she noted loudly enough to silence the rest of the gathered.

"Yes, it is," Neclan agreed.

"Is there any speculation as to why?"

All eyes turned to Farok again, who gave an elegant shrug. "The official story is simply retirement—after all, she is very old—but word in the halls is that Incasa has sent her a powerful and complex vision which requires the added clarity of her home village to sort out."

"A vision beyond the one she made public at Assembly?" Tanay asked.

"I don't know," he admitted with an apologetic smile. "Seed cake?"

"I have one, thank you."

"So what do you know about the new First Oracle?" Chamberlain Penir of Havo's temple asked.

Farok gave another elegant shrug. "Nothing unseemly or secret, I'm afraid. He's is in his late thirties. He comes from a wealthy Anavatanon family who've served Incasa's temple for at least five generations. He's intelligent, handsome, privileged, and very, very ambitious. He's well-liked and well-respected within the temple hierarchy; however, he's neither as powerful nor as beloved by the God as Freyiz and since he served under her as delinkos, he's naturally a bit intimidated by the position."

"Who wouldn't be?" Tanay observed dryly.

The gathered snickered, but a swift, disapproving glance from their Senior Abayos-Priest, stilled them at once.

"Will this cause disquiet in Incasa's temple?" she asked bluntly.

"I shouldn't think so, Sayin, not with Bey-Freyiz leaving so soon."

Neclan leaned back, turning her teacup peevishly between finger and thumb. "So," she said after a moment. "Momentous changes at Incasa-Sarayi and disturbance at Oristo-Sarayi. Does anyone else have something to add to this list of woes?"

The gathered glanced about at each other before Rakeed kicked Tanay under the table. With a yelp, she turned and swatted him in the back of the head before acknowledging his point with a glare.

"I don't know that this adds to any tale of woe," she said, daring Rakeed to gainsay her. "But there has been an unusual event at Estavia-Sarayi."

✦

"Kick me again and I'll see to it that every hospital bed at Usara-Sarayi is short-sheeted," she threatened as she and Rakeed made their way back along the opulent, tree-lined merchant street that linked the six main temples together.

Pausing before a line of carpets hanging outside a nearby stall, her fellow chamberlain just shrugged. "Are you saying that you weren't going to tell her?" he asked, studying the elaborate designs with an appreciative air.

Tanay gave no answer for a moment. "I don't know," she said finally. "But I *do* know that delon have no place in temple politics."

"And yet the timing is just as suspicious as Bey-Freyiz's retirement."

"Possibly, but I won't have Brax and Spar dragged into any nonsense about visions or prophecies regardless," she replied. "And I will *not* have them spied upon. Will you be long?"

"Not at all. In all fairness," he noted, feeling the texture of a small lap rug between finger and thumb. "I don't think that's what Neclan had in mind. She asked that you keep an eye on the situation, not spy on the delon. Yes, they are beautiful," he told the merchant hovering unobtrusively by the door. "I'll take twelve of the blue ones. You were saying?" he asked as they continued along the street, moving from linen and silk shops to incense and perfume stalls as Oristo's sphere of influence waned and Incasa's waxed.

"That I don't like it."

"Well, just think how impossible Farok's job is, then. He has to keep an eye on an entire temple of politically savvy, subtle, and dissembling seer-priests, arse-deep in these latest disturbances."

"I suppose. *Now* where are you going?" she demanded as he suddenly veered off toward a glassmaker's shop.

"I need blue bottles."

"I'm never going to get back in time to receive the day's supplies," she sighed. "Ah well, I suppose Monee can handle it." With a resigned expression, she followed the other chamberlain inside.

✦

"You know the delon might be pertinent," Rakeed continued a few moments later as they passed a row of incense sellers. "You said they were brought to Estavia-Sarayi by the Battle God Herself. That alone warrants attention. I'm surprised someone from Incasa's temple hasn't been over to interview them already."

"Well, they'd best not make the attempt," Tanay growled. "They haven't given us the whole story by any stretch of the imagination; I can feel it. And until they do, the delon are *off limits*. Kemal of Serin-Koy and Yashar of Caliskan-Koy are their abayon now and I want the whole family left in peace."

She glared at him and he raised both hands in surrender. "You don't have to convince me," he protested. "I'm sure they'll be fine abayon, and if you say Incasa's people are hiding things, I believe you. You're the one with a modicum of prophetic sight, after all."

"Don't let it get around," she sniffed in a mollified tone. "Most priests of Oristo think it's a pile of sheep manure."

"Don't you?"

Striding purposely through a mud puddle, Tanay gave a faint snort. "Perhaps," she replied, glancing darkly at the tall, wrought iron gates of Incasa-Sarayi before them. "But usually it's the seer that makes it so, not the sight."

✦

In her bedchamber, Freyiz paused in the supervision of her packing as a thread of sarcastic power trickled through her mind. She chuckled.

"You always were a swift one," she murmured in the direction of Estavia-Sarayi's chamberlain. "Too swift to be scooped up by Incasa and confined to the life of a minor seer." Turning, she stared out the window at the flickering red power signature of the Battle God's temple to the north. "So, Tanayin-Delin," she continued. "I leave the delon in your capable hands for now. But only for now, mind you. The time will come when they'll pull away from your protection as well as from mine."

With a sigh, she turned back into the room. "But then, delon always do, no matter how vital it might be for them to stay," she added sadly.

✦

Across the city, dusk came slowly to the first clear night of High Spring, gifting the sky with a hint of pink and orange before settling into darkness. At Estavia-Sarayi, the new abayon saw Brax and Spar safely tucked into bed in the delon alcove off their own rooms, then withdrew as Jaq clambered up at once and stretched out across their feet.

In their own bedchamber Yashar lit the lamp and closed the shutters while Kemal unrolled the pallet. Glancing over, the older man noted the pensive expression on his arkados' face. With an evil grin, he checked to ensure the door was locked, then suddenly tackled the younger man and tossed him onto the pallet. After a short wrestling match which Kemal won by jabbing the older man in the ribs, he glared down at him while Yashar just laughed.

"You had your serious face on," he explained. "I hate your serious face; it interferes with lovemaking."

He made a grab for him, but Kemal caught his hand. "You don't think that suddenly being given the responsibility of two delon is a reason to be serious?" he demanded.

"I do not. It's a reason for celebration. We finally have the bed to ourselves without your great, mangy dog stealing all the covers."

"So you're not worried?"

Pulling free, Yashar stripped off his tunic, flexing the muscles of his arms and chest with a lewd expression. "I was never worried. I knew *my* seed was potent; *you* just never had the natural field to sow it in. If you'd gone to Oristo's temple and petitioned the Hearth God, we might have had delon long before now."

This set off another wrestling match, but finally both men caught each other up in a more passionate embrace.

Afterward, while Yashar poured them each a glass of dark red wine, Kemal raised himself up on one elbow.

"You could have petitioned Oristo yourself," he noted wryly.

"I'm too hairy. I'd make a terribly ugly woman." Handing him a glass, Yashar held his up in salute. "To our delon, sensibly grown past the age of birthing and breast feeding."

"Yes, to the age of sulking and arguing."

"I'll handle the arguing, you handle the sulking."

"No, thank you."

Draining his glass, Yashar threw himself down beside the other man. "We'll do fine," he said, attempting a more serious tone. "So stop fretting. It's not like we'll be alone in it. We have all of Cyan Company to help us."

"We'll need them."

"There you are. Besides, if they do too much sulking and arguing, we can always pack them off to Bayard. After all, he survived yours."

"There is that." Draining his own glass, Kemal set it down carefully beside the pallet. "Estavia knows what She's doing," he allowed finally. "She wouldn't have given them to us if She hadn't thought we could handle it."

"It's settled, then." Stretching out on the rumpled blankets, Yashar placed his clasped hands behind his head. "Blow out the lamp, will you? I'm exhausted."

Shaking his head, Kemal rose. "Old man," he admonished over his shoulder. "You better start pacing yourself. Fade on me now and I'll find myself a younger arkados to fill my bed and raise my delon."

"I'd best get myself ready for your return, then."

"I guess you had."

Extinguishing the light, Kemal padded back to bed, finding the older man in the darkness with the ease of long familiarity. As the night breezes whispered through the shutters, they made love more slowly now, each taking comfort and gaining strength from the other.

7

Kardon

O N THE EDGE of the Berbat-Dunya, Graize rode seated before Kursk in the middle of the Rus-Yuruk's kazakin-host. Eyes half closed and focused on a point somewhere between his pony's ears and half a mile away, he floated in a heavy trance—made that much easier by the hypnotic swish, swish of the kazakin's slow gait through the grasses. It seemed to calm his thoughts. Above his head, the lights merged and flowed like an ever-changing flock of silvery birds and, reaching out, he ran his mind through their midst almost instinctively. Touching each tiny spark of consciousness, he began to idly gather them up, weaving and binding them together under the pressure of their guidance until a crude human-seeming began to emerge.

The lights bonded swiftly with this new form, moving faster and faster with each passing hour and, as their singular awareness and sense of purpose grew in strength so did his own sense of self. When the kazakin crested a low rise in a jingle of tiny bells, and the shimmer that represented their spring encampment stretched out before him, he remembered his life on the streets of Anavatan.

His gray eyes narrowed as he glared at the lights, realizing that they were responsible for this sudden return to memory.

"The past is gone," he told them sharply with more clarity than he'd felt since the attack on Liman-Caddesi. *"If you want to make yourselves useful then show me the future, the near future."*

With an icy breath, a hundred visions rose up around him like a cloud of crystalline butterflies; places and events yet to be, both near and far. He flipped through them impatiently, discarding each one like a gem merchant sorting through inferior goods until he sensed that he'd found the one with the appropriate amount of power and riches won quickly; the power and riches he had always dreamed he would have.

"*That one*," he demanded, pointing at the wavering image of a child of unformed potential hovering behind a dark-haired man surrounded by a host of silver swords. "*Give me that one.*"

The lights complied eagerly, throwing up the names and faces of the allies he'd need to make the vision a reality. The few he knew stayed still just long enough to be recognized: Kursk, Rayne, and Ozan of the kaza-kin; while the names of others he was yet to meet trailed faintly across his mind like spiderwebbing made of ice crystals: Timur, their oldest wyrdin, Ayami, Rayne's abia, Caleb, her youngest kardos, Ozan's delon—Rayne's kuzon—Briz, Gabrie, and Tahnan, and her oldest kardos Danjel hovering in a cloud of mist. His people, his . . . he strained to understand the sudden wash of icy possessiveness that came over him—his . . . generals, the ones who would lead his army against the shining city and crack open the walls of Gol-Beyaz as he'd envisioned earlier in Kursk's tent.

But there was something subtly different about this latest vision. He frowned.

His army?

The lights dimmed for just an instant and he knew then: not *his* army but *their* army, built to give them power and form. Folding his arms, he fixed them with a cold, unimpressed stare and the lights fluttered nervously about him, tempting and cajoling, promising him his power and riches and whatever else they could glean from his thoughts. After a long moment, he unbent enough to send them a morsel of reassurance. He didn't need bribes to attack Anavatan, he only needed . . .

The flicker of an image came and went almost before he could register it, but he knew whose face it was just the same; the dark-haired man, the one person who might upset all his plans; the one person who, in some far distant future, he might allow to upset his all plans for reasons he could sense but couldn't yet understand. The one person who was . . . key.

The lights gyrated in agitation, thrown into a panic by his train of thought and, almost absently, he sucked in a mouthful of tiny spirits and, holding the image of his beetle—cracked carapace and all—in his thoughts to focus him, he breathed a line of icy power through their midst, knowing instinctively that the spirits' life force would feed the lights as well as they'd fed him. He would build them their army, he assured them, and unleash it upon the shining city like an avenging storm because it pleased him to do so, but after that he had other plans for his future and for theirs. The game was all that mattered, and Graize had always been very good at the game.

"And you'll help me win it, won't you," he whispered. *"Because I know what you want now and you'll need my help to get it."*

Reluctantly, the lights agreed.

✦

A few moments later a pause in the steady gait of the kazakin interrupted his thoughts, and he looked up to see that the shimmer had become a sea of sheep and goats flanked by half a dozen mounted Yuruk. The same high-pitched whistle he'd heard before the kazakin had approached him sounded across the plains and, as the other riders stirred, Kursk glanced down at him with a smile.

"Almost home now."

He turned. "Standard-bearer, answer the call."

With a huge smile, Rayne raised herself up in the saddle, and putting two fingers into her mouth, gave a long, ululating whistle in return.

There was a moment's silence, then a series of short whistles, and Kursk nodded.

"All's well. Let's ride."

Urging his pony into a canter, he brought the kazakin down the rise.

✦

The animals engulfed them within minutes. For a heartbeat Graize was back in Anavatan on market day, with great flocks and herds crowding the narrow streets so tightly the people could hardly move around them. He smelled the strong, lanolin scent of warm wool, tasted the dust of the city streets churned up into the air, heard the tinkle of the thousand tiny bells woven into their wool to protect them from the spirits of the wild lands, then a small figure galloped toward them and he recognized the first of his new allies.

Caleb.

Perhaps two years younger than Rayne, with Kursk's hawk nose and a medium complexion burned brown by the sun, he had one arm tightly wrapped in thin strips of goat hide around two wooden splints, but still managed to guide his pony with ease. Staring openly at Graize, he halted his mount with a flourish just in front of them.

Kursk smiled warmly at him and Graize could see the blood tie stretch between them as it did with Rayne.

"What news, Calebask?"

"Abia's just returned from the west," the boy answered eagerly. "She wasn't too pleased to find you gone, Aba," he added with a grin.

"My arkados spent the winter with her family," Kursk remarked to Graize. "Go and tell her I've returned," he replied to Caleb. "And tell her I've brought her a new delos, one she didn't have to go to the trouble of birthing herself."

Caleb's black, almond-shaped eyes widened, but after nodding sharply, he wheeled about and galloped for the encampment, raising a great crowd of insects in his wake.

Beside them, Rayne snickered. "*He's* not too happy either, Aba," she noted.

Graize looked at her curiously.

"If you're Abia's new delos," she explained, "then you're Caleb's new kardos. New, *older* kardos."

"Is that a problem?"

"Oh, no, he's used to it. There's four older than him already."

"How'd he hurt his arm?"

She shrugged. "Showing off. He wanted Danjel to notice him." She twisted in the saddle to meet his eyes. "You see, it's not Caleb you have to worry about, Graize, it's Danjel."

"Danjel will welcome him as warmly as the rest, Raynziern," Kursk interrupted in an admonishing tone, urging his pony into a trot to end further discussion.

Behind him, Rayne just shrugged as Graize cast her a curious glance.

✦

Power and freedom, violence and wild potential; the inner life of the Rus-Yuruk washed over him like the tide. Sheep and goats, ponies, dogs, tents and paddocks, riders on guard, and children at play; the outer life followed a heartbeat later. Shaking his head to clear away the spirits that had suddenly clamped themselves about his face, he peered more closely at the encampment.

The paddocks were made of wood and wattle surrounded by perhaps a dozen goat hide tents. Two fire pits, cold now, flanked the entrance to a central clearing, and beyond that, several reed huts which Graize could only assume were for storing wool or drying fish stood by the water. As they cantered forward, people came out to meet them on ponies and on foot, but moved aside for a tall, angular-faced woman Graize recognized from his vision as Rayne's abia, Ayami. As she came forward, Kursk dismounted and took her in his arms, leaving Graize balanced precariously on the pony's back. The kazakin leader related their adventure quickly and, when Ayami turned a welcoming smile in his direction, Graize felt an almost violent twist in his chest. She gestured.

"Come down, child, and let me have a look at you."

Her voice broke against his mind like the waves of the Halic-Salmanak and without thinking, he swung off the pony's back. Unused to riding for any length of time, his legs were stiff and sore and buckled underneath him as he touched the ground; he would have landed in an undignified heap at her feet if Ozan hadn't anticipated this and caught him under the arms. Face burning, he glared at the lights for not warning him of this humiliating entrance, but Ayami chose not to notice it. As Rayne eagerly repeated the story of his rescue for all within earshot, she lifted his chin with two fingers, searching his face as her touch sent rivulets of warmth through his body.

"There's strength in your spirit," she noted approvingly, "if little in your body just yet. How old are you, child?"

The beetle's image supplied the answer from the still-foggy depths of his memory.

"Thirteen."

The gathered Yuruk began to murmur softly, but Graize ignored them, concentrating instead on Ayami's features as her expression hardened.

"Is this how the Anavatanon care for their children, then?" she asked bluntly. "Leaving them undernourished and alone?"

He could sense that her question was directed more toward the adults standing around them than to him, but he answered anyway, giving a careless shrug. "Only if they die," he answered harshly.

Her expression softened. "Did your abayon have no kardon to gift you to, then?" she asked.

The lights crowded forward, eager to give him this memory back, but he shook his head. He needed to think clearly right now, such memories would only muddy his heart.

"No."

Her expression shifted again. "Well, they do now." Turning, her hand moved from his chin to his shoulder. "Rayne, take your new kardos to . . ." she thought a moment, "Ozan's tent for now," she said at the man's nod, "and find him something to eat. Caleb lend him some clothes and Kursk . . ."

He smiled. "My love . . . ?"

"I need you in *our* tent. The winter apart has been far too long."

The gathered grinned openly at this, but Rayne looked up with a frown. "What about Danjel, Abia?"

Ayami's black, almond-shaped eyes flashed. "Danjel can wait."

✦

"So who is this Danjel, anyway," Graize asked around a large piece of cheese drizzled with olive oil and parsley, the food granting him more clarity of thought. "And why do I have to be worried?"

Caleb snickered but Rayne glared at him to be quiet. She'd brought Graize to Ozan's tent as instructed, shooing all but her younger kardos away so that he might eat in peace. Watching him alternate between staring intently at the dead beetle in his hand and stuffing his face was disconcerting, but one or the other seemed to be helping him stay in the present. He was certainly acting more like a child and less like a mad creature plucked from the wild lands now.

"Danjel's the leader of the kazakin youth," she explained, holding his gaze firmly locked in her own so his eyes wouldn't slide away from her words. "He's training with Timur to be a wyrdin. He'll be sixteen by the next moon and he's the best rider and the best fighter of us all."

"Yeah, and tell him why," Caleb interrupted, gesturing at Graize with his kinjal.

"*You* tell him why."

"He has spirit blood," the boy supplied promptly.

Graize's brows drew down while around him the lights dimmed slightly as if they were trying to escape his notice.

"They *say* he has spirit blood," Rayne corrected. "He and his abia came out of the Berbat-Dunya when he was three and she died a year later in the attack on Serin-Koy. He's been our kardos ever since."

"So why do you think he's got spirit blood?"

Caleb rolled his eyes. "Because he came out of the *Berbat-Dunya*," he said with exaggerated patience. "And because he's so good at everything, and because he's a wyrdin and because he's bi-gender even though he's living as a male right now."

"The Yuruk believe the spirits choose a child's gender and that their blood makes it . . . fluid," Rayne added. "Danjel goes back and forth from male to female whenever he feels like it because he has spirit blood, you see?"

Graize glanced at the gathered spirits hovering just out of reach. "In Anavatan most bi-gender live either as both or as one or the other, but they believe it's a gift from the Hearth God, not the spirits," he stated.

Rayne shrugged carelessly. "Spirits, Gods, they're all the same thing, Graize. It's only a matter of size."

Around him both the lights and the spirits suddenly crowded around him, agreeing noisily, and Graize brushed them aside with an impatient snap of his mind. "But why do I have to worry about him?" he persisted, holding tightly to his original question before it slipped out of his thoughts.

"Because if you're going to go anywhere or fight anywhere on horseback at your age, he's the only one who'll be able to teach you to use *your* spirit blood, or your connection to the spirits, whichever you have," she answered. "You're just too old to learn properly any other way."

Beside her, Caleb nodded. "And *you* came out of the Berbat-Dunya, too," he observed, "and you're a wyrdin . . ."

"Already," Rayne added.

"So he might see you as a challenge."

"A threat."

"You're not that much younger than he is."

"Graize is a lot smaller, though."

"Yeah. Hey, that might work in his favor."

"You mean Danjel might see him as a younger kardos, instead of a threat."

"Could be. If he played it the right way, kind of vulnerable, you know?

"Where are you going?"

Both of them stared at Graize as he stood up suddenly and he glanced down at them in annoyance, his eyes perfectly clear for the first time in days.

"For a piss," he answered caustically. "And for some peace and quiet. You're like two carrion birds squawking over a corpse and I'm not dead yet."

"We're just trying to help," Caleb grumbled.

"Then help by taking me to him and letting *me* worry about how to play it. *After* I go for a piss," he added.

Rayne stood. "He'll be waiting for you anyway," she said. "We shouldn't put it off any longer."

"Yeah." Caleb stood as well, sheathing his kinjal. "And besides," he added with a grin, all evidence of his earlier pique gone, "I have to piss, too."

"Figures," Rayne snorted.

✦

Moments later, trailing a host of lights and spirits like an ethereal dog pack, Graize let Rayne lead him to the far paddocks, feeling rather than seeing the eyes of the Yuruk following after them. A dozen figures waited for them, ranging in age from fifteen to nine and he recognized the tall, black-haired youth with the piercing green eyes and the air of command immediately. Much like Ayami, Danjel listened to Rayne's recount, then fixed Graize with an unblinking stare.

"So you can't ride, you can't shoot, and you can't herd. What *can* you do?"

Arms crossed, Danjel waited patiently while Graize considered his answer, his eyes awash with wispy white streaks of prophecy.

What can you do?

What could he do? He stared off into space, feeling his newfound grasp on reality slipping away as he tried to concentrate on the question.

And why did it matter?

Far away, the spirits that had not followed him from the Berbat-Dunya sang a jeering song in his ears.

What could he do?

The lights supplied the answer and he nodded, seeing the future take shape around their words, a future of riders and warriors, raids, battles, and bloodshed all in the name of power.

"I can make a God," he replied in a faraway voice. "A God that will lead the Yuruk to battle against the Warriors of Estavia and sweep them into the sea."

The gathered youths straightened at that, but Danjel simply raised an ironic eyebrow.

"How?"

"With an army," he answered, as the lights continued to spin the future out before him. "The greatest army in a century."

"An army of Yuruk?"

"Yes."

The youths glanced at each other as Danjel snorted.

"We haven't the numbers. And even if we did, you'd never bring us all together under one banner."

"I couldn't, no."

"So, who could?"

A green-eyed rider, dressed in golden scale mail, flashed before his eyes.

"You."

"Me?" Danjel asked sarcastically.

"In time."

"You're not funny."

"I'm not trying to be. In time, you'll lead one of the greatest kazakin in history." His eyes cleared for just a moment. "They say you have spirit blood; you *must* have seen this."

The gathered held their breaths.

"I've seen the *stream*," Danjel allowed in a faintly menacing tone. "I've seen *many* streams."

Graize nodded. "No future is certain," he agreed, ignoring the threat. "But when I said you, I meant all of you." A sweep of one hand took in the entire settlement. "The Rus-Yuruk."

"How?"

He looked up as the lights spun about his head like tiny spiders building a vast and complicated web.

"By being the first kazakin to beat the Warriors of Estavia," he answered.

"Again, how?"

"With my help." Graize leaned forward, his eyes now shining with a silvery glow, the original icy power that had burned a path through his veins helping him see past the lights to the many futures flowing behind his words that they didn't want to show him. "You have power, but so do I," he continued, the words bubbling from his lips in a rush, driven by a sudden gout of images spewing through his mind. "You can speak with the spirits on the plains to find a lost kid or a lost lamb. I can find an army. You know if a storm will give rain or pass by from the way the wind whispers in your mind. I can tell you where it will go and how to make it strike where we want it to. I can see our enemies before they see us, find their weak spots, and know when to attack them. And I know that if we ride against the village of Yildiz-Koy this season, we'll win. I *know* it. I've *seen* it and that future *is* certain if we move fast. The warriors will chase us until the snow covers the northern wild lands in drifts of white clouds, but they won't catch us and they won't know why until it's far too late. As word spreads of our victories, more and more Yuruk will flock to our banner. The Petchans will hear of it and they'll come down from their mountain keeps to share in the bloodshed. They'll come from the north sea and the south; every enemy Anavatan has ever made. We'll build and grow, year by year."

He froze as a new image suddenly loomed up before him.

"And then *he'll* come," he whispered.

"Who, this God you can build?"

"No, not yet." Graize turned to stare across the lake at the distant mountains and beyond. "Someone else." His eyes narrowed as the lights crowded in on him again, fluttering in agitation. "Someone who doesn't need Gods or temples to give him power. Someone from the north, yes, that's it, a sorcerer living in a faraway tower on the sea, brewing magics that no one's ever faced before and building alliances with our enemies, north and south, for just such a time as this."

"Our enemies?"

Graize blinked. "Anavatan's enemies for now, but they'll be our enemies in the future." He frowned as a golden-haired figure hovered just
behind the tower. "Someone who thinks he's hidden from me," he continued, "someone who thinks he doesn't need me, and who thinks he's
found someone better, but he's wrong. He'll hear of our victories and,
smelling blood and opportunity, he'll come to offer us his help to crack
the walls around the lake of power."

"Why?"

Graize laughed low in his throat as the lights whispered the answer
in a sibilantly sarcastic hiss. "Because he'll think he's using us. But we'll
be using him. We'll see him coming." He turned a wide, luminescent
gaze on Danjel's face. "We've already seen him, you see, but he won't
know that."

The gathered murmured their appreciation of this strategy, but
Danjel held up one hand and they silenced.

"And this *God?* Will you use It, too?"

Graize watched as the lights paused as if they were holding their collective breaths.

"No," he answered. "We'll strike a bargain with It."

The lights relaxed.

"What kind of bargain?"

Graize shrugged. "The kind that all Gods want."

"Worship," Danjel spat.

"Possibly."

The bi-gender wyrdin snorted. "The Yuruk don't pledge their worship to anyone or anything. And they don't shackle their lives to Deities
any more than they do to cities *or* to mad prophets that come out of the
wild lands spouting nonsense. If they did, my abia would have ruled the
Rus-Yuruk within a year."

Graize smiled faintly as the others snickered. Around him, the lights
pressed against his mind and he used the image of his beetle to shoo
them away as one might a cloud of gnats. "Alliance, then," he amended.
"The God is young. It will be satisfied with that for now," he said, sensing the truth of his words.

"For now?"

Graize shrugged. "When It's older, It'll want more. They always do,
but so will the Yuruk. And everyone will be haggling from a position of

strength by then. But for now, if the Yuruk will ride against Yildiz-Koy, the God will throw Its growing strength behind their cause."

"With no guarantee of worship?" Danjel pressed. "Again, why?"

Above him the lights froze as if fearing to reveal the answer Graize had already guessed at.

"For the chance to drink from the waters of Gol-Beyaz," he answered.

Danjel considered it.

"The waters will give It great strength, yes?"

"Yes."

"Enough to manifest in the physical world?"

"No. That's not how it's done."

"You've *seen* this?"

"I *learned* it from the priests of Oristo." Graize raised his head. "Look into my prophecy, delos of the wild lands, and you'll learn it, too."

Danjel locked eyes with him at once. For a long time the two of them stared at each other, their eyes as white as the snow on the faraway mountains, while the gathered waited in impatient silence; then, finally, as one, they broke contact.

Graize tipped his head to one side.

"Well?"

Danjel frowned as his eyes returned to their jewellike green tone. "You're playing a dangerous game, *Kardos*," he warned, fingering the pommel of the kinjal at his belt.

"But . . . ?"

"But one you just might win with our help. With *my* help."

"And *will* you help me?"

After a moment's thought, Danjel nodded. "Timur may not believe you and the Yuruk may not follow you, but *I'll* help you, if only to bring my own future greatness into being."

Graize laughed. "Yours and mine, *Kardos*. Done." As the others broke out into excited chatter, he tipped his head back, staring into the cloudy sky with a triumphant expression. The game had begun and nothing would break it up early this time, not Havo's Dance, nor any other God-made catastrophe, not until somebody's stag beetle was dead.

And this time it wasn't going to be his.

Above him, the lights grew brighter and brighter with the promise of strength and power. The spirits, however, fluttered nervously about his face, fearing a future that both Graize and the lights chose to ignore; a future where a dark-haired man and a hitherto unseen black-eyed, golden-haired woman could ruin everything with a simple glance, for creation and destruction were still far too intertwined for their comfort. But, with a dismissive wave, Graize swept them away. He would not allow past or future ghosts to interfere with his plans. Not again. Looking past the settlement to the wild lands and beyond, he bared his teeth in the direction of Anavatan.

Never again.

8

Gol-Beyaz

"*C*AN YOU READ and write?"
    "*No.*"
"*Can you cipher?*"
"*Some.*"
"*What weapons are you familiar with?*"
"*How do you mean, 'familiar'?*"

◆

After the initial excitement of Brax and Spar's acceptance had worn off, most of Estavia's senior officers'd had no idea what to do with them. Finally, Kemal and Yashar had brought them along to the Cyan Company training yard. After the beginnings of an awkward interview, Kaptin Julide's second-in-command, Birin-Kaptin Arjion, had pressed his fingertips to the bridge of his nose before fixing Brax with a stern expression from under his black brows.

◆

"What weapons do you know how to use?" he amended stiffly.
    "Oh. Knife and sling."
    "And?"
    Brax shrugged. "Fists."
    "Is that all?"
    "Pretty much."
    "I see. So, basically you've received no training whatsoever."
    "None you'd want to know about."
    "But you did serve a kind of apprenticeship?"

Brax straightened sharply at his tone. "I served a full apprentice-ship," he retorted. "In a year's time, Cindar and I would have been split-ting our take fifty-fifty. There isn't a lock I can't open and Spar could get behind you and cut your purse before you'd even known he'd moved."

Seated to one side, his arms draped about Jaq's neck, the younger boy nodded solemnly as the gathered warriors shook their heads. Arjion briefly closed his eyes.

"So you're dexterous and Spar is fast," he allowed. "Which is fine on the streets, but Estavia's warriors meet the enemy face to face, not from behind, and they don't split any form of *take*. They serve the God and the God's temple provides them with all they need."

Brax stared up at him in disbelief. "You mean, you don't make any shine at all?" he asked in a horrified voice.

Ghazi-Priest Tersar guffawed out loud and even Kaptin Julide broke a smile, but Arjion merely raised an eyebrow in Kemal's direction. "Clearly, your new abayon haven't explained our terms of service to you," he said in a voice dripping with sarcasm. "Having second thoughts?"

Brax narrowed his eyes, then gave a shrug of studied disdain. "No." As the God's presence tickled against the back of his mind, he frowned. "It just feels . . . wrong somehow," he added.

"As it should."

"What?"

"Estavia's warriors receive payment and tribute just like any other elite fighting force," the birin-kaptin explained, "otherwise we'd be pos-sessions, not soldiers. Does that make you feel any better?"

"So why didn't you say that in the first place," Brax muttered under his breath.

"What was that?"

"Nothing. How much do they get?"

"That depends."

"All right. How much do I get?"

"Delinkon chosen to serve at the temple receive a silver soldis in recognition of their achievement and another after their first year of service. I imagine you'll receive the same." Arjion glanced over at Kaptin Julide, who nodded. "And considering that the temple provides food, clothing, board, and weapons," he continued, "I'd say that's a more than adequate sum."

"How much do they get later on?" Brax pressed.

"Again, that depends."

"On what?"

"Your status, based on your achievements and dedication to the God."

Brax tipped his head to one side, debating whether to ask the most obvious, albeit the most tactless question, then gave a mental shrug. It's not like the man would be surprised.

"How much do you get?" he asked.

Arjion merely smiled tightly. "Forty golden soldon per year."

Spar straightened with a jerk, but Brax just nodded, his expression carefully neutral.

"When would I get that?"

"You want my best guess?"

"Yes."

"Never."

"Why?"

Arjion raised a fist, lifting one finger per point until he'd made an empty hand. "You're too suspicious, you're too argumentative, you're too undisciplined, you haven't had enough training, and what training you have had has obviously taught you to seek the less than honorable path. You can't do that when you serve the will of a God. They take offense . . .." he blew across his palm. ". . . and you end up with nothing."

"And if that changed?"

"Why would it change? Just so you can make a lot of *shine?* There are easier ways."

Brax folded his arms, but nodded stiffly. "Point," he acknowledged, echoing Yashar's phrase from earlier that morning. "But suppose I wanted to do it for Estavia? Suppose I wanted to rise in Her temple as high as I could go just for Her glory?"

"Do you?"

"Maybe. I don't know yet. Does anybody?"

"A few serve that selflessly, yes, but they don't tend to be interested in money."

"But they still get it, right?"

"Yes," Arjion sighed. "They still get it."

"So how long would it take for me to get it?"

Arjion gave a shrug as disdainful as Brax's own. "With tremendous effort on both your part and on the part of your instructors, forty years, give or take a few."

"That's a long time."

"You have a lot of ground to cover and a lot more to make up."

✦

"Up! Down! Up! Lift your arm, Brax! Higher, it's a sword, not a stick! Like you see Brin doing. Higher! All right, everyone stop for a moment."

"Square! Come on, faster! Brax, get into line! Hurry! No, beside Levith where I showed you before; we've been over this a dozen times!"

✦

After that first interview, Kaptin Julide had placed Brax in a unit of first-year delinkon, but when it became obvious that he needed more training just to keep in line, she'd added two hours of individual sword and spear practice in the early morning with Tersar and another two hours of bow practice in the late evening with Arjion. Three days later when his unit began formation drill in the central courtyard; his training increased by yet another hour in midafternoon. On the fourth day he could barely walk but had refused both Kemal and Tanay's ministrations. On the fifth day, his legs had collapsed underneath him as he'd tried to get out of bed. Gritting his teeth, he'd sworn Spar to secrecy and made his morning practice with moments to spare. Somehow he'd gotten through the day, the constant strengthening presence of the God the only thing keeping him on his feet, but on the sixth and final day before Cyan Company was to leave for Anahtar-Hisar, he'd vanished before dawn.

Kemal found him sitting against Estavia's onyx statue in the temple's central shrine, the secondhand sandals Tanay had managed to find him tossed into one corner.

He raised his dark eyes to the man's face with a look of stony acceptance.

"I can't do it," he said bluntly.

Kemal took a seat beside him, carefully avoiding the sharp end of the statue's downward pointing sword.

"No," he agreed. "Not like this, anyway."

Brax's jaw tightened. "I didn't run out on practice, you know," he said stiffly, misinterpreting his abayos' words. "She told me to come here."

"I don't doubt it." Looking up into the God's crimson gaze for guidance, Kemal felt a single name take form in his mind on the faintest breath of wind and nodded. "Have you ever heard of Kaptin Haldin?" he asked.

"No."

"He was Estavia's first and only Champion, many hundreds of years ago. He commanded the army which protected Anavatan's builders. He and Marshal Nurcan—the Warriors' first fighting-priest—laid the foundation stones for Her temple, right here before this very altar. He's buried under Her statue behind us."

Brax glanced over at the polished black marble slab beneath the God's onyx feet, but said nothing.

"Since that day, Estavia's ghazi-priests have trained thousands of warriors to follow in Haldin and Nurcan's footsteps," Kemal continued. "And they've been doing it the same way for centuries."

"If it's not broken . . ." Brax muttered, his voice tinged with bitter sarcasm.

"Exactly, because up until this point it hasn't been. Most of Estavia's fighters come from families that are already sworn to Her worship so they're familiar with Her ways. They begin at age six, serving under an abayos or older kardos, sometimes a ghazi or even a senior delinkos. They assist them, fetch and carry for them, get to know the life. What little formation training they do is carried out within their family or in small village groups. During battle they stay behind, sometimes at home, sometimes behind the lines. By the time they pick up their first real weapons at age eleven, it almost comes naturally."

Rubbing at one tightly swollen wrist, Brax frowned. "So Spar has two years before he even has to start real training?" he asked.

"Yes. He has two years to catch up on five instead of nine."

"Lucky him," Brax said under his breath.

"Hm?"

"Nothing."

Kemal frowned. "You really need to stop doing that," he admonished gently. "It's disrespectful to Estavia's officers and therefore disrespectful to the God Herself."

Brax glanced over at him with the beginnings of a scowl, then nodded sharply. "All right."

"What I meant before," Kemal continued, "was that we can't go on blindly assuming that your training can follow the usual path. You're not usual and neither is your circumstance. To believe otherwise is to fail you and so ultimately to fail the God."

Brax glared at the floor. "It all comes back to that, doesn't it?" he said after a moment.

"Always."

"And that . . . chews at you, to fail Her, I mean."

"Yes."

He shook his head. "Life used to be a lot more simple," he mused. "You did what you had to do and you didn't worry about what anyone else thought about it, especially not the Gods. I never thought that would change. I never thought it *could* change." He gave a deep sigh.

"It chews at me, too, you know, even with it being so soon."

"I know," Kemal said sympathetically. "I can see it."

When Brax gave him a suspicious frown, Kemal smiled.

"You're not very good at hiding your thoughts or your feelings," he explained. "You're the least subtle person I've ever met, even given your age."

Brax mulled over his words for a moment, trying to discover any criticism or sarcasm despite Kemal's warm tone, then just shrugged. "It doesn't matter," he replied. "I can't get it. Not even with Her help. Kaptin Omal's right. I'd get killed, or get someone else killed."

Kemal sighed. "No, you won't." As Brax frowned at him again, he stood. "Lesson one," he said, crossing his arms. "The essence of strategy is adaptability, to use what works and discard what doesn't. So, *delinkos*," he stressed the word with a smile, "the traditional training regimes aren't working. Why?"

"Because I'm too old."

"No, because you haven't had the nine years of preliminary groundwork that you require. So the answer is . . . ?"

"I dunno, to get them?"

"Exactly. Now, how?"

Brax shrugged wordlessly.

"Well, how would you learn any new skill?"

"You'd start at the beginning."

"That's right."

Brax frowned at him. "You want me to fetch and carry for five years before I pick up a sword?" he asked.

"Maybe. If that's what it takes. Could you do that?"

Staring intently at a spot just past Kemal's right shoulder, Brax considered everything that would mean while the God whispered Her demands of battle and glory in his ears. Five years. In five years he would be . . . old. Her impatience with the thought of waiting at all was almost audible.

So was his.

"I don't know," he replied finally. "Probably not."

"An honest answer. As it happens, you're forgetting the main point from the other direction. You're in an unusual circumstance requiring unusual strategy, remember. You haven't had nine years of training, but you haven't got nine years to catch up either." When Brax looked at him questioningly, he just shrugged. "Do you really want to be nineteen before you pick up a real sword and twenty-four before you become ghazidelinkos?"

"No."

"It would be detrimental anyway. You need to become familiar with your weapons now, but you also need the groundwork. So, the only answer is to take you out of traditional unit training and put you into individual training more similar to that of other non-temple apprenticeships."

"Under who?"

Kemal shrugged. "Myself and Yashar probably, but possibly not; we have to think this through very carefully. The Warriors of Estavia are not a collection of individual Champions, Brax, we're an army; we're soldiers. To take you out of that hierarchy could hamper your ability to work within it and you're already far too self-centered for the council's liking. And the decision—the order—to deviate from traditional training would ultimately have to be theirs anyway. All we can do is try to convince them that it's the right way to go."

"So how do we do that?"

"Well, precedents wouldn't hurt."

"What does that mean?"

"That it's been done before."

"Has it?"

"I don't know."

Brax laid his hand on the cool marble slab beneath the statue's feet. "You said Kaptin Haldin was a Champion, but he had to have been a soldier, too, right?"

"Yes."

"So how did he manage both?"

"I don't know. There aren't a lot of stories surviving from before the building of Anavatan."

"Why not?"

Kemal shrugged. "Some people believe that literacy destroyed the oral traditions that kept such stories alive—very few of Estavia's warriors could read and write before that time—only the stories that were written down are still with us and the priests of Ystazia, not Estavia, tended to be the ones who did the writing. So, naturally, more stories of the Art God's people exist. Others—mostly the priests of Incasa, for obvious reasons—believe that something happened during those years that the Gods want shrouded in mystery."

"But they're not sure?"

"No."

"Can't they just ask?"

"They have. No one's ever received an answer. Incasa's particularly aggressive in His silence, Estavia less so, but even Ystazia, the scholars' and historians' own God, won't satisfy their curiosity."

"Sounds like They've got something to hide."

"Possibly. Ask Estavia yourself. See what She says."

Brax closed his eyes. Then opened them again with a frown.

Kemal raised an eyebrow. "Well?"

"Nothing. It's like She didn't even hear me. Does that mean She doesn't want me to know?"

"Not necessarily. It may mean She wants you to find out for yourself. If the Gods tell us everything, we don't learn anything, do we?"

Brax made a face. "So what do we do?"

"We go hunting for what stories have been written down." Kemal straightened. "You need to start your reading and writing soon anyway or Spar will outstrip you there. Ihsan say's he's coming along very quickly."

"So that's what he's been doing. He wouldn't say."

"I imagine he thought you'd disapprove."

"He knows I wouldn't. He probably just wanted to show off what he could do later on."

"Oh?"

"When you're the youngest and the smallest, people underestimate you. In our trade that can be either good or bad; depends on how you play it. So it helps to have a few surprises up your sleeve."

Kemal raised an eyebrow at him and Brax shrugged. "All right, in our *old* trade," he amended. "The point is that Spar likes to play things close until he's sure it's safe."

"I see. Well, it's safe now, so why don't you give him the chance to show off and ask him to help you find stories about Kaptin Haldin. There's a reasonable library at Calmak-Koy."

"Where?"

"Calmak-Koy. It's a village and recuperative hospice southeast of Anavatan's Eastern Trisect on Gol-Beyaz. In the old Gol-Yearli lake tongue it means 'gathering place of many flowers.' I'd like to spend a day or two there and have the physicians get you back on your feet before you start training again."

"But I thought Cyan Company was leaving for Anahtar-Hisar tomorrow."

"They are, but we can catch up to them in a day or two."

"Are we allowed to do that?"

Kemal shrugged. "In all honesty, I'm not sure; we'll have to ask Kaptin Julide. But better to be a day or two late than to kill Estavia's latest, *personally chosen*, Champion-delinkos, don't you think?"

Brax snorted. "Probably."

"Then, come on. We have to speak with the kaptin before breakfast and . . ." he paused as the first notes of Havo's Invocation filtered faintly in to them, "the sun's rising. The breakfast bell won't be far behind." He held out his hand and, after only a moment's hesitation, Brax took it and allowed the man to help him stand, stifling a grimace as the movement pulled at his stiffened muscles.

✦

Calmak-Koy had been like nothing he'd ever experienced before.

Built up from the rocky shore in a series of low-walled tiers lined with flower beds, it was more like an orderly, wide-sweeping village than a hospice. Protected from the winds to the north by the promontory of Anavatan's Eastern Trisect, and from the mountains to the east by a thick woods of pine trees, it was warm and open, its lawns and surrounding meadows already green. Both covered barracks and small, open-air kiosks radiated from a large, central infirmary, with paddocks and stables to the north and herb and vegetable gardens to the south, intersected with walking paths lined with fruit trees. A similar path through the pines led to the foothills and a series of hollowed-out caves where hot springs bubbled all year.

It was here, in these warm, healing waters, that Brax spent the bulk of the three days Kaptin Julide had allowed them, soaking the pain and stiffness from his muscles and listening to Kemal and Yashar talk about the life of Estavia's warriors. Their low, hushed voices filled the lamplit caverns with echoing whispers that merged with the constant buzz of Estavia's own voice in his head and, as the sulfur-scented water lapped against his chest, the history of Estavia and Her people unfolded before him; from the early days when the farmer-cum-soldiers of the western villages dipped their weapons into the waters of Gol-Beyaz for the Gods' blessings to the great march north; from the building of Her temple and the raising of seven companies of elite fighting-priests, to the night when She manifested in all Her terrible glory on the streets of Anavatan to save two children from the spirits of the Berbat-Dunya. He could almost see Her plans for his own future, but every time he reached for them, they slipped away like trickles of water until, finally, he gave up trying and just drifted.

✦

During this time, Spar had taken his request for stories about Kaptin Haldin seriously and had been digging through Calmak-Koy's library with the help of several librarian-delinkon of Ystazia. The evening before they were to leave to rejoin Cyan Company at Anahtar-Hisar, he very carefully laid a fine-paged volume open in front of the other boy, gently moving Jaq's ever-present head aside before pointing at a large illustration.

Brax peered down at the brightly painted figure in the center with a suspicious frown.

"That's him?"

Spar nodded.

"What's he fighting; some kind of giant . . . centipede? They usually have more legs than that, don't they? And less teeth."

Spar rolled his eyes. "It's a spirit," he said darkly, his tone warning Brax to take it seriously.

The older boy grinned at him. "Like the ones we fought on Liman-Caddesi?"

Spar nodded. "Haldin had to cut it into ten equal pieces to kill it."

"But I thought they weren't physical?"

"I dunno. Maybe he had a special sword or something."

"Huh. I guess we should have thought of that the other night." Brax traced the lines of misty power spraying from the creature's wounds, then looked back at Kaptin Haldin. "What's that silver-and-red stuff coming out of his mouth?" he asked.

"Into."

"What?"

"In. To."

"All right, into. What is it?"

"Her power."

"Oh, right. They all get that. They call it up in their Invocations."

"Not like this."

"Oh?"

"This was stronger."

"Really?" Brax peered down at the picture carefully. "How much stronger?"

"Lots. It was more . . ." Spar thought for a moment. "Pure. More Her."

"Does it say why She gave it to him?"

"Nope."

"How about where he came from? How he got his training? How he died?" A negative after each question brought an exasperated frown to his face. "So, basically, it just says he killed giant spirit bugs?"

Spar showed his teeth at him as Brax picked up the book. "You know, I thought he'd be taller," he observed, flipping carelessly through the pages, then laughed as the younger boy snatched the book away with an indignant snort. "Still, we know She gave him this extra-strong power to fight with, and if She gave it to him, there's no reason why She wouldn't give it to me, right?"

Spar gave a noncommittal one-shouldered shrug as Brax smiled grimly.

"Keep digging."

✦

By the time they took to the water to rejoin the rest of Cyan Company the next day, Spar had found two additional stories about Kaptin Haldin, both detailing his military exploits against the spirit world, and both with a similarly lurid picture of him fighting some fantastical creature while Estavia's power flowed down his throat. Neither had said how or why. When Brax'd asked Yashar where they might find out, the older man had just shrugged.

✦

"There aren't a lot of stories surviving from that time," he said, repeating Kemal's words as he tossed his kit onto the barge that would take them south. "The only place they might have some written details of Haldin's early life is at Ystazia-Sarayi's main temple library at Anavatan, but since it's about Estavia's Champion and not Ystazia's, it's hard to say."

"When will we get back there?"

"Not for some months." Catching Spar under the arms, Yashar lifted him into the boat. "I'm afraid you won't find any magical shortcuts, Brax," he added as he moved aside to let Jaq leap in after the younger boy. "Kaptin Haldin trained like any other soldier of his time. The God's favor only increased his prowess later on. Besides, you want to be your own man, don't you, not a copy of someone else? Pass me that bag."

Brax handed it over with a scowl and refusing Yashar's help, joined Spar at the low railing as the sailors cast off.

✦

Now, staring down into the brilliant waters of Gol-Beyaz, Brax pressed his hand against his chest, feeling the crinkle of vellum beneath his tunic. Spar would kill him if he ever found out that he'd carefully sliced that first illustration of Kaptin Haldin and the spirit bug from his book last night, but it comforted him somehow. It was like a talisman. And besides, if it had been the wrong thing to do, Estavia would have told him so.

He frowned to himself, feeling the seed of truth in this line of thought. Following Kaptin Haldin's path was the right way to go, like Kemal had said—and he knew it, whatever Yashar might think—but he wasn't going to find the answers in some library of Ystazia. Only Estavia could tell him what he needed to know, and if She wouldn't answer him in his head, he'd ask Her face-to-face. Maybe She liked being asked that way; after all, it had worked on Liman-Caddesi; it could work again. And if he wasn't meant to know, She'd tell him that, too. Face-to-face. The God of Battles wasn't as subtle as Her people seemed to think She was. He'd learned that the first night.

Leaning over the edge of the low-sided barge, Brax trailed his fingers through the swiftly flowing current, ignoring the brisk wind that slapped his hair into his face. A school of small, silvery tchiros fish leaped from the water beside him, their shiny skins flashing in the late afternoon sun before flipping back under the waves again. They looked so much like tiny fish spirits that he wondered if they, too, were slowly changing, slowly becoming the Gods of fishes and mollusks and if they did, would the Gods eat them or erect them a temple shaped like a fish-monger's?

Leaning farther over the side, he peered down into the sparkling waters, shifting his feet in frustration as he tried to maintain a grip against the deck's smooth wooden surface. Chamberlain Tanay had come to Calmak-Koy late last night to make one final examination of their wounds and present them each with a brand-new pair of sandals along with a lecture on keeping them clean and supple. Listening to the leather creak, Brax wondered sarcastically if tossing them into the lake would violate those instructions. They didn't feel supple, they felt stiff and hard and his feet felt hot, confined, and sore.

Beside him, Spar had already stuffed his into his kit bag and was curled up beside Jaq, fast asleep and, making a swift decision, Brax pulled the sandals off, then, gripping the lower edge of the railing with his toes, leaned over the water again. Far below, he thought he could just see movement. He stared intently down into the depths, until a sudden touch on his shoulder nearly sent him overboard. Laughing, Kemal caught him by the back of the tunic as Brax shot him a furious scowl.

"What are you doing?" his abayos asked in as innocent a tone as he could manage as Brax pulled away from him.

"Looking for the Gods," he retorted from between clenched teeth as both Spar and Jaq awoke to stare up at them.

"Well, you'll never spot them that way; They don't manifest physically until they leave the water, and never when the wind has the upper current moving along this quickly."

"Upper?"

"Mm-hm. The upper or surface current flows north to south, the lower God-current—the one created by the movement of the Gods—" he expanded, "lies beneath it and it runs south to north. When the wind drives the upper current hard, the Gods go deep." Dropping down beside the railing, Kemal stretched out his legs and lifted his face to the last of the sun's rays with a contented sigh. "You'll have to wait until They rise," he finished, closing his eyes.

"So, when will They do that?"

"Hm?"

"The Gods, when will They rise?"

"You mean other than at the Morning Invocations?"

Brax's expression fell. "Oh, I'd forgotten about that. *Do* They rise at other times?"

"Mm-hm."

Brax waited a moment, then tapped one finger against his knee impatiently.

"Well?"

Kemal opened one eye. "Hm?"

"When?"

"When what?"

"When will They rise?"

"Oh. Anytime They want to." He closed his eyes again. "But generally at dusk," he allowed, sensing the boy's growing annoyance.

Brax stared back at the shimmering waves, now turned a translucent, golden-pink in the setting sun.

"It's dusk now," he pointed out.

"Mm-hm."

"So where are They? Where do They come up?"

Kemal sat up with a resigned expression. "They don't always *come up* at all, Braxin-Delin. And they don't always come up together. Some people say they can call Them, but . . ." he shrugged. "I've never been able to do it."

"But you have seen Them? The Gods? Rise?"

"Oh, yes." Kemal's expression grew distant. "When I was growing up in Serin-Koy I used to sit by the water and watch Them dancing on the waves, sometimes far away, sometimes close by. Once, when I was fishing with my kardon—I must have been, oh, seven or eight at the time, I think—I saw Usara and Ystazia dancing together across the surface like a pair of huge swans." He paused. "Except that most swans aren't blue."

"Or multicolored with three pairs of arms?" Brax asked sarcastically, remembering the many representations of the Arts God he'd seen in Anavatan.

"No, not that either," Kemal answered. "I have seen *black* swans, however. The scholars call them Estavia's Attendants; for sea battles anyway; it's crows on land. But They—the Gods—moved as gracefully as swans, is what I meant."

"And you've seen Estavia?"

Kemal nodded. "She prefers to rise closer to Her temple—I've watched Her from the southeast walls many times—but I saw Her from the battlements of Orzin-Hisar, that's Serin-Koy's watchtower, once when I was fifteen. I was on night duty and it was just before dark. The stars hadn't even come out yet. She rose up right in front of me like a great, ebony behemoth, a hundred feet high, looked me straight in the eye, then vanished without so much as a ripple on the water."

Brax exchanged a wide-eyed glance with Spar who was sitting up, as captured by the story as he was. "So, what'd you do?" he asked.

"Other than grip the wall so tightly I brought up a blood blister on my sword hand, not a lot."

"You mean you didn't even talk to Her?"

Kemal shrugged. "She took me by surprise. Besides, what would I have said that I hadn't already said in my mind before?"

"You might have asked Her why She came up in front of you like that. If maybe She wanted something of you."

"I might have, but if She'd wanted something of me, She'd have told me so. Gods have voices, and I think you've already discovered that They aren't shy about using them." Kemal raised one finger in a gesture of mock seriousness, "Patience, young delinkos, time generally brings an answer to most of our questions," he intoned. "Anyway, a week later I was chosen for the temple, so maybe She was giving me a heads up. Maybe She was trying to decide if I was worthy. Maybe She just wanted to startle me—even the Gods have a sense of humor sometimes. Who knows?"

Brax glanced back down at the waves. "I suppose. But *I'd* of talked to Her."

"And what would you have said?" a new voice suddenly inquired

Brax looked up as Yashar dropped down beside Kemal, draping his legs over the other man's with a contented grunt.

"I don't know," he answered. "Something, though."

"Well, when you get the chance, let me know what words you choose. I myself usually find that I'm so swept up by the force of Her power that I can't say much of anything."

"It's that way with most of us," Kemal added. "That's why it's so much easier to speak with Her in our minds."

"But don't you ever feel like you need to talk to Her face-to-face?" Brax asked. "You know, with real words?"

Kemal tipped his head to one side. "Not usually. Why? Do you?"

Brax looked away with a shrug. "Maybe," he answered, ignoring Spar's equally curious expression.

"Then do it," Kemal offered. "The first time you get the opportunity, speak to Her face-to-face. In fact, try to call Her up."

Brax glared at him, trying to decide if he was making fun of him. "Just like that?" he asked sarcastically.

"Why not?" Kemal grinned at him. "She's *your* God now, after all."

"And speaking of speaking," Yashar interrupted, "Kem, the barge-kaptin wants to know if we're to carry on south or if you wanted to stop at Serin-Koy for the night."

Kemal grinned. "The *barge-kaptin* asked?"

"Well, all right, she *might* have inquired *after* I *may have* mentioned it was your home village, but still, we wouldn't reach Anahtar-Hisar until early morning and the delon could use a night's sleep in a real bed. Couldn't you, Spar?"

He smiled down at the younger boy who nodded shyly.

"And *you* could use a night of Bayard's cooking?" Kemal asked in an unimpressed tone of voice.

"Why not? Just because you're not fond of spicy meat, or too much of Bayard's company for that matter," he added with a laugh, "doesn't mean I'm not. And besides, I doubt Cyan Company sailed right on through the night anyway, not at this time of year. They'd want to arrive in daylight." He turned to Brax. "Anahtar-Hisar's the only one of the nine village towers that isn't built on Gol-Beyaz. It sticks out into the southern Deniz-Hadi Sea on a narrow little promontory. There's nothing to fear from pirates or Petchans, but it's rocky and often foggy so it's always better to arrive in full daylight." He turned back to his arkados. "You know that."

"Point," Kemal acknowledged as he rose. "All right. Inform the barge-kaptin we'll put in at Serin-Koy, but this was your decision and you can tell Kaptin Julide that tomorrow."

"Done. Look, Brax," Yashar said with a wink. "There's Orzin-Hisar, the site of Kemal's life-changing meeting with Estavia."

Brax turned to the western shore as Kemal shot his arkados a sour look. The tall limestone watchtower loomed possessively over the distant rooftops, with a low, fieldstone wall butting up against its sides, separating the village from the pale green fields beyond.

Brax squinted up at the tower, then swept his gaze along the distant hillsides, sharing a frown with Spar who'd joined him at the railing.

Kemal glanced down at them. "What?"

"Nothing." He turned back. "Just . . . where's the Wall?"

"Right there."

As they watched, a flock of sheep flowed over a low place in the village wall like a wave of woolen mist.

Brax shook his head. "No, I mean *the Wall, the God-Wall,* the one they built to keep out the spirits of the wild lands."

"That's it."

"That? That's *the great wall of stone and power?*"

"Yes."

"But it's so small," Brax sputtered, remembering the great, snaking structure from his Invocation vision. "That wouldn't keep out a herd of rabbits!"

"Exactly. It only needs to be high enough to anchor the Gods' protection in the physical world. Any higher and the farmers couldn't get through to their fields and the animals couldn't get through to the lake."

"But what about the Yuruk?"

"As I said, it's God-protected. Here." Kemal took him by the shoulders and turned him slightly. "Stare into the sun, then look again."

His eyes dazzled by sunspots, Brax blinked. For just a moment, the air above the wall shimmered with a silvery-blue-and-purple light, rising nearly forty feet into the evening sky. "Maybe, but still . . ." he argued, refusing to be convinced. "No wonder they keep trying to bash through it. That's almost begging to be attacked."

"You think so?"

"Well, how many times have they gone against Anavatan?"

"Not many."

"And you don't think it's because of the thirty-foot-high stone walls?"

"I rather thought it was because of the one thousand temple troops and the very well armed city garrisons."

"And besides," Yashar interjected, "I thought you told us the spirits were beginning to worm their way through Anavatan's walls despite their great size."

"They are."

"So, obviously, size is not as important as strength."

"I suppose. But still . . ." Brax shook his head in disgust and even Spar looked bitterly disappointed.

Kemal just laughed. "Come on; let's go tell the barge-kaptin she can put in."

Frowning deeply, Brax stared indignantly at the wall one last time. "All I know is, I'd attack that, whatever might be protecting it," he muttered. "I wouldn't be able to help myself."

"Hm?"

"Nothing." When Kemal raised an eyebrow at him, he shrugged. "Really, I was just thinking out loud."

"A dangerous habit, that," Yashar teased.

"I know."

✦

Once the barge came closer to shore, Brax reluctantly pulled his gaze from the wall and turned his attention to Serin-Koy, a neat little village of wood and plaster houses to the north of Orzin-Hisar. Barns and drying sheds followed the net-covered shoreline, dotted with fishing boats, and a large, walled paddock stood beside Orzin-Hisar to the south. A troop of militia were shooting arrows into a line of stationary targets in the center of the village while beyond, farmers and oxen were still hard at work plowing up the western fields for the High Spring planting while sheep and cattle grazed beside flocks of geese and chickens in the newly green fields farther on, despite the lengthening shadows. As they watched, two children and a large black dog carrying a ball in its mouth vaulted over a low place in the God-Wall where it met Orzin-Hisar. Jaq immediately began to bark. The children stared out at the water and then began to wave enthusiastically, which just increased his excitement.

"All right, all right, go." Kemal gave the dog a light shove and he flung himself into the water at once, reaching the sandy beach in a few powerful strokes. Spar looked apprehensive and Kemal laid a reassuring hand on his shoulder. "Don't worry. They're old friends," he said as they watched the two dogs bound up to each other, tails wagging madly. Beyond them, the children set off for the houses at a dead run.

"Bayard will have received our letter about Brax and Spar by now," Yashar observed. "Five aspers says he makes the shore before we do."

Kemal just shook his head. "No bet."

"Who's Bayard?" Brax asked.

Kemal grimaced. "My oldest kardos."

"Kem's the youngest," Yashar added with a grin. "Bayard raised him after their abayon died of fever when he was four years old."

"And you don't like him?" Brax asked, noting Kemal's sour expression.

His abayos shrugged. "Oh, I like him well enough, he's just . . ."

"Loud?" Yashar suggested.

"Loud will do."

✦

In fact, half the village was waiting for them when they put in, but moved aside as a large bald and bearded man wearing a blacksmith's leather apron, a dozen years older than Kemal, pushed forward eagerly. He clapped his youngest kardos on the back hard enough to stagger him.

"Kemin-Delin!" he shouted, using the double diminutive that made the gathered villagers laugh and Kemal wince. "I wondered if we were going to see you this season, but when we spotted the company heading south, we thought we'd be disappointed. Yash!" He aimed a mock punch at the other man who took it against his forearm with a grin.

Kemal shot Yashar a look. "So they didn't stop, Bayard?" he asked.

"No, I heard they put in at Kinor-Koy. That's the birin-kaptin's home, yes?"

Yashar gave Kemal the look back. "That's right."

Bayard turned suddenly. "So, these are my new kardelon?" he asked eagerly.

Spar took a step back behind Brax. Without Jaq by his side he looked even smaller and more uncertain than when he'd walked through the temple gates. Brax just stared up at the man evenly as Kemal nodded.

"Well, the younger one has Yashar's eyes." Bayard noted with a booming laugh. "But the older one has your stance, Kemin, all prickly and challenging. Come on." He waved them toward the village before either Kemal or Brax could reply. "Your other kardon will want to see you, and meet them."

"How many more are there?" Brax asked as a look of panic crossed Spar's face.

"Dozens," Bayard supplied happily from over his shoulder.

"Seven altogether," Kemal corrected, and the older man shrugged.

"Only if you're just counting *actual* kardon, dozens if you count the entire family. But really only five at the moment, I suppose. I mean six with Kemin home now. Zondarin left for Anavatan a few days before Havo's Dance. She didn't stop by to see you?"

"I imagine she had duties pretty much at once."

"Point. Anyway, we'll still have a full, welcoming house once they all come in from the fields," Bayard continued as if the earlier subject had never been changed. "In fact, they should be on their way home any moment now."

"For supper?" Yashar hinted largely.

Bayard laughed. "For supper," he agreed. "So, Kemin, are you going to take a turn at the oven tonight?" he asked, grinning broadly as Yashar raised both hands in a gesture of mock horror. Kemal just smiled tightly.

"I wouldn't deprive my arkados of your cooking," he responded. "He'd never let me forget it."

"True enough. All right, I'll cook, you tend the fire. Come on." Throwing one huge arm over Kemal's shoulder, Bayard steered them toward the village. Spar and Brax trailed after them with equally apprehensive expressions while Yashar rubbed his hands together in anticipation of the evening's meal.

✦

Bayard's home, one of the few two-story dwellings in the village, was built just north of the main square, beside the forge. The inner courtyard, with its traditionally round herb and vegetable garden, was shielded from view by a comfortably tall stone wall and the house was ringed with unusually high but neatly tended flower boxes. Inside, the central room was as open and welcoming as their host, with an iron stove to the east sending out warm fingers of heat and a large loom dominating the west. A wide multicolored carpet covered the polished wooden floor and beautifully inlaid trucks lined the inset cupboarded walls which were decorated with iron lamp holders and various intricately forged weapons. Even the ceiling was an elaborate display of carved wood and brightly painted tiles.

Brax and Spar stared about in hushed awe, unused to such openly displayed signs of wealth. A look of speculative greed flashed between them, but the moment was swiftly swept aside as people began pouring in, dumping a huge pile of sandals and boots by the door. Kardon, kuzon, delon, kardelon, and more crowded into the house, all greeting Kemal and Yashar as enthusiastically as Bayard, then pouncing on Brax and Spar. The younger boy quickly became overwhelmed by so much attention and, when Jaq finally pushed his way through a sea of legs to his side, he nearly fainted with relief. Catching the animal by the collar, he drew him into a far corner where he could watch Brax field question after question. Meanwhile, the supper preparations swirled about the room like a storm; everyone talking and laughing at once, Bayard's shouted instructions just adding to the chaos.

"Kemin, Yash, you help Hadzin pull the divans into the center of the room!" he yelled, using the diminutive for nearly everyone, young and old alike. "Ekrubin, yes I see you hiding there, you and Covalin and, yes, Braxin, too, you can put the table together; Ekrubin, show him where we keep the sections! Arrianin, get the cushions, Hiesonin, the plates and cups—careful now, those are older than I am! Do we have enough dried fruit for everyone? No? All right, Aptullin you run over to your Teyia Badahir's and ask for some. Come to think of it, invite her for dinner, too; she'll be just coming off duty. And put your sandals on! It's still too cold to run about barefoot," he added as she made for the door. "Yes, Pausin, you can help me here." He carefully placed a bowl of olives in the arms of a very small girl, then caught an older boy by the collar as he raced by. "Hadirin, get the salt, then find wherever your abia put my cumin. Hello, Maydir, my love." He paused for breath long enough to kiss a tall woman who'd entered with a skein of carpet threads over one arm, then carried on barking orders. Finally, nearly twenty people sat down to a table laden with bowls of steaming curry, pilaf, stuffed grape leaves, fruit, and flatbread, the children seated cross-legged on the floor between the adults' feet, with half a dozen dogs and cats prowling about the perimeter waiting for scraps, and everyone still talking excitedly over everyone else.

Passing Spar the bowl of olives, Kemal glanced about.

"Where's Chian?" he asked over the din.

"At Usara-Cami with Evalaz," Bayard answered. "They won't be back until morning, but you and I can walk up there after supper if you like."

"I want to come, too," Aptulli said at once.

"Tomorrow if you finish up your curry. Slowly."

"How is he?" Kemal continued.

The older man exchanged a glance with Maydir, then shrugged. "A bit better. He looks at you more often when you speak to him these days, and sometimes he even answers, more or less."

"And his legs?"

"The same."

"Bayard's built him a set of braces," Maydir mentioned as she poured a cup of salap for an elderly woman bundled in shawls beside her. "They allow him to stand when he tends to the flower boxes, but he still can't walk without aid."

"I help him with the flowers," Ekrubi said loudly from between Bayard's feet, and his aba took him by the ears and planted a loud kiss on the top of his head. "Yes, you do. It's all that can really hold his attention for any length of time," he added quietly over the boy's head.

"Chian is Kemal and Bayard's kardos," Yashar explained before Brax could ask. "He served as Serin-Koy's leading battle-seer and priest of Estavia until he took a head wound in a Yuruk attack two seasons ago."

"Evalaz has been a great help to him," Bayard continued. "We'll lose that one to Usara some day soon, mark my words."

"Evalaz is Bayard and Maydir's eldest delos," Yashar supplied.

Spar turned a wide-eyed look on Yashar's face as Brax frowned. "But I thought families all served the same God," the older boy said in confusion.

"Most do. But if someone's called to serve another, they go."

"And They don't mind?"

"Who?"

"The Gods?"

"Why would They mind?" Bayard chuckled. "The Gods steal followers from each other all the time, like one kardos steals bread from another—give that back, Ekrubin, yes, I did see you. Maydir follows Ystazia and Zondar, our kardos, is a gardener at Havo-Sarayi in Anavatan," he continued. "But you don't have to be a gardener to pray to the God of Seasonal Bounty, or a farmer, either, for that matter. Who wouldn't give thanks to Havo for successful crops or fine fishing?"

"Or pretty flowers," Aptulli broke in.

"Or pretty flowers," he agreed, gazing at her fondly. "I myself serve Estavia in the village militia as a reservist," he continued, "but I also pay homage to Ystazia and Oristo in my chosen trade."

"Both the Arts and Hearth Gods lay claim to blacksmithery," Yashar explained.

"Teya makes the best iron lamps on Gol-Beyaz," Arrian interrupted proudly.

"So, it pays to stay on the good side of whatever God might help keep it that way," Bayard noted. "And so far none of Them have demanded my exclusive worship, although I swore oaths to Estavia when I was sixteen."

"But I still can't see why the Gods would let anyone do that?" Brax insisted.

"Unwilling followers bring the Gods no strength," Paus lisped in a singsong voice and Kemal nodded.

"Remember, all that we are and all we do either strengthens or weakens the Gods we worship," he said.

"Oh. Right." Catching up a piece of flatbread as the plate went by, Brax chewed on it with a grimace and Bayard laughed.

"What's the matter, Delin?"

"Nothing."

"Really? You look like you're eating a dung beetle instead of your new teya's best bread."

Brax shook his head. "It's not that, it's just that I'd thought the Gods were . . . I dunno . . . stronger."

"Stronger?"

"Maybe not stronger, just more . . ."

"Autonomous?" Yashar suggested.

"What does that mean?"

"Stand alone."

"I guess."

"No one's stronger when they stand alone, Brax," Kemal replied. "A dozen swords are always stronger than one."

"Sure, but the only one you can really trust is the one in your hand. If you start trusting too many others, you end up with one in your back."

"Estavia's ghazi-priests would never do that," Arrian said fiercely from between Yashar's feet. "They swear blood oaths to die for each other."

"And what happens then? When you're the last one standing and all your strength has died with them?" Brax retorted coldly as Spar indicated his agreement with a sharp nod of his head.

"Are we talking about Gods or people here?" Yashar asked in amused confusion.

"Either way. If you rely on others for strength, you're dead if they turn or run or die."

"Your new delos is quite a philosopher," Badahir noted, fixing Brax with a look that made him flush. "Be careful, Kemin, or you'll lose him to Ystazia's scholar-priests."

"Not much chance of that," Yashar answered, thumping Spar's back as he nearly choked on a cup of salap. "Estavia favors him. She likes the combative ones."

"Don't I know it," Bayard laughed. "She took the prickliest member of our family to Her temple in Anavatan."

"The Gods were formed by the collective will of Their followers," Kemal said to Brax, pointedly ignoring Bayard's remark. "They rely on us as much as we rely on Them. We're a family."

"And family sticks together," Coval added. "Everybody working to keep the family strong."

"Even when someone leaves to go to a new family?" Brax prodded.

"Especially then," Bayard answered. "That's how you build alliances, even among the Gods. Now, Covalin, fetch the asure, will you, I feel the need for something sweet after all this debate. You'll have some, too, won't you, Braxin?"

"Yes."

"And Sparin-Delin?"

He waited patiently until the younger boy nodded.

"Good, now, Pausin, what did Nathu teach you today?"

As the talk turned to less contentious subjects, Brax finished his bread with a reflective frown. Despite what Bayard and Kemal had said, there was something deeply wrong about Gods just letting Their followers walk away from Their worship, especially if They relied on those followers for strength. No one with power did that. Not willingly anyway.

Passing Spar a bowl of asure, he stared at a small iron-and-silver statue of Estavia standing in Its wall niche by the stove. Something else to ask the God when he finally spoke to Her face to face, he thought. The questions were beginning to pile up.

Beside him, Spar stifled a yawn. He'd said nothing throughout dinner but had accepted each offered plate, eating until his stomach grew distended and his eyelids heavy. Now he made no protest as Yashar lifted him in his arms and laid him by the stove on a sleeping pallet Ekrubi pulled out from a nearby cupboard for him. Jaq immediately lay down beside him, giving a contented sigh that ruffled the boy's hair, and Spar wrapped his arms around his neck. Within minutes the two of them were sound asleep.

Brax, however, stayed up for a long time, listening to the adults speculate on the season of fighting to come and the unknown threat growing to the south which had the temples so worried. But eventually even his eyes grew heavy and he allowed Kemal to help him into bed beside Spar. As people began to take their leave and the room grew quieter, he watched with a sleepy, half-lidded gaze as the older children laid out the pallets for the younger, then, as Bayard, Kemal, and Yashar left for Usara-Cami, he fell asleep to the rhythmic sound of breathing all around him.

✦

Outside, the three men walked through the village in companionable silence, taking the hard-packed path past the forge and the drying huts to the small temple of healing standing within sight of Gol-Beyaz in the very center of an orchard of mature fruit trees. A bright and airy building, it had wide, latticed windows to the east and a semicircle of rose and rhododendron gardens for the patients to sit or walk through in good weather to the west. A six-foot statue of Usara, looking both calm and stern, stood sentinel before the lantern-lit entrance.

Kemal set a small coin in its open palm before turning to Bayard.

"How is he, really?" he asked.

Bayard sighed. "Failing," he said simply before leading the way through the ornately carved black walnut doors.

✦

A junior physician met them in the anteroom and led them down the hushed corridors to one of the smaller, brightly painted, private rooms. On a low stool, a heavyset youth sat reading to a tall, emaciated, black-haired man, well wrapped in woolen blankets and propped up on a wide pallet by a number of silken cushions.

Moving quietly for all his bulk and exuberant personality, Bayard kissed his delos on the head.

"Are we interrupting, Evalaz?" he whispered.

The youth closed the book carefully. "No, Aba. We were just finishing up."

"Good." Crouching, Bayard took Chian's limp hand in his.

"Kardos," he said gently. "I've brought you a surprise. Look, it's Kemin-Delin and Yash, come all the way from Anavatan to see you."

Kemal stepped forward into the lamplight. For a moment it seemed as if Chian's dull gaze brightened somewhat, but then the faint light of recognition faded again.

"I didn't realize you were coming, Teya," Evalaz said apologetically. "We took him out for some air today. It must have tired him. He'll be more responsive in the morning if you'd like to visit again."

Kemal nodded, his expression working to remain light and cheerful.

"He was happy about your new delon," Evalaz continued. "I read him your letter several times. It made him smile."

"We'll write more," Yashar said, coming over to lay a comforting hand on Kemal's shoulder.

"Did Brax really stare down the entire temple command council?"

"More battered them into submission through sheer force of argument," Yashar replied with a chuckle. "He's very focused when he's certain he's right."

"He sounds like a battle-seer," Bayard said, glancing down at Chian fondly.

"Estavia forbid we should have another one of those in the family," Kemal answered, making his voice match the teasing quality in the other man's tone. "One is enough. No, Brax is a warrior through and through. He and Spar have been reading the adventures of Kaptin Haldin."

In the bed, Chian's dark gaze suddenly misted over with a thick white fog, but when the others turned to him, his eyes were closed.

"We should go," Bayard whispered.

"Yes. We'll come back tomorrow before we leave," Kemal promised.

Chian gave no indication that he'd heard, but as the three men filed out and Evalaz picked up the book again, he gave a slight jerk before his face relaxed into its usual slack expression once more.

✦

At Bayard's home, Brax gave an equally agitated jerk before sinking deeper into sleep.

He was dreaming; he knew that much. He stood on a flat, featureless plain surrounded by creatures of mist and claws. They came at him in twos and threes and tens and hundreds and he slaughtered each one, power slamming down his arm into the gem-encrusted sword She'd given him until he waded knee-deep in ethereal blood and entrails. But he never faltered; he was Estavia's Champion, Kaptin of Her Warriors, Builder of Her Temple, beloved and favored above all Her followers, and he could fight forever with Her blessing. Her power burning through his veins like fire, he raised his head and screamed out Her battle cry, challenging any and all to come and fight until it felt as if his throat would burst.

And they came; wave upon wave of spirits pouring from the Berbat-Dunya, driven forward by a creature of unformed potential and driven mad by the power denied them growing behind the wall; Her wall. But safe within its bounds he could feel Her power also growing, and he doubled his own attack knowing that together they were invincible. As the last of the creatures died at his feet, he slumped to the ground, his sword arm throbbing in time with the beating of his heart.

✦

He awoke with a start. For a moment, he stared wildly into the darkness, feeling the last of Estavia's power thrumming through him, then, as his eyes adjusted to the moonlit room, he remembered where he was. And who.

Beside him, Spar and Jaq slept on, undisturbed by his dreaming, and he sat up with a groan, running one shaking hand across his face as sweat dribbled through his hair and down his neck. He felt like he'd been run over by a donkey cart. His throat hurt and his arm hurt, and his chest hurt, but deep inside him, Her power still pulsed through his veins and he closed his eyes, savoring the sensation until it slowly faded away, leaving nothing but an aching void behind. Anxiously reaching for the familiar warmth of Her presence, he sighed in relief as he found it, then opened his eyes again.

Estavia's statue stared down at him from its shadowy wall niche, its tiny ruby gaze glittering almost sardonically in the moonlight. He frowned at it, then carefully eased off the pallet. As Spar stirred sleepily beside him, he placed a finger against his lips, knowing the younger boy could see it—he'd always had the better eyesight of the two of them.

"It's nothing, go back to sleep," he whispered. "I just have to piss."

The younger boy gave a faint snort and rolled over, arms about the dog again. As Brax groped for his clothes and his carefully hidden talisman, his thoughts chased themselves around and around inside his head. She'd sent him that dream; She had to have. She'd named him Her Champion, just as She'd named Kaptin Haldin all those centuries ago, and had gifted him with Her favor and Her power.

Having tasted it once, he had to have it again.

Slipping into his tunic, he made to step away from the pallet, then paused. Reaching down, his fingers found his practice sword almost by instinct. The hilt felt as comfortable and familiar as it had in the dream, but he knew this was no shining jewel-covered weapon of a God's favor, only a blunt and awkward piece of metal meant to strengthen his wrist, not slay his God's enemies.

But it would serve his purpose tonight.

Clutching it to his chest, he headed for where his memory told him the back door would be and, careful to avoid the dark shadows that made up each pallet and each sleeping figure, he slipped into the courtyard beyond.

The night air was chill, the ground cold but welcome beneath his feet. Making his way around the woodpile and the vegetable garden, he reached the back wall in half a dozen steps. Scaling it easily—his fingers and toes finding purchase on the rough stone despite the burden of the sword in one hand—he straddled the top, gazing out past the sleeping village to the bulk of Orzin-Hisar standing like a spike of shadow in the moonlight. He guessed he had about an hour before Serin-Koy's priests of Havo climbed to its top to invoke the dawn.

Plenty of time.

Swinging his leg around, he resisted the urge to look back toward the wall—if thousands of hungry spirits hovered just beyond its protective barrier, he didn't want to know it. Taking a deep breath, he launched himself into the darkness.

His feet hit cold, soft dirt. Something scratched across his face and he froze. Then, as his eyes adjusted to the gloom, he saw that he'd landed in a small grove of immature cherry trees. Grinning ruefully, he ducked under their slender branches and headed swiftly down the main street toward Gol-Beyaz.

✦

The wind had dropped when he reached the shore, leaving the lake to lie as clear and calm as a great pane of glass, as if even the currents were somehow moving under the shining surface rather than through it. Shivering, he made his way down the cold, sandy beach until his toes touched the water, then backed up a step.

"Now what?" his mind asked caustically.

"Now I call."

"How?"

"Um . . . I don't know. The last time She just sort of showed up."

"That was different."

"How?"

"You needed Her then."

"I need Her now."

"For what?"

The question echoed though his mind, making him suddenly doubt his intent. For what? For power? Was that enough? Closing his eyes, he remembered the intoxicating sense of invincibility Her presence had evoked, then the dull, empty ache as it dissipated.

"If She gave it to him, She can give it to me."

The memory of his own words made him start, then he forced himself to straighten.

"Yes, it's enough. It has to be."

He reached out.

Deep within his mind, he felt a faint shudder as the God of Battles stirred, drawn by his ambition and by Her very palpable favor for him. With an equal mixture of fear and anticipation, he reached out again, then gawked as one moment the moon was shining down on the clear, rippleless surface of Gol-Beyaz, and the next on Estavia, God of Battles, as She rose from the water before him.

Brax almost fell over backward.

In the small confines of Liman-Caddesi She'd been huge and terrible; here on the open waters of Gol-Beyaz She was that and so much more. Her flashing swords spun above his head in a constant blur of silver lightning while Her eyes bored into his like crimson flames, but all in absolute silence. When the tip of each sword blade snapped to a halt on either side of his jaw, his knees almost gave way. Struggling to find his voice, he could only make a slight scraping noise in his throat. The

God bared Her teeth at him and, to his surprise, that calmed him. He looked up into Her eyes and his back straightened as Yashar's words echoed in his mind.

"Estavia favors him."

The God's chuckle made him blush as he remembered that She could also read his thoughts. He almost backed up a step, then cleared his throat.

"I . . ."

He coughed, then, scowling at his own cowardice, drew himself up.

"I said I would talk to You if You came," he began, feeling stupid but not knowing what else to say. "So I have to . . ." he trailed off, then tried again. " 'Cause I said I would. 'Cause I said I *could*."

A ripple of amusement passed over the God's feral visage even as six words spoken in his own, irreverent cadence echoed in his mind.

"SO TALK. WHAT DO YOU WANT?"

A dozen answers came and went before he realized She already knew; She just wanted him to say it.

"I want what Kaptin Haldin had," he answered in a rush before he lost his nerve. *"Everything* he had."

The God's teeth gleamed in the ebony of Her face, Her expression fiercely eager, but with a warning deep within Her crimson gaze. He pushed on, regardless.

"He was your Champion. You gave him special powers, special . . ." he struggled to make sense of what he'd felt. "You loved him best," he said finally.

"HE SERVED ME BEST."

"So will I."

"EASY TO SAY."

"I'll prove it. But . . ." he paused, his mouth suddenly dry.

"BUT?"

"But I need Your help. I can't learn what I need to know by myself. I need You to . . . I dunno, make it take." He lifted the practice sword. "Make this take. Inside."

Her eyes flashed red, and for a moment he thought he might have asked for too much, then Her left sword slowed, descending until it rested against his chest where the picture of Kaptin Haldin lay. The surprising strength of it, given physical weight by the power of his own desire, pushed him backward but he braced his feet in the cold sand, feeling the point just barely pierce through vellum into skin. Looking into Her eyes, he dropped all pretense of strength and courage and allowed the frightening, overpowering need he'd always kept hidden fill his own gaze for the first time in his life. For a heartbeat, Her right sword winked out of existence and he felt the soft brush of Her hand caress his cheek, then, with a lightning fast motion, the sword was back and slashing across his wrist. Pain shot up his arm and he nearly dropped the practice sword in surprise, but he gripped the handle and rode it out, refusing to cry out. As it lessened to a dull throb, the God bared her teeth at him in savage approval, then pointed inland.

Brax turned.

The wall shimmered a brilliant yellow in the growing light of dawn, the God-Power stretching its protective surface a mile into the air. It seemed impregnable, unscalable, but beyond it he could see massive storm clouds gathering to the west and he knew it wouldn't be long before his dream was made real. The spirits were waiting out there, impatiently biding their time, testing and prodding each spring for some, for any, weakness they might exploit. One day they would find it and then they would attack.

And he would be there.

He turned back, nodding even as Estavia's words echoed in his mind.

"I WILL GIVE YOU WHAT YOU NEED TO BE MY CHAMPION. IN RETURN, YOU WILL GIVE YOUR LIFE, YOUR WORSHIP, AND YOUR LAST DROP OF BLOOD TO DEFEND MY BARRIER."

"FOREVER."

Then She was gone.

✦

He stood for a long time, staring out at the still water, feeling the last of the pain in his arm fade away. As the first note of Havo's Morning Invocation reached his ears, he glanced down, expecting to see a deep, blood-pumping gash across his wrist, but where Estavia's sword point had scored the skin, only the faintest outline of crudely drawn wall, like the symbols he painted each morning, remained. As he watched, it swiftly disappeared in the growing light, but he could still feel it, throbbing just beneath the surface.

For a heartbeat, he marveled at his own audacity, then a wide grin split his features. He'd called and She'd answered. He was favored of Estavia and he would become Her Champion, he would defend Her barrier, and nothing, *nothing* would get through it. Not ever. His head spinning with images of glory and of battle, he headed back toward the village. He couldn't wait to tell Spar what had just happened.

✦

In Bayard's main room, the younger boy had been sitting up in bed for half an hour waiting for Brax to return, and watching the last of the moonlight dance across the floor. As Havo's priests began the Invocation to their God, he cocked his head to one side. He should be back soon. Pushing away a tinge of worry, he absently stroked one of Jaq's silken ears. Brax'd be all right, he told himself. *She'd* protect him. She liked him. She'd give him whatever he wanted, and Brax wanted to be Kaptin Haldin. Whatever that meant.

But what did *he* want?

Something deep into his mind seemed to freeze in anticipation as he considered the question. He'd never really thought about it; Cindar and Brax had always managed to get him whatever he needed before.

"Need and want are two different things."

The words came into his head almost before he finished the thought on the heels of the now familiar tower image. He frowned. The image had been pressing against his mind again ever since they'd left Calmak-Koy, but it had never used actual words before.

"Are they?" he demanded experimentally.

"Aren't they?"

He snorted. The words were Brax's, but the voice was his own, probably just to confuse him and keep him in the dark about who was actually in that tower, he decided.

"Is it?" the voice prodded.

"Shut up."

"All right, but you asked what my price was before. Do you still want to know?"

"I don't care, actually."

"Don't you?"

"No."

The voice went silent.

"He's going to leave you, you know," it continued after a moment.

"Who?"

"Brax. When She turns him into this great and important champion of Hers, he's going to walk away and never come back. He won't need you and he'll forget all about you. He might even let you die, just like he let Cindar."

The words were spoken in his own voice now, but Spar just shook his head in disgust, recognizing the ploy.

"Grow up," he snapped. *"I'm nine years old, not five."* Lying back, he pulled the blanket over his shoulders as he heard Brax's familiar footfall outside the door.

"Don't you want to know when it's going to happen?" the voice insisted quietly.

"No."

"How about how to stop it?"

Spar made no answer, but as Brax shed his clothes and slipped under the blankets beside him, he shivered.

9

The Tower

PERCHED ABOVE A ROCKY PROMONTORY jutting into the northern sea, Cvet Tower stood like a spike of sullen red fire in the cloudy sky. Built seven centuries ago by Duc Leold Volinsk as a beacon for his ships returning with tribute from their conquest of Anavatan, its great signal fire had never been lit; the Warriors of Estavia had sent his fleet to the bottom of the ocean, and a year later the duc himself had been deposed by his cousin Anise Rostov. Believed to be haunted by the spirits of his long dead fleet, Cvet Tower was abandoned. It stood empty, staring blankly out across the sea at the distant shores of its defeat for six hundred and eighty years, until it was once again occupied by a Volinsk with designs against Anavatan.

In the south tower window, Prince Illan Dmitriviz Volinsk stood as still as the tower itself, watching the rain hammer rivulets of prophecy against the sea and mulling over the future. A tall man of twenty-one, dark-haired despite his ancient northern blood, with deep-set eyes that focused inward more often than out, Illan was believed to be one of the finest seers in Volinsk, but very few knew the true scope of his abilities. Or of his ambition. As the rain beat a steady pattern of possibilities against his mind, he turned from the window and crossed to the carved wooden atlas table standing in the center of the room.

Built in the southern style—in Anavatan itself, in fact, the knowledge of which gave him a deep sense of ironic satisfaction—its inlaid tiled surface had been designed to represent the sea and the three most powerful nations on its coastline; each one picked out in a different precious metal: silver for Anavatan, copper for Rostov, and gold for Volinsk.

On each one a number of marble figurines carved as horses, people, towers, ships, and siege equipment had been carefully arranged.

Lifting one between finger and thumb, Illan studied it carefully. Something portentous was happening across the sea, something that was going to transform the tedious prophetic imagery of streams and pools and raindrops to the more exciting and useful imagery of fire. It would finally be truly advantageous for Volinsk, but this time there would be no ill-prepared fleet of ships sent out against a strong and God-protected foe by a brainless and imprudent ruler. This time they would allow the rot to settle in first, then they would act behind a mantle of political dissembling so thick that even Incasa, their God of political dissembling, would be unable to penetrate it until it was far too late. And the pivotal piece was the Anavatanon child, Spar.

The small figurine gleamed in the dim light as Illan set it down on the southernmost point of Gol-Beyaz. Spar was unique. Most seers and oracles navigated the realm of prophecy from a passive position, interpreting the flow of imagery and emotions through the reactions of their minds and bodies, reactions very different from those of the prophetically blind. A very rare few, like Illan himself and even the boy Graize—should he not spiral down into gibbering madness—could use their abilities to touch the minds of other seers; in Illan's case, with actual words. An even smaller number could interact with the realm of prophecy itself, imposing their will upon the threads and streams of possibility. These few, like Spar, could be a powerfully dangerous force in the world if not properly controlled.

And Spar would be controlled, trained, and aimed in the direction of Illan's choosing. The boy's painfully transparent denial that he needed any training at all and the fact that Illan wasn't the only one to realize his potential made the challenge that much sweeter. He loved a contest of wills, especially against the overconfident God of Prophecy and His so-called Oracles. But, he cautioned himself, the rot had to settle in there as well.

The sound of a booted foot striking the tower's uneven nineteenth step interrupted his reverie and a moment later, his sergeant-at-arms, Vyns Ysav, entered the tower room. Some twenty years older than the prince, he'd served as his personal servant and bodyguard since before Illan could walk. He kept his tongue in his head and his ear to the ground and was a useful sounding board for those times when the prophetic streams became more muddied than simple ruminations could clear. Illan found him as valuable a tool as his atlas table. As the older man crossed to the center of the room, he turned his head to accept his salute, waiting for the message he was already aware of.

"A mounted company approaches along the coastal road, My Lord," the sergeant announced.

"Yes. It's Dagn," Illan answered, allowing a note of impatience to creep into his voice at the thought of his eldest sister. "With questions from our ducal brother, Bryv." Lifting a crowned figure from the center of Volinsk, he held it up to the light. "He wants to know if this season's fighting against Rostov will be successful."

Vyns tilted his head to one side. "Will it, sir?"

"No more than last season's." Taking the crowned figure and placing it among a host of mounted knights near the Rostov border, Illan shrugged. "However, since the fighting actually serves a better purpose than simply grinding Cousin Halv's armies into dust, it will do for now. As long as it's not too costly," he added to cut off Vyns' satisfied smile. "Which it's becoming."

"Dangerously so, sir?"

Illan's eyes misted in concentration. "Not quite yet," he answered after a moment's reflection. "Next season, if the harvest is poor, they may have to be reined in a little." Clearing his eyes with a brief shake of his head, he smiled coldly. "But for now, Dagn and Bryv are free to squander our resources as they see fit."

The sergeant frowned. "That isn't what you're planning to tell Her Grace, is it, sir?"

Illan sighed. "To some extent I plan to tell Her Grace the truth, or at least as much of it as she's willing to hear." Lifting the delicately carved figure of a south sea fighting ship, he studied the tiny royal flag on its bow with a dreamy smile. "Don't become fretful, Vyns," he assured the other man after a moment. "I'll not say anything too impolitic today; it's not yet time for that, and when it is, you'll have plenty of warning." He set the ship down facing the island of Thasos to the south of Gol-Beyaz. "But it hardly matters," he continued. "Unless I see a crushing defeat for Volinsk—or possibly his own death—Bryv won't change his plans. The campaign against Rostov is as comfortable and familiar as an old pair of boots. It will take a very special pair of *new* boots to dislodge it."

"And the new pair of boots is in Anavatan, sir?"

"The new pair *is* Anavatan, Vyns. But it's important that neither the cobbler nor the buyer realizes that, lest the latter get too greedy and force the former to close up shop."

Vyns gave him a confused look and, with a sigh, Illan lifted two gold-and-copper-crowned figures, bringing them face-to-face with each other. "As long as Volinsk and Rostov struggle over the same unarable stretch of steppe between them, the Anavatanon with their God-strengthened, self-righteous warrior-priests will believe we represent no immediate threat and will remain open for business with no added security on the door—on the passage through to the northern sea," he explained patiently. "And, as long as both Volinsk and Rostov believe the other is defeatable, neither will reach for Anavatan prematurely."

And belief was everything, wasn't it?

Vyns nodded. "I see now, sir."

"Good." Setting the figures back into place, Illan lifted two medium-sized Volinski fighting ships and, after a moment's reflection, set them down in the center of the sea. Then, with a nod, he returned his gaze to the window, his expression already drawing inward. "The company will be here within the hour," he said in a distant voice. "Have the kitchen lay out a meal and breach a cask of wine. They won't be staying the night, so you needn't prepare rooms. Say nothing of our conversation or my inclination. If Dagn should ask, inform her that I've been sequestered in my tower room all week, anticipating her arrival; that's all you know."

"Yes, sir."

✦

Two hours later, Prince Dagn Vanyiviz Volinsk stood by the fire, turning a glass of heavy red wine between finger and thumb while rivulets of water ran down her boots to pool on the flagstone floor. Four years older than Illan, she was similar in height and build, but with paler hair and eyes and a confident intensity that stood out in marked contrast to his carefully designed air of aesthetic disinterest. They'd once been close, but the war and the increasing demands of his prophetic sight had sent them to opposite sides of the country: Dagn to the fighting in the west, and Illan to the calm, focusing isolation of Cvet Tower. Both social and extroverted, Dagn had never understood her brother's need for solitude and had often accused him of removing himself from court on purpose so that Bryv was forced to seek his council like a petitioner.

And she was most probably right.

Now, she caught him in an impatient stare.

"Will one big push prevail against Rostov this season?" she demanded with characteristic bluntness.

Standing in his usual place by the window, Illan made a show of rubbing two fingers along the bridge of his nose in mock resignation. One big push had never finished either of them, but both sides always believed it would.

"No," he replied just as bluntly.

"Why not?"

"Because Rostov's no less powerful than they were last season and now they're drawing allies from the west."

"So? We're drawing allies from the east."

"Then our individual strengths will be equally balanced. Again."

Dagn's blue eyes glittered in the firelight.

"So what *will* tip this balance to our favor? What will *finish* Rostov?"

He made a show of considering the question seriously, but inside he was bored.

What will finish Rostov?

Who cares.

He was careful to keep any sign of this opinion from showing on his face. Only the riches of Anavatan could tip any form of balance in anyone's favor, but to obtain them, they had to be subtle and they had to be patient.

His family were not known for either.

"We could assassinate Cousin Halv," he replied, more as a stalling technique than an actual suggestion, but Dagn snickered.

"It's been tried," she answered, her own features relaxing slightly. "He has as many swords and seers protecting him as Bryv does." She paused. "Why? Have you seen something that might suggest it would be more successful this time?"

He sighed, weary of this line of questioning already; if he'd seen it, he would have said so at the beginning of their conversation. He considered the possibilities in saying yes, but then discarded the idea. Lying about prophecy carried its own weight of complications and—as tempting as it was—it actually muddied true visioning and undermined a seer's credibility.

"No," he replied, a note of testiness creeping into his voice. "So, short of a plague or a famine—which I have not seen, so don't even bother to ask—there's nothing to suggest that this year's campaign will be any different from last year's."

"So, basically, you've got nothing of importance to say to me at all."

"Basically, that's correct."

"Then what good are you?"

Illan smiled tightly. "In the short term, none. In the long term, perhaps a great deal."

"Oh, yes, I've forgotten. Your plots against Anavatan."

He was surprised by the sneer in her voice.

"You don't feel the shining city is a worthy prize?" he asked.

She grimaced in exasperation. "I think it's a risky and expensive dream that rears its ugly head above us once every few generations or so like a family malady."

"Unlike Rostov, of course."

"Don't go down that path again, Illan," she warned. "Rostov is a dangerous foe that must be defeated before we can turn any military attention elsewhere."

"I agree."

She frowned at him. "Then why do you keep this conquest of Anavatan alive in Bryv's mind," she demanded, her voice dark with suspicion.

"Because it's a risky and expensive dream *now*. But it's a reachable reality in the future—in the *near* future. I *have* seen that."

"But not this season?"

"No."

"Why not?"

"Because they're still too strong."

"You've told Bryv this?"

"His military advisers have told him this. You may tell him, however, that the Yuruk of the western plains are nurturing a new leader which could unite the wild lands to our advantage."

"Could?"

He shrugged. "When you sow a field of grain in the spring, you can only hope that it will yield a good harvest in the fall. It *could*, and the best you can optimistically say is that it *should*, but there are always variables."

"Like a plague or a famine?" Her tone was sarcastic, but her voice had lost its suspicious edge and he smiled.

"Or a flood, or a drought, or even something as simple as a clash of personalities. We'll know before the year is out. The Yuruk's new prophet is planning a small foray against the village of Yildiz-Koy to test his leadership skills. If all goes smoothly, in a year or two the Yuruk will be strong enough to attack the western shores of Gol-Beyaz in force while the Petchans attack the south and we attack the north."

"And if all doesn't go smoothly?"

"I have another field in reserve that could yield a similar harvest if properly sowed."

"Which is?"

"Too early to say. Its crop might blight; it's still a very young field."

Dagn shook her head, impatient with the agricultural analogy. "So your counsel is to wait, then?"

He shrugged. "Bryv could send some privateers to harass the Anavatanon merchant ships in the Deniz-Siyah if that suits him better. Two would be sufficient, I'd think. Their navy will be expecting something like that, and it won't raise suspicions of a plot elsewhere. They'll send a few extra ships to patrol the shipping lanes, but not too many due to this *new threat* brewing in the south."

She chuckled at his sarcastic tone. "Ah, yes, I've forgotten, those strange, *unidentified* ships hovering off the coast."

"Yes."

"Give my regards to Memnos when you write to him next. Tell him that the duc of Volinsk is ready to commit troops to his cause at a moment's notice. Bryv's very words."

"I shall."

Sipping at her wine, she smiled nostalgically. "Do you remember the summer we spent sailing with him off the island of Skiros?"

"I do."

"It was so warm and peaceful then. There was nothing to worry about, no wars, no intrigue."

"Do you miss it?"

"I do, sometimes." She chuckled. "You were nothing more than a self-centered brat back then."

"And you were nothing more than a bossy know-it-all. And Bryv?"

"Bryv." Dagn's expression grew sad. "Bryv laughed more."

"So did you."

She shrugged. "I suppose.

An almost comfortable silence fell between them and Illan glanced over.

"Will you be spending the night?" he asked, as surprised by the warmth in his own tone as he was by the question he already knew the answer to. He could see her considering it, remembering closer times when they were younger, wondering if those times might be re-created, their friendship rebuilt, by one long, quiet talk before the fire. For a moment he thought he might have seen it wrong, and then she shook her head with an expression of genuine disappointment and the faint prophetic stream that had warmed his thoughts for just a moment, faded.

"No, I have to get back."

"Another time, then."

"Perhaps."

✦

An hour later, watching her lead the envoy back along the coastal road, he was again surprised to find that he shared her disappointment.

"Another time, then."

"Perhaps."

But unlikely.

He turned back to the atlas table. Another time, perhaps, but not now; there was still too much to do now. Something portentous was happening and he needed all his concentration to detect its most vulnerable aspect. Spar was the key. Lifting the boy's figurine to eye level, he stared at it until the room slowly faded from his sight, then sent his mind speeding south toward Anahtar-Hisar. The tall granite tower standing high above the bright blue waters of the southern sea filled his vision, then began to waver precariously as another image rose up beneath it.

Another time, then.

He frowned.

Perhaps.

With an impatient sigh, he returned Spar to the table and lifted the well-worn figure of his sister from its permanent position amidst the crowded border garrisons, searching for some subtle, prophetic warning that would keep their conversation in the foreground but, after finding only regret for lost opportunity, firmly set it back in place. There was still too much to do now, he repeated. His relationship with Dagn could wait. They had time. They always had time.

Lifting Spar once again, he bore down, calling up the image of Anavatan's southernmost stronghold and its newest charge. His vision steadied and Spar came into focus, crouched like a tiny gargoyle on the turreted roof of Anahtar-Hisar, his blue-eyed gaze as faraway as Illan's own. The Volinski seer nodded to himself. Most latent prophets were solitary by nature, unconsciously seeking out the high and lonely places where their abilities could grow without the distractions of everyday life swirling about and cluttering up their thoughts. When they were ready to see, their minds took flight like birds leaving the nest. And Spar's mind was almost ready; he could feel it from here. They'd been interacting carefully over the last two weeks and Illan could feel the link between them growing stronger and more solid with each passing day. It only needed the smallest—most enjoyable, he allowed—kick in the tail feathers now to make Spar's abilities take wing. Holding the boy's figurine up to eye level, Illan reached out to deliver it.

✦

"Shield arm up! Right leg back to support the body! Now, sword arm out, thrust and back! Always pull back, ready for your next attack!"

Crouched on the roof above the private officers' training yard, Spar watched as Yashar went over the first strike position with Brax for the twentieth time. They'd been at it most of the morning and Spar could feel the older boy's frustration growing.

"Again! And again! Slowly, Brax, slowly!"

"I *am* going slowly!"

"Go *more* slowly!"

"If I go any *more* slowly, I'll fall over!"

"Then *fall* over! You have to learn control; control always comes before power and always, always, before speed!"

From the tense set of his shoulders, Spar could see that Yashar's patience was wearing as thin as Brax's. One of them was going to blow any minute, he thought with a snort, although they'd lasted a lot longer than he'd expected.

And that was because of Brax.

They'd been at the southernmost tower of Anahtar-Hisar for twenty-two days and, true to their word, Kemal and Yashar had separated the two of them from the rest of the garrison delinkon, concentrating on individual rather than on unit training. The older boy had responded with the same level of fevered intensity coupled with agitated impatience he'd shown at the temple in Anavatan, but despite this, Spar could see a marked difference in his demeanor: he was calmer and more willing to listen—whatever Yashar might think—held himself with greater confidence, and seemed much less likely to throw his shield across the courtyard in frustration.

"This is stupid! No one's ever gonna come at me this slowly!"

All right, maybe only a little less likely, Spar amended.

"I think we should take a break."

Striding forward, Kemal held out a bulging waterskin and, bristling with indignant disinterest, Brax very carefully set his sword and shield to one side before accepting it. As he followed the two men into the shade of a nearby potted palm tree, only Spar could see the effort it took him to keep from simply falling over. Estavia didn't seem to be helping him as much as Brax had said She would. And again, only Spar seemed to notice this.

The older boy himself had been wildly excited when he'd finally returned to bed that night at Serin-Koy, blurting out all that had happened in a barely contained jumble of words that had made no more sense to Spar then than it did now.

✦

"She came to me. She talked to me. She said She would make me Her Champion."

"How?"

"By giving me what She gave to Kaptin Haldin."

"Which was?"

"Everything."

✦

He never had explained what that everything was supposed to be—and Spar wasn't even sure he could—whenever he talked about that night, he got such a dazed and awestruck expression on his face that he looked as if someone had hit him over the head with a barge pole.

A chuckle sounding deep within his mind interrupted this cynical observation and his expression hardened. The tower's voice in his head had grown increasingly pushy in the last few weeks, interfering with his thoughts and offering up wholly unwelcome advice on his actions while still refusing to identify itself. It was really starting to piss him off. Drumming his fingers against his knife handle, he waited for it to make some further annoying observation but, after a few moments of silence, he cautiously returned to his earlier line of thought.

Brax obviously believed the Battle God had gifted him with special powers—although strength, endurance, flexibility, patience, and wisdom didn't seem to be on the list—but what disturbed Spar the most was that he was just as vague on what Estavia wanted in return as he was about what these great powers were supposed to be. Nothing came free, especially when it came from Gods. Cindar had hammered that into their heads all their lives; Brax had taken less than a month to forget it.

"She probably wants his life," the tower voice now sniffed. *"Or more likely, his death. That's typical of the Gods as you know."*

"Who asked you?" Spar snarled back, unable to resist rising to the bait.

"No one. I was simply observing that Gods are never satisfied with worship alone. They want it all, and that usually consists of blood, pain, and death."

"Horse shit."

"Are you telling me you don't believe that?"

Turning his face toward the brisk, salt-encrusted breeze blowing in from the sea, Spar snorted. *"I'm not telling you anything,"* he replied tersely.

"You don't have to; your emotions speak it plainly enough. You don't put your trust in Gods any more than I do."

"*And I don't put my trust in mysterious, free-floating voices either, so bugger off.*"

"*As you like, but don't you want to know what those special powers were that Estavia gifted Kaptin Haldin with so many years ago?*"

"*And I suppose you can tell me?*"

"*I can.*"

"*And it's gonna cost . . . what?*"

"*Nothing too expensive; perhaps only conversation.*"

"*Forget it. I can find out on my own.*"

"*How? In that pathetic excuse for a library?*"

"*It's not that bad.*"

"*Four volumes? One thin, little, out-of-date tome on southern growing practices, another outlining Ystazia's festive rituals, and two journals written by almost illiterate tower commanders? Please.*"

"*They weren't ill . . . whatever you said.*"

"*Of course they were; they could barely spell their own names.*"

"*So what? They were warriors; they didn't need to learn any more than they already knew.*"

"*And obviously didn't. Is that what you want out of life as well?*"

"*None of your business.*"

"*If not mine, then whose? Your new* abayon?"

Ignoring the sarcasm in the voice's tone, Spar turned his attention, almost unwillingly, back to the courtyard. Kemal was holding his sword out at arm's length, explained something to Brax. As he watched, the older boy lifted his own sword, mirroring the movement with an intense expression. As Yashar nodded his encouragement, Spar smiled.

"*How nice,*" the voice sneered. "*He's learned how to hold it properly. One move down and only a thousand more to go before he's thrown, all too unready, into battle. Is that what true abayon do for their delon?*"

"Shut up."

Lying on the ground beneath the rooftop, Jaq raised his head and whined. The dog didn't like it when Spar came up here and not only because he couldn't follow. With an inward glare, Spar scrambled farther up the roof, hopefully out of the animal's earshot. The movement caused the small delos-drum at his side to vibrate gently and he covered it quickly with his hand to quiet it.

Yashar had given him the traditional instrument of the youngest delinkon before they'd left Anavatan. Usually he kept it with his belongings, but in the last day or two he'd taken to carrying it about, tied to his belt by its short leather strap. Yashar had been pleased to see it and, for some reason, that made Spar feel warm inside. Now, as the sounds of the village militia training beyond the tower—adults and delinkon moving to the constant thump of the same drums—filtered up to him, he ran his fingers along the soft, faded vellum, squinting down at the markings along the body.

"That's the symbol for Caliskan-Koy where I was born," Yashar had told him, pointing to the outline of a small boat. *"The finest ships on Gol-Beyaz are built there. That there's my father's mark,"* a grain flail. *"It was his drum first, you see—and this mark's mine,"* a short sword standing upright beside a cypress tree. *"If you find it useful, you might set your own mark on it before you pass it on to one of your own delon some day."*

Spar had been more pleased then he'd wanted to admit, but somehow the older man had sensed it in the short duck of his head and had smiled at him.

"Yes, yes, yes, he gave you a drum just like a real abayos would," the voice allowed impatiently. *"But shouldn't a real abayos also give his delon every chance to realize their full potential when he isn't passing down terribly valuable family heirlooms? I mean, be honest, how much time have either of those two spent teaching you something actually useful, like how to read and write for instance?"*

"I know *how to read and write,"* Spar shot back. *"A little,"* he added grudgingly when the voice scoffed at him.

"Exactly," it agreed. *"A little. You'll need a lot more than that if you're going to make anything at all of your life."*

Spar just shrugged, but inside he had to admit—if only silently—that he knew neither Yashar nor Kemal cared much about reading and writing; he'd had to find the library on his own, and Brax had yet to pick up a scroll, never mind an actual book. Spar had a suspicion that their new abayon had forgotten that part of their young *Champion's* training altogether, and the older boy obviously had no intention of reminding them.

"So, why don't you *remind them?"*

"Why should I? If Brax doesn't want to read and write, that's his business."

"And you're willing to remain ignorant as well, are you? I thought you might have more ambition."

"Piss off."

Below, Jaq let out a yip.

"I don't need any more ambition," Spar snapped inwardly, feeling his temper rising. *"I'm safe, I'm fed, and I've got lots of skills I can work just fine."* Glancing up, he watched an immature eagle land on the tower ridgepole, a hamsi fish dangling from its beak and, pulling his knife, flipped the thin handle through his fingers and around the back of his hand, catching it before it came close to falling. He cocked his arm.

"Very physically dexterous," the voice interrupted in a patronizing tone. *"But if you throw it, you might lose both bird and knife."*

"I might and I might not."

"With proper mental training, you'd know.*"*

"And I suppose you can *give me it?"*

"I can."

"For what?"

"For nothing. Abayon don't charge their delinkon."

"I'm not your delinkos."

"No, you're not." The voice was getting definitely snippy now, and Spar sneered at it. *"Because if you were,"* it continued, ignoring his response, *"you wouldn't be wasting your time reading books on Ystazia's equinox tea ceremonies and learning how to gut your enemies—and your birds—you'd be learning how to wield your considerably powerful, although deeply latent, mental abilities before they wither on the vine for lack of use."*

"They do *have seers* here, *you know,"* Spar retorted, his own tone dripping with disdain, as he resheathed his knife. *"Don't you think they'd have said something if I really had all these* great *latent abilities?"*

"What, Sable Company?" Now it was the voice's turn to sneer. *"You can't be serious. Not one of them could find their arse on a sunny day. Besides,"* it continued in a more mollifying tone, *"you have the strongest natural shields I've ever felt—nearly as powerful as my own—I doubt that lot could even see you to look at you. No, use your head, Delin; if they were really any good, they'd be sworn to Incasa, wouldn't they?"*

"Whatever." Despite the voice's very good point, Spar was getting bored with the argument. *"It all comes down to one thing,"* he said. *"The*

Warriors of Estavia took us in, they fed us, and they clothed us. You *didn't, so* they have the right to direct our training *and* you *don't."*

"And far be it for me to cast aspersions on such a noble enterprise as expecting two hungry delon to offer up their lives in exchange for temporary food and shelter," the voice sniffed, refusing to back down, *"but the least they could do is ensure that they* direct *that training properly."*

"They are."

"So, you'll be ready for battle when it's thrust upon you, will you?"

"Yes."

"Willing and able to die for Estavia? Such confidence. Is that why you're hiding up here instead of taking your turn with the sword down there? Don't tell me you think She's granted you special powers as well?"

"I'm not hiding; I'm watching Brax. He needs to be ready before me."

"Too true. Do you think he will be?"

"Yes."

"Really? By this summer?"

"What?"

"The Yuruk are planning an attack this summer, and when they do, the Warriors of Estavia will be called upon to fight. Your precious abayon will be sent and you'll both go with them."

"So what? We won't be in the battle. Delinkon never are."

"They will be if the Warriors are slaughtered and the village overrun."

Spar frowned, knowing the voice had dropped the word village in as bait.

"What village?" he asked suspiciously.

"Whatever village."

Spar snorted, convinced now that the voice was just lying to get a rise out of him. *"It won't happen."*

"Won't it?"

"Will it?"

"You tell me."

"Drop dead."

The voice chuckled. *"I will tell you this much: Brax, at the very least will be drawn into danger. He's Estavia's new Champion, and, in case you've forgotten, She's not the God of daisies and love poetry. She'll call him and he'll go. He'll either live or he'll die. You could know which it will be, and knowing, you could do something about it, unless of course, being fed, clothed, and safe really is all you care about."*

"Spar?"

About to deliver a scathing retort, Spar started at the sound of his name. Glancing over the edge of the roof, he saw Kemal gesturing at him.

"Come down please. Jaq's whining is drowning out the lesson."

Spar nodded. *"Thanks a lot,"* he growled as he began to make his way toward one of the small, tower windows. *"You made him notice me."*

"Your thrashing about made him notice you. You have to learn to control your body when you use your mind."

"Yeah? Well, control this. GET STIFFED."

The voice chuckled. *"As I said, considerable, although deeply latent, mental abilities. I wish you had the time to see if they develop naturally, I really do, but you haven't, so I'm going to help you access them whether you want to or not."*

"Don't do me any favors."

The responding icy laughter which echoed through his mind made the hair on the back of Spar's neck rise.

"Oh, believe me, Delin," the voice replied. *"I'm not."*

✦

We have a new enemy.

"Not now."

With an impatient shake of his head, Graize waved the lights away. They'd grown stronger over the last two weeks, coming closer to the integrated Godling he knew they would one day become. Weaving in and out of his thoughts, using his experiences to build a rudimentary understanding of the world, they whispered newly audible words in his head with an increasingly annoying sibilant hiss; words he had no interest in. They'd already made him aware of the northern sorcerer's ambition and increased interest and Graize had patiently explained his own lack of concern. Whatever the foreign seer now knew, or thought he knew, was of no importance at the moment.

He told the lights so and, buzzing hungrily, they reluctantly withdrew, merging with the ever present spirits swirling just out of reach as Graize returned his attention to the task at hand.

Seated on one of the kazakin's more docile mounts, he'd accompanied Timur and Danjel out onto the plains that morning to taste the signs on the winds of an approaching thunderstorm. Unwilling to take his abilities at face value, the ancient wyrdin had been teaching him to see the spirit world as the Yuruk saw it, as simply one aspect of the world as a whole, and the spirits themselves as no more than the wild sheep that dotted the faraway mountainsides, as creatures to be ignored or domesticated as he saw fit.

Licking his lips, Graize stared out at the vast horizon of power and potential that shimmered all around him like a silvery sea. Resisting the urge to draw all that power to him, he stroked the smooth length of the new bow Danjel had gifted him with before bending an ear to Timur who had been speaking to him for the last few moments without a response.

"Hm?"

"I said, what do you see, Wyrdin-Delin?" Timur repeated patiently. Like Danjel, the old wyrdin was bi-gender although, unlike Danjel, Timur preferred to remain physically ambiguous, to more easily converse with the spirit world.

Graize licked his lips, catching up a tiny, imprudent spirit with the tip of his tongue. "Power," he whispered.

"And?"

He frowned. "What else is there?"

"Life."

"It's the same thing."

"Not necessarily," Timur retorted, shaking one thin and gnarled finger at him. "Life is the smooth, rhythmic ebb and flow of all things, great and small. Power is simply life's fuel." A wave of one hand took in the entire landscape around them. "Every event in life's rhythm sets up its own pattern of ripples, like insects touching the surface of a still pool of water. If you know how to look, how to listen, how to *ask*, you can learn many things." Timur leaned forward, the bells on the old wyrdin's pony chiming softly. "Such as, we're expecting the banners of the first kazakin of the Khes-Yuruk from the west. Are they near? Ask the ground beneath your feet; ask the wind on your face and the hills it's traveled over." One arm swept up. "Ask the sky."

Graize stared out at the distance horizon with a frown. Some of what he'd told Danjel that first day had been the truth, some: more bravado than certainty. With the lights and spirits as his guide, he *could* sense an army coming, find an enemy's weak spot, and know when to attack it, but only if they knew. The lights were more interested in their own internal growth than the external world these days and spirits, anxious about the future, crowded so close to his body that all they could tell him was the beating of his own heart. Likewise, the ground, the wind, the hills, and the sky showed him nothing more than the vast expanse of power spread out for the taking. It made him hungry; it made the lights hungry; hungry like the spirits were hungry, desperately and angrily. He narrowed his eyes. *It always came down to hunger, didn't it?* he thought; hunger and need.

"*Ask the ground beneath your feet.*"

Tipping his head to one side, he made a pretense of studying the flattened grasses under his pony's hooves while Timur and Danjel waited either patiently or impatiently as their nature dictated.

Nature.

Hunger.

Need.

In the shining city he'd needed money to satisfy his hunger; other people's money. To get it, he'd needed the game. He was good at the game. Here he needed more, here he needed the Yuruk. But to get them, he still needed the game. Yet what was the game here?

Nature.

Reaching into the hide bag at his belt, he gripped the dead stag beetle at the bottom, rubbing at the cracked and jagged carapace to collect his thoughts. The Yuruk believed he was a prophet. To be one, he had to act like one—whether or not he really was one was again unimportant—but it helped if he could really do the things they expected him to do, and the spirits and lights could only tell him so much. The Wyrdin-Yuruk used the spirits in their augury as he did, but they also studied the natural signs all around them; signs they'd expect him to know as well; signs of the game.

Graize had always been very good at the game.

The tiny spirit he'd sucked up had tasted of rain, but that wasn't enough.

"*Ask the wind . . .*"

Closing his eyes, he raised his face to the breeze and felt . . . something. The air was damp and chill. It smelled like the tiny spirit had tasted . . . of rain.

". . . and the hills it's traveled over."

Encouraged, he opened his eyes. Stretching before him, the tough meadow grasses undulated like a green sea, the thick, ribbed underside of each blade turned upward. Upward towards the rain, so the rain would be soon.

"Ask the sky."

The darkening clouds above his head stretched across the horizon, swollen with power and driven by the rising wind. The wind was from the west. The rain would come from the west. His eyes narrowed. But that hadn't been Timur's question, had it?

Confused suddenly, his mind began to drift, listing to one side like a leaky boat. The lights pressed forward, sensing his returning receptivity, and he pushed them away with an impatient shake of his head. What had Timur's question been, he demanded silently. He'd just heard it. Something about banners, the regiments of a Yuruk kazakin.

His expression cleared as he remembered. No, not *a* kazakin, *the* kazakin; the first kazakin come from the west to answer the new wyrdin's call to arms. His call to arms; his and the Rus-Yuruk's. He remembered.

The elders—Kursk, Ayami, Timur, and the rest—had needed little convincing to agree to attack Yildiz-Koy. With the long, tedious winter over and the sharp spring breeze calling them to ride and to fight, the promise of victory was as unnecessary as any outside motivation; they'd only needed someone to name the place. And although they wouldn't trust him to lead, not yet, one village was no better or worse than another and so they would trust him to name the place. The place would be the test of further trust to come.

Still, Yildiz-Koy was walled and well guarded and so Kursk had sent messengers out across the plains: *come and fight with us; come and bloody the nose of the great Warriors of Estavia with us; come and loot a fat farming lakeside village with us.*

Come and see with us if our new wyrdin is truly as powerful as he pretends to be.

The first kazakin from the western Khes-Yuruk was due to arrive any day now. Was it near? Graize had to know, but he didn't know. But he *had* to know. But he *didn't* know. His mind began to splinter under the dual pressure of panic and doubt and suddenly, buzzing impatiently like an angry wasp, a single light darted forward and exploded across his vision. Startled, he jerked back, and then began to smile. He'd forgotten. The lights needed this attack to grow. They needed it to feed. The lights would know, and they would tell him. Gesturing them forward, he formed the question in his mind.

"Is the kazakin near?"

Finally understood, the lights cavorted about his head, then streaked into the air, forming their answer in the sky, and Graize laughed out loud, his mind suddenly clear and clean for the first time in days, almost as if the rain had already swept past, carrying off each loose, chaotic thought like a swollen river might carry off debris. He turned, his eyes purposely blank, the game already forming in his mind.

"I see horses," he said in a distant, singsong voice, "wearing the scent of moisture on their flanks."

"And on the horses?"

The lights formed his new answer at once.

"Riders. Many riders, dressed in furs with curved blades in their belts and destiny surrounding them like gray mantles."

"Are they near?"

The lights pulled back, lines of mist streaming down to pool upon the ground. He shook his head.

"Not yet. It's raining in the west, storming. They're standing beneath a steep escarpment, protected from the storm. When it's done and the sun comes out of hiding to bathe the plains in light, then they'll come."

Beside him, both Timur and Danjel nodded in satisfaction and he felt their thoughts as if they'd shouted them aloud. The riders he could have made up, but not the reasoning, he was still too new to the plains. Or so they thought.

"When will the storm come?" Timur prodded.

This time he knew the spirits could tell him, feeling their excitement and suddenly understanding why. His lips pulled back from his teeth in a triumphant grimace more a snarl than a smile as the wyrdin's own words echoed in his mind.

"Power is simply life's fuel."

And what a fuel it was, he agreed.

"Tonight."

"Plenty of time, then. We should get back."

Turning, Timur and Danjel led the way back to the encampment as Graize took one last look at the sky. The lights swooped in on him again like a flock of seabirds, their newly found hunger almost screeching in his mind.

"*We have a new enemy,*" they insisted.

"*It doesn't matter,*" he answered.

"*But he's allying himself with an old enemy.*"

"*It still doesn't matter.*"

"*But . . .*"

"*No.*" Lifting one hand, he ran a caressing finger through their midst, bleeding off their anxiety. "*He can't stop us,*" he assured them. "*You'll feed; I promised that you would.*"

"*When?*"

"*Soon. Very, very soon. There's a storm coming. You can feed from the storm. We can* both *feed from the storm.*"

"*How?*"

"*I'll show you how. When the storm comes. You'll feed and grow strong.*"

Comforted, the lights calmed. They were still hungry, but they would feed. Graize had promised that they would.

His own mind racing with excitement at the thought of this new stream of possibility, Graize brought his mount awkwardly into step beside Danjel's. The game was on. The lights would feed and so would he. As soon as the storm came. Catching up another tiny spirit, he tasted the approaching rain and laughed out loud.

✦

Thunder rumbled in the distance, far away but coming closer. As the sun set slowly behind the heavy, western storm clouds, Graize crouched outside the tent he shared with Danjel and five other youths, breathing in the thick cluster of spirits that hovered about his face. Their small allotment of power sent a cooling track of ice down his throat, filling his belly with prophecy. Like the lights, they could sense the storm was coming; unlike the lights, they knew that they could draw power from its strength. That's what they'd told him; the secret they'd shared with him.

"Power is simply life's fuel."

He nodded. The spirits had been born on a thousand nights like this one; out over the wild lands, each and every one of them. Closing his eyes, he reached out to the west, feeling the storm front drawing closer, knowing something else.

So had he.

And he could lose himself in its embrace as easily as they could if he wanted to.

The memory of that first night above the plains caused a sudden twist of spirit-fed excitement to ripple through his body, but he suppressed it. Not now, he told himself sternly. He had too many other things to do right now.

Ignoring the well of disappointment that followed, he pulled his mind back, then sent it flying out across the slumbering encampment on the wings of the spirits.

✦

By the time the kazakin had returned that evening, the breeze had been so filled with the whispers of wind and rain that anyone could have read the signs, so much so that the shepherds had brought their flocks and herds into the paddocks for the night. Now, a single delinkos sat cross-legged beneath a makeshift tent to guard them, her dog standing protectively by her side. The rest of the Yuruk were all battened down, the tents tightened, and the people lying in their riding clothes in case the storm brought flooding or, worse, fire. But in the tent behind him, his new kardon: Rayne, Caleb, Briz, Gabrie, and Tahnan all slept soundly, trusting that their elders would rouse them if need be. Only Danjel tossed fitfully under his woolen blanket, his wild blood stirred by the power of the approaching storm. For a heartbeat they shared a dream of flying freely over the plains, then, with a gesture, Graize settled the other youth into a deeper slumber. He would be the only wyrdin awake tonight. He had things to do, important things, and he didn't want to be disturbed.

Excited by his thoughts, the lights spun around him as the wind picked up, sending his hair whipping about his face.

"Whisper, whisper, whisper," he chided them out loud. "It's like sitting in a nest of hungry sea snakes. Be still."

The lights calmed, then began to spin again as a dozen tiny drops of moisture scattered across Graize's cheeks. It would be soon. He stood.

✦

When the storm finally broke over the camp, he was ready for it. The wind battered against his tent, sending sheaves of rain coursing over his face and, as he threw his arms wide, his mind leaped into the sky. Released, the lights hurtled after him.

In the heart of the storm, lightning flashed almost continuously, sending out a dozen, jagged streaks of energy at a time to shatter across the rumbling clouds. As each one touched the air, it became a tiny, new-born spirit, swollen with prophecy and, opening his mind wider than he ever had before, Graize drew each one in, feeling them fill him with a power so raw and strong he thought it might tear him into pieces. All around him, the lights cavorted in a near drunken frenzy, growing and swelling as they followed his lead, sucking up the spirits as fast as the storm could spew them out, the immature presence Graize had fashioned within the lights growing stronger and more self-aware with each passing moment. When the storm moved on, it followed, drawing Graize along behind it.

Spread out across the clouds, Graize hardly noticed until he found himself far out above the gray, wind-tossed waves of Gol-Bardak. Then, as the eastern shore came into view, he felt a sudden tugging at his chest. He looked down.

Far away he saw himself standing as still as death, rain-drenched features raised to the sky, the pupil of one eye pinprick tight, the other wide and staring. A silver thread of power, fine as a strand of spiderwebbing, held him in place, but as he watched, it stretched almost to the breaking point, causing his heartbeat to falter. He paused, still pulled by the power of the storm, until he felt something touch his face as if from a great distance. He used the feeling to anchor himself in the physical world, then slowly, he began the painful journey back into his body, hauling in the lights behind him like a school of struggling fish in an overburdened net.

The presence within them fought him, but eventually he pulled it from the storm as well. As it smacked back into the deep recesses of his mind, his body crumpled.

Physical sensation returned slowly, a sharp pain just below his right eye, a copper taste in his mouth, the sound of his own ragged breathing, and finally, the sight of Rayne looking down at him, her expression a mixture of concern and annoyance. He stirred, realizing that he was lying cradled in her arms and when she saw the light of recognition return to his eyes, annoyance won out over concern.

"You shouldn't do that," she scolded in a harsh whisper so as not to wake the others. "You're not ready to follow the spirits. And don't try and tell me that wasn't what you were doing because I know what it looks like. Only Timur can do it safely. And Timur is *old*."

He tried to rise, but the faintest tensing of her muscles held him in place.

"I don't care if you think you're strong enough," she continued, sensing his thoughts from the look on his face. "It's not about strength. It's about temptation. And you almost lost out to it."

He frowned at her angrily and she glared right back at him. "I know the spirits sing to you, Graize. We can all see it. It makes you a powerful wyrdin, but it also makes you wide open to attack. They're dangerous. You can't trust them. You think just because you can understand their words, they want to share what they know with you? They don't; not any more than any wild animal wants to share its den."

Hearing the truth in her words, Graize cast a jaundiced look toward his ever present crowd of spirits who fluttered back in agitation.

"They'll try to distract you," Rayne continued. "And you're distractible enough already." She smiled smugly down at him. "I had to take drastic measures to bring you back."

Suddenly recognizing the copper taste in his mouth, Graize ran the back of his hand along his lips, feeling a thin trickle of blood smear across his knuckles.

"I hit you," Rayne explained matter-of-factly. "Twice. It was the only way to snap you back to yourself. Otherwise you would have flown away like your beetle birth fetish."

"Birth . . . ?"

Rayne shook her head in exasperation. "Townies," she muttered. Twisting slightly, she made herself comfortable, leaning her back against the tent pole. "The first creature that sees you when you're birthed into this world is your birth fetish. It helps you, especially when you're a wyrdin. Aba figures you were reborn over the Berbat-Dunya so the first creature that saw you was . . . ?" She paused expectantly.

He frowned. "My stag beetle?" The force of the storm had scoured his mind clear of the usual foggy clutter that pressed upon his thoughts, but her words still made very little sense to him. "It can't see me, Rayne, it's dead."

She cuffed him absently as she might have done to Caleb.

"I know it's dead," she snapped. "I'm not talking about the actual creature; I'm talking about its spirit. It links with you, becomes part of who you are and how you see the world. And how the world sees you."

"So I'm a beetle?"

"Yes. Beetles can live anywhere, eat anything, and stag beetle males have huge nasty mandibles for fighting. But they also have wings. Wings are a problem. If you fly too far or too long, you lose track of your body and then the spirits eat you." She made a ferocious face at him. "But don't worry. I'm here, and I'll smack, kick, or bite you back to the world any time you need it. My birth fetish is a *marten*."

"A weasel?"

"That's right, and weasels eat anything, too, including beetles."

He chuckled thinly. "Just remember," he warned, "beetles bite back."

She sniffed disdainfully at him. "Maybe, but just *you* remember they make a tasty snack well worth the risk." Hunkering down, she pulled a soft, sheep's wool blanket over the two of them. "Now go to sleep," she ordered. "The storm's passed. Everyone's safe."

Feeling the last of his energy drain from his body with her words, Graize closed his eyes, allowing the spirits to return to cocoon his mind in a misty white blanket of newly born potential, then opened them again.

"What's Danjel's birth fetish," he asked.

"Swallow."

"Kursk's?"

"Fox."

"Ozan's?"

"Nightingale."

"And Caleb's?"

She snickered. "Mouse, whether he likes it or not. Now *go to sleep*."

Nodding, he called the Presence to him, wondering idly what creature had first seen it birthed, before drifting off to dream of shining, white waves and a figure with eyes the color of snow.

✦

An hour later he awoke, feeling the storm center spitting the last of its fury against a mist-wrapped tower on the northern shore of the Deniz-Siyah. Wrapped in blankets and wedged safely between Danjel and Rayne, Graize could still feel it dancing across his nerves, heightening his newly strengthened awareness. Without even trying, he could feel the others sleeping all around him, their dreams lying open to his thoughts as easily as if they were speaking them aloud. Then, despite Rayne's warning, in one breath his mind took wing on the backs of his spirits soaring beyond the tent, to touch the sleeping minds of his new people: Kursk and Ayami, their dreams as well as their bodies entwined together, Ozan, his sleeping mind filled with music, Timur ever mindful and alert even in repose, all the way to the single shepherd asleep in her small tent, leaving the dog to stand watch over their slumbering charges. He breathed in the scent of fleece, heard the soft wicker of ponies, then reached out to the rain-drenched plains and the sparkling slivers of power that identified every living creature, from the tiniest insect hidden in the grass roots to the hosts of faraway Yuruk kazakin waiting for the dawn to continue their journey to the shores of Gol-Bardak and the raid on Yildiz-Koy.

He smiled in the darkness.

Yildiz-Koy. Where he and the new Presence would feed from more than just the spirits of the wild lands and their songs.

Roused by the thought, the Presence buzzed sleepily against his mind.

"Soon," he crooned to it. "Soon, you'll feed from spirits so strong this feast will seem like famine. Soon, you'll feed from the Warriors of Estavia." "And so will I."

Closing his eyes, he reached for the ebbing storm once more, felt it touch the sleeping mind of the northern sorcerer across the sea and pulled his thoughts back quickly before the man could sense him in return. It was not yet time to engage with that potential ally-cum-enemy, but—he chuckled to himself—soon, very, very soon. Everything would be soon. Rayne was wrong. He was strong enough to follow the spirits and they would share their den with him whether they wanted to or not. Beetles ate anything, and he would eat the spirits, eat every last one of them, if they didn't give him what he wanted. And the Presence would help him. It had been birthed into this world, and the first creature that had seen it was himself, whatever snowy-eyed Incasa might think.

Pressing himself against the warm curve of Danjel's hip, Graize wrapped the new Godling he'd formed from lights and lightning and prophecy about his mind, and fell into a dreamless sleep as his storm faded into the distance.

10

Seers

THE MIDAFTERNOON SUN BEAT DOWN upon the white cobblestones of Thesa, the only town of note on the island of Amatus. Her golden hair falling loose about her shoulders, Panos walked freely through the northern market, the dust and the heat whispering fine lines of music across her toes as she made her way through the crowded stalls, shops, and carts. She'd been coming here ever since she was a very small child and all the merchants knew her by sight as well as by reputation. Ignoring the many calls of greeting, she followed a faint line of pale light as it led her inexorably toward a familiar artisan's tent, the counter lined with wooden toys and small stone sculptures. Lifting the figure of a white dolphin, she marveled at how the purely physical chill of cold marble battled the equally strong sensation of wind blowing through her mind.

The shop's proprietor stepped forward, a pleased expression on her face.

"You honor my humble craft as always, Oracle," she said with a bow, carefully keeping her gaze from locking with Panos'. "How may I serve you today?"

Enjoying the taste of plums that the woman's words evoked, Panos gave her a dreamy smile.

"How many colors do your marble creatures come in?" she asked, stroking the smooth length of the dolphin's flank.

"As many as can be found on the bottom of Gol-Beyaz Lake, Oracle. What color do you seek?"

"A green tasting of spring rain beating down on tiny shoots of grain, and at the same time a green so dark it transforms your mouth into a forest of dark mystery."

Used to such analogies, the artisan merely nodded. "And the creature?"

"A sea turtle." Panos lifted her head to stare directly into the sun for a single breath, allowing the dazzling brightness to wash over her like the morning tide. "Young and fresh." She returned her attention to the artisan. "About the size of my hand. It entered the water this morning and its spirit led me here on a trail of seaweed."

"Ah, yes. I knew it was for something special." Bending, the woman lifted the figure of a small turtle from beneath the counter. The light green of its back and belly was streaked with a much darker green that gave it a slightly striped quality. "I carved it last year," she said, "as I watched the young struggle to the sea."

"Yes." Panos lifted the turtle until she could stare into its tiny marble eyes. "It's so hard to be born, and harder still to grow. But we'll help it." She set it down carefully. "Wrap it up, please; it's going on a very long journey."

"Of course, Oracle. Will there be anything else today?"

Panos swept her gaze across the displayed figures, her black eyes narrowing in concentration. "No," she decided after a moment. "I only need one gift in marble and anything wooden would only get burned up."

The woman immediately looked concerned. "Burned, Oracle?" she asked worriedly. "Is there to be a fire?"

"Oh, yes, but not here. It's being set far, far to the north in a tower by the sea."

"Ah. Well, I hope it won't get out of control," the woman said politely as she handed Panos the figure wrapped carefully in oilcloth.

"I imagine it will," Panos answered. "But I'll be there soon to keep an eye on it." Glancing back toward the mansion perched on the hill overlooking the marketplace, she watched as a royal delegation from Skiros arrived, standards rippling in the breeze. "Right on time," she said happily. Stretching out one hand, she stroked it down the length of an imaginary lover in gleeful anticipation before she turned and made her way back to her mother's home and the message from King Pyrros.

✦

Far to the north, Illan Volinsk felt an unusually warm breeze whisper through his hair as he settled himself by Cvet Tower's highest window and closed his eyes.

He smelled burning.

Lifting his face to the tantalizing aroma of smoke that drifted through his thoughts, he opened his mind to accept the powerful new vision taking form before him.

Burning. Burning grain and burning grass, burning fields and burning homes. A new power had been born into the world on the wings of last night's storm, with creation and destruction in equal measure crouched beneath its feet waiting to do its bidding, waiting for three children to light the fire of its birthing bed; a fire that might catch up the whole of the southern lands in flame, scorching the land in preparation for something wholly new and terrible.

Three children.

Illan reached out and drew their names from the coals of possibility on a trail of whispering gray smoke:

Graize and Brax and Spar.

He knew it. His breath quickened in excitement as each one paraded his destiny before him: standing on the brink of adulthood, Graize had already taken on the mantle of power and prophecy and Brax awaited nothing more than his God's direction to throw his life away at Her command. Only Spar remained uncommitted to this new fire, standing in the wings, half hidden behind the God of Prophecy's gray mantle, still so young and inexperienced despite all his untapped potential to shift the future from one stream to another. It only needed a gentle nudge to set his feet upon the path of Illan's choosing before he was old enough to truly choose one for himself.

Outside the tower window, rain pelted against the sea in ribbons of gray mist, warning him that a fire could as easily be snuffed out as unleashed. He must be cautious still. He nodded. Just a nudge for now.

Sergeant Ysav's characteristic thump against the uneven nineteenth step brought him back to himself just before the man advanced to the center of the room and saluted.

"You sent for me, sir?"

Illan turned from the window, his eyes as misty as the sky outside.

"It's raining," he said simply.

The sergeant frowned. "Sir?"

"It's raining," Illan repeated. "Rain brings first obscurity and then sweet-smelling clarity to both the physical and the metaphysical worlds." He took a deep breath and slowly his eyes returned to their naturally dark color. "But first it brings obscurity." Crossing to the atlas table, he began to clear an area along the western shoreline of Gol-Beyaz. "Let me pose a question of clarity to you on this rainy day, Vyns. Let us say that this," he gestured, "is the enemy's territory—which, of course, it is. And these," he held up half a dozen armed figures, "are their forces." He set them down carefully in a line along the shore. "Let us also say that these," he held up another half a dozen mounted figures, "are their traditional enemies. Not," he raised one finger, "their traditional *northern* enemies—those remain in a position of watchfulness for now." He turned the figure of Cvet Tower so that it faced the western shore. "Nor any possible new enemy from either the south or from their own midst, but rather, their traditional *western* enemies, the Yuruk." He set the mounted figures in a line facing the others.

"And the first enemy is . . . the Anavatanon, sir?" Vyns hazarded.

"Yes, Sergeant, the Anavatanon, with their warriors, and their Gods, and their great wall protecting all that they hold." Illan set a strip of pale blue-painted wood between the two forces. "So, here we have two peoples, the Anavatanon and the Yuruk. Now, if these two peoples are resolved to fight, to whom goes the advantage?"

Vyns shrugged. "The Anavatanon, *traditionally*, sir."

"Agreed, and," Illan gestured at Cvet Tower, "the Volinsk, for there will be deaths on both sides and this is always to our advantage, albeit in the short term. However, there are always variables which might extend the advantage to the long term if handled properly." He frowned down at the table. "If handled properly," he repeated.

"The Yuruk are massing to attack the village of Yildiz-Koy," he continued with uncharacteristic bluntness. "Despite their so-called seers," he added, his lip curling in disdain, "the Warriors of Estavia seem blissfully unaware of this. So what is the most likely outcome?"

Vyns scraped at a bit of stubble on his chin. "Does the village have adequate militia to fend them off, sir?"

"Ordinarily, yes, but the Yuruk have amassed a much larger force than usual due to the emergence of a new prophet in their midst; a charismatic young savage with madness in his eyes and the destiny of a thousand at his fingertips."

"Sir?" Vyns asked, confused.

"Never mind." Illan set the newly painted figure of a mounted seer on the table. "The outcome, Vyns."

The sergeant shrugged. "If the village militia cannot drive them off, then the village is taken."

"Yes. But if the village is taken, will the spirits that hover about our new prophet's head like moths around a flame have the strength to break through the wall and reach Gol-Beyaz and by doing so tip their hand?" He stared at the expanse of white-and-silver painted waves in the center of the table as if the answer could be found amidst their swirling patterns. "I had thought perhaps they might have been strong enough this spring but that did not materialize," he mused, "so I'm thinking not quite yet. So our young prophet is not planning to breach the wall this season; rather this is simply a raid to test the strength of his forces and build his leadership skills. And if they weaken the wall even a little, this will be all to the good. But will it also be all to the good for us?"

He turned to stare at the sergeant, his eyes paling to the color of summer clouds.

"There's a new power rising, Vyns, a power that could destroy the Warriors of Estavia utterly. It's still young, weak, and vulnerable, but it will quickly grow stronger and my question is: will this attack help it or hinder it? Will it rouse the Gods enough to cause Them to take the field, and if They do, what then?"

"If the Gods take the field, They'll likely destroy this new, young power to keep it from destroying Their warriors, my lord," Vyns answered.

"Yes, likely They will."

"But the Yuruk have been raiding the villages around Gol-Beyaz for centuries," the sergeant continued. "It doesn't generally rouse the Gods, sir, does it?"

"No, but that's because the Gods' seers generally have a *slightly* greater modicum of true sight than they seem to have of late and so the Warriors of Estavia have always been able to mount an armed response." Illan frowned. "So why are they so blind to this attack?"

"Something's shielding it?"

"Some thing or someone." Illan lifted the mounted prophet between finger and thumb. "Are you strong enough to accomplish this, Graize," he asked it, staring into its tiny, painted face. "I wouldn't have thought you were, but then you are a tricky little creature, aren't you, and you've made some very tricky friends of late." He set the figure down again, with a thoughtful expression. "It could be Incasa," he considered. "He's a tricky little creature, too. However, regardless of who or what may be shielding it, I don't think I want the Gods involved just yet," he decided, "so the Warriors of Estavia must be warned."

"How, sir, if all their seers are blind?"

Illan smiled coldly. "By lifting that blindness from the one seer least likely to raise suspicion," he answered, "The one seer they really should suspect, but never will until it's far too late." He smiled. "*My* seer." Lifting Spar's figure from its place atop Anahtar-Hisar, he reached out.

✦

He smelled burning.

Lying beside Brax, Spar jerked in his sleep as his dreams filled with smoke. His eyes began to sting. He couldn't see, couldn't breathe. He found himself falling and threw out a hand to catch himself, but just before the panic awakened him, the tower's voice rose up and he knew it had put the smoke into his head just to frighten him.

"*Bastard!*" he spat.

The voice ignored him. "*The wall,*" it intoned.

Spar growled inarticulately back at it. Even since its ominous promise above the practice yard, the voice had been nagging at him, invading his dreams as well as his thoughts with insistent messages of misery and death delivered in such a smugly superior tone that it made him want to slap it. It was hard enough to ignore it in the daytime, but at night it was nearly impossible and it knew it.

"*The wall,*" it repeated, "*will not hold.*"

And suddenly his mind was filled with the image of tumbling stones. A choking fog of smoke and dust broiled out toward him and he stumbled back in fear. Then, as if from far away, Jaq, pressed tightly against his side, grumbled in his sleep, and Spar turned to drive his face into the dog's neck, breathing in the heavy scent of earth and fur and . . . manure.

He'd been rolling again. In seagull shit.

The very commonality of the thought calmed him.

"*It's a just a buggerin' dream,*" he told himself sternly. "*It isn't real.*" Folding his arms, he planted his feet in the dream's dust and regarded the pile of rubble with a deeply cynical sneer.

"*The wall's always held,*" he told the voice in a tone of cutting disdain.

"*No, it hasn't,*" it replied, unimpressed by his bravado, "*and you know it.*"

The image faded to become the rain-spattered cobblestones of Liman-Caddesi and Spar felt his heart begin to pound overloud in his chest as the faintest tracery of silver-white mist began to drift toward him.

"*Stop it,*" he grated.

"*Stop what?*" the voice asked in a curious tone that belied the underlying spark of triumph beneath the words. "*This is no vision of mine. This is a memory.*"

And suddenly lightning skipped across the sky and Spar saw Drove, alive again, leap forward to jab his blade at Brax's face. As the other boy fell back, he swept his own knife up, slicing through Drove's jacket but missing the arm.

The slow, numbing panic that had taken hold of him that night came over Spar again as the memory played itself out. He found himself bending down, scrabbling in the sand for the rock he remembered throwing at Graize, who was even now running toward him, intent on stealing their one, their only chance of safety.

"*Safety from what, Spar?*"

"*Shut up.*"

The rock's jagged edges scraped against his palm as he let it fly. For a second he thought it might hit the other boy this time, but Graize only swayed out of the way and kept coming, but slower now as if he waded through deep water.

Spar looked down.

The mist had thickened, clinging to his feet and legs like strands of sticky sea grass. He kicked out at them, but for every strand that released its grip another took its place. He squeezed his eyes shut, trying not to see the savage teeth and claws that he knew were rising from their midst, but then the other boys were screaming and he opened his eyes.

Drove was struggling against a swarm of ghostly beings that tore frantically at his body, sucking up the blood that welled from a dozen wounds across his face and chest while Graize stared past him, frozen in terror. Brax was shouting at Spar to hide, but as he turned, Graize shook off his fear and, catching him by the collar, sent him spinning into the street toward a sea of blood-maddened creatures spewing out from between the buildings. Skidding on the slippery cobblestones, he tumbled into their midst.

The creatures leaped upon him at once, tearing at his hair and clothes, reaching flesh a second later. He heard himself scream, felt a blazing, numbing pain shoot through his mind, freezing his ability to sense the possibilities, and then Brax was wrapped about him, shielding him from their attack with his own body and, knife hand thrust into the air like a fiery brand, was shouting out the words that had saved their lives that night; the words that had summoned a God.

"Save us, God of Battles, and I will pledge you my life, my worship, AND MY LAST DROP OF BLOOD, FOREVER!"

The words seemed to explode all around them, blazoning across the night sky like a beacon. As the dream shattered under the force of Brax's promise, Spar felt the voice flinch away from the brightness of it, and struggling to his feet, he began to laugh.

"That's right!" he crowed. *"Brax called Estavia and She came! He saved us!"*

"What of it?" the voice replied. *"The wall is breached. Next time it will fall, and everyone you know will die, including your precious Brax."*

Spar's hands balled themselves into fists. *"No, he won't!"* he shouted. *"Brax'll be Her Champion, the greatest ever since Kaptin Haldin, and he'll keep your stupid wall from falling; you'll see!"*

"Oh, will he? And how do you know that, little seer? How do you know that for certain?"

"I just do!"

The faintest outline of a figure cloaked in a spinning vortex of power suddenly towered over him. *"Oh, no, you don't,"* he said darkly, *"but you soon will. You're nine years old—remember, Spar—you're not five, but neither are you fifteen. You're a child, a child who may not make it to adulthood without my help."*

Hands snaked out from the vortex, clamping around Spar's head like a pair of iron bands. He fought against them, but then his head was splitting open like an egg, sights and sounds and smells spilling out faster than he could catch them. He saw Brax struggling against a hundred sharp-clawed creatures of power and need in a sea of blood-flecked mist. He saw the waves crash over him, saw them knock him off his feet, and saw the creatures closing over his head as he went down. And for one brief moment he saw himself standing on a battlement in the pouring rain, holding the future in his hands before Brax's death washed over him again.

"I told you I would aid your sight and so I shall," the voice thundered at him as a howling wind rose up all around them. *"See! Incasa drew this vision from the very depths of prophecy, the God of Battle's Champion overrun and vanquished! They know he will not stand!"*

"That's the past!" Spar shouted, knowing even as he said it that it was the truth. *"I can feel it!"*

"What of it?" the voice scoffed. *"The vision wasn't altered when Estavia took his oath, it was only delayed. The spirits drew strength from the unsworn on Havo's Dance, and when they join forces with the Yuruk this season, the wall will topple. The riders of the wild lands will cut through all resistance like a scythe through a grain field and the spirits will flow after them. If they reach the shining waters of Gol-Beyaz, neither Gods nor Warriors, nor even gifted young Champions thrust all too unready into battle will be able to stop them. You know this; you can feel it, too."*

"So, what do you care?" Spar demanded, eyes narrowed in the wind.

"I don't, but you might. You might care just enough to stop it."

And from somewhere deep within his mind a field of flaming grain rose up all around him. He heard screaming and the sounds of battle and, as the fire raced toward him, driven by a thousand years of madness and hunger denied, he knew this was the future unless—he struggled to catch the one illusive image that refused to come to him—unless . . .

"That's right, little seer, reach for it," the voice urged. *"Unless what? Unless the Warriors of Estavia take the field? Unless Brax does? Do they need your great Champion so soon? And will he survive it if they do?"*

Throwing his mind out like a fishing net, Spar jerked the answer from the fire and saw Brax, bloody but alive, rising from the smoke, his eyes the color of blood. The relief he felt was almost physical.

"And so he lives, then," the voice agreed. *"That's very good. And it would seem that he also takes the field, but how? You told me that delinkon never do. What draws him into battle, Spar? And where will that battle take place?"*

The fire refused to answer. Snarling in frustration, Spar gathered all his strength and threw his mind out once again only to have it slam against a rock-hard barrier that suddenly leaped up before him.

"What the crap is that?" he shouted.

"The wall of power. The God of Prophecy's trying to stop you. He believes that Brax will fail. He's seen it and so he won't help you. Or maybe He's planned it all from the beginning: Cindar's death, Drove's, Brax's surrender to the will of the Gods. But the question is: will you surrender, too, little seer? Will you let His wall stand between you and your natural right to see the truth?"

And the fire rose up again, filling his mind with the screams of the dying. He saw Yashar fall, and then Kemal, saw a thousand creatures of power and need pour into Gol-Beyaz on a rolling tide of mist and death, and saw a figure mounted on a snow-white pony—a figure he almost knew—appear out of the smoke. He saw Brax throw himself forward to meet him, and then the wall slammed up once again. Balling his hands into fists, Spar hammered against its glittering surface.

"Break through it!" the voice urged.

"I can't!"

"Then go over it!"

With a yell, Spar leaped into the air, fingers and toes scrabbling for purchase on the wall's smooth surface. He hung there for a heartbeat, then fell back.

"I can't! It's too slippery!"

"Is this how you plied your trade in the city, little thief?" the voice sneered. *"No wonder you let your abayos die."*

"Shut up!"

"CLIMB!"

Spar lunged forward once again and suddenly his hands gripped stone and he was clambering upward, faster and faster, the memories of a hundred such ascents driving him on.

"Where will the battle be joined?" the voice demanded. *"Reach the top, see the place, find the name!"*

The open sky loomed just above his head. Throwing out one hand, he touched the top, and then the wall turned to mist beneath his feet.

He cried out and the figure, now darkened to the color of heavy storm clouds, appeared above him.

"*Climb!*" he insisted.

"*I can't!*"

"*You must or all is lost!*"

"*Then help me, you piss-head!*"

And suddenly he was hanging in midair, held up by the figure's will alone as the wall collapsed around him. Far below he saw a tiny village appear out of the smoke and dust and just as suddenly he knew its name.

Yildiz-Koy.

He fell. As the ground rushed up to claim him, he heard the voice again, its tone much gentler now.

"*Well done, Delin. Now go to them and tell them, tell him. Yildiz-Koy will be the first but not the last to fall. They can stop it, Brax can stop it, but only if they know. Only if you tell them.*"

And Spar smelled burning.

✦

"Shield up, and then counter with the sword."

In the practice yard, Spar crouched under a plane tree watching as Kemal flung his shield up to knock Yashar's attack aside, then sweep his own weapon around to be caught in return. He frowned.

It had been two days since the voice had shown him the raid on Yildiz-Koy; two days since it had urged him to go to his new abayon and tell them what he'd seen. Since then, it had seemed content to lie quietly and wait for his response, but Spar didn't fool himself into thinking it had gone.

"*So, what do you care?*"

"*I don't, but you might. You might care just enough to stop it.*"

Spar shook his head at the memory. Despite what the voice had said, he knew it had to have some kind of personal stake in all this or it wouldn't have pushed him so hard. Nobody gave anything away for free, especially information. No, it would bide its time until the last possible moment and then, if he hadn't moved yet, it would rise up again with a new form of attack. When it did, he had to be ready to meet it; he'd learned that much strategy at least.

"*You might care just enough to stop it.*"

But the question was, did he?

"A shield is best used to deflect, not to block," Kemal continued, breaking into his reverie. "Never take a blow directly if you can help it. The shield may not be able to withstand the force of it and, if it breaks, your arm certainly won't withstand another. A broken shield is preferable to a broken arm, but an intact shield and an intact arm are the most preferable of all."

Bringing his shield up again, Kemal tilted it slightly as Yashar aimed another blow at his head. The sword skittered off to the side, sending the larger man to Kemal's left and Kemal brought his sword point up to freeze an inch away from his arkados' ribs. "And, as you can see, a deflection might overbalance your opponent, opening him up to your own attack." He traced the sword point along Yashar's tunic and the older man showed his teeth at him. "Any questions?"

He glanced over at Spar who shook his head impatiently. That was what he'd be doing if he went to Kemal and Yashar, his thoughts continued, refusing to be sidetracked; taking a blow directly—maybe on the shield—but definitely directly. On the streets he'd never taken any kind of blow at all, that's what made you a mark. And that's what the voice was trying to do, turn him into a mark by making him think the raid on Yildiz-Koy was his responsibility, making him commit openly to the life of a seer.

"And as for Spar, they'd sell him to the God of Prophecy's white-eyed lunatics at Incasa-Sarayi in a heartbeat if they ever found out what he could do for them. They'd addle his brains with their seeking so fast he'd go mad from the strain."

Spar shook his head, impatient with the memory. He knew the priests of Incasa were dangerous, but the voice was equally dangerous. There had to be a way to accomplish what Kemal was talking about: deflect the voice so that it overbalanced and opened itself up to a counterattack; so that it became the mark, not him, so that when and if he took on a seer's life, it was on his terms and nobody else's.

The thought of turning the voice into a mark appealed to him and he returned his attention to the lesson with renewed interest. Brax was standing now, mirroring Kemal's movement with an intense expression and suddenly Spar felt an irrational stab of jealousy. Brax had no doubts, no questions. His path was clear: learn to fight, then fight. He trusted

Estavia to protect him, or more likely, Spar amended cynically, he believed he was unkillable. But Spar knew better. He could die in a heartbeat, they all could; he'd seen it.

"It all comes down to one thing: the Warriors of Estavia took us in. They fed us and they clothed us, so they have the right to direct our training."

But did they also have the right to get them killed?

With a scowl, he leaned back on his heels and drove the point of his wooden practice sword into a crevice between two flagstones. And why did he have to worry about any of this, he thought, suddenly feeling petulant. He was *nine*. Tanay had said he didn't have to make any decisions yet. And he *shouldn't* have had to anyway. *Brax* was supposed to take care of them. This whole plan of letting Cindar die and then handing them over to a temple full of guards and soldiers had been his idea, but now some mysterious know-it-all voice was making Spar take responsibility for *all* of them, not just for him and Brax, whether he wanted to or not. *And* get his own life ruined in the meantime, he added with an indignant growl, because he *knew* that as soon as he told anyone that he could see things, *really* see things, Sable Company would be on him like a flock of eyeball-picking crows, never mind the priests of Incasa, just like the pain-in-the-ass voice probably wanted. *And* why hadn't *they* seen all of this themselves, anyway. It was their job, after all.

It wasn't fair.

With a dark scowl, he stabbed his sword point down into the crevice again, but at Yashar's warning frown, he thrust it back into his scabbard. He was sick of thinking and sick of practicing, he thought sulkily; it was too hot for either. Glancing up, he glared at the sun as it blazed down on him from high in the shimmeringly pale sky. The air was unseasonably heavy and humid, the small amount of lake breeze able to work its way past the tower walls and buildings no match for it. He felt sleepy and sticky, and horribly confined in the padded practice tunic. All he wanted to do was tear it off and toss it into the inlet, then throw himself after it. In the old days he and Brax would never have been out in the sun with this many clothes on, not at this time of day. They would be off dozing under a wharf or tucked up against the side of a tree-shaded hostel waiting for the cool evening breezes to bring the drinkers and gamblers—the most unwary marks in Anavatan—out into the streets. But not anymore. Oh, no. Now they had to pretend to stab people to death until they passed out from the heat.

He snorted. Brax looked pretty close to it. His face was beet red, his hair plastered to his skull. Even Kemal and Yashar were dripping with sweat.

Wishing that some God of shade and leisure had risen from Gol-Beyaz with the rest of Them, Spar caught up Yashar's waterskin and pulled the hide-wrapped cork as loudly as possible. If they all wanted to die of thirst, they could, he thought taking a deliberately long drink. He wasn't going to.

As if reading his thoughts, Yashar called a halt. Brax threw himself down beside the younger boy as Kemal set his shield carefully against the tree trunk. Spar glanced over at it, noting the many scrapes and gouges across the surface. With a start, he realized that each one represented a blow—a possible killing blow—that Kemal had avoided. Seeing his expression, his abayos turned the shield so that he could see it more clearly.

"Those are from sword and spear deflections," he said, pointing at four long indentations, "and this pattern of smaller damage is from arrow fire, the only force a shield is meant to absorb," he added, continuing the lecture. "And even then, with a metal shield the most skillful can deflect that as well, allowing the arrows to be retrieved and sent back at the enemy."

"Always my favorite strategy," Yashar noted. Catching up a nearby bucket, he emptied its contents over his head, shaking vigorously as water poured down his face and beard to soak the front of his tunic. "A metal shield is always best."

Spar's face grew cloudy. Kemal's shield was twice the size of his own small wooden one and that was heavy enough to carry. He doubted he'd ever be able to even lift one made of metal. Beside him, Brax frowned as he liberated the waterskin from the younger boy, obviously thinking the same thing.

"It does have the advantage of deflection," Kemal allowed, noting their expressions, "but its disadvantage is the sheer weight of it, which hampers both speed and coordination; something I believe our young delinkon are quite adept at, yes?" He smiled at them reassuringly.

"Point," Yashar agreed. "Plus a deflected arrow might also strike an ally."

"And point again," his arkados nodded. "In that instance all you can really do is pray that Estavia will further deflect the arrow into the ground for you."

"And pray that She'll direct your own arrows to their intended targets," Yashar added.

"Does She?" Brax asked, tipping his head up to take a deep drink from the waterskin.

"Not generally, no," Kemal answered sternly, before Yashar could say something humorous about Brax's aim which up until this point had been extremely erratic. "She expects you to practice with as much diligence as is necessary to become proficient on your own."

"I'll be an old man by then," Brax groused, wiping his mouth on his sleeve.

"Very likely," Yashar agreed.

Ignoring the conversation, Spar ran his finger along the gouges, his expression pensive. So either Kemal had managed to avoid all these attacks, or Estavia had deflected them for him, he thought. Whichever it was hardly mattered; what mattered was that he was still alive. He frowned. So why was Kemal's safety *his* problem, he grumbled, returning to his original line of thought. Why was any of theirs? Kemal was a warrior, so was Yashar. They knew what they were risking. Obviously they had protections in place.

But did Brax?

He saw him struggle against a hundred sharp-clawed creatures of power and need in a sea of blood-flecked mist. He saw the waves crash over him, saw them knock him off his feet, and saw the creatures close over his head as he went down.

He frowned. Protections or not, death could come so easily; all it took was one misstep. The Warriors of Estavia died all the time just like the council had reminded Brax—their memorial ritual in High Summer sometimes took hours.

He smiled wistfully. That had been the best time to work in the old days, when the warriors and garrison guards were all busy remembering friends and lovers who had died too young. He shook his head in renewed anger. Why would any of them ever want to risk it, anyway?

"Spar? Are you all right?"

He blinked, then looked up to see Kemal watching him with a concerned expression. Shaking his head irritably, he glanced over at Brax.

"He's wondering what it's like," the older boy supplied, taking a wild stab at Spar's expression.

"What? Battle?"

It was close enough so Spar gave a careful, noncommittal shrug.

Kemal stretched his legs out in front of him, crossing one ankle over the other before answering. "Frightening and exhilarating," he said as he accepted the waterskin from Brax, "but then Estavia fills you and you forget your own feelings in the rush of the God's passion for combat."

Brax had his foggy barge-pole expression on his face again and Spar snorted.

"And when you die?" he demanded, his voice harsher than he'd expected, but knowing Brax would not ask this question for him.

"The God will take us down into the depths of Gol-Beyaz to sleep by Her side."

"So you don't care if you die?"

"We care, but we also accept."

"Why?"

"Because it's what we do."

"Think of it this way," Yashar explained, coming over to sit next to Spar. "All trades have purpose, technique, and tools. In your, uh, earlier trade your purpose was to . . . thieve, I suppose, yes?" When Spar gave a careless nod, he continued. "The technique was to rob people in such a way as to get away with it, I imagine, and the tools were some form of lock-picking needle or pocket-picking hook?"

Spar bridled indignantly at the last word and Brax chuckled.

"Spar never used a dip," he explained proudly. "He was far too good for that. Always was."

Kemal chuckled and Yashar shot his arkados a disapproving look from beneath his heavy, black eyebrows. "The point I'm trying to make is a serious one," he said sternly. "Your old trade was theft, your new trade; *our* trade is, to put it bluntly, death. Now, there's a lot more to it than that, of course; we protect the followers and the property of the Gods, but we do it by killing. That is at the heart of our worship. We kill in Estavia's name, for Estavia's reasons, and at Her order. Our techniques are those of battle: strategy and tactics, and our tools are the sword, bow, lance, and spear. We kill, and sometimes we die, again in Her name, for Her reasons, and occasionally at Her order."

"You see, everyone dies, Spar," Kemal added gently. "The best anyone can hope for is to die well."

The best anyone can hope for is to die old, Spar thought cynically, but said nothing as Yashar nodded his agreement with Kemal's words.

"And, just as the God draws strength from the deeds we perform in life, as we explained before," he added, "so does She draw strength from our deaths. In this She is the God of Death. It is Her domain."

Brax and Spar exchanged a look. "But I thought all the Gods shared death," Brax said with a frown.

"And so They do," Kemal answered. "Each in Their own way: Usara oversees death in the sick, Oristo in the aged or the very, very young, while Havo lays claim to the cycle of deaths and rebirths in all of nature. Ystazia gives death meaning through poetry and song, while Incasa lays out the time and place for His Seers to use for His purposes. But only Estavia sends Her people out to cause death and to risk it. We know what may happen and we go willingly. Anyone unwilling does not go."

And Brax would go; he'd seen it.

"You just might care enough to stop it."

"Shut up." He flicked one hand impatiently, and Kemal made an inquiring noise.

"Fly," he answered simply.

His abayos gave him a sympathetic smile. "A quarter hour more and we'll go for a swim in the inlet where the Gods still keep the water fresh; they can't reach you in the water. All right?"

Spar nodded, trying not to show the relief on his face as they stood once more.

"Good. Now again. Shield up . . ."

✦

Two days later he dreamed again. The wall fell in a crash of rock and a spray of power and, eyes streaming in the broiling dust, Spar watched as a line of torch-wielding riders winked in and out of sight along the crest of a hill. The same familiar, mounted figure rose up like a beacon in the saddle, and as they stared at each other, the figure gave a signal and the riders bent down, touching the fiery ends of their torches to the dry fields below. Flames shot into the sky.

He tried to shout a warning, but the smoke filled his lungs, making him choke. Scrabbling frantically in the bedclothes to find Jaq, he struggled to wake up, but this time even the dog's comforting presence could not halt the stream of images. He saw battle joined, saw the defenders fall, and once again a thousand creatures of power and need rose up to close over Brax's head.

Nearly hysterical by now, Spar's mind hurled outward, seeking help from someone, from anyone he could trust. Streaking down the paths of memory, it hit Tanay's sleeping mind like a thunderbolt, almost throwing her from her pallet. The force of it awakened first Oristo deep in Gol-Beyaz, then First Abayos-Priest Neclan, before it ricocheted back toward him. He cried out, and then the image of a frail old woman seated in a room of warm wood and colored glass rose up to steer the vision in the proper direction, and suddenly at Serin-Koy's Usara-Cami, a blank-faced man with Bayard's features sat bolt upright in his bed. For an instant he and Spar locked eyes, then, with an almost physical jolt, the man caught up the boy's latent ability and hurled it toward the shining net of Battle-Seer Elif's prophetic sight hovering above her sleeping form at Estavia-Sarayi. The old woman's cataract-filled eyes snapped open to stare into Spar's, and then she whipped out one mental hand toward him.

Almost crying with relief, he caught it.

The vision tumbled over him and through him, falling faster and faster like the stones of the collapsing wall he'd first seen, but this time they did not fall before the eyes of a frightened and inexperienced child, but those of a cunning and powerfully dangerous battle-seer. With an impatient gesture, Elif stripped the subterfuge and extraneous details from the vision, called up one clear image: a horde of Yuruk attacking Yildiz-Koy, then banished it. It vanished like so much mist in a windstorm and the last thing Spar saw before the peaceful darkness of a dreamless sleep came over him was Elif thrusting the vision into the sleeping mind of Kaptin Liel with the metaphysical equivalent of a smack to the back of the head. As Sable Company's most powerful seer jerked awake in surprise, Elif and Spar allowed themselves the pleasure of one cynical snort.

✦

Far away in Cvet Tower, Illan Dmitriviz Volinsk nodded in satisfaction. Although his little seer had—very skillfully he admitted—managed to keep his figurine from the board for the moment, the game had only just begun. All that mattered now was that the Warriors of Estavia were moving in the direction he desired. Returning to his place before his window, he stared out at the moonlit waves as the warm breeze returned to whisper playfully about his face.

The Wall

THREE DAYS LATER, four barges carrying two hundred archers and infantry set out from Anahtar-Hisar. Three made for the eastern shore to pick up reservists from Caliskan, Camus and Adasi-Koy while the fourth, carrying Estavia's newest Champion, went west to Ekmir, Kenor, Kepe, and Serin-Koy. Picking his way carefully along the crowded deck, Brax supposed that he should be thankful that the complement of Bronze Company cavalry had ridden out the day before. The return trip was already three times longer than the journey south had been—then it had just been a question of filling the sails, now it took a line of rowers on either side of the barge to fight their way north—but at least they weren't doing it covered in horse-shit.

"The current's stronger in High Spring," the barge-mate had explained the first day. "That's when the Gods are at Their . . . " he'd paused for dramatic emphasis . . . "friskiest like everything else."

Brax had shot him a look cynical enough to impress even Spar, but hadn't been able to resist leaning over the side to see if he could spot any . . . friskiness going on. There had been nothing but tiny bubbles rising from the smooth surface, just like the last time, and both Kemal and Yashar had laughed at him.

"It has nothing to do with the Gods," Kemal had explained. *"The upper current runs north-south, remember, and with so many people on board, it's natural that it would take longer."*

Brax had just shrugged. He hadn't been particularly interested in anything Kemal'd had to say to him right then. Squeezing into a small spot at the larboard railing, he stared back at the receding turrets of Alev-Hisar, the tower both Kinor and Kepe-Koy shared, remembering

the frenzy that had gripped Anahtar-Hisar when they'd heard the news:
the Yuruk were planning a raid on the village of Yildiz-Koy and one
third of the garrison was being deployed to meet the threat. Including
Kemal and Yashar. Brax had been wildly excited about the prospect of
carrying out his promise to Estavia so soon, but the older of their two
abayon had squashed his mood almost immediately.

✦

"You'll only be coming with us as far as Serin-Koy."

"What?"

Yashar cut off Brax's budding protest with a short chop of one hand.
"No arguments, Delin. This is battle, not practice, and you're still far
too young."

"I can stay at the back."

"There is no back; only the last line of defense."

"Other delinkon go into battle."

"Not at your level of training."

"But . . ."

"No. You'll remain behind in Serin-Koy with Bayard and your new
kardon. End of discussion."

"There'll be plenty of battles to come," Kemal added, trying to take
the sting from the decision. "There's no need to face them all at once."

"I told Her I would fight for Her," Brax answered between clenched
teeth.

"And so you will, when you're old enough."

Seething with resentment, Brax made to protest again; then the God
touched his mind with the faintest of caresses and he bit the words back
at once. Kemal eyed him suspiciously, but ignoring the penetrating look,
Brax simply turned on his heel and left the room.

✦

Some time later, Spar and Jaq found him standing on a low spot on the
God-Wall, shooting arrows at a straw target with a dark expression on
his face. The younger boy crossed his arms, his own expression demanding an explanation for Brax's sudden acquiescence, and the older
boy just shrugged.

"She told me to wait," he said simply, fitting another arrow to his bowstring.

Spar's eyes narrowed.

"She did. She told me to wait."

Something moved behind the younger boy's eyes for an instant, and Brax cocked his head to one side.

"What?"

Pulling one of Jaq's ears, Spar just shook his head.

"No, really, what?"

"Nothing."

Now it was Brax's turn to narrow his eyes. "Yeah, so, how come you've got that 'gotta take a piss' look on your face?"

Spar showed his teeth at him, then shrugged. "I was just wondering . . ." he began, then paused again.

"What? Where the latrine is?"

"When you started obeying anyone on the first order," the younger boy snapped.

Brax snickered. "Since now. I guess I'm just more mature these days." Laughing at Spar's familiar sneer, he unstrung his bow. "I had to talk to Estavia and do some thinking," he allowed, "and I couldn't do either with everyone flying about like bees around a hive someone had just kicked over, now could I?"

Spar gave his usual one-shouldered shrug. "So, what're we doing, then?" he asked.

"About what?"

"About Serin-Koy?"

"What about Serin-Koy?"

Spar gave an annoyed snort. "Are. We. Going?" he asked tightly.

" 'Course we are." Brax jumped down. "Kemal and Yashar are our abayon now, like Cindar was, yeah? So, we do what they tell us to do, but . . ." he held up one finger, "we keep our eyes and our ears open, just like in the old days." His expression grew serious. "And if you get any bad feelings about anything at all, you tell me right away and we go to ground. Just like in the old days, too. Got it?" When Spar nodded, he threw his arm over his shoulder. "All right, then, let's go play nice and let them think I was just off sulking."

Spar shot him a cynical glance and he laughed.

"Don't be an idiot." As the sound of their names filtered out to them, he jerked his head toward the tower. "C'mon. They probably want us to practice *not* going into battle today."

✦

Although his expression had remained doubtful, the younger boy'd allowed Brax to draw him back to Anahtar-Hisar and Brax'd smiled in satisfaction. They would go to Serin-Koy, just as he'd told Spar they would, but the God had a plan for him—he could feel it—and if She told him to go to Yildiz-Koy, he would go, whether their new abayon said he could or not. But at least this way Spar would be safe.

Now, looking out at the western shore, it seemed impossible to believe that they could be hurrying toward battle on such a perfect day. The grain fields beyond the villages were awash with the pale green spread of new growth and the distant hills already looked lush and wild. If he stared long enough, he could almost see each blade of grass and each tiny blue-and-yellow wildflower stretching all the way out to the horizon. Everything was so still, so peaceful, and so . . . he felt his chest tighten . . . open. He swallowed, his throat dry. Anyone could see you out there in that huge empty place with all that sky. How could anyone live and work out there without feeling horribly . . . stared at.

Suddenly wishing he was back home amidst the safe, concealing buildings and wharves of Anavatan, he turned away, concentrating on the crowded deck until his heart stopped pounding. Around him, the warriors of Cyan Company played dice or dozed in the warm afternoon sun, content to treat the journey like an extended leave. Even Spar was curled up asleep, arms wrapped around Jaq, unconcerned about the future. Taking a deep breath, he thrust the sense of panic away.

Don't be stupid, he chided himself. *She wouldn't let anything like that happen to you. So shut up, calm down, and get some sleep.*

Reaching in to touch the comforting warmth of the God's presence, he slid down until his back pressed against the railing and made himself close his eyes.

✦

They put in to Serin-Koy just before dusk. So close to Yildiz-Koy, the village conscript of twenty-four archers, fifty infantry, and twelve battle-seers had gone overland the day before, but Bayard was waiting for them on the wharf, having guessed their purpose in stopping. On deck, Yashar and Kemal took their leave of their new delinkon with little fanfare, the older man simply taking each boy in a great bear hug that made them gasp, the younger staring searchingly into their faces for a long moment.

"You'll take care of Jaq, Delin?" he asked Spar seriously.

One fist wrapped tightly around the dog's collar, the younger boy nodded.

Kemal smiled. "Well, that's a relief. I have to admit that, even though the God loves him, I was always a little afraid for him on the bat-tlefield."

"You don't have to be afraid for him anymore," Spar answered firmly.

Kemal nodded, then, after giving him a brief hug and ruffling Jaq's ears, turned to Brax. "Be safe, Delin," he said earnestly. "Obey Bayard and Badahir. They could teach you a lot if you're willing to learn."

"I'm always willing to learn," Brax answered stiffly.

"Yes, well . . ." For a moment Kemal looked as if he might disagree, then he squeezed Brax's shoulder with a distracted smile. "We'll be back soon."

Brax nodded, surprised by the sudden lump in his throat. "Don't get killed, all right," he said fiercely, scowling up at his new abayos to mask his concern.

"We'll do our best."

"You better, 'cause I still don't have that arrow deflecting trick down, you know."

"I know. We'll work on it as soon as we get back."

"Good. Well. Good-bye." Brax abruptly caught Spar by the shoul-der and maneuvered him and Jaq onto the wharf without another word. As they took their place beside Bayard, the dog let out a single, loud bark and Spar dropped to one knee. Arms about the animal's neck, he watched as the barge headed slowly back toward deeper water, then craned his head to look up at Brax. Unable to offer him any comfort, Brax just shrugged. He had no idea if they'd just lost two more abayon. He hoped not.

✦

Two days later the village elders received a message. The collective relief force had reached Yildiz-Koy and its tall tower of Kumas-Hisar and
had taken up their position between the fields and the hills. The scouts
had fanned out across the plains but had returned with no word of the
enemy. All was as quiet and peaceful as it had been for the last two years.

✦

Holding court before a dozen children gathered outside Bayard's forge,
his delinkon Hadzi stated darkly that it hardly mattered.

"All they have to do is journey along one of the deeper gullies that
follow the western ridge," Badahir's eldest bi-gender delos said in an
ominous voice. "There's places there permanently shrouded in mist and
pockets of ancient power so thick no seer can pierce through them. The
Yuruk could be creeping along there right now and no one would be any
the wiser."

The children glanced uneasily at each other, but Brax just bent to
whisper a cynical comment in Spar's ear and the younger boy snickered.

✦

That evening, however, when the two of them climbed to the top of
Orzin-Hisar—Jaq padding up the spiral staircase behind them—they
were both unusually somber. Leaning against one of the shorter para-
pets, they stared out past the God-Wall, watching it shimmer with the
bluish glow it took on in the setting sun, each one thinking his own
thoughts.

They'd been coming up here several times a day since they'd arrived, partly to get away from Bayard's noisy and chaotic household but
mostly because Spar had become obsessed with the wall, staring intently
at it for hours as if trying to memorize every nuance of its ever-changing
facade. Or at least staring at it for as long as Brax would allow him to.
The older boy was usually good for about half an hour before—growing
bored—he'd make Spar come back down again. He'd been willing to let
him climb up here alone, but ever since Spar had watched their abayon
sail away from them, he'd become a little—Brax tried to come up with a
gentler word than needy, and settled for clingy—and didn't like having

the older boy out of his sight. So that meant that every time he could convince him, the two of them made the long ascent to the quiet, breezy top of Orzin-Hisar.

Still, he supposed that if Spar had to stare at something, the wall was a better choice than the warehouse he'd been obsessed with all last winter.

"You mean the one we lifted those three bags of spices out of?" his mind supplied.

"Yeah that one, but I doubt the wall's got any hidden treasures like that in-side its stones."

"So why's he staring at it?"

"I dunno, maybe he thinks it's pretty."

His mind just sneered at him and Brax shrugged. He knew there had to be more to it than that, but Spar wasn't ready to tell him yet and be-sides—he returned his gaze outward—it *was* pretty. At dawn the rising sun, reflecting off Gol-Beyaz, changed its nightly opaque indigo to that of a rosy orangey-yellow, then paled it to a nearly opalescent pink at its height, only to darken it once more to blue and back to indigo as the sun set behind the western hills. Last night at midnight, leaning against the parapet, half asleep, he'd marveled at the hints of green and purple and blue that sparkled like living stars across its face. It was as if the wall were alive, dancing and flowing to the rhythm of the sun and the moon.

Absently he'd wondered if the wall also changed color with the sea-sons, at the whim of the Gods, or as the fields and hills gave way to buildings and wharves. Back home he'd never even seen it—in fact he'd never even been farther north than the Western Trisect dockyards. The lake and village merchants that filled Anavatan's many outdoor markets said it stretched a mile above the high stone walls of the city, but back home it hadn't mattered. On the streets of Anavatan it was easy to ig-nore Gods, armies, enemies, and walls in the day-to-day struggle to get by, but here it dominated every part of people's lives; a physical reminder that there were other concerns besides bread.

Chewing at a hangnail on his sword hand, he sighed. Life used to be a lot simpler.

Estavia stroked a responding warmth through his mind reminding him that life used to be a lot colder, too, and he acknowledged Her point before glancing over at Spar.

"So what do you think?" he asked. "You figure a blacksmith's delinkos who's never been outside of Serin-Koy knows anything about . . . anything?"

Standing in his usual position with one hand buried in Jaq's ruff and the other cupping the delos-drum at his side, the younger boy quirked up the corners of his mouth but said nothing, continuing to stare out at the wall as if hypnotized.

Brax leaned over the parapet and spat an experimental wad of spittle at the ground. "Hadzi oughta shut up, though," he noted with a scowl. "Everyone's getting scared. Both Aptulli and Paus had nightmares last night."

Spar nodded absently.

" 'Course it could be, yeah?" Brax continued, giving the other boy a questioning glance. "The Yuruk could be creeping along south, just out of sight behind the ridge and we'd never even know about it. Not if they're hiding from the seers in some mind-blocking misty place like Hadzi says they are."

His expression grim, Spar nodded again.

Rubbing his palm absently over the pommel of his sword, Brax grimaced. "Still, they have to come east eventually, and then we'll see them—I mean, then Kemal and the rest will see them," he amended, scowling darkly as he remembered once again about all the fighting he was going to miss. He straightened suddenly. "Well, I say let them come, the Warriors'll crush every last one of them. They can even come here. *I'm* not afraid of them."

Staring out past the wall at the distant hills painted a vivid orange and purple in the setting sun, Spar just shook his head at him.

✦

The next day, Birin-Militia-Kaptin Badahir gathered the older children together in the central courtyard. A tall woman, with Bayard's eyes and Kemal's thick black hair, she'd earned her position in a decade of fighting the Yuruk. Now she stood in the center of the courtyard, her delinkos Coval beside her, looking self-important.

Brax tried not to glare at him.

"All right," Badahir said when they were all, more-or-less, quiet. "Since none of you seem able to talk about anything else, let's talk about the Yuruk. Good riders, good archers, but poor infantry. Anyone know why?"

Seated beside Spar and Jaq, Aptulli dutifully raised her hand.

"Yes, Kardelin."

" 'Cause they don't walk anywhere."

The children snickered, but Badahir nodded her head. "That's right," she answered and the girl stuck her tongue out at the others. "The Yuruk live in small, mobile family groups. They follow their flocks and herds from winter pasture to summer pasture, relying on small sturdy, plains-bred ponies to cross the vast expanse of territory they have to cover every year. It's said their delon are taught to ride before they can walk. They're known for their skills with the bow and the spear, so they might be a force to be reckoned with except for what? Ekrubi?"

Bayard's middle delos looked up from the blade of grass he was methodically shredding and frowned. "Um . . . 'Cause there aren't enough of them?"

Badahir smiled. "And here I thought you weren't paying attention. Right. There aren't enough of them. They maintain no more than a very loose, very temporary alliance with other Yuruk families, formed when they have a set objective. They have no council or leaders, so there's no one to mold them into a solid disciplined, fighting force, and no hierarchy—that means nobody tells them what to do, Aptulli," she added in response to the girl's confused expression.

"Not even the Gods?" she asked, her eyes wide.

"They don't have Gods, dummy," Ekrubi sneered. "*Everybody* knows that."

"Yeah, like everybody knows you peed your pallet last night," she shot back. Her kardos made a lunge for her, but at Badahir's frown, he returned to his place, muttering darkly.

"Everyone does not know it," the birin-kaptin said sternly. "Very little is known about the Yuruk. What is known is that they value the quality of our livestock, but they would rather try to steal it than pay for it. This is nothing new; they make raids against the western villages every year. So, why don't we have to fear them? Hieson?"

"Because our militia is the strongest on Gol-Beyaz," the oldest delinkon present promptly replied and Badahir smiled.

"Well, that may be why Serin-Koy doesn't have to fear them," she allowed. "But what about the rest of the villages?"

"The wall protects them," Arrian piped up.

"And?"

"Um, the battle-seers always see them coming first?"

"A very good point to remember, yes," Badahir acknowledged, drawing a pleased smile from her delos. "And? Anyone?"

"The Warriors of Estavia kill them all whenever they try anything," Brax added darkly.

The other children glanced over at him uneasily, but Badahir nodded, her expression serious. "Sometimes that's exactly why," she agreed. "Being willing and being able to kill your enemies. The Warriors of Estavia are both and they got that way by consistent, diligent practice. And, yes, that's why we're here today," she added as the children began to groan at the word practice. "Even those of you who won't be pledging your service to the God of Battles need to know how to defend yourselves and your village if called upon." She turned. "Coval, hand out those practice swords to anyone who needs one." As her delinkos hurried to obey her, she continued. "Obviously, the willingness to kill or even die in defense of those under your protection is only the beginning. You also need discipline, focus, perseverance, patience, strength, flexibility, coordination and stamina. So let's talk about discipline." She grinned as several of the children began to groan again at the even less popular word.

"All right, fine, how about stamina? Contrary to what you might think, stamina is not being able to go full out all day. Stamina is knowing when to move and when to rest, knowing what muscles to use, and what muscles to relax, knowing when to take a breath and when to release it, knowing how to pace yourself so that you don't waste the reserves of power and energy you might need before the battle's over and, finally, knowing exactly how much force is necessary and using no more and no less. On that note, Coval, get Ivasik up and ready."

As Coval heaved a large, straw figure covered in a tattered brown tunic into the center of the courtyard, Ekrubi leaned toward Brax.

"My aba named it after this famous Rostovic general he heard about once," he whispered. "But after Kemal went to Estavia-Sarayi, he saw a woodcut of him, and he says it doesn't look anything like him, but we kept the name anyhow."

Badahir cleared her throat loudly and the boy swung his attention back to her as she raised her sword, pointing the tip at Ivasik's chest.

"Now, this is a practice sword and that is a practice dummy," she explained. "You'll find that if, and when, you close with a real opponent the resistance may be quite different depending on what kind of armor they may be wearing. However, with the battle lust on you and the God's power coursing through your veins, you may not even realize you've thrust." She slashed at the dummy's midsection and Aptulli gasped, clutching her delos-drum to her chest. "In this place you're both powerful and vulnerable," Badahir continued. "That's where practice comes in so that instinct immediately prepares you and your weapon for another attack." Continuing the movement, she snapped the blade sideways and stepped forward with it raised to strike once more. "Otherwise you may never feel the enemy's strike either, and then . . ." She looked pointedly around and Hadir's hand shot into the air.

"You die," he stated emphatically.

"You die," Badahir repeated. "But if you pay attention, *Ekrubin-Delin*, your enemy will die instead."

The boy started guiltily, dropping the handful of pebbles he'd collected as the others snickered.

"Now, generally the young have the advantage of speed and flexibility, the old, the advantage of power," Badahir continued. "So let's see where we all fit in with that. Who wants to go first?" She made a show of glancing around as half a dozen hands began to wave. "How about you, Brax. Let's see what our Kemin has taught you, eh? Give Ivasik a mighty whack there."

With all eyes staring curiously at him, Brax stood, pulled his sword and, feeling the God's power suddenly rise in anticipation, screamed as loud as he could and threw himself at the practice dummy, dealing it a blow that would have decapitated it if the force of his attack hadn't sent them both hurling to the ground. A great puff of straw and dust exploded all around them as they landed.

The gathered stared at him, openmouthed, as he disentangled himself. Rising with a scowl that dared any of them to say anything, he sheathed his sword, and after a moment, Badahir cleared her throat.

"As I was saying, the old *generally* have the advantage of power." She paused, but when Brax simply glared at her, she shrugged. "Generally."

Coval chuckled. Lifting the dummy, he began to stuff the straw back through the split seam in its throat. "It was a good strike," he allowed with a smile as Brax began to help him with the repairs.

"Yes," Badahir agreed. "The enemy is definitely down, but this might be a good time to talk about control. Without it, you're also vulnerable. And on the ground," she added unable to resist the comment. Brax scowled but said nothing. "With it, you're unassailable; control yourself and you control your opponent."

"If Brax came at me like that, I don't think I could control my bladder," Ekrubi pronounced with a laugh.

Badahir raised one dark eyebrow at him. "Well, then I suggest you stay on his good side, Delin," she suggested. "And how about you go next? See if you can hit the enemy without crushing him into the dust."

As the younger boy jumped up and advanced on the dummy with a feral grin, Brax threw himself down beside Spar. The pressure of the God's awakened passion buzzed through his body like a thousand bees, making it difficult to sit still and, as he watched Ekrubi aim a wobbly slash at the dummy's chest, he grinned to himself. Control or not, he was definitely catching up to the delinkon his own age. Sooner or later, they would have to take his promise to Estavia seriously.

Deep within him, the God thrummed Her agreement.

✦

An hour later, Badahir called a halt to the afternoon's training. Every one of the children'd had a chance to take out their fear and trepidation on Ivasik, and it was with a buoyant air that they scattered toward their various homes for supper. Ekrubi aimed a swing at Brax, then ran in mock terror as the other boy advanced on him, while Hieson and Arrian chased Hadir from the courtyard shouting out that they were going to steal his livestock. Even Spar unbent enough to allow Aptulli to show him a new rhythm for his drum, but as they passed within sight of the wall, his attention returned inexorably toward it, his expression grim. Beside him, Brax just rolled his eyes.

✦

The next evening, however, as the two of them took up their usual position on the battlements, Brax was more concerned. Spar had become increasingly subdued all that morning, refusing to acknowledge anyone who spoke to him and glaring at Brax when he'd caustically asked what kind of flea was climbing up his arse. He'd disappeared with Jaq right after the noon meal, missed training, and only reappeared just before supper, but had refused to talk about it. Knowing that he would eventually spill whatever was bothering him, Brax had waited him out and, after stuffing his face as if he hadn't eaten in three days, Spar'd finally jerked his head toward the tower. They'd slipped away, managing to avoid the cleanup even with Jaq tagging along behind them.

Now, Brax leaned his elbows against the parapet, waiting for the other boy to speak, but after a long silence, glanced over at him. Spar was staring out at the wall, his expression fearful.

Brax frowned.

"Spar?"

When he didn't answer, Brax touched him lightly on the arm, scowling down at Jaq as the dog whined at him.

"C'mon Spar, what is it? What's wrong?"

The younger boy took a deep breath. "Something's different," he whispered.

Brax turned to stare at the wall but could see nothing unusual. "How?"

Spar frowned. "I don't know, just different," he replied vaguely. "It's changed. Something's changed it."

"Some *thing?* Like a God maybe?"

Spar shook his head, his face twisted into a grimace of frustration. "No. I don't know. I can't . . . *see* it." He turned suddenly, his blue eyes gone a frighteningly misty white, and Brax felt a chill run up his spine. "Something's happening," he said softly.

"Something."

Spar nodded. "Something big." He pointed out past the wall at the distant horizon. "Out there."

Beyond the wall something moved under his regard, then slipped away.

"Out there. Somewhere."

✦

"WHERE WILL IT BE?"
  "Somewhere."
"SOMEWHERE WHERE?"
  "Somewhere near."
"SOMEWHERE NEAR WHERE. TELL ME."
  "Later."
"WHY LATER?"
  "Because now's not the time to speak of it."
"WHY NOT?"
  "Because there are too many ears listening and too many eyes watching now."
"WHEN WON'T THERE BE?"
  "Soon. Very soon."

✦

Hidden deep in one of the many crevices of the Berbat-Dunya's western ridges—just as Hadzi had supposed—Graize and the growing army of Yuruk stopped for the night. While the elders raised the tents and the youngsters tended the ponies, Rayne and Caleb took their new wyrdin with them to find water. Setting their bows carefully to one side, they began to fill a number of waterskins from a thin, winding stream, one of the many, both above and below ground, that fed Gol-Beyaz far to the east. Graize could feel its tiny allotment of power flowing past him like a school of silvery hamsi fish and, bringing a dripping handful to his mouth, he sipped at the chill, living water, then tossed the rest into the air. The spirits around him snapped at the droplets like so many greedy seagulls while, high above, the Godling watched hungrily, waiting with poorly concealed impatience for Its own time to feed.

✦

"When will it be?"
  "When will what be?"

✦

Graize returned his attention to the water, casually deflecting the unfamiliar thread of power that rippled past him on the breeze, his expression drawing inward as he recognized its source. The Battle God's seers had discovered the place of attack some days ago—as he'd known they would; they weren't completely blind after all—but not the time nor the size of the attack force. They'd been seeking the kazakin with all their might ever since; the spirits could feel their movements and had passed their feeling along to Graize, but Danjel had led them along a secret silvery path of power, hidden from all eyes save those born to the wild lands themselves. The seers would remain blind for as long as Graize wanted them to be. After that, his only fear was that they might remain blind past the time he needed them to see, but the northern sorcerer would help him with that whether he wanted to or not. Baring his teeth at the sky in a grimace of anticipation, Graize licked his lips. The Godling had shown him that possibility hiding behind the clouds this morning. The northern sorcerer would tell Spar and Spar would tell the others. Who'd have thought he'd ever see that particular little dockyard rat again.

The memory of the younger boy, eyes wide with shock and fear as Graize was snatched away from him by a host of blood-maddened spirits, caused his thoughts to suddenly spiral down into a swirling mist of bewilderment and uncertainty. Spar was dead, wasn't he? Sucked dry by the very same spirits that had murdered Drove? How could he be hiding behind a veil of mist and clouds if he was dead? And if he was there, who else might be hiding there beside him?

The faintest outline of a half-remembered dark-haired figure began to take form, and Graize shook his head savagely. No. He would not see that one. The past was only necessary to drive the future and his fellow lifters existed only in the past. If Spar truly lived, then he was the only one to have survived that terrible night intact. Graize would see to it that he didn't survive too many more.

Reaching into the pouch at his belt, he brought out his badly damaged stag beetle, stroking its cracked carapace to soothe his mind as he told the Godling to take the images away. He would not think of the others and they would not think of him. The game was all that mattered; the game and the moves necessary to win it.

As his thoughts stilled, he reached out confidently. The first move began to form in his mind with an almost painfully clear, crystal clarity, then a shimmering pattern of sun and shadow dappled across his vision, causing his thoughts to scatter once again and he snapped his teeth together in irritation.

"Now what?"

He glanced up with a frown to see Danjel standing over him, a lacquered hide and iron helmet in one hand, a wineskin in the other. Smiling at Graize's annoyed expression, the other wyrdin silently held out the wineskin.

Graize set the stag beetle to one side with a sigh. Ordinarily, he found comfort and even focus in the older youth's presence; however, the long trek through the Berbat-Dunya's powerful heartland had brought Danjel closer to a truly bi-gendered form than ever before and the change was unstable. The constant ebb and flow from male to female was making it harder and harder to see him. See her. See Danjel. Accepting the wineskin, Graize fixed the other youth with a narrow-eyed stare.

"You're blocking my view of the river, Kardos," he growled, "either choose a sail or stay in dock, but this back-and-forth tacking is making me seasick."

Features shifting obligingly closer to the female, Danjel dropped down beside him, pulling off her riding boots and dipping her feet into the water before bringing her bright green eyes to bear on Graize's face.

"What are you doing?" she demanded as the younger wyrdin took a drink, then tossed the wineskin to Rayne and opened a goatskin bag he'd been carrying since they'd left their spring encampment.

"Creating the future," Graize answered, dumping the contents out onto the ground.

"With turtle shells?"

"Yes, with turtle shells. Caleb collected them for me before we left," he said gesturing at the younger boy, who gave Danjel a smug smile.

"Why turtle shells?"

"Because turtles carry all possible futures with them in their travels. They carry them in their shells." Graize stroked the pile gently with his fingertips, his expression distant. "And what are they for, Kardos?" he asked suddenly, mimicking Danjel's modulated accent.

The older youth frowned at him. "Well, *children* use them to shovel sand," she sneered, "adults make them into bowls."

"Indeed; bowls to carry shoveled sand in."

Danjel shook her head impatiently. "Bowls to hold humus or yo-gurt in."

Graize shook his head. "Oh, no; bowls to hold the *future* in. Re-member they're *turtle* shells." Laying each shell in a line along the water's edge, he turned them so that the older wyrdin could see the sym-bols he'd etched inside each one. "Turtle shells carrying a future of sand and sea and land and stone and power and . . ." he paused, watching the lights spin lazily above his head.

Beside him, Rayne jabbed him with her elbow. "And?" she prodded, passing the wineskin back to Danjel despite Caleb's protest.

"And death, little marten," Graize finished. Taking up the stag bee-tle between finger and thumb, he touched it to each shell in a parody of walking. "The death of all our enemies," he purred.

"I like the sound of that," Caleb chuckled, mollified by the thought of battle.

"Mm-hm. However," Graize raised one warning finger, "there are nasty little traps everywhere that our turtle-future might still fall into," he added, his expression darkening. "Nasty little traps with nasty little spies hiding inside them, like sneaky little crabs waiting to eat our turtle."

Danjel paused, the wineskin half lifted to her mouth. "Spies?" she asked with a frown.

Graize nodded sagely. "Mind spies," he answered, touching one fin-ger to his temple.

"You mean the Anavatanon seers?"

"Them and others, too."

"Oh, right, your northern sorcerer." Danjel finished her drink and Graize watched as the thin rivulets of power in the wine trickled down the smooth length of her throat, wondering idly if she ever needed to shave or if whiskers were too far toward the male for her to manage even when she was . . . a he. He would have to ask her someday. Some day when it mattered.

The image of another, golden-haired, woman fluttered across his thoughts like a butterfly and he brushed it aside impatiently. Golden hair was not in his future. Not in that way anyhow.

"Yes, my northern sorcerer," he agreed. "He's spied on our plans and then he's told someone else." Spar's face swam in front of his mind's eye. "A little baby spy," he continued with a sneer, waving his hand to banish it. "And that baby spy's probably told the others, told the spies of Estavia. But it doesn't matter because they aren't the right kind of spies, anyway." He reached up to run his fingers through his ever present host of spirits. "There are two kinds of spies, aren't there, my shiny ones," he crooned at them as they rubbed lovingly along his knuckles. "The first is the simplest: the kind that spies on the land and on the people." He cocked his head to one side, his expression sly. "You're that kind of spy, my sleek and lovely swallow-kardos."

Danjel frowned at him but Graize continued. "Most of the Lake Gods' spies are that kind, too. They spy on the enemy, and on the enemy's movements. They have spies right now whose only job it is to spy on us."

"Yes, you said they would," she commented.

"I did."

"And that it didn't matter."

"It doesn't."

"And that you would tell Timur why before Kursk agreed to commit our people to battle."

"And so I will."

"So is it time?"

"Almost."

"What do we do in the meantime?"

"Rest. Eat. Sleep."

"I think we have that covered. And the seers, the spies?"

"They'll likely do the same."

"And they don't worry you because they're not the right kind of spies?"

"Them?" Graize chuckled, lifting one of the turtle shells up to eye level. "They don't worry me because they're nothing. They're like minnows swimming behind a whale; all they'll ever see is its tail."

Rayne rolled her eyes at the analogy, but Graize just smiled at her. "The other kind of spy is a very special kind," he continued. "They're different. They don't spy on people, they spy on the bright and bubbling streams that feed the future and they see far more than the tail. They might even see the turtle if they look very, very closely, but they don't worry me either because they aren't likely to tell the little minnow spies even if they do see it because most of the special spies worship the whale."

Rayne grimaced impatiently at him. "What?"

"Incasa, the God of Chance," Graize explained.

"I thought He was the God of Prophecy."

Waggling the beetle in her face, Graize shook his head. "They're one and the same says my little birth fetish here. All prophecy does is spy on multiple streams and figure out which one is the most likely. And little birth fetish says that the problem is that if these very special spies can spy on your mind, then all the streams you might consider sailing down are being watched." He cocked his head to one side with a sly expression. "Or are they? If the mind is mad, how could they ever make sense of any of it, especially if that mad mind also has a cunning plan, a cunning little beetle's plan." His right pupil drew inward until it was nothing more than a tiny pinprick, then snapped back out again. "Supposing you were planning an attack but you knew the enemy would find out about it? What would you do?" he asked suddenly.

Caleb straightened. "Make it a feint," he said eagerly. "Send the main body somewhere else."

Graize grinned mirthlessly. "Simple, isn't it? Just like in a shell game. Which one has the pea under it? Only the one running the game knows for sure and the trick is to make the mark look somewhere else for it. Battle tactics are no different; you make the enemy look somewhere other than where the pea is."

"Is that what we're doing?" Caleb asked.

"Maybe." Graize formed the turtle shells into a wide oval pattern. "Pretty little possibilities," he whispered, "all sitting so cozy and warm around a bright and shiny center.

"The far eastern streams are out," he said, sweeping four of them away abruptly. "How would you cross Gol-Beyaz without being seen—and the Yuruk are notoriously fearful of boats, anyway."

Caleb bridled, his hand dropping to the pommel of his kinjal. "We're not fearful," he growled.

"Are, too."

As Caleb made to argue, Rayne reached over and casually swatted him in the back of the head. "Be quiet," she ordered, "or we'll never get through this."

"Besides, what kind of spoils do they offer even if we could get there," Graize continued, ignoring them both. "Calmak-Koy is full of sick people—what use are they? Adasi and Camus-Koy are mostly pots and goats—we have plenty of pots and goats."

"And bowls," Danjel noted dryly.

"Shh. Caliskan-Koy's tower, Kapi-Hisar, guards the strait from the Deniz-Hadi Sea so it's far too strong," Graize mused, more to himself than to the other youth. "And how would you ever take Satos-Koy with its mighty Anahtar-Hisar standing so straight and tall above the world. No, it's out, too." He flicked the southernmost shells away. "So let's go north. I hear Bahce-Koy's beautiful this time of year, just bursting with fruits and flowers," he said in a mocking voice heavy with what the Yuruk might have recognized as a Western Trisect merchant's accent if they'd ever walked the streets of Anavatan's many markets. "And it's such a pretty little village and so close, so very close . . ." Graize paused, one hand raised. "No." He swept the northernmost shell away too. "It's also so very close to the shining city with all its nasty little warriors. That leaves six." He peered down almost myopically as if he couldn't quite see them all. "Wait, five," he amended, his eyes clearing. "Yildiz-Koy can't count, can it? *After all, It's just a feint.*" He giggled suddenly, happy to finally voice the main thrust of his plan. "Yes, pretty little Yildiz-Koy all bright and sparkly, like a pear made out of crystal. Send enough people to take a bite of it, but don't eat the entire pear or there'll be none left for later." He very carefully picked up the central shell and set it to one side, away from the carelessly flung pile. "That would be greedy, especially with all those armed and ready gardeners waiting for us. So, that leaves Sardiz-Koy to the north, and Serin, Kepek, Kinor, and Ekmir-Koy to the south. All on this side of the lake, all rich, and all worth the risk."

"Ekmir's very close to Anahtar-Hisar," Danjel noted, "and it's stuck out in a kind of peninsula. We could get trapped there."

"And it's too far away for an orchestrated attack with Yildiz-Koy, anyway," Rayne added.

"Likewise Kinor-Koy."

"Indeed." Two more shells were flung onto the discard pile.

"Sardiz-Koy or Serin-Koy seem the best choices," Danjel noted. "They're on either side of Yildiz-Koy. Close enough for the orchestrated attack."

"True, but we need Kepek-Koy to keep the streams from silting up,"

Graize answered, "and to keep the spies confused by the number of possible peas under the shells, so we have to consider it seriously."

"Very well. Um . . . It shares the protection of Orzin-Hisar but sits farther south, so it would take some time to rally the garrison to its defense. That's all I can think of to recommend it."

As Graize remained silent, staring down at the three remaining shells, Rayne cocked her head to one side. "So which is it going to be, Kardos?"

Graize smiled. Turning the shells onto their faces, he began to move them about in a complicated three-way figure eight. "Which one, which one, which one has the pea beneath it," he murmured to himself. "Place your shine; place your shine, which one, which one. Swallows and martens and mousies and minnows all want to know which one." Abruptly he gathered them up. "If the seers of Incasa are watching, all they'll see is three streams, equally navigable." Lifting the one he'd set aside, he placed it in between. "And one certainty: Yildiz-Koy. By the time they realize what that certainty really is a certainty of, it'll be far too late. And who knows, their God might even keep them in the dark. Incasa's an unpredictable old bastard and He likes to hide His peas. Even from His other peas," he added, the image making him giggle.

Danjel frowned at him. "How do you know that?" she asked, refusing to be distracted by the flow of words.

"Because He saved me that night above the Berbat-Dunya, and it would have been a much better idea to let me die," Graize said, a dark light gleaming in his pale eyes. So I'm a pea, too, but what kind of a pea? That's the question." He closed his eyes, lifting his face to the evening breeze. "I felt my death as clearly as if I'd fallen into ice water so cold it burned my flesh instead of freezing it," he said in a singsong tone. "I fought it, but it was too strong." His voice hushed. "Too strong. But then I saw a great pair of dice hurtling toward me." He opened his eyes. "They came up life and I lived."

"The God claimed you? You didn't tell us that before."

Graize shook his head. "Gods don't claim, They accept. No, He just saved me so that He could see what was going to happen next: destruction or creation, it could go either way. Like I said, he's an unpredictable old bastard."

"So, should you really be talking about Him like that?" Caleb asked, unable to stop from glancing over his shoulder.

Graize shrugged. "Why would He care? He's a God."

"What about your northern sorcerer," Danjel pressed, "and the—what did you call it—baby spy? What if they find out?"

Graize gave her a chilly, almost death's-head grin. "Oh, I hope they do find out, I really do. In fact, I might tell them myself. The one with his smug superiority and his certainty that all things are going his way instead of mine, I want him to know when it's too late and he realizes that I've won this round of the game. Because it's *my* game. And as for the baby spy, he's so far out of his depth he could drown in a bucket of water. And he just might." Graize's eyes widened as the Godling, eager to add its two cents' worth, whispered the image of Spar standing on the battlements of Orzin-Hisar through his mind, and another: himself, bow in hand, standing above the dark-haired figure of his dreams who lay clouded by death. "Yes, he just might indeed. Let's do that. Let's make *something happen*." He laughed out loud, beckoning the Godling toward him. As It swarmed joyously around his head, covering him in a mist of silver-white power, Graize pulled a shell from the four in his hand and pressed it into Danjel's palm without bothering to look at it, then caught up his bow. "Find Timur. Tell her that, with their approval, of course," he added with a deep, almost sarcastic bow, "the kazakin have a new destination, one rare and ripe and ready for the plucking."

All three youths looked down at the unfamiliar symbol etching into the shell. "So, which one is it, Kardos?" Rayne asked.

Catching up his bow, Graize laughed harshly.

"Serin-Koy, little marten," he answered. "And we're going to take a very big bite from it."

12

Serin-Koy

"GHAZI?"

Kemal opened his eyes to see Birin-Kaptin Arjion's delinkos bending over him in the darkness, face illuminated by a small lamp held in one hand. He blinked.

"Brin?"

"There's word from Kaptin Liel, Ghazi. The enemy's been sighted in vision. They'll make their attack at sunrise."

"Which is in?"

"Three hours' time, Ghazi. All commanders are to get their people into position at once."

Kemal nodded fuzzily. "At once." He twisted about to poke his arkados in the back. "Yash. Up. Battle."

As the older man grunted incoherently, then continued to snore, Kemal turned back to Brin.

"Food?"

"Is coming, Ghazi."

The youth withdrew and Kemal bent over Yashar's ear, cupping his hands around his mouth. "Yash!" he shouted.

The older man jerked up into a sitting position. "What?"

"War. Get up." Fumbling for his tunic, he ignored the other man's snarled response. In the seven years they'd been together, he'd seen Yashar greet a predawn formation with pleasure exactly . . . never. He'd be all right once the sun came up and he could actually see the enemy. Probably.

A short time later, fed and warded, he helped Yashar settle his leather-and-iron-studded cuirass more comfortably across his shoulders, the two silver swords of Cyan Company worked into the front, gleaming in the lamplight.

"The delinkon could have come in handy today," his arkados groused as Kemal wrapped Yashar's belt around his waist, fastening the heavy iron buckle with the ease of long familiarity.

"You know we never could have kept Brax away from battle," the younger man answered. "They're safer at Serin-Koy. For that matter, so is Jaq." Kneeling, he fastened Yashar's bronze greaves about his legs. "Besides, we've never had delinkon before." He glanced up at the other man with a suggestive smile. "And we've always managed."

"*You've* always managed," Yashar argued, refusing to be mollified as he pulled a small stone from the sole of one sandal. "I go into battle with my vambraces too loose and my helmet strap too tight."

"Be thankful it's not the other way around." Catching up the other man's sword, Kemal slid it into its place within the shallow cavity in his shield. Then, after placing it beside his spear and bow, he took up Yashar's cloak, allowing the heavy blue wool to spill out between his fingers. Fastening it to the older man's throat with a heavy pin in the shape of a boat, he then stood back to survey the effect. "You took terrifying," he noted.

"I feel it." Hefting Kemal's cuirass in turn, Yashar straightened one of the shoulder straps before holding it up. "Come. Time to become terrifying yourself."

✦

Eventually, when they were both armored to the other's satisfaction, they caught up their weapons and helmets and joined the lines of the warriors streaming from their own billets into the night. Kemal took a deep breath, staring up at the stars with a smile. "Good morning for a fight," he observed.

"What morning?" Yashar groused. "The moon's still carousing in the sky."

"You can smell it coming on the breeze." He took another deep breath. "It will be cool and clear today."

"I'm thrilled to hear it. Azmir!" Yashar gestured at a delinkos running past them. "Find coffee!"

"Yes, Ghazi!" She changed direction at once, darting off toward the makeshift commissary in the village square as Kemal shot his arkados a reproachful glance.

"You could have gone yourself," he chided.

"I have troops to shout at."

"Ah, yes. Well, there they are, all ready for you." He pointed to a knot of Cyan Company standing with the muster from Caliskan-Koy, their silver fishing boat standard snapping smartly in the breeze.

Yashar grinned. Catching Kemal by the chin, he kissed him fiercely. "The God give strength to your sword," he growled, then turned and stumped over toward his command before the younger man could answer.

Kemal watched him go with a smile. "And yours," he whispered, then jerked his head toward Serin-Koy's militia kaptin, his kuzos Duwan. The woman fell into step beside him, gesturing to the others who followed them toward the God-Wall and the darkened fields beyond.

The path between the sown fields was narrow, the grasses to either side wiping across their legs to leave wet stripes along their greaves. As they took their positions, Kemal glanced past Serin-Koy's sheep's horn standard at the four contingents of temple infantry and their militia support silently moving into the traditional three-line rows; in this case between the first two sets of pasture and grain fields stretching from the southern livestock paddocks at Kumas-Hisar to the northern fishing huts at the far end of Yildiz-Koy. The mounted archer companies with their accompanying militia cavalry would be lining up on the flanks, leaving the temple cavalry free to maneuver, while the village militia would stand behind the God-Wall beside the battle-seers—both theirs and Sable Company's—as the last line of defense.

But they wouldn't be needed. Not today.

As Duwan maneuvered their own troops into line, Kemal turned to stare at the dark, western hillsides in the distance. He'd been fighting the Yuruk his entire life and it was always the same. They'd come streaming through the breaks in the hills, screaming and whistling their strange battle orders, carrying torches to light their arrows, and using what spirits of the wild lands they could coerce to their command to obscure their attack. They would swarm forward in a wave of flashing hooves, then break into individual streams; some to pepper the defending flanks with arrow fire, then wheel off to turn, regroup, and attack again; always trying to weaken their foe bit by bit, to lure some small company away from the protection of the line to be destroyed; others to work their way around to the flocks and herds. The village shepherds would scramble to bring whatever livestock they could to the safety of their tower's walled paddocks, aided by whatever mounted cavalry they could muster, the noncombatants would flee for the tower, and the militia would take up position behind the God-Wall. If they had warriors with them, the warriors would stand before them to absorb the brunt of the assault, archers answering the enemy fire with barrages of their own, aiming into the darkness with the help of the battle-seers; then cavalry charging forward in a wedge to herd the enemy toward the entrenched infantry. If they were alone, they would stand behind the God-Wall and answer barrage with barrage, strike with strike, until the Yuruk broke off the attack and the village could stand down.

Today would be no different.

Turning, Kemal watched the steady stream of lamplights bobbing in the misty darkness as Yildiz-Koy's priests guided the young and the old to the safety of Kumas-Hisar while the delinkon ran back and forth from the village well, hurrying to fill the many buckets of water needed to douse any fires set by the enemy. One youngster, staggering under the weight of a bucket almost as large as he was, called for help and Kemal smiled as two of the boy's kardon ran to assist him.

He remembered how proud he'd been when Bayard had entrusted him with this important duty at age eleven. The buckets had been heavy and awkward and he'd splashed more down his legs then he'd carried, but by thirteen he was leading the brigades that protected the storage barns. At fifteen, he'd stood with Badahir behind the God-Wall, listening to the sounds of arrow fire slicing through the air and the rhythmic thunking as the first barrage fell short. He remembered the invocation of Serin-Koy's priests of Estavia calling on the Battle God to come and fight with them, and the awe and fearsome triumph he'd felt the first time he'd watched Her explode into being before them. He'd almost gone over the God-Wall after Her and would have if Badahir hadn't caught him by the back of his cuirass and hauled him back.

✦

"Estavia favors him. She likes the combative ones."

A sudden pang of guilt made him wince as the memory brought up Yashar's words about Brax. Perhaps they should have brought him to Yildiz-Koy, he thought. He was more than old enough to carry buckets and he would have been in no more danger than any other village delinkos. It might have been good for him, taught him to behave as part of a team: the value of planning, and of keeping a clear head in the midst of chaos and danger. Perhaps they'd done both him and the Battle God a disservice by being so cautious.

"The Warriors of Estavia are not a collection of individual champions, we're an army; we're soldiers. To take you out of that hierarchy could hamper your ability to work within it and you're already far too self-centered for the council's liking."

And wasn't that exactly what they'd done, his thoughts continued, pulled him out of that hierarchy and trained him like a champion and not a like soldier? And what kind of champion could he possibly be if he had no knowledge of working as a unit? No knowledge of actually being a soldier?

"I told Her I would fight for Her."

Driving the butt of his spear into the ground, Kemal shook his head impatiently, telling himself firmly that they'd made the right choice. If Brax were with them today, he might begin by carrying buckets, but once battle commenced he'd be drawn into the thick of it, driven by his oath to fight for the God who'd saved his life, regardless of his orders. And he'd be killed. He was better off at Serin-Koy. If the God had other plans for his future, She would make that plain. But for now, he was safe and Kemal had other things to concentrate on. Leaning against his spear, he locked his knees and, closing his eyes, willed his mind to a state of calm preparation for battle.

✦

"Seer!"

The priests of Havo had barely begun to sing the dawn when the call went up, carried along the lines of infantry to the commanders at the rear. The small, black-clad scout galloping from the hills west of Yildiz-Koy didn't even pause as the lines opened in a ripple of movement to let her pass, then closed behind her again.

"Seer!"

The second scout was spotted a moment later. Like the first, he raced through the lines and disappeared, engulfed by a moving bubble of clear passage. Once he'd passed Cyan Company, Kemal set his helmet on his head, tightened his chin strap, then strung his bow. Around him, the others did the same at Duwan's command, and after a swift glance to the right and left, Kemal nodded in satisfaction, then swung his attention back to the western hills. It would be soon.

He felt rather than heard Sable Company begin the invocation that would ready Estavia. Closing his eyes, he imagined Kaptin Liel—androgynous features softened by the flow of pure power—surrounded by a dozen battle-seers, their swords raised and pointed toward Gol-Beyaz. When the seer kaptin's first call came as a single, high tenor note of obligation, it rippled through his thoughts like the thread of a familiar dream, stirring Estavia's lien within him, drawing his head up, and peeling his lips back from his teeth in an anticipatory grimace. The second call—a modulated harmony of battle-seers promising victory and violence—tightened his fingers around his weapons as it sizzled through his veins. The third—a call to arms—drew a note of response from his own throat which merged with the unit commanders to become a single voice swearing allegiance and obedience. Kaptin Liel reached out to gather them up into one large, cohesive mental force and, as the final call rose from every throat on the battlefield to become one long, undulating chord of strength and supplication, it spread across the surface of Gol-Beyaz like a heavy mist.

Deep within the Lake of Power, Estavia began to stir and as one, Her warriors turned to the shimmer of sunrise on the distant hills.

When the attack came, they were ready for it.

✦

At Serin-Koy, standing in his usual place atop Orzin-Hisar, Spar frowned, turning his head from side to side as if testing the predawn air like a nervous dog trying to catch a scent, his well-honed sense of danger making the hair on the back of his neck rise. To the east, the sun touched the sky above the dark, pine-covered slopes of the Degisken-Dag Mountains with the faintest of pale brush strokes which traced themselves across Gol-Beyaz to merge with the pink-and-orange glow rising from below. To the west, the God-Wall faithfully reproduced the bright colors of the lake's emerging power while beyond it, the fields sparkled with dew and the distant hills showed a glimmer of green. Behind him on the battlements—to the south as it happened to be— Serin-Koy's priests of Havo took their places, preparing to answer the blackbirds and finches already in full song and to call the village to wakefulness. But to the north, the faintest hint of lightning skipped across the sky, causing his newly strengthened abilities to buzz irritably in response. As he peered into the gloom, the northern fields shimmered like slivery-gray puddles reflecting a cloudy sky—shimmered with the movement of horses and standards—and he nodded in understanding.

Yildiz-Koy.

Beside him Jaq began to whine and he reached down to lay his hand on his head.

"It's all right," he told him quietly. "The warriors are with Kemal and Yashar. Everything'll be fine."

He never saw Incasa rise silently above the waters of Gol-Beyaz, a frightful purpose in His snow-white eyes, one hand raised above His head.

When the God's vision hit him, he was completely unprepared.

It struck his mind like a physical blow, knocking him against the turreted wall with a cry. Fire rose up all around him, fire carried by dark riders on dark horses, whistling and screaming and racing toward him on the crest of a violent whirlwind. They flowed over the hillsides toward the livestock in the western pasture fields, cutting down the shepherds and their delinkon in a hail of arrow fire. He smelled burning, heard screaming, and, struggling against the fear that threatened to overwhelm his mind, he fought to call up the image of the long, steady lines of warriors he knew were there, ready and able to throw the enemy back beyond the hills. But when a single, familiar face, drawn in terror, swam before his eyes, he fell back in shock. Hieson. Sent to guard the cattle with his kuzon on this warm High Spring night. Sent because it was safe, sent because their enemies were miles away, and suddenly Spar knew: he wasn't seeing a wakeful village guarded by lines of armed and ready defenders strengthened by a God; he was seeing a slumbering village alone, unprepared, and undefended.

He was seeing Serin-Koy.

His head jerked back, hitting the tower wall with an audible crack. Stars spun before his eyes and he tasted blood as his teeth snapped down on the tip of his tongue. Hands clasped over his ears to block the terrifying sounds of battle that overwhelmed his mind, he fought to clear his head; to think, to do *something*, to do *anything*, but the enormity of what he'd just discovered froze him in place. They were going to attack here. *Here.* Attack Bayard and Badahir, Maydir, Aptulli, Paus. And Brax. No one had seen it yet, but they were coming. They might have even reached the outer fields by now. Hieson might already be dead. And *he* should have seen it, he should have known it. All his life he'd known when to run and hide. All his life until now. He'd known something was wrong, but he hadn't known what. Why hadn't he known what? All the signs had been there. A blind beggar could have seen it. He should have seen it. Why hadn't he seen it?

A cold nose shoved itself into his left ear and he grabbed Jaq around the neck, using the animal's solid presence to thrust the shock and growing panic aside. It didn't matter why he hadn't seen it. He saw it now and now was all that mattered. Pulling himself to his feet, he gripped the edge of the battlements and locked his eyes on the empty hillsides beyond the western fields. "So it's a vision," he panted, taking a long, shuddering breath. "A big one, a new one, but just a vision. It's no different than before, not really. Get a grip. There's no one out there yet. It hasn't happened yet. It's gonna happen, but it hasn't happened. Not yet. You've still got time."

Time to do what, the panic hovering just below the surface of his mind demanded.

"Something, anything. *Warn* somebody. Warn Brax. You always warn Brax."

Soothed by the artificially calm sound of his own voice, Spar made to turn, but his feet seemed frozen in place. Cursing himself for a useless baby, he tried to move, but deep down inside, the tiny voice that had always warned him of the approach of danger began to scream in fear as the flames rose up before his mind's eye again, threatening to engulf his mind and he realized for the first time Brax wasn't there.

He smelled burning. Coming closer. Cindar was gone, Brax was gone, and he was all alone.

Slowly his knees gave way beneath him. Pressed against the tower wall, he curled into a tight ball, rocking back and forth as the dying began to scream in his head. It was too much; they were too many. They were going to attack Serin-Koy and he couldn't stop them. He couldn't make an entire village run and hide; he couldn't distract the Yuruk or drive them off. He wasn't a fighter; he wasn't even a seer; he was a lifter. He'd never wanted to be anything else.

But Brax did, he thought suddenly, his practical nature finally winning out over the fear. Even though Brax wasn't right there beside him, Brax wasn't gone, he hadn't left him. Brax was down there in the village, sleeping and unaware of the danger. He had to warn Brax, he always warned Brax, he had to get him to safety; that was his job, that's what he did.

But even as he thought it, he knew Brax wouldn't listen; not this new Brax with a weapon in his hand and Estavia's lien on his life, on his loyalties—on his brain, Spar's thoughts added angrily. Brax would fight. Brax would die. He didn't want his protection anymore. He thought he didn't need it.

But he did need it.

"I see we're in the same quandary as before."

"Shut up!"

Spar lashed out instinctively, striking his fist against the hard stone of Orzin-Hisar as the voice in the faraway tower sounded overloud in his mind. The pain brought him back to himself and he glared angrily into the darkness as he sucked at one scraped knuckle.

The voice gave a murmur of patently false sympathy. *"I've remained silent long enough,"* it replied. *"And now your time has run out. There's too much at stake to let you run and hide up on your rooftops any longer. You have to grow up today, Spar, or the God of Prophecy's going to manipulate you forever."*

> *. . . something flickered past the lamps.*
> *. . . a thousand creatures of power and need pouring into Gol-Beyaz.*
> *. . . a rolling tide of mist and death.*
> *. . . tumbling stones. A choking fog of smoke and dust.*
> *. . . burning . . .*

"Stop it!" Spar almost screamed out loud as the images began to tumble through his mind too fast to comprehend.

"I'm not doing it; you are," the voice snapped back. *"Your mind is wide open, untrained, undefended, and vulnerable to any attack just like that village down there. And it will be attacked if you don't do something right now!"*

"Like what?"

"Like See who your true enemy really is!"

And the vision rose up again as a choking fog of smoke and dust broiling toward him. But then the mist was suddenly blown away and he saw Graize, mounted on a snow-white pony, crest the western hills, a vast cloud of power and potential hovering over him like thunderstorm.

He gaped in astonishment.

Graize?

✦

And riding in the midst of Kursk's lead banner, Graize let out a howl of laughter as he drank in the shock of Spar's understanding as it hit the streams like a boulder flung into the waves. Standing in the saddle, he gave a mocking bow in the direction of Orzin-Hisar, knowing the younger boy could sense it.

"Yes, oh, yes, soon there'll be more than just shock," he shouted at him, sending his hate flying back along the streams of power. *"Soon there'll be panic and screaming and villagers running about in terror like ants around a drowning anthill, and you'll be as powerless to prevent it as you've always been! The spirits'll suck out your eyeballs and throw your body from the ramparts to*

be trampled by my Yuruk; but not before you see me put an arrow in someone's eye and then our precious northern busybody'll know I've beaten you both!"

The sudden image of the dark-haired figure rose up, threatening to send Graize's mind listing to one side and he slapped the image of his stag beetle across it with an impatient gesture. He had no time for madness today and no time for ghosts, no matter how real they might be growing. No time for pathetic little dockside seers either, he sneered. He had a village to attack. With a howl of triumph, he flung one hand forward as Kursk led wave after wave of Yuruk down the hillsides.

✦

Atop Orzin-Hisar, the voice reached out and tore the final shred of protective caul from Spar's latent abilities with a single, savage gesture.

"SEE AND RESPOND!"

And Spar's warning vision spewed from his mind like a pillar of flame.

✦

Across the village, people came screaming to wakefulness as images of fire and death in the hands of the Yuruk exploded across their sleeping minds. In Bayard's main room, the sense of sudden danger slammed into Brax's dreams so hard he awoke with a gasp. His heart pounding in his chest, he stared uncomprehendingly into the darkness. How could the Yuruk be here, he thought fuzzily. They were supposed to be at Yildiz-Koy; all the seers had said so. Turning, he reached out for Spar and found nothing. The pallet was empty.

Sudden danger slamming into his dreams.

Tossing the blanket aside with a curse, he fumbled for his clothes as Bayard's family began shouting and crying in confusion all around him then, after jerking his tunic over his head, he snatched up his weapons and ran for the back door, making for the garden wall without thought for anything but Spar.

✦

Outside, the village was in chaos, people running everywhere while the militia officers shouted for their troops to come together. Above the din, Brax could hear Badahir's calm, distinctive voice calling her people to form up in the central square and he nearly checked at the sound, Estavia's lien demanding a physical response. But he had to find Spar first; he had to know he was all right, then he would fight, he promised, just help him find Spar. The God's presence rose in willing response, compelling him toward Orzin-Hisar and he sprinted for the tower as its great, bronze bell began to toll.

"Be there," he panted. "Just like you've been every morning since we got here. *Be* there."

The tower's stone bulk rose up before him and he rocked to a halt as he caught sight of a small, blond figure standing on the battlements, arms raised awkwardly toward the rising sun as if warding off a blow. He swayed dangerously close to the edge, but just as Brax was about to shout to him, he saw Jaq's great head rear up to catch the younger boy by the back of the jacket and pull him out of sight. Heart in his throat, Brax started for the tower door, but with Spar's safety assured, the Battle God's lien stopped him in his tracks and he nodded in acceptance. Estavia had kept Her word, Spar was safe, now Brax would keep his word, too. Turning, he ran for the streams of militia heading for the village square.

✦

Badahir was shoving the adults into line when he arrived. As soon as they managed a simple cohesion, they made for the God-Wall, bows at the ready, and Brax joined them, his vision already covered with a fine red mist.

"I told Her I would fight for Her."

"And so you will."

The excitement that rose with the memory drove whatever fear he might have been feeling away as they reached the wall, but rather than go over it, to his surprise, the militia began to form a long, thin line behind it. He snapped his teeth together in frustration even though he understood why. The wall was their only real physical defense; they couldn't, and shouldn't, race out to face an unknown enemy; they'd be slaughtered, but everything he was wanted to leap over it anyway.

Pulling back behind the line, he made himself take a deep breath to still the insistent internal itch that kept trying to take control of his sword hand. A good lifter never just leaped over anything, he reminded himself sternly. A good lifter waited patiently for the right opportunity; for the *safe* opportunity to act, ignoring need and greed alike, or he'd get pinched. A good fighter had to be the same, or he'd get *killed* and that would end his service to Estavia before it even began.

"So, stop being an idiot," he growled. "You're Her Champion. Act like one."

Crouching, he drew his fingers through a muddy puddle, bringing them up slowly and deliberately to draw the outlines of the wards he painted every morning on his arms and chest: Anavatan, Estavia-Sarayi, Cyan Company, himself, Spar, Jaq, Kemel and Yasher, and Her Wall; using the familiar movements to still the buzzing in his body. Then, feeling Her lien thrumming through him in approval, he headed back the way he'd come. When he reached the end of the line, he clambered onto the wall where it met Orzin-Hisar and, using the tower's bulk to shield himself from both the militia and the steady streams of noncombatants alike, he peered over at the empty livestock paddocks where a second line of militia were already forming up. A good lifter—and a good fighter—chose the best ground and waited for the mark—the enemy—to come to him, his thoughts continued in a deliberately lecturing tone. And the enemy would come here because although most of Serin-Koy's livestock were out in the western pasture fields he could already see the frightened shepherds driving them back toward the safety of the walled paddocks and that was what the enemy wanted: Serin-Koy's sheep and goats and oxen, even the horses if they could get them. So any attack they made elsewhere was a feint; the *real* attack would be here. Drawing his sword, he pressed the hilt against his chest, feeling the Battle God stir in anticipation of bloodshed and glory.

"I told Her I would fight for Her."

"And so you will."

"And so I will. I swear it."

Taking a deep breath, he peered out at the western fields.

The Yuruk were in sight now, a dark, swirling mass of horses and riders fanning out across the newly planted fields, racing the morning wind. A hail of arrow fire fell short and he heard Badahir shouting for the militia to hold their own fire and not waste their shafts. As a dozen Yuruk peeled off toward the paddocks, a company of mounted villagers leaped over the God-Wall to defend them, and for the first time in his life Brax wished he could ride as the pounding of hooves sounded over-loud in his ears. This close to real combat, the God's lien rose up inside him, and he suddenly felt himself standing on the fields of Yildiz-Koy, lines of infantry and cavalry facing the enemy to either side of him. As they closed, he felt rather than heard the seers' invocation to Estavia.

✦

"God of Battles, I pledge you my strength!"

✦

With the rest of Her people, he felt Her response begin as a grow-ing sense of bloodlust in his veins and a tingling in his hands.

✦

"God of Battles, I pledge you my blood!"

✦

The tingling became an overpowering itch and he clutched at his sword, feeling the far-off ranks prepare to move forward toward the Yuruk.

✦

"God of Battles, I pledge you my worship, my will, my service, and my life!"

✦

Eyes half closed, he felt the God's power compel him forward and he gave himself up to it, leaving the safety of the tower's bulk to stand facing the enemy, sword raised defiantly toward them, the God-Wall's power crackling all around him like lightning.

✦

"God of Battles, come into this world and use me as you will!"

✦

As the need to do battle in Her name swept through his body, he felt Estavia burst into being above Her warriors at Yildiz-Koy just as he re-alized that he'd forgotten his shield.

13

Battle

AS THE SUN ROSE above the eastern peaks of the Degisken-Dag Mountains, the battle for Yildiz-Koy raged across the pasture fields. Filled with the power of Her followers, the God of Battles towered a hundred meters above the village, her twin swords spinning above Her head like wreaths of crackling fire. At Her feet, Kaptin Liel screamed out Her invocation in a voice gone harsh and ragged while the rest of Sable Company directed the power of their kaptin's words up into the waiting arms of their God. As swarms of spirits hurled themselves upon Her like so many tiny leaches, Estavia sucked up a huge mouthful, then spat the transformed energy at the rest in a great gout of flame. It tore through their midst like a brand, scattering as many as it destroyed and opening a path for Bronze Company who thundered forward to drive the attacking Yuruk toward the first line of waiting infantry. Spears planted in the ground, the rear ranks began to chant Estavia's name as the enemy met Azure Company with a crash of steel on steel. A hail of arrow fire streaked toward the militia entrenched behind the God-Wall, but with a howl of laughter that bounced off the distant hills, the Battle God reached out to scoop them out of the air in one sweeping motion, crushing them into powder, before hurling them back at the line of Yuruk leaders standing on the crest of the hills.

On the rise, Danjel sent her own defiant scream back at the Battle God as she called up a new swarm of spirits to throw themselves at Her while beside her, Ayami's high-pitched whistle sent a new wave of Yuruk streaking down the hillsides. They surged forward then split into a dozen lines which streamed around the Battle God like water. Another whistle and those lines split again, some making for walled paddocks, others for the storage sheds, and still more to lure the more heavily armored cavalry away from the supporting infantry. Behind her, Danjel called up another swarm of spirits to obscure their movements and, as Estavia left the village proper to give chase in greedy anticipation, she sent a triumphant thread of power flying toward her fellow wyrdin-kazak on the hills above Serin-Koy.

✦

From his vantage point above the village, Graize accepted Danjel's message with a laugh and, lips drawn back from his teeth in a savage grin, threw a great swarm of his own spirits forward. With no God to stop them, the very first wave had already reached the Wall, hitting it like a storm, but slamming back again just as quickly. They'd begun to batter at it with frantic intensity as more and more of their numbers streamed forward on a tide of rage and need, but as always the Wall held firm. Above him, Graize could feel the Godling growing impatient.

"Soon, very soon," he promised. "Let the spirits weaken it a little first, then it'll be your time. And mine."

Turning, he watched as Kursk brought a fresh wave of Rus and Wes-Yuruk together for another assault against the militia guarding the storage sheds. He could almost feel the defenders bracing to take the hit and he sneered down at them contemptuously. They were so thinly strung out along the God-Wall that they would be vulnerable to any concentrated attack, but with so few fighters remaining in Serin-Koy, they could do little else; pool their defenses in one spot and the Yuruk would simply attack elsewhere; all they could do was dig in and hope that their numbers would hold out longer than their enemies' numbers. It was the traditional defense against the Yuruk's traditional wide-sweeping hit-and-run attack, and it usually worked. But not today.

With a snicker, Graize sent another swarm of spirits streaking out before Kursk's lead banner. Today the Yuruk had numbers to spare and, as soon as the village militia was weakened enough, they would form up into one highly *untraditional* wedge and smash their way through the defenders at the walled paddocks like a rock slide over a flower garden and one single defender would get the final shock of his very short life. Then he would no longer hover above Graize's dreams

and plans like some dark-eyed storm cloud. Stroking his fingers along
his bowstring, the Yuruk's new wyrdin-kazak gave a mocking salute in
Brax's direction, before gathering up yet another swarm of spirits to
throw at Serin-Koy.

✦

Unaware of his old enemy's presence, Brax set an arrow to his bow and
drew it back, trying to remember not to let the string hit his forearm
when he released it. With only a few weeks of training he doubted he'd
hit anything else that morning, but it hadn't mattered; the God's lien
sang in his veins so loudly that he could hardly focus enough to aim the
weapon anyway. As a new wave of Yuruk charged forward, he fired up
and over the paddock wall, then caught up another arrow as they passed.
The deadly whistle of returning fire dropped him almost instinctively,
but not before a feathered shaft hit the wall above his head with a shower
of dust and stone. Eyes narrowed, he snatched it off the ground and, fitting it to his bowstring, rose and fired it back. The sound of a muffled
scream made him bare his teeth in derision, and drawn by his aggres-
sion, the God's lien began to rise even higher as, beside him all along the
wall, Serin-Koy's battle-seers began a fresh Invocation to Estavia; calling on the God of Battles to bring them strength as they had since the
attack had begun. Brax had no idea how She could manage to support
both Yildiz and Serin-Koy, but he was grateful for the responding spike
of energy that shot through his body every time they started singing.
Early on, the force of Her lien had driven him into the line of entrenched militia, and he could feel a growing fatigue begin to eat away
at his reserves; the only thing holding it at bay was Her will. As yet another wave of Yuruk thundered forward, he fitted a new arrow to his
bowstring and, as the battle-seers began to scream Estavia's name once
more, he allowed the now familiar surge of energy to lift him to his feet
again.

✦

The fighting continued throughout the day. Wave after wave of Yuruk
riders charged the village of Serin-Koy and, by noon, hand-to-hand
fighting had broken out all along the God-Wall. Despite the battle-
seers' efforts, gaps began to appear in the lines as, hopelessly outnum-

bered, the defenders began to crumble. As the sun dipped toward the western mountains, the Yuruk finally broke the line at the storage sheds. Villagers scattered before a full banner of torch-carrying riders that surged over the wall, cutting down anyone who stood against them. Exhausted militia hurried to close the breach, but it was too late; one by one, the buildings went up in flames.

✦

On the rise, Graize gave the signal and standing in the saddle, Rayne swept her yak's tail standard up in a great arc, calling the banners of the Khes-Yuruk waiting in reserve forward into battle. As they thundered over the hills, whistles sounded across the field, and the engaged kazakin of the Rus, Wes, and Irmak-Yuruk now flowed together to form one solid wedge that drove itself toward the paddocks and the thin line of militia guarding the herds of frightened livestock. The heavy wooden gates held for less then a moment, then splintered inward and the kazakin surged inside, some making straight for the defenders, while others began to drive the flocks and herds out into the fields.

✦

Long out of arrows, Brax hurled a fist-sized rock at the head of the rider barreling down on him, then snatched up his sword and vaulted onto the wall. The man swung a huge, curved blade toward him and Brax ducked instinctively, nearly toppling over backward as the weapon whistled over his head. He struck back and missed and then the enemy's blade was streaking toward him again, moving unbelievably fast. He barely got his own sword, two-handed, up in time. As the weapons connected with a clash of steel, he felt the God-strength within his arms hold fast and then the man gave a wrenching twist and Brax's left elbow twisted with it. He heard a crack, felt a shock of pain shoot up his arm, then, as his sword went spinning off, he fell, hitting the ground beyond the wall so hard it knocked the air out of his lungs.

✦

Graize saw him fall and, standing in the saddle, he sent a scream of triumph into the air. His enemy was down and the Gods' ancient defense lay writhing and shrieking in his newly awakened sight like a mortally wounded snake. It was time to chop both their heads off. Now. Raising his arms, he summoned the Godling to him.

It streaked from the clouds above with all the speed and power of a blazing comet, trailing a legion of spirits behind it in a trail of silvery fire. Graize allowed It to flow around him and through him, filling him with an icy cold power that nearly froze his breath in his body, then Godling and wyrdin together raced toward Yildiz-Koy. When they reached the pasture fields, they kept going, scattering the remaining defenses as they went, aiming for the single figure staggering to his feet before the wall.

✦

On the battlements of Orzin-Hisar, the smell of burning wood and wool drew Spar to his feet. Holding the wall like a vise, he watched Brax's death hurtle toward him. He felt numb and heavy, unable to think or even feel. The tower voice had done its damage and gone, leaving him wide open to a constant barrage of images that battered against his mind like a whirlwind.

Brax standing in the center of a broiling sea of blood-flecked mist.
A hundred sharp-clawed creatures of power and need.
A rolling tide of mist and death.
Burning.
And something flickering past the lamps.
Something.

Above him, the sky darkened perceptibly as a new power streaked from the clouds toward Orzin-Hisar. It filled his mind with a screaming howl of hunger and his legs gave out from under him as blood began to trickle from his nose and ears. He fell against the battlements to lie, staring upward, unable to look away, as the vision played out in front of his eyes gone a pale, misty white.

The power enveloped Brax in a swirling mass of silvery teeth and claws. In its midst, Spar saw Graize ready his bow; as he fired, a legion of spirits swarmed in to catch the spray of blood that shot out to cover the setting sun in a veil of golden fire. The power caught Brax in an icy embrace, newly formed teeth tearing frantically at Estavia's protections. Screaming in fury, pain forgotten, Brax fought them both with all the strength and rage his fourteen years on the streets of Anavatan could summon, but as his body weakened, the juvenile wards on his arms and chest faded.

And Spar began to cry, knowing that this time he couldn't save the older boy, feeling as if everything since Cindar's death had been leading up to this one final moment when he would be left all alone. Deep within his blistered mind, he felt the tower voice rise up again and, with a gesture of almost gentle triumph, draw back a curtain of darkness to reveal a fine, silver light that undulated in the distance.

No longer caring what it wanted in return, Spar closed his eyes, and reached for it.

And paused as a hand touched his. Opening his eyes, he stared up at a blank-faced man sitting propped up against the battlements, iron-braced legs splayed out before him, a heavyset youth with Bayard's features lending him a shoulder for support. He seemed somehow familiar and Spar frowned as Kemal's words filtered down to him from far away.

"... served as Serin-Koy's leading battle-seer and priest of Estavia until he took a head wound in a Yuruk attack two seasons ago."

A blank-faced man sending Spar's mind flying toward the shining net of Elif's prophetic Sight . . .

The name came slowly.

"Chian?"

The corners of the man's dull eyes crinkled in response. With a featherlight touch, his mind reached out to still the flood of images, then brought one single vision forward.

As the creatures closed over Brax's head, he managed one choked-off cry for help. His call shot through the mist like a blazing arrow and, drawn by the violence of his desperation, ESTAVIA LEAPED FORWARD.

Recognizing his purpose, Spar shook his head, jerking up the rest of the vision and almost throwing it at him.

Only to have him disappear before She could reach him.

With a dismissive mental shrug, Chian played the final unseen image out before them like a skein of wool.

Estavia reaching out into darkness for the one man able to save the future: Kemal.

And Spar's clouded eyes suddenly brightened with hope as their abayos' words echoed in his mind.

"I took some injuries last night conducting a ritual to manifest the God of Battles."

A surge of new energy drew him to his feet and he nodded excitedly. Kemal had called up Estavia that night to save them from the spirits on Liman Caddesi.

"She favors the combative ones."

Kemal could get Her here to Serin-Koy and, once here, She would save Brax.

Below him, Graize swept his sword down again, the image of the streets of Anavatan shimmered into being, Brax cried out, his call shooting through the mist like a blazing arrow as it had that very first night, and Spar and Chian joined their minds together to hurl their cojoined abilities out with all their strength to amplify his past and present desperation.

✦

"Save us, God of Battles, and I will pledge you my life, my worship AND MY LAST DROP OF BLOOD, FOREVER!"

✦

The pure force of his belief hurtled along the streams of possibility, slamming into Kemal's mind with all the power of a hurricane. It ricocheted off the Battle God's lien within him, then, sucking up enough energy from every warrior on the field to stagger them, it blazed across the sky.

Estavia froze in mid strike, Her feral visage snapping to the south as She saw what it revealed: the village of Serin-Koy on fire, its militia dead or overrun, and Brax, *Her* Champion, unarmored and unprotected, fighting a savage creature of power and need that hammered against Her wards.

Against *Her* wards.

With a scream of rage that deafened every person on the field, the Battle God exploded out of being, the shock wave flattening half the fishing huts on the western shores of Gol-Beyaz.

✦

Her appearance at Serin-Koy was no less violent. One moment Brax was striking out, one-handed, at a spirit a thousand times more powerful than those he'd faced on Liman-Caddesi; the next It was swept away and he was catapulted into the air, every limb outlined in fire, as Estavia's presence slammed into him, stripping away all his pain and fatigue in a single blow. Brax gave himself up to it as the now-familiar figure of Kaptin Haldin rose up to encase him in golden light, the gem-encrusted weapon from his dream appeared in his hand, and once again he stood on a flat, featureless plain surrounded by creatures of mist and claws. Once again, he fought them with the same ferocity and unwavering belief in his own invincibility and Hers, and once again they shredded before the power of a God.

And then he saw Graize.

The other boy appeared out of the mist like a wraith, his eyes gone white and wild, a legion of fresh creatures swarming about his head. He spat a curse at Brax so powerful it smacked against Estavia's protections, and then he was galloping toward him, a curved Yuruk saber in his hand. Brax raised his own weapon and when they met, there was an explosion of energy that sent them both flying. Brax was the first to rise, the power of Estavia driving him to his feet; Graize lay stunned for half a heartbeat longer and then he, too, was up and hurtling toward his enemy.

They met with another crash of steel and power. Brax bore down, forcing Graize toward the ground, his lips drawn back from his teeth in a feral grimace. The other boy snarled back at him in unbridled hatred, then screamed out a single word.

Atop Orzin-Hisar, Spar looked up to see the power become a savage-clawed creature of rage and hunger streaking from the clouds above. He stood frozen for an instant, the memory of Liman-Caddesi catching his breath in his throat, but then, as Chian's mind wrapped about his in a mantle of strength, he flung their combined power out like a sling, spinning it into a great net of darkness to entangle the creature in mid-strike.

Shrieking in fury, It tore at the net's black strands while, from the ground, Graize surged upward, knocking Brax away with one blow. He gave a piercing whistle, and just as Estavia turned to face this new threat, a whirlwind of spirits spewed forward to obscure Its presence. She waded into their midst, shredding as many as She sucked in and showering Brax and Graize with their tattered, half-physical bodies.

Spar and Chian held their ground against the creature as It twisted about to batter at their minds while Graize sent a hail of tiny spirits against them like a cloud of gnats. Chian's already weakened abilities began to buckle. The creature renewed its attack, jerking just enough of its sinuous body from the net to sink its half formed teeth into Chian's cheek. The former battle-seer faltered, but as a spray of blood caught Spar across the face, his eyes snapped open almost unbearably wide and he saw the past.

The shining waters of Gol-Beyaz began to churn as the lake dwellers' prayers for prosperity and power formed a dual future of creation and destruction. Across the wild lands a host of spirits driven by the rage and pain of a latent seer came together as one, and within the lake of power Incasa formed a vision to mold a God: an unformed child of power and potential born under the cover of Havo's Dance. Spar saw his own part in Its birthing, saw what might become his own part in Its fate and then, as Chian's strength began to fail, he saw behind the battle-seer, a single, shining path leading down into a darkness so total it froze his bones to look at it. Together, he and the creature stared into its depths, watching as a shimmering black tower began to take form, and together they felt Incasa's sudden consternation as He, too, saw this new, dark future. He raised His dice, and then a white-eyed man standing in the window of a tall, red tower rose up between them.

For a heartbeat, he and Spar stared across the waters at each other. The man beckoned, but mesmerized by the darkness, Spar turned away and the man held up a marble figurine of a mounted seer in sarcastic salute before turning to send a spike of warning across the sea so hard it slapped against Spar's mind with a crack as it flew past.

✦

Below the wall, Graize's uneven pupils snapped open at the contact. For a moment it seemed unfamiliar and then he recognized the mind of the northern sorcerer. He almost refused to heed his warning, but as the man stripped away the mist around the streams to show him what would occur if the God of Prophecy took hold of his new Godling, he gave a reluctant whistle to call off Its attack. Caught up in Spar's visioning, It resisted at first, then turned, trailing a line of crimson blood and ebony power behind It, and shot through Spar's now-ragged net to lose Itself in the clouds.

As Brax surged to his feet to renew his attack, Graize turned and ran for his mount as well. The battle was won, dozens of sheep and cattle were taken, and the village was burning. It was enough. Holding the Godling's presence in his mind, he gave the signal and the Yuruk wheeled about and galloped back to the western hills behind him.

✦

At Yildiz-Koy, Danjel felt Graize break off the attack. She gave a long, undulating whistle to call her own kazakin back from the God-Wall, then turned and vanished behind the hills. As Bronze Company gave chase, the infantry slowly lowered their arms. There was silence on the field.

✦

Pressing two fingers against the bridge of his nose to stem the trickle of blood caused by Spar and Chian's violent contact, Kemal glanced up as Yashar pushed his way through the milling militia to his side.

"It was a feint," the older man said bluntly.

"I know."

"Why didn't *they* know? Why didn't Sable Company *see it?*"

Kemal just shook his head.

"They should have seen it," the older man insisted. "Then we never would have . . ." His deep voice broke over the words. "We thought they'd be safe, Kem, and we left them there all alone."

"I know." Handing his helmet to Duwan, Kemal stripped off his cuirass and dropped it to the ground. "Come on," he said darkly. "We have to find out what happened and then we have to get back there."

With Cyan Company falling in immediately behind them, the two men ran in search of Kaptin Liel.

✦

On the field of Serin-Koy, Her expression as sated and sleepy as a well-fed house cat, Estavia watched the Yuruk retreat, then reached down to draw Her fingers through Her young Champion's dust-and-sweat-encrusted hair, before slowly disappearing.

Brax stood watching Her pass with a dazed expression, but as the golden presence of Kaptin Haldin gradually faded along with Her, he gave a long, shuddering breath and sank to his knees, one hand pressed tightly around his wounded arm.

On the battlements, Chian drew Spar's mind up from the depths of Gol-Beyaz with his final breath before the wake of the Battle God's passing burned his own mind to ashes. Spar's eyes slowly returning from white to blue, the young seer stared up at the place where the Godling had disappeared, his expression blank and shocked then, with one hand clasped around Jaq's neck and the other holding a dead man's hand, he deliberately closed his eyes, allowing his mind to drift back down to the edge of the dark place where Chian had dwelt for so long.

✦

At Cvet Tower, Illan Volinsk laid one finger atop Spar's figurine before very gently pushing it over on its side with an expresion of genuine regret. For a moment, he considered removing it from the board entirely, but then shook his head. The streams had become so muddy at this point that the boy might just survive with enough of his abilities left intact to influence the newly formed God of Creation and Destruction. Spar had the potential to affect the streams of possibilities and that potential had not been completely destroyed. Incasa had seen it, too, and despite the very real danger to His power base, Incasa might still have a use for Spar, as damaged as he was; the oldest of the Lake Deities was a greedy old bastard after all. Like all gamblers, the God of Chance liked to hedge His own bets and Graize wouldn't be nearly enough insurance for Him.

"Any more than he would be for me," Illan mused aloud. Spar might never trust him now, but that possibility hadn't been completely destroyed either. It was something to consider as the game progressed.

As was the new possibility of gaining Graize's trust, his thoughts continued. His acceptance of Illan's aid on the battlefield of Serin-Koy was encouraging. Lifting the young wyrdin's figurine from Serin-Koy, he set it back in its place beside Gol-Bardak. However unstable, the boy had, nonetheless, done very well in his first engagement. He'd remained focused on one clear and simple vision, had advanced toward it along the cleanest stream possible, and achieved his goals: the Yuruk now believed in his prophetic and leadership abilities and the Godling was well on Its way to a controlled, physical awakening outside the influence of the Gol-Beyaz Deities. Illan would soon need to have a new figurine created.

Casting his gaze across the board, Illan nodded in satisfaction. The streams were progressing exactly as he had foreseen. Estavia's battle seers had been easily herded from the south to the west like a flock of sheep driven from summer to winter pasture with their warriors obediently following along behind like so many sheepdogs. Now it was time to herd them back again as the *mysterious ships* sighted in the Deniz-Hadi inlet that spring were about to enter the game. He'd dreamed of them and their very special passenger that night.

Reaching below the atlas table, he retrieved a polished olive wood box before turning toward the sound of footsteps. His eyes cleared as Sergeant Ysav entered the room.

"You sent for me, sir?" the older man asked.

Illan inclined his head. "A ship from Skiros will be arriving within the hour, Vyns. Take an honor guard to receive it and return with the envoy and his retinue at once."

"Sir."

"They'll be dressed as Ithosian merchants," Illan continued, setting the box carefully on the table. "But don't treat them as such," he cautioned. "The envoy's a powerful general and cousin to King Pyrros who's conquered much of the southwest coastline of the Deniz-Hadi Sea in the last two years. You'll remember him, Memnos of Taurus."

"I do, sir. He fought with your ducal father for three years against Rostov. Part of his martial training as I recall."

"Yes." Illan's expression warmed. "He taught Dagn and me to sail in the southern manner when I was five."

"I remember, sir," Ysav groused. "I nearly drowned that summer. So did you."

"Nonsense, neither of us were in any danger." Illan turned. "He'll be traveling with a bodyguard of half a dozen soldiers and one formidable seer; you'll know her by her eyes." His own paled slightly. "They'll be unusually dark, unlike those of the northern seers, Vyns. *Do not* meet her gaze. Stronger men than you have lost themselves in the power of her abilities."

"I'll remember that, sir."

"Have the second level made up with the southern-facing bedroom for the seer and the northern for the envoy. The main storage room will need to be cleared for the guard and the smaller made up as a private dining room."

"And the ship, sir? Will it need to reprovender?"

"Likely. Offer whatever fresh water and stores they require for the return voyage. I don't imagine they'll wish to sail on to the capital when their business is complete. They'll not want to waste the fighting season any more than I do."

The sergeant glanced up with an expectant expression and Illan chuckled. "Yes, Vyns. The game is moving swiftly. We may be sailing against Anavatan sooner than you think."

"My lord?" The man's countenance brightened at once.

"Yes, so treat the envoy well. He's the key to Volinski mobilization."

"I will, sir."

As the sergeant left to carry out his orders, a new spring in his step, Illan opened the box's delicately wrought golden lid and drew the first of a dozen intricately carved single-masted warships from their velvet settings. He placed each one in a circle around the figurine of Anahtar-Hisar, then lifted a small figure beautifully wrought in gold before closing the box with a satisfied expression. The game was moving very swifly indeed.

✦

As he had predicted, the envoy from the southern maritime realm of Skiros arrived within the hour. Illan met them in the small private audience hall on the first floor, coming forward smoothly to embrace the heavyset older man who strode into the room well ahead of three others.

"Memnos," he said with genuine warmth in his voice.

The man returned the embrace, then held him at arm's length for a moment before smiling in return. "Prince Illan. You look well."

"As do you. It's been a long time."

"Too long. I was sorry to hear of your father's death."

"Thank you. We received your mourning gift, and King Pyrros'. It was generous of His Majesty."

"He remembers his friends, as your father did."

"Indeed. And I hear you've become a father yourself."

"I have, with a brood of four already. This is my eldest, Viktor."

Illan inclined his head as the youth standing just behind Memnos' right shoulder bowed. "A Volinski name, Memnos?" he asked.

"To honor the man who treated me as a son so many years ago." Memnos now gestured an older man forward. "This is my cousin Hares."

"Ah, the famous mapmaker," Illan said with a smile. "Your reputation for accuracy and beauty precedes you even across the northern sea."

Hares bowed. "You're too kind, Highness."

"And," Memnos continued, "may I introduce you to Panos."

The figure from last night's dream now stepped forward. She was dressed as an Ithosian sailor, but her eyes were as black as onyx, giving her thin face a mysterious, otherworldly cast. Illan met her deep, swirling gaze with a guarded one of his own, but it was her hair, as bright as spun gold beneath her plain woolen cap, that drew his attention. It was said that only Pyrros of Skiros threw children with hair the color of the summer sun, but only a fool would point that out as *King* Pyrros of Skiros was, as yet, unmarried—a ploy to keep his allies hoping to make a political match with him. Illan bowed politely as one would to an equal, taking in her measure as she took in his.

"Be welcome in my home, Panos," he said formally. "No door shall be closed to you if you desire it to be opened."

She smiled suddenly, the years falling away to reveal a youth of seventeen or eighteen at best. "Thank you, Highness. I may avail you of that offer. I've heard a great deal about the *prophetic* gifts of the Volinski seers," she said, moving her gaze languidly up the length of his body.

"And I those of the Skirosian oracles," he replied.

"And I," Memnos interrupted pointedly, "have heard a great deal about the skill of the Volinski vintners, but I've yet to see any evidence of it."

Illan laughed. "My apologies. Come, sit, eat, drink, and rest from your long voyage."

✦

An hour later, when his guests had eaten their fill, Illan sat back, turning a wineglass between his finger and thumb, watching as it caught the last of the evening sun in its crystal depths. "I trust your journey was uneventful," he observed.

Memnos shrugged. "The trip across the Deniz-Siyah was as cold and damp as I remembered it to be. Gol-Beyaz was warmer, however, and more interesting. The villages have grown prosperous in the years since I passed them last."

"Prosperous," Illan agreed, "and complacent."

"They look to have good reason. Anahtar-Hisar was an impressive sight, very large and very tall, but the three towers at the mouth of Anavatan's strait, now those are truly a work of military prowess. I was sad that Viktor and Panos did not get to witness the fabled chains of Oristo. When were they last laid across the waters, in your great-grandmother's time, wasn't it?"

Illan nodded. "Ivagn Volinsk was a pirate at heart. She raided the coastlines of the Deniz-Siyah for much of her reign. The fleet she took up the Bogazi-Isik strait was the largest of its time."

"They say she brought a piece of Siya-Hisar home with her," Hares noted.

"Yes. It's housed with the ducal regalia in the capital."

"I'd love to see it someday."

"I should be only too happy to show it to you. Any season but this one, of course."

"And on that note," Memnos said, straightening in his chair. "I've brought you a gift." He gestured and Viktor passed him a long, leather case tied with a silken ribbon. Inside was a creamy-smooth vellum map finely drawn with colored inks and gold and silver embossment. "The Deniz-Hadi," he said with real pride as the two youths held it up to the light. "Made by Hares, of course." He gestured at the other man who smiled diffidently.

"It's beautiful," Illan breathed. "I'm particularly impressed with the areas outlined in red. The coastal holdings of the Skirosians?"

"Obviously," Memnos grunted. "As you can see, we now control the bulk of the western shore, and all of the southwestern islands. Pyrros is ready to move on Thasos and Ithos next season, but this, as you know, will alert the Gol-Yearli and their Warriors of Estavia to our growing military strength."

"Yes," Illan agreed. "They might even respond in force if Thasos called for aid; they've been trading allies for many years."

Memnos gave an elegant shrug. "They might," he allowed, "but they're a walled people with a walled people's mentality."

"And Skiros?"

"We're a maritime people."

"The Gol-Yearli have a marine force."

"They have a lake force; it's not the same thing."

"So you don't assume they'll be any threat to your designs on Thasos and Ithos?"

"None at all." Memnos sat back. "Especially if the Volinski are as prepared to throw their support behind us as I've been given to understand that you are."

"We are." Illan bent toward the map. "The duc would like nothing better than to come to the aid of the man who once tried to drown his overly-ambitious little brother."

"He could try to drown mine," Memnos suggested absently. "He's more ambitious than you and much less useful. All he can do is lead troops."

Illan laughed politely. "In the meantime," he said, returning his attention to the new map, "I've been in negotiation with the Petchans of the Gurney-Dag Mountains," he said pointing to the area just northeast of the Deniz-Hadi. "For a price—which I've already paid—they'll cease their raids on the southern villages this season so that the Warriors of Estavia will keep their focus north where the Yuruk nomads have been testing the skills of a new military leader. The Battle God's people have already drawn the bulk of their fighting force away from the southern towers, so you'll have no trouble from that quarter if you move quickly. Thasos and Ithos may call for aid, but the Gol-Yearli will be too busy to answer with anything more than foodstuffs this season."

"And their oracles?" Panos asked. "They won't see through this strategy?"

Illan smiled. "Their *oracles* will be all too occupied with other business this season. Will you have another glass of wine?"

She smiled back at him, her black eyes sparkling in response to his obvious challenge. "Yes, thank you, I will."

✦

Later, after the men had retired, Illan found Panos where he'd expected to, standing on the rocky shore beneath Cvet Tower, staring out at the waves and listening to the faint sounds of merriment coming from the ship at anchor beyond the point. She'd removed her cap, allowing her hair to spill out across her shoulders like a golden mane. They said nothing for a long time until, finally, Illan glanced over at her.

"And how did you find the journey, Oracle?" he asked formally.

She turned her dark, fathomless eyes on his face.

"Gol-Beyaz tingled," she answered. "I could feel it singing in my mind."

"What did it say?"

"Come and lose yourself in my embrace, and be one with the Gods."

"Naturally you did not obey it."

"Naturally. But I was tempted. It sang so sweetly, and the song was so familiar, like honey on my tongue, once tasted, never forgotten."

"I'm not surprised. They say the Oracles of Skiros are the children of the Gods," he noted.

She shrugged. "I'm from Amatus."

"That's far to the east. Pyrros has a long reach these days."

She gave him a shrewd glance but made no answer. "I felt a lot of activity beneath the waves," she noted after a time. "Its marble floor was alive with music and dancing. Is it always so energetic?"

"These are unusual times."

"How so?"

"The Lake Deities have birthed another of their number."

"Ah, yes, my little sand swimmer." She turned, her golden hair spilling across her shoulders. "I've brought you a gift, my tall tower prophet," she said. "Would you like it now?" Her black eyes were teasing, but before he could respond, she pressed an oilcloth-wrapped object into his hands.

Opening it, he marveled at the small marble sea turtle. "It's beautiful," he said.

"It's for your prophecy, so that you might keep an eye on your new God. They can be tricky, you know . . . Gods."

"Yes." He met her gaze deliberately, feeling the heat of her regard wrap about his mind like a balm. "But It will not be so easy to mold to Their desires as they imagine."

She stepped closer, lifting her face to his. "And why is that?" she asked.

"There are other desires at work."

Her laughter fell about him like raindrops in the moonlight. "Desires such as yours?" she asked.

Reaching out, he ran his fingers through her hair, marveling at how vibrant and alive each individual strand became under his touch. "Yes, mine," he answered, "and others. Perhaps yours."

"Perhaps," she allowed. "But mine involve the southern sea. What possible interest might I have in more northerly climes?"

"Wouldn't you like to swim in the waters of Gol-Beyaz without fear of losing yourself in its embrace? To see if you might draw up some of its legendary power to aid in the working of your own will? With Anavatan in ruins and the Gods sorely weakened, this is entirely possible."

"The thought of losing myself in any embrace is no fear," she breathed. "It's a heady challenge, like a deep, dark wine. But won't these Gods have seers and oracles of Their own in place to prevent this very thing?"

"Of course. But of the two most dangerous, one is old and one is young. Little match for the two of us together."

"And the rest?"

"Are of no consequence."

"I see." She smiled demurely up at him. "And what would I have to do for this delicious little swim," she purred.

"Perhaps the swim itself would be payment enough," he answered, "if it occurred at just the right time to suit us both."

"And how would you ensure that it was?"

"Well, I would have to study the matter . . . intimately," he answered.

He leaned down to kiss her and she met his lips with a smile.

"Mm. I like a man who studies his subject," she murmured. "The more intimately the better." Taking his hand, she led him back the tower.

✦

Standing discreetly in the window above them, Hares accepted the gold coin Memnos ruefully handed him. Panos had a great many more weapons than just her eyes, he mused, as Prince Illan of Volinsk was about to discover.

14

Visions

*A*IM, DRAW, RELEASE.

"See the target."

Feel the target.

"Don't see the enemy; see only a target."

The enemy is *the targe*t. Always *see the enemy.*

"Aim, draw, release."

Ignore everything but the target.

"Delon."

Birin-Kaptin Arjion's voice feathered across Spar's concentration with barely a ripple to mark its progress as he squinted down the length of the arrow shaft.

Go down deep to the very edge of the dark place. See the enemy from there.

"Spar."

He blinked, coming up just far enough for his inner sight to ring the practice dummy in a silvery-white glow.

"Spar, release."

Release.

The arrow streaked forward to join a dozen others in the very center of the target. With a cold smile, Spar lowered his arm, allowing the surrounding physical sensations to return to the forefront of his mind. Sound returned first: the rhythmic thumping of the delos-drums from across the temple's central training ground, the grunts and explosive breaths of those training, the ringing of steel against steel; his own breathing, his own heartbeat. Then odors: jasmine and magnolia, leather and sweat. Finally sight: flagstones and dust, Jaq, ever vigilant, standing to one side, Arjion, his usually stern demeanor marred by the faintest hint of approval, looking down at him. The man gave one brisk nod before gesturing at the practice dummy.

"Good aim," he said gruffly. "But you're still too slow. Go again."

As Spar pulled another arrow from the quiver at his back, he felt his mind return to the dark place.

Concentrate.

"Now concentrate."

All sensations faded once again.

✦

"Concentrate. Are you concentrating?"

"Yes."

"You don't seem to be. Concentrate properly."

Elif's voice, nagging, pressing, training as much as he would allow her to; the dark place often repeated lessons he'd already learned from Elif, Yashar, Cindar, even Chian from the short time they'd had together in their minds.

Aim, draw, release.

The arrow streaked toward the center of the target and, expression blank, he reached for another.

✦

It had been four months since the battle at Serin-Koy. Four months since Yashar, finding him sitting vigil by Brax's bedside in the infirmary, had caught him up in a desperate bear hug and practically squeezed the breath out of him. Four months since they'd returned to the temple of Anavatan with the rest of Estavia's infantry while Bronze and Sable Companies had gone chasing off after the supposedly ill-trained nomads who'd wounded their pride. And four months since Chian had shown him and the strange God-creature the dark place where he could protect his mind and his powers from the spirits who would destroy him and the seers who would use him. The dark place on the very edge of death.

Spar's eyes narrowed. Four months; most of Havo's High Spring and all of Ystazia's Low and Estavia's High Summer, spent avoiding the scrutiny of seers and priests. The first few days after the fighting had been easy; the Battle God's commanders had been too busy hurling accusations and questions at each other to bother about anything else, but that single moment of power on the battlements with Chian had marked him as a latent seer of powerful ability and, eventually, they'd come looking for him.

"They'd addle his brains with their visioning so fast he'd go mad from the strain."

Spar snorted. He hadn't spent nine years ensuring the western dockside marks underestimated him for nothing. He'd been ready for them and it had been ridiculously easy. Arms clasped tightly about Yashar's neck, he'd stared dazedly back at Kaptin Liel. One tiny shudder was all it took to have his new abayos break off the interview with a warning growl. After that, the dark place had provided him with all the protection he needed. They couldn't reach him there. Nothing could.

He shook his head irritably. Like Estavia's seers, the spirits of the wild lands had discovered his abilities and constantly pressed against his mind, scrabbling at his defenses like rats in the night. The God-creature was there, too, hovering just out of reach, drawn to Brax by the blood he'd shed at Serin-Koy, and drawn to the black tower It and Spar had seen together but afraid of the net Spar had built to entrap It. He could feel It, pacing back and forth beyond his dreams, waiting for him to lower his guard, but that was never going to happen. Not again. Brax needed him. The God-creature could come to him, but on his terms only.

Spar frowned. Everyone would come to him on his terms only from now on.

The sound of a familiar curse broke into his thoughts, causing him to turn his gaze to where Brax was practicing shield work with Bazmin in the center of the training ground. His hair and clothes were drenched with sweat, but he advanced on the older delinkos with an intensity so aggressive that only Spar could see the fatigue underneath it. He frowned.

✦

After the battle of Serin-Koy, Bayard had found Brax lying facedown before the paddocks, one arm twisted unnaturally beneath him, his hair and clothes covered in a sticky patina of blood and fine, silver-colored ash. He'd carried the unconscious boy to the infirmary in Orzin-Hisar, but even after the village's physician-priests had sewn and splinted his arm and forced a horrible-smelling concoction down his throat, he'd just lain there, pale and unmoving, staring vacantly at the ceiling. Finally, Spar had brought Jaq in to cover him in dog spit. Then his face had twisted into a familiar expression of annoyance, his right hand had risen weakly to ward off the dog's ministering tongue, and his eyes had finally come back to life. More relieved than he'd wanted to admit, Spar had glared down at him.

"Were you asleep during the 'carry a shield' lecture?" he'd spat.

It was High Summer before Brax could carry any kind of a weight with his shield arm despite Usara's priests.

His left arm. Don't get into the habit of seeing the world from the warrior's point of view. It limits you.

His own voice now, not the voice in the tower's.

Spar shrugged anyway. For Brax, it *was* his shield arm, he reminded himself. He'd given up their old life; their old *point of view* for the chance to die young so that the God of Battles might smile at him. Once back in Anavatan he'd thrown himself into his training with a new strength of purpose that only Spar recognized as a desperate pretense that he was fit and whole. Everyone else thought he'd been blessed by Estavia and treated him like some kind of mystical hero raised from the dead.

Like Kaptin Haldin raised from the dead.

"If you ever tear up a book again, you'll wish you were dead. What the bugger do you think a shield is for?"

Spar had dropped the ragged illustration on Brax's chest in the infirmary the next day with a baleful expression and at least the older boy'd had the decency to look contrite. Not that it mattered. Blessed or not, he'd set himself on a path that would get him killed unless Spar could prevent it. He'd better hope that Spar could.

Expression wrathful, Spar sent the arrow whistling toward the practice dummy and, even without concentration; it buried itself in the very center of its chest.

"Lucky throw."

"My ass, he's the best shot in dockside."

Spar's eyes lightened at the memory; Brax protecting him from Cindar as he always had, protecting him, defending him, looking out for him.

"He needs a new jacket."

"*Now, then, clothes. Do you mind castoffs for the time being?*"

Lifting his arm, Spar measured it against the arrow shaft in his hand with a thoughtful expression. Tanay had made sure they didn't wear castoffs for long, but he'd still need another jacket by this autumn. *Blessed* by good food and warm blankets, they'd both grown two inches that summer; he'd ripped the back of his tunic getting it on last week, and Brax had gone through three pairs of sandals in four months. It was unlikely either of them would ever be as big as Kemal, never mind Yashar, but Brax was already filling out, the pinched, sallow cast that hunger and suspicion had stamped on his features slowly fading before confidence and security.

Spar snorted cynically. It was fading before pimples and facial hair, both of which were making Brax unbearable in the mornings. *He* was aging, too, but you didn't see him obsessing over his looks, he thought, shaking his head.

"*I'm going to finish my tea. If you'd like to join me, there's a cup on the shelf there and the pot's beside you.*"

He smiled faintly. Eleven days after they'd returned to Anavatan, Tanay had brought him to the kitchens for a special meal of roasted lamb kebaps, halva, and lokum to celebrate his tenth birthday. Apparently, the priests of Oristo *knew* these things, but Spar had always suspected that, with all the excitement over Brax, she'd just wanted him to feel special. He didn't mind. He already felt special when he was with her. That was enough.

Besides, around here special was overrated, he thought as he watched Brax take a blow to the shield that nearly sent him flying. Face set in a carefully neutral expression to hide the pain the blow had caused him, he advanced on Bazmin again and Spar shook his head; around here, special caused bruises and broken bones.

Beside him, Arjion called an end to the archery practice and, after carefully unstringing his bow, he turned and made his way through the pairs of training warriors, Jaq at his heels. He was the youngest delinkos ever allowed on the training ground, thanks to Brax and his unswerving belief that Estavia had brought them both here for some great purpose. That belief had put a specially shortened bow in Spar's hands a full two years before most delon became proficient with a sling, a weapon he'd mastered years ago. The infantry fighting masters had been so impressed with that and his abilities with a knife—abilities any half decent lifter his age had managed—that there was talk about beginning him with a short sword in a few weeks.

A scornful expression crossed his face as he took the stone steps to the infantry quarters at a run. Spar had no intention of learning any other weapon earlier than he had to. He'd had seen what happened when you faced the enemy at any age and that wasn't going to happen to him. He'd been raised as a thief and thieves didn't face their marks, and although he might not be thieving anymore, he didn't see any reason to change that basically sound strategy.

The dark place agreed.

"Never let them see you. If they can't see you, they can't identify you to the Watch."

Cindar's words, spoken before the raki had addled his instincts. The dark place often threw up images of the first father he'd ever known although it always made him feel vaguely uncomfortable and guilty. Sometimes he put Yashar's face in front of them, sometimes Brax's, if he didn't want to see it, but he didn't do it often; Cindar's words were usually too sensible to ignore, especially now that he was surrounded by teachers who believed the best way to survive a battle was to kill the enemy.

"The best way to survive a battle is not to be in one," he thought derisively, *"as a warrior or a seer or anything else; and no gloried city guard's gonna tell me any differently."*

Seated across the courtyard, Elif turned her milky-white gaze in his direction. The painted protections on her cheeks seemed to glow ominously and he ducked quickly through the infantry doorway, only pausing once he was well inside the cool corridor.

"And no four-hundred-year-old battle-seer is either," his thoughts continued as he headed through the dormitory wing. He'd made that decision when he'd come to after the fighting, still clutching Chian's cold fingers on the battlements of Orzin-Hisar. All their training only got you crippled and finally killed. Chian had shown him that.

With that in mind, he'd managed to avoid both Elif and Liel—after the seer-kaptin had returned from the wild lands—for nearly thirty days, retreating to the dark place when he couldn't physically retreat to a dark corner or a shadowy rooftop. But finally Brax had caught up with him on the western wall overlooking the mouth of the Halic-Salmanak as he'd known he would.

The older boy had climbed up beside him and Jaq, leaning his back against the cool stone of the corner sentry box. Setting his left elbow carefully into his lap, he'd stared out at the city's many rooftops, watching the flocks of starlings turn and wheel in the sky, with a speculative expression.

✦

"You can't see them from here," he said after a while.

Spar's eyes tracked across Brax's face suspiciously without moving his head.

"The Western Trisect docks," the older boy explained. "They're too far up the strait."

A sarcastically raised eyebrow was Spar's only response and, a faint smile quirking the corners of his mouth, Brax leaned his head back and closed his eyes.

" 'S a hot day," he noted after a few moments.

Spar just shrugged.

"If we were still on the street, we'd be down at the docks right about now, I guess," Brax continued. "Sitting in the shade under a pier; maybe sharing an apricot or a few dates, or walking in the shallows looking for fishhooks or buoys. Hey, you remember that fishmonger's cat that used to go swimming in the surf, looking for baby crabs?"

Spar nodded warily, but Brax just smiled. "Yeah, it'd be too hot to work for a couple of hours anyway," he continued. "Not until after the sun had set a little."

Spar glanced over, drawn by the unusually nostalgic tone in the other boy's voice despite himself.

"Those were good moments," Brax continued. "When we were warm and fed, and safe for a while, yeah?"

Spar gave a one-shouldered shrug in neutral agreement.

"But soon enough we'd get back to work," Brax continued. "We'd go up to where the crowds were watching the northern ships unloading, or where the merchants were fighting over customers in the market-places, anywhere we might not be noticed, anywhere we might lift an asper or two."

Spar cocked his head to one side, curious about where this was going. The dark place inside was silent as well, waiting.

Brax absently shifted his left arm a little, his face relaxing as the pressure eased on his injury. "It was exciting sometimes," he said, "especially when we got away with it, you remember?"

Spar nodded.

"But I was always scared that it wouldn't last," Brax added with a frown, "that Cindar or I'd get pinched and you'd end up at Oristo-Cami. We never made enough to put anything by, and we never would have. We just weren't good enough."

Spar's brows drew down. "We made out," he said defensively.

"No. We made do. That was all. And it wasn't gonna be for long. If Cindar hadn't been killed that day, it would have been the next day or the day after that." He looked away.

"You know, all my life I could never do anything better than anybody else," he continued after a moment. "I couldn't run faster or climb better. I wasn't stronger or meaner or smarter. I wasn't a great lifter; I was good, but only just good. Now I have all this," he gestured back toward the temple, "but nothing's really changed."

"I thought you were a *champion*," Spar said, allowing a slight sneer to color the last word.

Brax shrugged. "That doesn't make me any better at doing it. I can't fight or ride half as well as the others. I never will, not now, not with this." He made a stiff gesture with his left arm. "And one day that'll probably get me killed."

"No, your stupid habit of diving headfirst into battle'll probably get you killed."

"Whatever. My point is that I was only a good lifter, I'll only be a good warrior, but I'll learn whatever I have to learn to keep from getting pinched or killed. But you're different. You know things. Even on the streets you were better at knowing things than anyone else I ever knew."

"That's 'cause you never knew any seers."

"I knew Graize."

Spar blinked in surprise. In all the time they'd been at the temple, even before the battle where the gray-eyed boy had reappeared like an apparition, Brax had never spoken his name.

"Graize is powerful," he answered distractedly.

"You told me he was just a cheap trickster."

"He was."

"And now?"

Spar shrugged. "Now he's a powerful trickster."

"Whatever. You may think he's better than you, but he's not. He's just older, but he's gonna *get* better if these rumors about him being trained by the Yuruk wyrdin are true."

Spar shifted uncomfortably. "What's your point?" he demanded.

"That he's dangerous and that he's not gonna go away. It doesn't take a seer to know that he's our enemy; he always was, and he always will be. But he's never gonna get past my guard with an edged weapon ever again. All I can do about it is to get better with the sword and the bow, but you can get better in your head. And don't give me that *I was too messed up at Serin-Koy to face it* crap. Yashar may buy it, but I don't."

Spar cast him a glance of mock injury and Brax gave him an exasperated look in return. "I'm not saying you weren't messed up," he allowed, "but that vision you had didn't burn out your abilities any more than this injury took my arm. You know it and I know it. You're ten years old now; this young and scared routine's not gonna fly much longer. You gotta make a choice. You wanna protect yourself from them, that's fine, but just make sure you don't protect yourself so hard you lose your best weapon against them all, including Graize. That would be playing right into his hands."

That would be playing right into Illan Volinsk's, hands as well, the dark place agreed.

Now it was Spar's turn to look away. "I know what I'm doing, Brax," he replied quietly.

"Well, just make sure you do, 'cause if you let Graize get stronger in his head than you, he'll take you down." The older boy caught and held his gaze. "And I won't be able to stop him."

Any more than he could stop him before, the dark place supplied bluntly.

And that had been Brax's unspoken point.

✦

After that day, Spar had allowed Elif to begin drawing him out, playing a cautious game of cat and mouse with her, letting only the faintest bit of his abilities show through the dark place and clamping them back down as soon as he felt her push too hard. He had no illusions about what she would do if she discovered their true scope, but Brax was right. He was ten years old now. He wouldn't be able to play the young-and-scared routine for much longer. But Brax was wrong about making a choice. He didn't have to choose anything, not yet. Tanay had said so.

"Age will bring about its share of decisions; you don't have to make any of them now."

And he wasn't going to make them with the limited options Estavia's warriors were willing to offer him either. He would make his own options.

Opening the inner door which separated the infantry wing from the more public areas of the temple, he peered around it cautiously before slipping through, closing it behind Jaq who still padded along behind him. One finger to his lips to keep the animal quiet, he made his way along a wide, open colonnade, the finely-wrought marble rails along the outside thickly entwined with blooming morning glories, the wall side regularly punctuated by polished wooden doors and delicately arched doorways. One such doorway led to a winding set of white marble stairs streaked with sunlight from a line of thin, latticed windows. He and Jaq took them silently, emerging into a small passageway with a single door at the end. After listening for a few moments, they slipped inside.

The room was a small, rectangular gallery, the floor and two outside walls covered in heavy woolen carpets and two large windows flanked by wooden shutters, easily closed to keep out the weather, but thrown open today to allow the sunlight to pool across the floor. The far wall was open, showing a two-story room beyond, the edge denoted by a black iron railing. On the inner wall, beside the door, a single shelf held twelve small embossed-leather-and-gold-bound books. Running his fingers along the spines, Spar selected the second volume from the left and carried it carefully to a pile of silk cushions by the window.

"Learn, Spar, learn everything you can."

Chian's words, his last words, spoken as he drew Spar's mind up from the brilliant waters of Gol-Beyaz.

"Don't let them turn you into something you're not."

The final image that had followed Chian into death was of flowers strewn across a sunlit floor. Spar had no idea why. But he was going to find out because something was happening.

He frowned. He didn't know what or when. He had only the vaguest sense of it tickling at the back of his sight like a hair caught in his throat. But he would find out.

"Learn."

When he was five years old, Cindar had grudgingly paid a drunken, half blind former-scribe to teach Brax and him a few written words, just enough to make out the occasional faded signboards in the Western Trisect dockside markets. (Which was why Spar could easily write out the words *Potions to cure boils and weeping sores: three aspers.*)

Before they'd left for Anahtar-Hisar, Marshal Brayazi had arranged for a priest of Ystazia to teach them how to read and write properly. It had been slow going, especially since the older boy had managed to avoid each and every lesson, just like he had with the old scribe. But Spar had suffered through the long lectures on letters and words, held to the task by his memory of the bright, jewel-encrusted book on the central dais in the armory. Ihsan, the priest, had read it—apparently he'd even written part of it—and he'd promised that Spar would also read it one day, once he mastered the pile of tattered vellum he laughingly called an *apprenticeship book.*

So, once they'd returned to the temple, he and the priest had met twice a week in the meditation room below the gallery, struggling through the first, a grubby piece entitled: "A Delon's Life of the Gods." It was nothing like the books at Calmak-Koy or even at Anahtar-Hisar, but Ihsan had insisted that this was the only way to gain a proper respect for the knowledge so carefully gathered and handwritten in each and every volume. However, it wasn't until he'd climbed the thin iron staircase ten days ago and found the dozen beautiful books that made up Estavia-Sarayi's nearly forgotten library that he'd begun to understand what Ihsan really meant.

"The written word is both the most illuminating and the most terrible of all powers. It gives form to all it touches, but that form is static, so what is written down must be at all times accurate and respectful to that which is being written about."

"In that pathetic excuse for a library? One thin, little, out-of-date tome on southern growing practices, another outlining Ystazia's festive rituals, and two journals written by barely literate tower commanders?"

The memory of Illan's voice sneered at him from the dark place and Spar snapped another memory of Ihsan's voice back at it.

"It doesn't matter how many books a library has, it only matters that they exist in the first place; exist and are available to anyone who wants to discover the knowledge they preserve."

Dropping into the cushions, Spar opened the book to the first page, breathing in the heavy scent of linen, leather, and ink with pleasure before peering down at the beautiful, curving letters.

"A tre . . . tre . . . tise on the stir . . . rup."

"It doesn't matter what a book contains either, again, it only matters that it exists at all."

"Learn."

And he would learn from any quarter he could. Each day he allowed Yashar, Kemal, and Arjion to teach him about weapons and armor and strategy and tactics; he listened while Elif and Battle-Seer Eren spoke about breathing, mind control, and the symbolism thrown up in vision, and Ghazi-Priest Ayse of Bronze Company described the charges she'd led over the years.

But he also listened while Tanay's assistants argued and bartered with the many potters, farmers, carpet sellers, vintners, masons, carpenters, tilers, painters, spice and perfume merchants, colliers and ratcatchers that passed through the temple's main gates every day. He hid in a shadowy gallery far above the main audience hall while Marshal Brayazi handed down discipline and reward to the warriors and delinkon under her charge, and Birin-Marshal Ginaz meted it out. He made his way into every room and hall in Estavia-Sarayi, from the tinsmith's tiny workshop off the kitchens to the huge blacksmith and weaponry forges off the far northern courtyard. He slipped into the herbariums to watch Usara's delinkon bending over tables cluttered with potions and infusions and tinctures, and peered through the infirmary doors while the Healer God's physicians spoke words of comfort over the dying and sometimes dealt out death itself in the name of comfort. He saw the launderers wringing the black dye of Estavia's wards from silk shirts and woolen tunics, and Havo's cultivators carefully tending the many breathtaking gardens inside the walls; gardens that had no practical purpose other than the strange understanding that Estavia, God of Bloodshed and Killing, loved flowers and scented plants.

But most often he visited Tanay, watching as she supervised and orchestrated every aspect of temple life, from the cooking and baking which began long before dawn, to the complicated lists of supplies and provisions she consulted each night after the kitchens had closed. And afterward, sitting on the windowsill of the small delin-room he shared with Brax off Kemal and Yashar's bedchamber, he would mull over everything he'd learned that day. Sometimes Brax would sit with him like he used to in the old days, content to talk or keep silent, whichever Spar preferred. Sometimes he would sit by himself, no longer afraid to be alone.

The God-creature often pressed upon his mind during these times, almost as if It, too, were hungry for learning. He would allow it a few seeds of knowledge at a time, much as he might have thrown a few crumbs to a feral cat to tame it. The God-creature would suck them up in greedy desperation, then spin away, back to Its mad prophet on the plains, and Spar would continue his musings alone.

On nights when the God-creature was inexplicably absent he would send his mind flying out across the Deniz-Siyah to hover about a tall, red tower on the edge of the sea: Prince Illan's Cvet Tower on the southern coast of faraway Volinsk.

Kicking off his sandals, Spar began to rub Jaq's belly absently with one foot as he remembered his first sight of the northern seer. Illan hadn't made contact with him since Serin-Koy, but that didn't mean that Spar hadn't made contact with Illan; Chian had taught him how to do that. The bulk of his mind safely housed in the dark place, he'd sent the finest tendril of consciousness out across the sea to hover above a strange, single-masted ship anchored off the tower promontory while two men, one old and heavyset, the other young and smooth-faced, took their leave of Illan and a beautiful golden-haired woman whose mind shimmered with ebony power much like the dark place itself. Something about her warned him to keep his distance, but all the same, he'd returned often to hover like a bird just beyond the window of Illan's scrying room, watching as the two of them planned the conquest of Anavatan.

And as the days grew warmer, and Ystazia handed Her dominion over the summer to Estavia, the God-creature began to join him on these forays especially on the nights when Illan and Panos, her name was, set their plotting aside to join together in Illan's bedchamber. Spar was not so interested—he'd seen plenty of people having sex before—but it mesmerized the God-creature and Spar often used these times to slip away and touch the lives of the Yuruk spread out across the wild lands.

It was a dangerous game. Their wyrdins could sense a presence far more subtle than his ever could be, and the one they called Danjel's ever changing power signature was a constant threat. As for Graize, his mind was like an autumn storm, darting this way and that, exploding with the fury of a hurricane one moment, then pattering the clouds with a shower of silver lights like a fresh spring rain the next, but Spar was learning to read his movements the same way he was learning to read the waves on Gol-Beyaz and Brax was wrong if he thought Spar believed Graize to be the more powerful seer. He never had. But that didn't make Graize any less powerful.

Setting one finger between the pages of his book, Spar closed his eyes, imagining the pale-eyed boy standing before the practice dummy in the training ground.

Always see *the enemy.*

Something was happening and it had to do with Graize.

"Once upon a time, a very long time ago, there was a shining silver lake of power called Gol-Beyaz."

Kemal's voice was so loud in his mind that he started, jerking his eyes from the book with a cough of surprise.

"And deep beneath its surface dwelled six mysterious beings of vitality and potential, for in the beginning the Gods of Gol-Beyaz were spirits."

He frowned darkly. Gods and Graize?

"So the God Incasa reached into the future to pull forth a mighty vision."

And Spar's eyes widened as the faintest glimmer of understanding began to tickle at the back of his mind. Gods and Graize. Incasa and Graize. Incasa and Graize and the God-creature.

"For in the beginning the Gods of Gol-Beyaz were spirits."

"You sneaky old bastard," he breathed.

A scratch on his leg drew his attention back to the room and he glanced down at Jaq who thumped his tail against the floor with an anxious expression.

"Don't worry," he said in a reassuring tone. "It's all just aim, draw, and release."

✦

Days passed and Estavia's High Summer slowly gave way to Oristo's Autumn. In the villages the crops were gathered, the livestock slaughtered and their meat salted or dried, and the heavy red wine and pale green olive oil the Gol-Yearli were famous for, sealed into earthenware jugs and laid up in a hundred cool, brick-lined cellars. Out on the sparkling waters of Gol-Beyaz and the deep, dark waters of the Bogazi-Isik, the gray fishing nets teemed with palamut, lufer, and mercan migrating south to the warmer waters of the Deniz-Hadi. As the dolphins raced the fishing boats back to their wharves, the fishmonger's white cat played in the surf and watched as the long lines of drying fish sprang up all across the docksides.

With the fighting season also coming to an end, the mounted Warriors of Estavia returned to their temple and their home villages to aid in those preparations while the Yuruk banners disbanded into individual kazakin, and made for their own winter encampments, driving their flocks and herds before them. And at Estavia-Sarayi it was decided that Kemal and Yashar would remain at the temple with their delinkon to continue their training until spring.

✦

Seated in her usual place on her divan, wrapped in heavy woolen shawls, Elif glanced up as Marshal Brayazi crossed the training ground to stand beside her.

"You've a frowning aspect, Bray-Delin," she said, her voice slightly amused. "Hasn't the chamberlain laid up enough boza and raki for the winter?"

The marshal gave her an unimpressed look, but just shook her head. Crouching, she leaned one elbow against the arm of the divan, her many long braids falling forward over her face. "I have a frowning aspect because I was summoned before one of my own seers as if she were the marshal and not I, she answered stiffly.

"Is that all?" Elif gave a disdainful sniff. "Injured pride?"

"Abandoned paperwork. I have to find a diplomatic way to tell the doyen of Thasos that we cannot expand our naval presence in the southern strait."

"Then you should thank me. I summoned you here to discuss a potentially *serious* prophetic situation."

"Which couldn't be discussed in my office or in the audience chamber over a cup of hot salap?"

"Samlin says I need the fresh air. Apparently, my lungs are beginning to fail."

An expression of concern replaced the one of mock annoyance on the marshal's face. "Is that what you wanted to talk to me about?"

The old woman just shrugged. "As odd as it may seem, no," she said, watching a flock of storks make their way across the sky toward Gol-Beyaz. "When Estavia feels the need to call me to Her bosom, I won't be bothering to discuss it with you or anyone else; you'll just find me dead. Oh, don't fret," she added in response to the other woman's concerned expression. "The Most Learned High Healer keeps filling me up with nasty little tinctures made from fish oil and whatever else he can scrape off the bottom of his shoe. Apparently, they're strengthening. No, I need to talk to you about Bessic, the new First Oracle of Incasa who's been writing me some very pressing and worrisome letters about Spar as of late. The delon's abilities are waxing, despite his young age."

The marshal glanced over to where Spar was standing in his usual place, systematically piercing a practice dummy in the chest with shaft after shaft, his expression blank and staring.

"Age," she repeated. "Was it his upbringing or his experiences since that's aged Spar so quickly, do you think?"

Elif gave an eloquent shrug that dropped the shawl about her shoulders into her lap. "Both, I would imagine." She paused as Murad came forward to readjust it, then retreated out of earshot again. "But he's not so old as he pretends to be," she continued, her tone softening. "He still needs both nurturing and discipline."

The marshal snorted. "You're one to talk about discipline. You let him run away from lessons whenever he pleases."

"He's a seer. His lessons are different than mere weapons training and strategy."

"Exactly. He needs religious training and practice in the seer's circle, neither of which he's had."

"I'm waiting for a sign."

The younger woman glanced over at her. "You know, I've always suspected that was just a seer's ploy to get people off your back."

Elif smiled. "Suspicion is not proof, Delin," she answered, her cataract- and vision-filled eyes warming. "Besides, how much training outside the weapons' circles has Brax completed?"

"That's different."

"Is it? Can he even write his name yet?"

"Writing's an overrated skill for a soldier."

"But not for a priest, and if he's to be consecrated as ghazi-delinkos, he must be educated. Come Bray-Delin, it didn't kill you, it won't kill him. He's close to his oath-taking, he needs more academics."

"How close?"

"Tanay says he crossed fifteen ten days after Havo's Dance. He should be ready by next Low Spring. But . . ." she held up one warning hand. "Brax glows with the silver light of Her favor. And it's a hot light; too hot for his age. It might burn him out or the God might bear him up. Delinkon may not make their oaths before sixteen, but whether they receive the Gods Themselves before that has always been mere speculation."

"So what you're saying is that the ritual is actually meaningless?"

"Don't get smart," Elif snapped irritably. "You know very well that the ritual has meaning, it's age that's sometimes meaningless. But in this case Brax's age is acting against him. He needs to learn how to read and write, *Ghazi-Priest* Marshal Brayazi."

The younger woman raised both hands in a gesture of surrender. "Fine. I'll have Kemal throw him in a sack tomorrow morning and force him to take lessons from Ihsan with Spar. Happy?"

Elif inclined her head graciously. "Yes, and in exchange I'll suggest, but only suggest, mind you, that Spar join Brax in the shield circle in the afternoon. He'll likely go, he wants Brax to be learned as much as I do, and so he may be willing to honor our exchange of hostages, but he may not. Don't be surprised if he vanishes before then."

The marshal shrugged. "If he vanishes, he's easily found; he's generally in the kitchens, and before you wonder, no, Tanay has not approached me regarding any shift in his training away from weapons and toward baking and pushing people around. But apparently Senior Abayos-Priest Neclan also wants to interview him."

"I would imagine that's because, like all of Oristo's priests, she believes theirs is the only temple that can raise delon properly."

"They may be right," the marshal said, watching as Spar jerked a handful of arrows from the practice target with an angry expression.

"Bollocks," Elif retorted bluntly.

"Hm. So you don't think she wants him for his prophetic ability?"

Elif gave a dismissive wave of one gnarled hand. "Seers with such a strong gift as Spar's do not serve at Oristo's temple," she sniffed. "Only Incasa's and Estavia's. But," she held up one hand. "Don't be so quick to rule out Tanay, regardless. I've always had my suspicions about her abilities and if she wants him, she may get him. They spend a lot of time together. Nothing is constant, Brax has proved that."

"So, what do we do?"

"Nothing. It's a long shot and if it happens, we'll see it coming." Her expression grew serious. "The machinations of Incasa's temple, however, are an entirely different, much more dangerous, matter. And that's why I *summoned* you, Marshal-Delin. As I said, the new First Oracle's been taking far too strong an interest in Spar recently. The delon's forays into vision have begun to disturb the streams."

"The streams or the God of streams?"

"Both, likely. Bessic has asked for permission to interview him."

"Why? Can't their people see the future around the ripples caused by a ten year old?"

Elif just shrugged.

"Have you told Kaptin Liel?" the marshall asked.

"No, but Liel will be resistant, of course."

"Good. Incasa's temple's never been happy with the autonomy of Estavia's battle-seers. They're always trying to lure the less combative ones away and they're not getting Spar. He's ours."

"I shouldn't worry about his being less combative," Elif said mildly. "He's far more aggressive than he seems. But it helps that we're agreed; it saves us from having to convince you to hide him when Bessic arrives."

"Which will be when?"

"Whenever you *invite* him."

"How about next High Spring?"

Elif snickered. "I don't imagine he'll want to wait that long, but . . ." she shrugged. "It's your temple."

"Not to hear Tanay talk. Or yourself for that matter." Brayazi sat back on her heels with a grimace. "I suppose it had better be sooner than later," she sighed. "But do you think we could we stall him for a few weeks at least?"

"Possibly. I've stalled him for as long already." Elif frowned. "Something's about to happen, Bray-Delin. I can feel it in my bones. And the visioning is changing from water to fire."

"But isn't that good? After all, Estavia's imagery is fiery, isn't it?"

"No, it is not good, *Marshal*," Elif snapped. "Estavia's *manifestations* are fiery, not Her imagery."

When Brayazi just gave her a mystified expression, she clucked her tongue in annoyance. "Never mind. You'd understand that if you were a seer." Her milky-white gaze tracked across the sky, watching the swirls of power wheel and turn like a flock of starlings seeking autumn berries. "A child of great potential still unformed standing on the streets of Anavatan. The twin dogs of creation and destruction crouch at its feet. The child is ringed by silver swords and golden knives and its eyes are filled with *fire*. It draws strength from Anavatan's unsworn and will be born under the cover of Havo's Dance."

"Freyiz's prophecy." The marshal tipped her head to one side. "Incasa's temple has never fully explained its particulars to anyone's satisfaction. At every Assembly it's always the same: what is it, is it dangerous, what do we do about it? They always answer: wait."

"The waiting may soon be over."

"How soon?"

"Within the year, I'm thinking. The future is in motion, caused by something greater than whatever our little oracle over there is disturbing," she added, nodding toward Spar who was now standing talking quietly with Brax on the other side of the training yard. "Something that's been in motion for some time."

"The prophecy."

"Likely; a stream with many strands swaying back and forth like fine sea grass drifting in the ocean." Her voice had gone wispy and soft and the marshal had to lean over to hear her. "A hundred futures, some ending in blood, others in flowers. Now where have I seen that imagery before?" She glanced up. "I'm getting old, Delin, old and forgetful."

"Nonsense. You're just tired." As a fine, cool rain began to fall, the marshal stood, gesturing to Murad who came forward to lift up the old woman, blankets and all. "I think it's best to be blunt with the First Oracle," she decided. "I'll write to him that he cannot see Spar this autumn whatever the streams may be doing. He's too young and too vulnerable since he experienced Chian's death. Perhaps sometime in winter if Samlin agrees."

Elif nodded wearily. "Bessic was a patient delon as I remember," she mused. "Good at teasing the wilier fish from the waters around Adasi-Koy. I don't know if this new position has changed him, but I should think we have until Havo's Dance at the latest before he gets really snippy." She laid her head against her attendant's shoulder. "I'll let you know if that changes."

"And what about the prophecy?"

The old woman grinned mischievously. "As Incasa's temple keeps saying: wait. I'll let you know if that changes, too."

"Sayin . . ."

"Delin." She turned. "Murad, I'd like to visit the infirmary for a few moments. I feel the need for one of Samlin's nasty little tinctures." As her attendant turned to go, the seer reached out from her nest of blankets and shawls to touch the marshal lightly on one arm. "Our own stream should open up by Havo's Dance at the latest," she said. "Until then, be patient and do nothing."

"Yes, Sayin." Stepping back, Marshal Brayazi watched as Murad carried the old woman through the pairs of training fighters, all of whom paused to smile or salute her as she passed. Brax and Spar followed their progress with their eyes until they disappeared through the infirmary door, then they turned and made their own way to the infantry quarters, Jaq keeping close behind.

"Havo's Dance it is," the marshal said thoughtfully. "But no longer."

15

Champions

ORISTO'S AUTUMN PASSED and, as Incasa's winter squalls darkened the waters of Gol-Beyaz, those warriors remaining at Estavia-Sarayi settled down to a quiet routine of storytelling, gambling, and guard duty. The days grew shorter and the rains colder. The sun hid its face behind a constant veil of heavy, gray clouds and a bone-chilling mist that covered every surface, inside and out, with a damp, slippery coating of moisture. In Cyan Company's quarters, Kemal and Yashar divided their time between their duties and their orders to keep Spar and Brax focused on religious and academic training. It was hardest with Brax who seemed increasingly unable to concentrate on anything that did not involve the sword, but even Spar had begun to show an uncharacteristically stubborn disinterest, often disappearing from their rooms well before dawn. As the final days of winter brought a violent storm sweeping in from the northern sea to drive even the hardiest warrior into the dormitories, they eventually gave up. Spring would see warmer weather and then they could all concentrate a little better. Spar took the news with his usual élan; Brax breathed a sigh of relief.

✦

Making his way down the quiet, spiral staircase that led to the temple's central shrine, Brax shivered despite the warmth of a heavy woolen jacket. His face and hair were plastered to his skull from having spent the morning on the eastern battlements with Spar, standing below the great black marble statue of Estavia which stared out across the strait at Dovek-Hisar. The waves below'd had an icy sheen to them.

It had been the same six days ago when Spar had first led him there. The younger boy had stared down at the water for a long time before turning a pale, unfocused gaze on Brax's face.

✦

"Something's happening," he said bluntly.

Brax felt a corkscrew of worry twist in his belly. "Yeah?" he asked carefully, resisting the urge to rub his left elbow which had suddenly begun to throb dully. "Like what?"

The younger boy shook his head.

"You know, the last time you said that we ended up in a battle," Brax observed, allowing a faint tone of reproof to enter his voice.

Spar just blinked the rain from his eyes before giving his familiar one-shouldered shrug. "I know."

He fell silent again and Brax studied him with a worried frown. A season's worth of warm clothes and heavy soups and stews had kept the winter pallor from the younger boy's cheeks for the first time in his life. He was taller and heavier, and his hair which had always fallen limp and lifeless about his face, was now thick and shiny—or would have been if it hadn't been soaking wet. He'd taken to wearing it long and loose like the temple's battle-seers, with a single brown bead woven into one lock. He looked better than he ever had, but his gaze was drawing farther inward every day; sometimes it was hours before he even noticed there were other people in the room with him.

"Something?" Brax prodded as the wind began to whistle through his own hair. "That doesn't involve us getting blown off the wall and drowned?"

The faintest hint of a smile touched Spar's lips. "Maybe."

"I'm glad to hear it. I'd hate to think I was out here for no good reason." Resting his right elbow on the stone wall, he purposely ignored the irritated frown the younger boy turned on him.

"I needed to talk to you," Spar said stiffly.

"And you couldn't do it someplace dry?"

"No." Spar's brows drew down. "It's too misty back there. I can't see."

Glancing up as the rapidly rising wind brought a heavy fog rolling in from the Bogazi-Isik Strait, Brax sighed. "So, what do you see out here?"

"Flowers the color of blood and gold strewn across a sunlit floor."

Of all the things he'd been expecting to hear, that hadn't been one of them.

✦

Now, as Brax reached the bottom of the stairs, the sounds of the wind and the rain faded. Passing under an archway, he made his way along a narrow corridor until he came to a familiar wooden door reinforced with iron. A small wall niche to one side held a tiny bronze statue of Estavia and he laid his sword hand on his chest in salute before pushing the door open.

More a mausoleum than a chapel, most of the residents of Estavia-Sarayi avoided the central shrine out of respect for the man interned here, so Brax knew from experience that it would be empty of worshipers, but that the oil lamps to either side of the door would be over half full, the tall incense brazier in one corner no more than a third empty; the altar would be clean of dust, and its bowl of lotus flowers would be fresh and sweet-smelling. Crossing the shadowed room, he drew his sword and, after laying it across the altar, came around to stare up at the Battle God's much larger statue standing in its high, domed alcove above Kaptin Haldin's tomb. Under the weight of its crimson regard, he slowly felt himself calm as he had the first time he had come here so many months before.

Brax had been coming here every day since they'd returned to Anavatan last spring. It was the only place he could gain any respite from the God's lien which kept up a constant, buzzing demand that he train, rain or shine, day in and day out, from the time he rose in the morning to the time he collapsed exhausted into bed at night when even his dreams were filled with images of conquest and battle. Here in the shrine, however, the lien calmed as if willing to accept quiet homage in place of violent action for at least a little while.

Breathing in the deep comforting silence like a balm, he knelt to press his hands against the black marble slab that covered the body of Kaptin Haldin.

Traditionally, the Warriors of Estavia stood in ranks or sat astride before their God as they would do on the battlefield and, when he stood with them, he stood as one of them. Every morning and every evening he took his place with the older delinkon of Cyan Company, feeling the power of their God course through his body to join with every other worshiper on Her parade ground and beyond. On the first day of Her High Summer he'd stood in the company shrine, listening while the adult warriors repeated the oaths they'd sworn the day they were accepted into Her service. The delinkon around him had stood rigidly silent, overawed by the heavy solemnity of the words, but he'd seen their lips moving as they'd spoken their own private oaths or repeated prayers of thanks or supplication they'd sent to Her in the past. Brax himself had breathed the words that had changed his life.

"Save us, God of Battles, and I will pledge you my life, my worship, and my last drop of blood forever."

Even at a whisper, his voice echoed overloud in the empty shrine, and he closed his eyes as the resurging memory of Her response on Liman-Caddesi made him feel young and desperate again, the cold of the stone slab seeping through his fingers making him feel a little sick. Surrounded by Her soldiers he stood as one of them, but here, where the man She'd loved above all others lay beneath Her feet, he knelt as Her Champion. Reaching out with his mind, he imagined the body of Kaptin Haldin lying beneath him, still and quiet, while his spirit rested in the warmth of Her presence deep below the waters of Gol-Beyaz. It made him feel better somehow, closer to both of them. If he could have sunk down beneath the slab himself to become one with Haldin's dust and bones, he would have.

He reddened, imagining what Spar would think of this feeling were he ever stupid enough to actually tell him. The sneer the younger boy would turn on him would be so cutting it would likely kill him on the spot. And in a way he'd be right. It sounded far too melodramatic and gruesome, even a little bit obscene, to actually be real, but it was the only way Brax had to describe what was more of a deep, bone-filling need than a simple emotion. He had no idea if the rest of Her warriors felt this way. He was far too embarrassed to ask Kemal or Yashar, but he supposed that it didn't really matter. Estavia knew it and accepted it, was greedy for it in fact, as greedy as a child standing beside a traveling confectioner handing out free rahat loukoum; greedy for them all, the sweets, the tray, even for the confectioner. For that matter, greedy for the sweet shop, the market it resided in, and the city which held the market. The tingle of amused and avaricious agreement made him smile.

Now, closing his eyes, he reached into that tingle, feeling Her presence in the underlying warmth that always began in his chest, then spread down to his belly and groin, his arms and legs, his hands and feet, and finally to his face. Once it had filled him like a pool of deep, liquid fire, he asked that it be directed down and through the stiffened scarring that curved along his shield arm. The responding trickle of warmth made him tip his head back with almost drunken pleasure.

The physician-priests of Usara at Serin-Koy had been uncertain if he'd ever regain the full use of his arm. At Kemal's request they'd petitioned the God of Healing for aid, but even after that God's gift of power their prognosis had been doubtful; the Yuruk's attack had shattered his elbow, Graize's corresponding blow had torn the surrounding tissue almost beyond repair, but Brax believed that Estavia would not let him be crippled. He'd suffered the healers' ministrations, both there and in the temple infirmary after they'd returned to Anavatan, following their orders about medicine and exercise, but every day he'd come here to the very center of Her temple and sent his need to his own God, the Battle God; his need and his unshakable belief in Her love and in Her power. And every day She responded, sending a thin line of Her own hot and blood-red power through the damaged bones and muscles, making them stronger—not healing them perhaps, for that was not within Her sphere of influence, but definitely making them stronger. Now, although his arm often felt thick and heavy, like it was carved out of wood, there was very little pain or weakness in the joint. He could carry a shield and wield it well enough to ward off a blow. That was all that mattered.

As this latest line of power grew, then faded, he sent Her a quiet prayer of thanks, laying his right hand on his chest once again, then turned and sat at the edge of the tomb, resting his back against the altar as Kemal had done so many months before. Now that he was calm and hale, he could mull over the rest of Spar's strange revelation in peace.

The younger boy had turned eyes gone unusually dark on Brax's face, and he'd felt a thrill of disquiet as Spar had begun to speak.

✦

"We've been here almost a year," he said in a tone that suggested that Brax would understand the underlying meaning in the words, but when the older boy just gave him a blank look in reply, he snorted impatiently. "A year this Havo's Dance," he expanded. "*Last* Havo's Dance the spirits of the wild lands broke through the wards on Anavatan's walls and flowed through the streets like a river of death."

Brax made a face at him, wondering why, in all the years of near silence, Spar had chosen this time to get poetic, and wishing he'd done it inside by a warm mangel instead of outside in the fog and in the wind.

"*This* Havo's Dance will be in nine days," Spar continued.

"So?" Brax finally answered, forcing his voice to remain casual as he realized where the younger boy was going with this. "It's different now; everyone's been warned, yeah?"

"So?" Spar threw his word back at him.

"So, they're ready for it this year."

"They are. You aren't."

"Me?"

Something soft like a flying insect flitted past them and Spar turned a dark gaze in its direction. "Don't even try it," he hissed, before returning his attention to the older boy, then frowned. "What?" he demanded as Brax favored him with an alarmed expression.

"What was all that about?"

"Territory."

"What?"

"Never mind, it's not important right now. Something's gonna happen," he said, repeating his earlier words. "Something's that's already started. They can't stop it." He turned away to stare down into the churning water below them. "They might not want to," he added quietly almost as an afterthought. "But I don't care what they want; I don't care what any of them want!"

His tone had become so savage that Brax took an involuntary step backward and Spar shook his head ruefully. "But I do care about you," he continued in a slightly more moderate tone. "So I need you to listen to me, *really* listen to me like you used to. Do you remember?"

"Sure."

"No, I mean actually, really remember! Like when I said you were in danger back then, you listened! You have to listen now!"

Brax raised both hands. "All right, Spar, I'm listening now."

"You're in danger. I've seen it."

"All right. How?"

Spar glared at him as if he'd been expected a different answer and suspected a trick. "Something's gonna happen on Havo's Dance; something with the spirits. You're gonna get dragged into it, and if you go in unprotected, you'll die."

"I'm protected by Estavia."

"No, you aren't."

"Spar . . ."

"Shut up!" The younger boy turned on him furiously. "You're not! You're so . . . so . . . delusional!" he shouted. "And don't ask me what that means, you know what it means! You wanna be Kaptin Haldin, *you want everything he was, and everything he had*, right? Well, he wasn't fifteen, Brax!"

The look on his face dared the older boy to make some facetious comment about being almost sixteen, but Brax just held his mouth closed and waited. After a moment, Spar turned back to the waves.

"Do you remember the book," he asked suddenly.

Brax blinked. "What book?"

"The jeweled book we saw that first day, the one you said was so ugly."

"No."

"The book on the dais. In the armory," Spar said between clenched teeth.

"Oh. Yeah, that book."

"Did you ever wonder what was in it?"

Brax fought back a sarcastic smile. "Um . . . since I didn't even remember looking at it, you can figure that would be a no, right," he ventured. "Why?"

Spar closed his eyes for half a moment and Brax could see him counting slowly. When he opened his eyes again, they were back to their usual color. "It's a history," he said more calmly. "A journal, from ancient times to now. The priests of Ystazia write in it sometimes."

"Yeah? So why is it here instead of at Ystazia-Sarayi?"

"To guard it."

"Against what?"

"Readers."

Brax risked a disbelieving face. "I thought the priests of Ystazia figured reading was a sacred duty. Aren't they always after everyone to learn how?"

"No, they're always after *you*. Most people would be thankful for the gift of it."

"Most people can't afford the *gift* of it," Brax countered gently. "The priests usually *charge* for it."

"Whatever. The book," Spar repeated.

"Right. The history."

"It's a history of the things the Gods won't speak of."

Brax went quiet.

"Others—mostly the priests of Incasa—believe something happened during those years that the Gods want shrouded in mystery."

"Can't they just ask?"

"They have. No one's ever received an answer. Ask Estavia yourself. See what She says."

Brax closed his eyes, remembering the heavy silence that had greeted his request. When he opened them again, Spar was regarding him with a knowing expression.

"So, how come the priests of Ystazia can write it down at all?" the older boy asked.

"It's what they do."

"Huh?"

"The priests, they write down what happens as it happens. They give it form." Spar explained. "The Gods can't stop them 'cause it's what they do, it's what they are, priestly *scribes*. If the Gods tried to stop them, They'd lose worship." His expression grew bitter. "So they'd lose *power*. But that means that even years later when the Gods have decided that they don't like what happened or maybe don't want anyone to know *how* it happened, the words are still there, written down. Given form. Words have power, especially written words."

"So, what'd the words in the book say?"

"I don't know."

Brax shot him an exasperated glance and Spar just waved a dismissive hand back at him. "Ihsan let me look at it a couple of days ago. The first few pages are written in a language no one can read anymore, but it's also got pictures. The first one was of Estavia standing above a woman, Marshal Nurcan, I think Ihsan said her name was; the first Marshal ever. She looked just like Estavia; kinda like Marshal Brayazi looks like Her. Kaptin Haldin was standing beside them with red-and-golden power coming out of his mouth."

"You mean into," Brax interrupted.

"No, I mean *out of*," Spar growled in reply.

"Last time you said into."

"Last time was different."

"How?"

"Because it was!"

The anger was rising in Spar's voice again, and Brax made a quick gesture of surrender. "Fine, out of. So what's the problem?"

The younger boy looked searchingly into Brax's eyes for a moment as if trying to decide how much to tell him, then turned abruptly to stare out at the waves again.

"Do you remember how we used to sit on the rooftops in the morning and talk about what was going to happen during the day?" he asked suddenly.

Brax nodded cautiously.

"And how we never told Cindar? He never knew what I saw or how much? We'd just sort out whatever we had to by ourselves?"

"Yeah."

"Well, I don't want anyone else knowing about this either. It's for you and me to sort out. Only. All right?"

"All right."

Spar took a deep breath. "I had a dream last night. I saw a new picture in the book of it happening again, to you, this Havo's Dance."

"What, Estavia and Marshal Brayazi sucking a bunch of red-and-golden power out my mouth?" Brax asked with a confused frown.

"Not exactly. Not Marshal Brayazi, anyway."

"So who, exactly, anyway?"

"I'm not sure. The dream was kinda hazy," Spar replied in a defensive tone. "But Estavia was involved somehow."

Brax gave him an even look. "And?" he asked simply.

"And you need to make your oaths to Her before then or you won't survive it. I saw that, too."

Taken aback by an answer he wasn't expecting, Brax poked at the inside of his cheek with his tongue for a moment, before turning his head to regard the younger boy out of the corner of one eye. "If She wants my death, I won't deny it to Her, Spar," he said seriously. "I can't."

Spar showed his teeth at him. "I'm not asking you to."

"But I'm not sixteen."

"It doesn't matter."

"What if they won't let me make my oaths yet?"

"Elif will let you. She'll know it's important."

"How?"

"Because she's a seer, stupid! She'll have *seen* most of this herself by now!"

"Why won't she see it all?"

"Because the Gods have hidden most of it. And don't ask me why, it doesn't matter."

"But how come you can see it?"

" 'Cause They can't see me."

"Why?"

"That doesn't matter either." When Brax continued to look doubtful, Spar tugged a hand through his hair in frustration. "Look, this was what you wanted wasn't it?" he demanded. "What you've been after ever since we arrived?"

"Well, yeah."

"So, what's the problem?"

Brax looked away. "You know I can't read," he said finally.

"I know you *won't* read," the younger boy snarled back at him.

"Whatever. They won't consecrate me as a ghazi-delinkos without it."

"Well, you should have thought of that before now."

"I figured I'd have more time."

"You don't."

"So what do I do?"

"Suffer."

"Not funny."

"Not meant to be."

They locked eyes for a moment, then Brax gave a rueful nod. "Fair enough. All right, so beyond that, what do I do?" When Spar shrugged, he raised an eyebrow at him. "You're the one who said I had to listen to you, so I'm listening. What do I do?"

Spar glared at him, but in the face of Brax's seeming compliance his expression grew more thoughtful than angry. "Cindar once told me that the difference between sworn and unsworn delon is that the oaths of their abayon cover them until they're sixteen."

"Doesn't sound like him," Brax noted mildly.

"Yeah, well, actually he said that the sworn shackle their delon to a life of groveling servitude."

"Now *that* does sound like him."

"Either way, we were unsworn because Cindar was unsworn."

"So Bayard's delon are sworn because he and Maydir are sworn?"

"Basically."

"But aren't we sworn men? Because Kemel and Yasher are."

"Yes. But it won't be enough. So what, exactly, are these big oaths the Warriors of Estavia are supposed to make?"

"You mean you don't know?" Brax replied, unable to resist the prod.

Spar ignored the tone. "No," he said.

"They're called First Oaths. Everyone who swears to a God makes them at sixteen. They're supposed to . . . I dunno, symbolize being an adult; you know, making adult choices about your life and what you're gonna do with it. The followers of Estavia swear their lives, their service, and their training to Her. Inside." He pressed his hand to his chest. "Private-like, just to Her, even though they're standing with other people when they do it. There's more . . . bits of, you know, ceremony, to it than that, but that's essentially it."

"But haven't you done that already?"

"Didn't you tell me Tanay said it didn't count until you were sixteen?"

"Yeah, but she's not a warrior."

"Well, apparently, she's right. *The temple, all temples* think you don't know your own mind until you're sixteen—even if you do know it—and so they think any oaths you swear before then don't really take."

"What does Estavia think?"

Brax gave a passable imitation of Spar's characteristic snort. "She knows I'm Hers."

"And what do *you* think?"

Brax laid his hand on his chest again, smiling as he felt the God's responding tingle. "The same." Glancing at the younger boy, he nodded in understanding as he'd done each day they'd sat on the Western Trisect dockside roofs and planned their day. "All right, so I don't make ghazi-delinkos this year," he said. "Some delinkon don't right away either, so there's no real reason I ought to, except for your dream. Will the rest of the oaths be enough?"

"You better hope they are," the younger boy snarled back, but when Brax continued to stare at him, he just shrugged. "Probably," he allowed.

"So how do we get me sworn without telling anyone why I need to be?"

"I'll handle that part."

✦

Later that night, Spar had awakened him with a scream of terror that had roused half the Cyan Company dormitory and sent Jaq into a frenzy of frightened barking. Their abayon had come pounding into the room, and while Kemal'd half wrestled the dog from the pallet, Yashar'd caught up the now hysterical boy in his arms. All he could make out from the stream of incoherent crying and babbling was that Spar'd had a terrible nightmare. Rocking him back and forth, he'd murmured as many comforting words and snatches of lullabies as he could think of into the boy's sweat-dampened hair, until finally, spent and exhausted, Spar had fallen asleep in his arms.

It happened again an hour later.

The next morning he could remember nothing more than the frightening image of Brax's death.

Kemal and Yashar took him to see Elif at once and, after a long day of careful probing she'd managed to discover the core of his *nightmare:* Brax, standing alone on Havo's Dance, facing a death that his immature oaths to Estavia could not prevent.

From Elif they went to Kaptin Julide, Kaptin Liel, Marshal Brayazi, and finally to the command council. After an hour's deliberation it was agreed. Brax would make his First Oaths on Usara's Last Day, thirteen days before he turned sixteen.

No one but Brax had seen the look of triumphant disdain that had flashed in the younger boy's eyes for one brief instant, and Brax had no time to do anything about it. Usara's Last Day was in eight days. The council hoped that would give him enough time to master enough of his letters to be consecrated as ghazi-delinkos.

It hadn't been. Warrior-delinkos would have to be enough.

✦

Leaving yet another frustratingly failed lesson with Ihsan this morning, he'd allowed Spar to draw him back to the eastern battlements, knowing that a hailstorm would not deter the younger boy from whatever high, lonely place he was currently obsessed with. At the wall, Spar had held out one hand.

"Here. This will help." Opening his hand, he offered Brax a small, brown bead like the one in his hair, strung on a finely-braided leather cord. "Tanay gave me three on Oristo's Last Day. The Petchan hill fighters wear them as protections against the spirits," he explained in response to Brax's confused expression.

"I thought Ihsan said they covered themselves in sheep's blood," the older boy said with a frown.

"They do that, too."

Brax held the bead up to one eye, then raised an eyebrow in Spar's direction.

"I don't know," the younger boy snapped at the unspoken question. "Maybe the color, maybe the ceramic. Does it matter? Just wear it."

"All right, all right." Brax passed the cord over his neck, tucking the bead inside his jacket. "So where's the other one?" he asked.

Spar frowned questioningly at him.

"The other bead," he expanded. "You said Tanay gave you three?"

"Oh. I wove it into Jaq's collar."

Glancing back at the corner sentry box, Brax could just make out the dog's large, red nose sticking out from the shadows. "Well, at least he has the sense to stay out of the rain. Can we please go in now, I doubt this thing's gonna protect us from the cold."

"Not yet."

"Spar . . ."

"No. Not. Yet. There's something you need to see."

✦

He stared out at the strait, his eyes gone the more normal misty-white, staring until Brax began to tap his fingers against the rain-slicked battlements, then pointed suddenly.

"There."

"Where?"

"Just above the waves before Dovek-Hisar."

Brax squinted past his finger. In the distance, nearly invisible in the gray, driving rain, a silvery creature, almost like a fine flying insect, flitted back and forth above the waves.

"What is it?"

"A very special kind of spirit."

Brax frowned. "I thought the spirits couldn't get anywhere near Gol-Beyaz," he said.

Spar made his standard one-shouldered shrug. "It isn't near it, not really."

"Huh?"

"It isn't really in the actual world yet. Or maybe It's not actually real Itself yet. I don't know. It doesn't matter. Just remember It."

He fell silent and, after a long time, Brax glanced over at him.

"All right. Um, is that all? Can we go inside now?" he asked.

His eyes slowly returning to their usual blue, Spar glanced up at the statue of Estavia before giving a weary nod. "Yeah," he said. "That's all I can do."

Together they made their way back to where Jaq sat sentry, while out on the strait, the Godling made one final pass, then turned and sped up the Halic-Salmanak towards Gol-Bardak.

✦

On the hillside overlooking the Rus-Yuruk's winter encampment, Graize watched as a great mass of spirits merged and flowed over the Berbat-Dunya in preparation for their yearly assault on the Gods' wall of power.

A change in the air caused his right pupil to contract suddenly and he turned to see the Godling streaking along the surface of the lake, sending up great spouts of water in Its wake. He raised one hand, and It immediately changed course and raced toward him. Spinning about his face, It tickled his mouth and nose with power, then shot upward into the air as another figure appeared above the narrow, winding path. As Danjel joined him on the edge, Graize stared thoughtfully down as the Godling dropped toward the encampment, giving Rayne's yak's tail standard, bobbing above the largest of the pitched tents below them, a hearty smack before spiraling up into the air again. It was getting impatient. Sucking up a tiny spirit that had latched itself to his upper lip, he grimaced. So was he, but the next move in the game was going to be tricky.

Graize had ridden with Kursk's kazakin all summer, harassing the shepherds and farmers from one village to another, leading the Warriors of Estavia on an increasingly enjoyable chase back and forth across the plains, then vanishing as autumn brought an end to the warring season. The winter had been a time to pause, regroup, eat, rest, mend cloth and leather, and learn the ways of his new people and their wyrdins from Timur and Danjel. Now, with spring so close the smell of new, green earth invaded his dreams, it was time for the first move in the season's new game. Laying each of his shells out in his mind's eyes, he held up the pea.

Turning to Danjel with a wide gaze, his uneven pupils almost completely obliterated by a fine, white mist, he gestured at the setting sun.

"Drops of blood and gold," he said, making his voice go thin and misty.

Twirling a hawk fetish between finger and thumb, Danjel nodded. "Blood and gold feed the people," he agreed absently.

"Yes, and the people are hungry for action. Spring will be in nine days. In nine days we'll feed that hunger."

"How?"

In his mind, Graize set the pea under the first of his turtle shells. "By attacking Anavatan," he answered.

"What?" Danjel stared at the other wyrdin as if he'd gone finally, truly mad, while a nearby spirit took the opportunity to knock the fetish from his grip and send it spinning down to land at Graize's feet.

And now the shells began to move. "It's time, kardos," Graize said, retrieving the three-tied feathers and pressing them into the other wyrdin's hand.

"To attack the city of the Gods? To what purpose?"

"To pay a debt."

"Whose debt?"

"Ours." Sucking the spirit into his mouth, Graize smiled as he tasted the hint of new spring growth in its power, then deliberately brought his attention back to the other wyrdin, making his words both clear and determined. "The Godling fought beside the Rus-Yuruk all year, asking little in return. Now It needs to bathe in the waters of Gol-Beyaz to build its strength or there can be no more fighting and the Yuruk will have lost a powerful weapon. It was the bargain we struck with It on that very first day, if you'll remember."

Danjel cast him a suspicious look. "I remember that you said It would be satisfied with alliance."

"I did," Graize agreed. "And now It needs Its allies to break It through the God-Wall of Anavatan to the shining lake of power, as It once helped them to break through the defenders at Serin-Koy," he reminded him.

"A wall of spears about a village is one thing; the *God-Wall* is something else again. That wall cannot be broken, *kardos*."

"Yes, it can." Closing his eyes, Graize lifted his face to the rising wind. "We shall attack the shining city,' he murmured. "My Godling will guide us and the spirits of the wild lands will hide us. We'll flow over the walls like a river and the spirits will flow with us. The drops of blood and gold will fall upon the cobblestones and yield a harvest of power and death the like of which no one has ever seen."

"Horseshit," Danjel spat. "The wall will hold as it always has."

"No, the wall is weak and it will crack."

"Even if it did, the Gods'll see us coming a mile away."

Graize laughed harshly. "Of course They will. Or He will anyway, the God of Shadows and Secrets. *And a child of great power and potential will be born under the cover of Havo's Dance.*"

The Godling flitted past him in Its insect seeming, and he raised one hand to stroke Its iridescent wings as It passed. "It's what Incasa's been waiting for, after all," he continued. "So, it would be such a shame to disappoint Him. He wants the child to be born and so do we, but we have to make sure It's born in our bed, not in His."

"Or Incasa wins the game," he thought with a snarl. *"And only I win the game. That's the most important rule."*

Danjel shook his head. "Kursk will never agree. Neither will Timur."

"They will if we convince them of the merits of our plan."

"Our plan?"

"Our plan, or did you think your future greatness would come in your dotage?"

"Big word, kardos," Danjel warned.

"Maybe, but without the Godling's strength the Yuruk will never beat the Warriors of Estavia, and your greatness will wither on the vine."

"My *life* will wither on the vine," Danjel retorted. "It's too risky. They're too many. Most of us would never live to feed from your drops of blood and gold."

"Yes, we would. Which one, which one, which one has the pea underneath it? Place your shine, place your shine." Graize raised a hand to forestall Danjel's next protest. "Remember, Kardos it's just like a shell game, you make the mark look anywhere but where the pea really is. Last time we used a mass attack of kazakin. This time we only need a few, well chosen people. We're not smashing the wall; we're just cutting a tiny little hole through it to let a tiny, little turtle shell inside. It's worth the risk for the blood and the gold." He leaned forward. "The Godling's almost fully in the game now, kardos," he said urgently, "almost in our very dangerous game. It only needs one more move to win, but to make it, It needs your help. Will you help it?"

Which one has the pea? Place your shine.

Tipping his head up, Danjel watched as the Godling turned and spun in the air, so close to a true form now that It resembled a fine, translucent dragonfly to almost anyone who knew how to look for It. "You'll need a lot more of the details fleshed out to convince Kursk and Timur," he warned.

"And to convince you?"

The other youth frowned, the green of his eyes paling to a fine, northern jade streaked with white. "With your few well chosen people I can see the stream," he allowed, then he nodded. "Yes, I'll help It."

"Then let's go place our shine, Kardos."

Turning, Graize plunged down the hillside at once, the Godling trailing along behind him like a feathery comet. After a long, thoughtful pause, Danjel tucked the hawk fetish safely away in his belt pouch and followed them.

16

Preparations

AT ESTAVIA-SARAYI, Usara's Last Day dawned much as it had the year before, with a rising wind and a heavy, concealing bank of storm clouds to the west. As the first note of Havo's Invocation filtered through the room's latticed windows on a breath of cold wind, Brax painted the Battle God's final protection along his right forearm and then gently wiped the brush clean before laying it across its white marble drying rack. As he turned, he caught sight of Kemal standing just inside the door holding a silk shirt draped across one arm. His brows drew down.

"I can get dressed by myself," he said, then scowled at both the petulant tone and the poorly masked quaver of nervousness underneath it. "Everyone's treating me like some kind of invalid."

Behind him, a muffled snort from deep within the bed clothes made Spar's opinion quite plain.

"Yeah, well, who asked you?" he shot back. "This is all your fault, anyway."

"Today's a special day," Kemal replied as he came forward with a smile.

"That's what everyone else keeps saying. It's no different than any other Oath Day."

"It's entirely different," Yashar noted from the doorway. "First Oaths are a time for family to celebrate together and, as you're the only delinkos to ever take First Oaths at Estavia-Sarayi, everyone at Her temple is part of your family, and so everyone wants to celebrate with you.

"I did warn you," he added as Brax began a new protest, "ten thousand abayon, remember?"

Brax just sighed.

He'd been up since well before dawn. Tanay herself had come to wake him, handing him a cup of hot salap before leading him into Kemal and Yashar's bathing room. It had been crowded with junior priests of Oristo and he'd almost balked at the door, but one firm palm in the small of his back had propelled him into their midst.

An hour later, soaked, washed, shaved, trimmed, brushed, and covered in scented oils, he'd felt like a prize ram on market day. He'd said as much to Spar as he was being hustled back into their room and the younger boy'd just snickered at him before disappearing under the covers once more. Stretched across the bottom of the pallet, Jaq had lifted his head to peer reproachfully at him, then he, too, had lain back down again.

"Great. Everyone gets to sleep in except me," Brax had muttered.

A muffled, *"Serves you right,"* had been Spar's only response.

Now, as Brax lifted his arms at Kemal's gesture, he shivered slightly as the cold silk whispered across his skin, then tried, more or less successfully, not to back away as Yashar stood aside to allow half a dozen more junior priests into the room, their arms laden with armor, weapons, and, thankfully, food. He accepted a piece of dried kilic fish from a gold-painted plate, then shook his head with a snort.

"What?" Yashar asked as he caught up a dark blue woolen tunic from one of the priests, the twin swords of Cyan Company embroidered on the front gleaming in the lamplight.

Brax just shrugged. "Nothing. I was just remembering something I told Spar a long time ago about the Warriors of Estavia."

"Something positive, I hope."

"Sort of. I guess. I think I missed some of it." Lifting his arms again, Brax waited until Yashar had pulled the tunic over his head before stuffing the fish into his mouth.

"Try not to get oil on your clothes," Kemal admonished gently.

"Sorry." About to reach for another piece of kilic, Brax chose a hunk of bread dripping with honey instead, ignoring Kemal's expression. He was hungry all the time these days and if people were going to shove food under his nose, he was going to eat it; he hadn't had a moment's peace to eat quietly in over a week. Taking a deep breath as Kemal wrapped a red linen belt around his waist; he caught a bit of honey as it dribbled toward his tunic with an expression of both guilt and annoyance equally mixed.

✦

Once the council had decided that he would take his oaths on Usara's Last Day, the temple had exploded in a frenzy of activity. What little time Brax had off from the training yard had been taken up by lectures from Kaptin Liel's battle-seers on the upcoming oath-takings, a series of painful pokings and proddings by Chief Healer Samlin's physicians, and a steady barrage of downright bullying from Tanay's servers. Peppered into the mix had been a constant stream of handling by the temple's resident artisan-priests of Ystazia who'd descended on him like a swarm of panicking locusts. Every square inch of his body had been measured and remeasured by weavers, leather workers, embroiderers, and armorers until he'd wanted to scream at them to get away from him, but every time, one look from Spar had brought him up short.

"This was what you wanted, wasn't it? What you've been after ever since we arrived?"

The younger boy had deliberately repeated his words on the battlements after Brax's first and only bolt the day after the council's decision.

Brax had just glared at him in resentful silence.

"So what's the problem?" Spar had demanded again.

The *problem* was that he still hated being stared at as much as he'd ever hated it, and he *really* hated being lectured at, poked, prodded, bullied, drawn on, pinched, and stuck with little pins.

"I feel like I'm being measured up for a really expensive shroud," he'd replied through gritted teeth after a half a dozen tailors had handed him over to as many metalworkers.

"So next time drag us both to Havo-*Sarayi instead of* Estavia-*Sarayi and they'll just measure you up for a really expensive gardening apron."*

"Next time."

Spar had turned an impatient glare in his direction. *"Look, it isn't all about you, all right? But it has to seem like it is on the surface. I told you things were happening, big things, scary things, things we might not want to happen. And if the people making them happen figure out that we're on to them, they'll make them happen someplace else where we're* not *ready for them. But everyone's ready for them here 'cause they've all come together here for your oaths."*

Brax had cocked his head to one side. *"If that's your first attempt at cryptic seer talk,"* he'd noted, *"it needs work."*

Spar had glared at him. *"Fine. You want it simple? You're the distraction, I'm the lifter, everyone else is the mark."*

"So, what's the shine?"

"Your pretty little outfit not all covered in blood, Warrior of Estavia.*"*

His expression had dared Brax to make another joke, but after a moment, the older boy had just shrugged. *"Fair enough."*

Now as Kemal held up a small iron-studded leather cuirass, he noted that, at least the one benefit of all this attention was that everything he was about to put on fit him like a second skin. If the rest of Her warriors were treated with even half so much deference as this, it was no wonder they all carried themselves with so much pride. The cuirass settled across his shoulders with an ancient familiarity that made the breath catch in his throat and he closed his eyes, feeling the lightest whisper of a warm caress across his mind. When he opened them again, Yashar was smiling at him in understanding. He held up a pair of new sandals.

"If you like, you can put these on yourself," he offered graciously.

Brax accepted them with a grimace.

After he'd straightened, noting sourly that Yashar might have mentioned how hard it was to reach your feet while wearing a cuirass—and after Yashar had stopped laughing—his abayon together fitted the finely-etched bronze greaves and vambraces onto his arms and legs, then Yashar wrapped a second old and worn leather belt around his waist as Kemal unwrapped a fine, iron sword from a piece of heavily embroidered blue cloth. Brax raised an eyebrow at it as he slipped it into the plain leather scabbard that matched the belt.

"Your village or home garrison provides your weapons when you go to your first posting," Kemal explained. "This was the first sword I ever wore in Her temple when I was sixteen. It was Bayard's before that. The scabbard, too. I thought you might be able to make some use of it."

"And speaking of home garrisons," Yashar interrupted, digging Kemal in the ribs before Brax could answer. "The cloak pin."

"Ah, yes." Accepting a heavy blue woolen cloak from a junior priest, Kemal draped it across Brax's shoulders with a smile. "The traditional First Oath gift, given to all delinkon by their families to symbolize the underpinning of the future by the past, is a cloak pin fashioned to represent your home village or home garrison. We debated over the form it should take for a long time . . ."

"Argued about it is more accurate," Yashar interjected. "Kemal hated all of my *very* reasonable suggestions."

"*As you've seen,*" Kemal continued, pointedly ignoring the interruption, "Yashar's is fashioned in the shape of a boat for Caliskan-Koy, mine is a sheep for Serin-Koy. The Anavatanon garrisons are all affiliated with one gatehouse tower or another, so their pins are usually in that shape . . ."

"But we didn't think that would suit you, given your history with the city guard." Yashar said dryly. "I thought about a pickpocket's dip," he added with a grin, "but you said you never used them."

"I said *Spar* never used them," Brax pointed out mildly.

"Ah, well, it's too late to change it now."

"Finally," Kemal said firmly, "the God Herself gave us the answer." He held out his hand to reveal a silver, rectangle-shaped pin fashioned to resemble a section of wall. "Defend my barrier. Wasn't that what She told you?"

The final protection on his arm feeling as warm as his face, Brax ducked his head, suddenly unable to speak as Kemal fastened the pin to his cloak.

"Your past: the city itself; and your future: its defense in Her name. And now . . ." Taking him by the shoulders, he turned him toward a heavy, gilt-framed mirror held by two of Oristo's delinkon. "You'd hardly recognize the delon who faced down Estavia's council a full year ago, would you?" he asked as Brax stared at his reflection in wonder.

An unfamiliar, armored youth of medium height, with long, thick, black hair woven with strands of silver and gold and wide, dark eyes stared back at him with far more maturity and confidence than he really felt. He glanced up and down, noting how the cuirass widened his shoulders and how his right hand automatically reached down to rest on the pommel of his sword. With the cloak pin at his throat gleaming as if it were made from the waters of Gol-Beyaz itself, he looked . . . he swallowed . . . he looked like a Warrior of Estavia. Feeling the warm, internal caress once again, he glanced up at his abayon. Both men were grinning widely at him.

"So what happens now?" he asked, suddenly suspicious.

Kemal made an innocent gesture in the direction of the door. "Now we go to breakfast."

"Dressed like this?"

"It's your Oath Day. You'll be dressed like that until after dusk."

"But breakfast. I thought . . ." Brax tipped his head at the plates of food.

"That's just to keep you going through dressing. You'll find there'll be a lot of eating today. Eating and celebrating."

"But only if Spar will haul his lazy carcass out of bed sometime this morning," Yashar added loudly.

Sharing a piece of halva with Jaq and Tanay who'd just rejoined them, Spar gave his older abayos an exaggerated salute with the last of it before sliding off the pallet. A few moments later, dressed in his usual blue training tunic and sandals, he fell into step beside Brax, nodding in satisfaction as he caught sight of the brown bead hanging from the older boy's neck. As their abayon led them from the room, he reached up and tucked it under his tunic. Brax glanced over at him curiously.

"Most of the temple's Oristo-priests know it's there," he noted.

Laying his hand over the bead woven into Jaq's collar, Spar shrugged. "Just humor me," he ordered.

Behind them, Tanay chuckled to herself.

✦

The corridors between the infantry quarters and the refectory were crowded with warriors from every company. Each one slapped Brax on the back or shoulders, called out well wishes, or shouted unnecessary advice. By the time they reached their own dining hall, Brax was reeling and Spar's hands were locked, white-knuckled, on Jaq's collar. Even knowing the dining room would be full to bursting, the roar which greeted them as they walked into the room almost caused both boys to make a run for it, but with Kemal and Yashar blocking their escape they had no choice but to move forward. The crowds parted at once for Kaptin Julide and Birin-Kaptin Arjion who led them to the center table like an honor guard and, distracted as always by food, Spar grabbed for a plate while Brax looked around with an open mouth.

"The entire Company must be here," he said in astonishment.

"The final few arrived from Anahtar-Hisar last night," Kaptin Julide agreed.

"But who's guarding the southern strait?"

"The militia garrison at Satos-Koy."

Yashar sputtered with laughter as he caught sight of Brax's expression. "Why, Delin? Don't you think they're up to the task?"

Brax scowled at him. "Well, sure, but . . . it's just . . . Never mind." He fell silent as the older man stuffed a plate into his hands.

"Don't fret," his abayos said gently. "Eat. There'll be plenty of time for worrying about the future later. Just remember, the sun will rise and set as quickly as it always does today, but *this* day, *your* day, will never come again. Try to enjoy it if you can."

Glancing over at Spar who was already carrying a mountain of food toward their usual table, Brax nodded reluctantly. "Yeah." Eyes tracking to the heavy storm clouds gathering beyond the dining room's latticed windows, he shivered. "Later."

✦

Beside him, Kemal followed his gaze with a concerned expression. First Oaths were a serious matter, but they were also a time for celebration, and as Yashar had said, this day would never come again no matter how many ceremonies, oath-takings or triumphs he might observe in the future. He hoped this worry over Spar's nightmare wasn't going to cloud the day for Brax. Elif and Sable Company had gone into vision every day since and had seen no more than the usual spring danger building over the Berbat-Dunya. But they had agreed; Brax was vulnerable because of his experiences on Liman-Caddesi and at Serin-Koy and just as Spar had predicted, Elif had seen that this day's oath-taking would take care of that. Kaptin Liel also believed that Brax's link with Estavia's first Champion would further protect him so he and Spar were to spend all three nights of Havo's Dance in Kaptin Haldin's shrine while the rest of the Battle God's warriors stood ready to send their combined strength to the God of Battles as they had a year ago. They were prepared. Brax had nothing more to fear than any other delinkos had on his or her First Oath Day.

Reaching for the coffee urn, Kemal shook his head with an embarrassed smile, remembering his own.

✦

Chian had rolled him out of bed long before dawn. Still six years away from the battle that would rob him of his mind and his body, his older kardos had towered over him like a giant. He'd caught Kemal up in his arms and carried him, struggling and protesting, into the bathing room and tossed him into the scented water with a great roar of laughter.

Badahir had pounced on him when they'd emerged. After she'd satisfied herself that he was armed and armored to her exacting standards, she'd handed him over to the rest of his kardon. Zondar had draped a huge garland of flowers around his neck while Radiard and Nathu had grilled him over the details of the oath-taking. Ever the most demonstrative of the family, Bayard had taken him in a huge bear hug, declaring in a voice loud enough for half the village to hear that their abayon would have been proud of him. Kemal would have run from embarrassment if he'd had any breath left, but he'd been too busy trying to pry his cuirass out of his rib cage.

The memory was enough to make him flush even now. But now, as then, it caused a lump to grow in his throat. He hadn't wanted to admit to Bayard that he couldn't remember their abayon anymore; that his huge, loud, balding kardos and his gentle and quiet arkados had been the only abayon he knew. But somehow the older man had seen it in his face and his own eyes had grown damp before he'd stepped aside to allow Maydir, the infant Aptulli on her hip and their three older delon crowding around her, to come forward with his cloak pin. Kemal hoped he and Yashar had made Brax feel as loved as he had when'd she'd pinned it to his throat. Laying his fingers over it gently, he smiled at the memory before catching up a mince borek and following the boy to their table.

✦

The single note of preparation a few moments later caused a general stampede toward the central parade square. By the time they reached their positions it was already filled to bursting. Brax started to take his usual place in the rear with the other delinkon but Kemal quickly caught him by the shoulder.

"Not today, Delin," he said. "Today, you stand with us."

Spar shot them a dark look before leading Jaq to their usual seat beside Elif, but as one gnarled hand reached out from her blankets to take hold of his, Kemal was relieved to see the younger boy's face relax. He hoped that was a good sign. Resisting the urge to glance up at the cloudy sky, he straightened as an anticipatory hush fell over the court-yard, the occasional creak of armor the only sound above the rising wind. As the final note of Usara's Invocations faded, a thrill of anticipa-tion rippled through the ranks. Standing between himself and Yashar, he felt Brax tense, one hand straying to the pommel of his sword to grip it convulsively.

Kemal smiled in sympathy. He'd felt the same eight years ago. Standing between Chian and Badahir, his palms damp with sweat, he'd locked his knees, afraid that everyone would be able to see his legs shak-ing and stared out at the morning sun rising bright and red above the Degisken-Dag Mountains, their slopes black with fallen pine nuts. The first stirring of Estavia drawn up from deep within him as Militia-Kaptin Davak had begun to sing had made him feel dizzy with relief.

Now, the heavy clop, clop of Marshal Brayazi's huge mount sound-ing overloud in the hushed square brought him back to the present. Re-leasing a breath he'd hadn't known he was holding, Kemal gripped the pommel of his own sword. As the marshal swept her weapon from its scabbard, he felt the familiar buzz of the God's lien within him begin to rise.

"You make your oaths as the first note sounds, speaking directly to Estavia in your mind."

His own words to Brax last week overlaid the memory of Badahir's words to him eight years ago.

"But what do I say?"

As Brax's words overlaid the memory of his own.

"Whatever you want to say, or need to say, in your own words."

"But what if my mind goes blank?"

"It won't."

"It might."

"Then ask Her for help. She's your God; She'll answer you."

As the marshal sang the first note of Estavia's Invocation, Kemal glanced down to see Brax, his eyes squeezed tightly shut, begin to move his lips silently.

"So, how do I know if it takes?"

"It?"

"You know, the whole sworn thing."

New questions he'd never thought to ask.

"She'll tell you. They talk, remember? And loudly?"

"Oh, right."

New questions but same ancient and familiar fear: what if She won't accept me? What if I'm not really worthy?

As the marshal's first note was picked up and repeated from Anavatan's three Hisars, to the ships on the Bogazi-Isik Strait, to each and every village along the shores of Gol-Beyaz, Kemal could feel Estavia's presence rising in response; feral, eager, and greedy for worship and for power.

What if She doesn't accept me?

She will. She has to. It's what She is. It's what They all are.

Deep within him, he felt the Battle God's exultant agreement. It caught him up as it always did, snapping his head back, and drawing his lips off his teeth in a snarling grimace. As he swept his sword into the air to channel the streams of crimson fire that streaked down the blade, he felt the minds and oaths of every warrior in Her service join to call the God of Battles into the physical world. Beside him, the intensity of Brax's newly sworn oaths blazed across his inner vision like a field of stars, so bright and hot it hurt his mind to look at them, and when Estavia burst into being above the courtyard, he felt Brax's own power take flight to meet Her. The boy's arms flung wide as She caught him up in a violent, ebony embrace that nearly blotted out the sun, and Kemal felt his own oaths explode into the sudden maelstrom that was their greeting. As the power of each of Her followers was sucked up beside him, he felt himself shredded and re-formed over and over until he could no longer tell where he ended and the God began.

The return to earthly mortality was almost painful.

Silence echoed across the parade square for one endless moment, and then, one by one, the Warriors of Estavia broke ranks to collapse against each other. Holding a nearly unconscious Brax up with one arm, Yashar glanced over at his arkados with a dazed expression but, his body feeling as flayed as his mind, Kemal could only shake his head. Finally, Marshal Brayazi pushed herself up from where she had fallen over her horse's neck, to give the boy an awestruck look.

"I swear, Delin, if this is how Her Invocations are going to go from now on we're all going to die happy."

The responding flush across Brax's face brought the gathered back to their feet and suddenly he was swarmed by rejuvenated warriors.

Across the square, Spar watched them with a somber expression, but when Brax finally broke free of the press to catch his eye, he nodded.

✦

"You're for Assembly, Ghazi."

As a light misting of rain began to fall, Kemal scowled as he hurried toward the Derneke-Mahalle Citadel. Kaptin Julide had pounced on him directly after the Invocation and he'd just stared at her in surprise.

✦

"Today, Kaptin?" he asked, glancing over at Brax who'd managed to work his way through the crowds of warriors to Spar's side.

"You'll be back long before his midmorning feast, never mind before dusk," she replied sharply. "We need to send a proxy-bey. Havo's Dance begins tonight and there'll be questions the marshal doesn't want answered."

"There've been questions all year," Kemal pointed out.

"Yes, and our answers all year have been that Estavia's warriors are prepared to meet any and all challenges to Anavatan's security. As always. You'll say the same today." She gave him a stern look from under her brows. "Spar's vision and our preparations regarding Brax are not to be discussed. It's private temple business, period."

"And the spirits, Kaptin?"

"What about them?"

"Shouldn't we warn the other temples that they may have increased in strength or numbers this year?"

"No. The temples were warned last spring. The spirits will do what they've apparently done every Havo's Dance: attempt to breach the walls of Anavatan. The citizens and the temples will also do what they've done every Havo's Dance: barricade themselves behind strong walls and shutters to wait out the storms. This year should be no different. We'll be ready; Incasa's oracle-seers probably will be, too. The city is secure." Noting his recalcitrant expression, the kaptin made an impatient gesture. "It may seem that we're always devolving a petty and annoying duty onto you arbitrarily, Ghazi, but Estavia-Sarayi has good reason for whom we chose to represent us among Anavatan's leaders. You're for Assembly. Now."

Closing his teeth on what would have been an unwise and likely insubordinate reply, Kemal merely saluted stiffly.

"Yes, Kaptin."

✦

Now, stepping around a bit of broken cobblestone, Kemal growled low in his throat. "Good reason, my arse," he muttered. "The good reason is that no one else wants to risk getting caught in an early thunderstorm."

Glancing up at the heavy clouds gathering overhead, he quickened his pace. The residential area situated between Estavia's temple and the center of Anavatan was mostly given over to the homes of the more prosperous warrior families and, with no Usara-Cami nearby, it was not unusual for the surrounding streets to be nearly empty of people today, but even with that knowledge, it seemed to Kemal that the air hung more heavily and the trees rustled more ominously than in previous years.

Brax's words from last spring echoed in his mind as he hurried along the street.

"The spirits attack the unsworn on Havo's Dance. That's why nobody goes out. They used to just suck the life out of things like spiders and mice, sometimes a sick rat, but last year they started on the feral dogs and cats. That made them strong enough to go after people, but they can only get to the unsworn, so we keep under cover when they're out hunting."

And Proxy-Bey Aurad's.

"There are no unsworn in Anavatan. It's the City of the Gods; everyone follows one Deity or another here."

Purposely ignoring the dark recesses between the houses, Kemal had to agree that at least there were no unsworn in this particular district. Nonetheless, he was still relieved to leave the quiet, shadowy mansions behind and exit into the vast, bustling marketplace that surrounded the Citadel.

A dozen people asked after Jaq as he made his way through the maze of tents and stalls—a dozen people whose only interest was in taking advantage of the buying frenzy that always occurred just before Havo's Dance sent most of their customers into a self-imposed house arrest for three days. The scene was so familiar that it almost banished both his worry and his pique. Almost.

As usual, he arrived late but was surprised to see that the Central Assembly Chamber held no more than six people today, a young server standing by the side table, one scribe, the three representatives from the city's Trisects, and Aurad. The server offered him a cup of very black tea and, as he grimaced at the taste, Ystazia's proxy-bey favored him with a sympathetic expression before gesturing at the empty cushion beside him.

"Just hasn't been the same since Dorn died last summer," he noted, saluting the other man with a small china coffee cup.

"Point."

"Where's Jaq?"

"With my delinkon, as usual."

"And I thought cats were the only fickle pets. You'll have to get a new one, old friend."

"I just might." Kemal glanced about as he took his place. "Where is everyone? I'd have thought Assembly would be half over by now."

"No such luck. We'll take a drenching before the day is over, mark my words." The musician leaned back, large hands clasped behind his head. "Usara's temple sent a very old retired potion mixer who's been in the loo since I arrived because Jemil and the rest are likely still hard at work ministering to the poor at this time of day, First Cultivar Bey Adrian is taking a drink in the upper gallery with a dozen followers—discussing last-minute party arrangements I'd imagine—and won't be coming down until we *actually* begin, Incasa's Bey is always fashionably last, as you know, and Neclan . . ." he paused dramatically, "has been delayed, but she's on her way."

"*Bey* Neclan, late for Assembly?" Kemal grinned. "What is the world coming to?"

"An end, no doubt. Ah!" Aurad sat up straight in gleeful anticipation as a figure entered the chamber, but the sight of Proxy-Bey Niami of Incasa-Sarayi gave him pause. "Huh," he said as she accepted a cup of tea from the server before taking Incasa's traditional place at the head of the table. "Well, that never would have happened in Freyiz's day."

Kemal said nothing, but the sight of the junior seer did not surprise him. It seemed that the God of Prophecy's First Oracle didn't want to answer questions any more than Marshal Brayazi did. That didn't bode well for the day.

✦

Once Assembly finally began the questions started at once. Already in a foul temper, Bey Neclan fixed Incasa's young representative with a cold stare.

"It's been one year since Sayin Freyiz brought us word of a new power born on Havo's Dance," she said bluntly. "Since that time our respective temples have followed the direction of our Gods and the *suggestion*," she said with a barely disguised sneer, "made by Incasa's temple that we prepare and that we wait. Well, we have prepared and we have waited, and now Oristo-Sarayi would like to know just what we have prepared and waited for. What is this child of power and potential? Is it a danger to us? Are the spirits of the wild lands in league with it and, if so, are they now a true danger as well? Quite bluntly: Is Anavatan safe, *Seer*?"

Niami gave the head of the Hearth God's temple a misty-eyed smile.

"My superiors have charged me to say this in answer, Sayin," she began respectfully. "The child of the prophecy is no threat to the City of the Gods."

She fell silent and after a moment, Neclan narrowed her eyes. "And?" she demanded.

"And that is all, Sayin," Niami answered almost apologetically. "There's nothing to fear, not on this Havo's Dance, nor on any other."

"Well, that's lovely, I'm so relieved," Aurad interjected, leaning his elbows on the table. "But it doesn't answer the rest of the question. *What is it*, this child of yours? You've had a year to snoop about the creeks or trickles or whatever you call them; you must have discovered something: hair color, eye color, pets, favorite foods, its *abayon*, maybe."

"Its present seeming is spiritlike, Sayin. What Its true being may become is still shrouded in the mists of time," Niami answered, ignoring the musician's suspicious tone with tactful élan.

"How very convenient," Neclan observed, her own voice dripping with sarcasm.

"But, Sayin," Niami said, opening her hands in a helpless gesture. "The temples are prepared, yes? And the city streets are swept of the unsworn?"

"Swept?"

Incasa's representative just shrugged. "Any danger that may arise from the prophecy or from the lowly spirits of the wild lands can't harm the *sworn* and Oristo, Usara, and Ystazia-Sarayi have all been aggressively recruiting among the unsworn all year, have they not?"

"Oristo-Sarayi is prepared for Havo's Dance," Neclan said, refusing to rise to the somewhat pointed accusation. "Our halls are full, *as always*, with those seeking refuge from the *weather.*"

"As are ours," Aurad answered. "And," he fixed the God of Prophecy's proxy-bey with an uncharacteristically stern expression. "You may tell your superiors at Incasa-Sarayi that *Ystazia*-Sarayi will be *prepared* to Invoke our own God should anything untoward occur during the next three nights, regardless of the state of the sworn or the unsworn."

"As is Oristo-Sarayi," Neclan agreed coldly. She cast an expectant glance toward Usara's representative and, after a brief moment of confusion, the old man nodded.

Niami cocked her head to one side. "If the temples of Hearth, Arts, and Healing feel it's necessary, then Prophecy has no objection to such prudent provisions, of course," she said. "It is after all, not the time of *our* God's accession. But I shouldn't wonder if Havo's temple mightn't have something to say about it, however."

All eyes now turned to the tall, bi-gender First Cultivar who was sitting, bare feet crossed at the ankles, staring out the high west window at the sky, and sipping at a crystal glass of raki with seeming disinterest. Setting the glass to one side, Bey Adrian just tucked a lock of disheveled black hair behind one ear before giving an eloquent shrug in reply.

"Havo isn't interested in prophecies, old or new. Change is necessary for growth. If the other temples want to place their people on alert, that's their business; we'll be doing what we always do, celebrating. But," Adrian raised one hand to forestall an indignant remark from Bey Neclan. "Havo will be out in force tearing up the city for the next three nights. Any spirits or prophetic children that get in the way will likely get shredded. Or eaten. Spring change belongs to *our* God and our God gets *very* hungry in spring."

With a smile, Niami now returned her attention to Bey Neclan. "And so the city is prepared, Sayin," she said pleasantly.

Oristo's bey favored her with a haughty look down the length of her nose. "So it would seem," she answered frostily.

"Then, perhaps, we might move on to other business. That is unless Estavia's temple has something else to add regarding Anavatan's security," Niami added with exaggerated politeness.

Kemal cast the young seer a jaundiced look as the Assembly, and most particularly the three Trisect representatives, now turned their attention his way.

"Estavia's temple is on alert," he said truthfully, "standing ready to send strength to our God should She need to do battle with the spirits of the wild lands or any other being that threatens the safety of our city. As we were last year and every year before that since Kaptin Haldin's time," he added.

"Do you anticipate any such attack, Sayin?" the Western Trisect representative asked anxiously.

Kemal gave a gesture of studied indifference. "We anticipate an *attempt*," he said, stressing the final word. "But," he shot a grin in the direction of Bey Adrian, "with Havo and Estavia's *appetites* being what they are, we don't anticipate an attempt coming to anything more than a midnight snack. Do you?"

The representative gave a relieved laugh. "No, Sayin."

"Good."

✦

The Assembly broke up quickly after that. Niami left at once as did the three Trisect representatives. After huddling together for a moment, Aurad and Neclan followed, supporting Usara's proxy-bey by one elbow each. Bey Adrian gave Kemal a jaunty salute, then headed off as well, the dozen junior priests in tow, their arms already laden with last-minute supplies. Standing a moment, staring down at the wide, mahogany table, Kemal swallowed the dregs of his cold tea, then handed the cup to the server and took his own leave, feeling just as unsettled as when he'd arrived. As he made his way through the still-bustling marketplace, the rising wind sent a splash of rain across his cheek and, with an involuntary glance at the darkening sky, he quickened his pace.

Across the courtyard, Bey Neclan watched him go with a thoughtful frown on her thin face, before making for the tree-lined avenue that led to Oristo-Sarayi.

✦

The temple was bustling with barely controlled chaos when she arrived. Handing her damp cloak to a junior priest, she strode down the wide, marble entrance hall, taking note of the many preparations already in full swing. Priests and servers rushed here and there, their arms laden with food and linens, all driven by the loud, booming voice of Chamberlain Kadar. An untrained observer might believe they'd never be ready for the glut of people who were already beginning to crowd into the public rooms, but Oristo's temple had opened its doors to the needs of Anavatan's citizens every Havo's Dance since the founding of the city itself. They'd be ready.

Pausing before the ten-foot-high ruddy-brown statue of Oristo which dominated the entrance, Neclan stared into its polished mahogany eyes. There was a different feeling in the temple this year, an air of underlying tension that made her want to snap at everyone around her. The God was unsettled and that put everyone on edge.

Behind her, the Head Launderer stormed from the main dining room, his face a dangerous burgundy.

"If you yell at me one more time, Kadar, you'll end up in the northern strait with a bag over your head!" he shouted. "Creases, my arse," he snarled as he stomped toward the lower level staircase.

Neclan raised an eyebrow at the statue.

Everyone.

✦

Her delinkos met her at the door to her private study.

"Chamberlain Tanay's waiting in the conservatory, Sayin," he said respectfully. "You were to meet after Assembly?"

"Right." Neclan huffed a breath of air through her nose in annoyance. The late start at the Citadel had set her entire schedule back by at least a half an hour. The God alone knew how she was going to make it up before dusk.

"Shall I bring tea or will you take an early supper, Sayin?" he continued.

"You will bring a large carafe of raki," she said darkly. "And three glasses."

"Three, Sayin?"

"Yes, I imagine Kadar will want to see me as soon as my business with Tanay is complete."

He chuckled at the resigned note of weariness in her voice.

"Yes, Sayin."

✦

Tanay was deep in discussion with the Chief Gardener over the state of the temple ferns when Neclan entered the large, glass conservatory. Noting the sour expression on her superior's face, one corner of her mouth quirked upward as she disentangled herself from the long, trailing fronds.

"I take it things didn't go well at Assembly?" she asked, as a server bustled in with the raki and a tray of confectionaries.

"Things went as they generally go at Assembly," Neclan sniffed. "With dissembling and political nonsense." Seating herself on a low divan, she rubbed irritably at her fingers, before stretching them toward the lit mangel in the center of the room.

"Here, let me." Tanay came forward to take the older woman's hands in hers. Rubbing them gently, she examined the red, swollen knuckles with a frown. "They look sore today," she noted.

"Don't fuss. It's just the damp, it makes them ache."

"Are you using the cream that Rakeed brought for you?"

"Yes, *Abia*."

"Good." Taking her own place beside her, Tanay poured them each a glass of raki. The two women sat in companionable silence for a moment until the deep lines about Neclan's eyes and mouth relaxed a little.

"Oristo is disturbed about Havo's Dance this year," Neclan said at last.

"Freyiz's prophecy?"

"No doubt. It's become clear over the months that your two charges are involved, and the Hearth God doesn't like it when delon are put in danger by adult concerns."

"The Hearth God's not the only one," Tanay agreed darkly.

"Brayazi *politely* declined my offer of a place for them here until after Havo's Dance," Neclan continued. "So we'll have to extend the God's protection to them in their absence. You gave the young one, Spar, the beads you dreamed of?"

Tanay nodded. "I don't know how much protection they'll be able to convey, but yes, he has one, Brax the other."

"Good. Well, then, that's all we can do." Glancing up, she spotted Kadar standing by the conservatory door arguing with the Temple Chef. "And now . . ." she said, the lines returning to her face, "I have battles of my own to mediate and you should get back before the rain begins in earnest."

"Yes, Sayin." Bowing, Tanay took her leave, shaking an admonishing finger at Kadar as she passed.

✦

Above the city, the sun began its downward trek toward dusk and the First Night of Havo's Dance behind a mask of heavy storm clouds. In Anavatan's harbors the ships and fishing boats were already battened down, their cargo safely stowed away, and their crews sequestered in the many inns and taverns along the wharves. In the marketplaces which still teemed with people, Oristo's abayos-priests fanned out, cajoling and bullying everyone who was still on the streets into heading for an early refuge, offering their already crowded halls to whomever needed them while Ystazia's people brought every tent, stall, table, and cart set up around their temples and camis that could be moved indoors.

The vast and sweeping public rooms and theaters of Ystazia-Sarayi quickly came to resemble a covered market on a high festival day with jugglers, musicians, dancers, and puppeteers all setting up shop as quickly as the relocated potters, jewelers, scribes, and many who might have gone home chose to spend the night right there. Others made their way to Havo-Sarayi in the hopes of joining in the revelry and cadging a free meal.

At Usara-Sarayi the physicians quietly laid out bandages and counted their remaining medicinals while at Estavia-Sarayi, the Battle

God's warriors honed their weapons, and tucked between the Healer God's and the Hearth God's temples, Incasa-Sarayi exuded an air of deep stillness and uninviting solitude, its gates already closed.

✦

Seated on a soft woolen cushion in the center of the God of Prophecy's most private meditation tower, Freyiz tasted the combination of excitement and anxiety emanating from the five other main temples with a neutral expression as she cast her farseeing prophetic gaze westward across the city, noting the areas of strength and weakness with equal objectivity. When First Oracle Bessic approached, she gestured him forward without turning her head.

"Niami has returned, Sayin," he said respectfully despite his position. "The city is prepared."

"And the temple-seers?"

"Are waiting for nightfall."

She nodded. "I'll rest until then. Call me when everything is in readiness for the High Seeking. You will lead it, of course; I'm here only in a purely advisory position."

"Yes, Sayin."

The tinge of disbelief in his voice made her smile.

She felt rather than heard him withdraw a moment later, and took the opportunity to tug at a fold in her cushion which was irritating her left buttock in a very undignified manner. She'd forgotten about the many sacrifices made to appearances at Incasa's main temple, but it was of little importance. She wouldn't be here that long. With a sigh, she gave the cushion a final, irritated tug.

When she'd left, she'd felt as old and used up as a candle stub, but the year spent at Adasi-Koy had given her the strength and clarity needed to face the coming trials. It had given Bessic a chance to solidify his position as First Oracle as well, she allowed, which was all to the good. Incasa-Sarayi needed a strong, single hand at the rudder if it was to weather the coming storms in one piece. She had no intention of undermining his authority; however, she was old enough to realize that intention and actuality were two entirely different streams, which power and appearance had a habit of silting up all too often. She would be glad to return to the more peacefully retired world of Adasi-Koy's lighter duties and softer cushions when this was all over. Reaching for the glass of salap at her elbow, she allowed her mind to return there ahead of her body.

As it was here, her own small meditation room back home held windows on all four sides, the specially-made and very expensive glass panes lightly tinted with color to represent the four directions of prophecy contained within the passage of time: yellow to the east for the dawn and for the past, pink for the north and south and the choices they offered in the clear, high light of the present, and blue to the west for the setting sun and its journey into a shadowed and enigmatic future. As a delinkos she had used those colors to hone and focus her gift; now they existed only in her memory and in the variations of warmth the sun cast through them and onto her face and hands. She remembered how the pink and the blue glass had transformed the shining, silvery waters of Gol-Beyaz and how the yellow had covered the slopes of the Degisken-Dag Mountains with a fine golden-wrought mist.

She snorted suddenly. She'd never much liked the look of that. Mountains should be green—clean, healthy green. Of course, to her eyes now the mountains would always be black as would the rest of the physical world. With a sigh, she returned her frosted, prophetic gaze to the west and the blue-and-silver-streaked Citadel below.

After months of careful sifting through a hundred streams, she'd finally sorted out the vision Incasa had sent her a year ago. A child of great potential, still unformed, born under the cover of Havo's Dance; a child, *a God*, created by the raw and uncontrolled power of the wild land spirits, solidified by hunger and by bloodshed, and fashioned out of madness, quickened by battle, and ready to be brought into the physical world by Anavatan's champions or by its enemies; a God for whom creation and destruction were two very real possibilities in equal measure. A God who stood poised on the edge of a dark place no God had any business going. And so, armed with the first and possibly only clear message she'd ever received from the God of Prophecy, she'd returned to His main temple with one simple directive: raise a High Seeking so that Incasa might ensure this child took its place beside the Gods and thus maintained the safety and security of Their people and Their city.

Or perished before It could be used against Them.

"Oristo and Usara's temples are responsible for the well-being of the city and Estavia's for its safety."

Freyiz sniffed as the First Abayos-Priest's words from a year ago filtered through her mind. Temple politics always muddied the streams. The Healer, Hearth, and Battle Gods might be responsible for such things as the well-being and safety of Anavatan, but Incasa temple-seers were responsible for its future and without that there was no Healing, Hearth, or Battle.

Staring out the southernmost window, Freyiz watched the prophetic waters of Gol-Beyaz turn from silvery-pink to silvery-blue as the final afternoon of winter began to wane. The future was still muddy and uncertain, so all the chosen champions of the Gods must be protected and all those who dipped into the streams made use of, both old and new. Brax and Spar were covered by Oristo, that left only Graize. To that end she had sent a dream to the golden-haired one from the south. Graize must be protected if the streams were to flow cleanly to any destination at all. She must do it, Freyiz had seen that clearly, and so they must form a tenuous alliance for now and worry about future conflict when it came. Creation or destruction was too close for more than just a God-child of prophecy this night.

✦

Far to the west, standing with a small, mounted complement of Yuruk on an escarpment overlooking Anavatan's great walls, Graize flung his arms wide with a howl of laughter as he felt the preparations of Incasa's temple wash over him. The rising wind sent his ragged brown hair whipping about his face, and he swept up a handful of newly born spirits and flung them toward the Godling. It snapped them out of the air much as a seagull might snap up a spray of tiny hamsi, then shot down to wrap Itself about his shoulders. His pony sidestepped nervously as the Godling passed its head, and Danjel glanced over, her green eyes showing a flash of annoyance in the more feminine face she'd chosen for this night.

"Control yourself, Kardos," she hissed. "They'll see us if you keep that up!"

"Nonsense!" Graize shouted, sucking in a mouthful of spirits of his own, delighting in the cold burst of power that shot down his throat.

"The God of Sharks already knows we're coming! He's holding out His hand and almost begging us to do it! It's going to be like snapping up fish in a barrel!"

The confusing comparison threatened to send his thoughts skittering off in a dozen directions, but he slammed the image of his stag beetle up before his mind's eye and jerked his thoughts back to business.

"Eight people; that's all we need, my swallow-kardos," he said, his uneven pupils glowing with an unnatural light. "That's what I saw, and that's what we've got. Eight. You and I for the present, bird and beetle, flight and fight. Rayne and Caleb for the future. That's a sharp-toothed marten and a cunning little mouse. And Kursk and Ozan for the past, fox for craft and nightingale for song. Oh, wait. That's six. Oh, well, the Godling can count for two. It needs to be two anyway for creation and destruction, doesn't It?" He tipped his head to one side. "Or Brax and Spar can join in," he allowed, "if they live through the night." He began to giggle to himself. "Which one, which one, which one has the spirit-turtle-dragonfly-pea beneath it," he said in a singsong voice. "Place your shine; place your shine, which one, which one."

"Graize."

Kursk's firm voice snapped him back to himself for a moment, but as the setting sun suddenly shone through a break in the clouds to illuminate the blue-cast God-Wall anchoring Anavatan's great defenses not a hundred yards away, he began to giggle once again, remembering.

✦

As Danjel had predicted, it had taken some time to convince Kursk and Timur of the plan they'd beaten out: to take a small kazakin to the very walls of Anavatan during this, the most dangerous time of the year. It took even longer for Kursk to agree to Graize's choice of combatants. The leader of the Rus-Yuruk had scratched at a thin scar running through the beard by his upper lip before shaking his head.

"Rayne's old enough," he'd agreed, *"but Calebask's still very young and very reckless. If he came to harm, his abia would skin us both. He can't come."*

Forcing his wayward mind to stay on topic, Graize had fixed the kazakin leader with an intense stare. He needed Caleb for the game, to balance the Godling's birthing with the mouse balancing the marten, otherwise there would be too much spleen, so youth or no youth, he needed him. *"Caleb* won't *come to harm if* you're *with us,"* he'd stated with as much sincerity as thirteen years conning delinkon on the streets of Anavatan could muster.

Kursk had frowned. *"And you've* seen *this, child?"*

"I have. Ask Timur, she'll see it, too."

And she had seen it—just as the spirits had told Graize she would. That future stream was wide and fast flowing, almost a certainty with Incasa's plan pushing it along. And within that stream Caleb would come to no harm if Kursk were with them. But Timur hadn't seen the trickle of blood carried along by the stream, the trickle of blood that washed over the older wyrdin's features. Only Graize had seen that.

✦

Now, he returned his attention to the present as Rayne poked him in the ribs to bring him back into the present. "Don't worry, my kardon," he said carelessly. "Everyone's so afraid that the spirits will attack Anavatan again this year that they'll miss our attack until it's far too late." Slipping off his pony, he caught up a stick and drove the point into the ground at his feet. "They're crouched beside this deep, dark, little pool that they think is the sea monster's front door," he said, removing the stick to peer down at the indentation in the dirt. "And there they wait, weapons at the ready for when it pops its head out, and when it does . . . wham!" He drove the stick back into the ground with so much force that it snapped in half. He glared at it for a moment, then tossed it aside. "But what they don't know is that there's a back door and that Incasa's going to open it for us. The old bastard wants my Godling all to Himself, but He can't have It. It's *mine.*"

Craning his neck to see past Ozan's mount, Caleb frowned at him. "How are you going to stop Him?" he asked.

"The same way you stop a well from eating a bucket," he answered. "You tie a rope to the handle and draw the bucket back up after it's drunk its fill."

"Won't the well see the rope?"

Graize raised a lecturing finger at him. "The best way to defeat a well, Kardos, is to use Its own arrogance against It." Climbing back into the saddle, he turned his mount and headed down toward the God-Wall at a gallop, following a great host of silvery spirits, the Godling still wrapped about his neck like a mist-colored scarf.

Danjel glanced over at Kursk, who nodded, then she turned her own mount to follow him, Caleb and Rayne close behind. "We'll keep that in mind, Kardos," she said thoughtfully.

Behind her, Ozan and Kursk exchanged a cautious look.

✦

Two miles away, two figures wrapped in furs and wool crouched beside a small fishing boat drawn up before the base of Dovek-Hisar. The one passed the time drawing maps in his mind while the other let the sand-and-grass-colored ripples caused by the Yuruk's presence filter through her mind. As the first few heavy drops of rain began to fall, a single strand of brilliantly golden hair strayed from the depths of her hood, only to be tucked away almost primly.

"*You're very arrogant, my young oracle,*" Panos said in Graize's direction. "*Arrogance is red and so is blood, but water is blue and you can't breathe it, even if you think it might taste delicious.*"

Glancing down, she studied the cold, lake water with a frown. "It tastes of ice and snow still."

Hares made an inquiring noise and she shook her head, her black eyes narrowing. *I should have stayed in Volinsk whatever that pushy old woman wanted,* she thought. *I hate being cold.* Leaning against the boat, she pulled a silver flask from her pocket. "*But you need me to help you breathe, don't you, so here I am. Being cold.*"

Saluting the huge statue of Estavia standing silent guard above Her temple across the strait, Panos took a deep drink. "*You're cold, too, my dark warrior, much colder than my lovely warm tower to the north.*"

She handed the flask to Hares who tipped it up thankfully. "*Ah, well,*" she sighed. "*As soon as the first of Your number finishes with His plan, I can get warm and so can You. Then we'll both be happy.*" Tucking deeper into her furs, she settled down to wait.

17

The Twin Dogs of
Creation and Destruction

CROUCHED ON ESTAVIA-SARAYI'S easternmost battlements, Brax squeezed his eyes shut as the wind sent a scattering of fine rain mixed with ice pellets scoring across his face, causing the old scar on his cheek to burn sharply. Squeezing the pommel of his new sword, he risked a glance at the western horizon, but the sky had grown so dark in the last few hours that it was impossible to know the time.

As if in answer, the notes of Usara's Evening Invocation filtered across to him, carried by the sounds of the Hearth temple's revelry to the southwest. He sighed glumly. It looked like this year's First Night was going to be just as cramped, damp, and miserable as last year's. Thanks to Spar.

Shaking the rain from his hair like a dog, he shot a jaundiced glance in the younger boy's direction, but Spar ignored him. Only partially protected from the weather by Jaq who'd insisted on following them outside, the younger boy stood, staring fixedly down at the churning waves of the Bogazi-Isik. And he'd stay there, too, Brax grumbled to himself, until whatever he was waiting for happened or until they were blown off the battlements. And even then Spar'd find a way to get them back up here again, so he might as well make himself as comfortable as possible.

If possible.

Digging at a drizzle of rain running down his neck and under his cuirass, Brax pressed his back against the sentry box wall and, closing his eyes against the weather, went over the day's events.

◆

The time had passed as quickly as Yashar'd said it would, the excitement over his oath-taking marred only by the darkening sky. As the day'd moved toward dusk, more and more people had turned their attention to the west, their expressions both distracted and concerned. When, just after noon, a spattering of hail had swept across the rooftops, Marshal Brayazi'd ordered Estavia-Sarayi locked down early.

The temple delinkon had fanned out at once, closing doors, windows, and shutters, while Brax and Spar had watched from the gallery as Sable Company's black-clad sentinels had muscled the main gates closed. The solid boom echoing across the courtyard had caused Spar to jump nervously, but when Brax had glanced over, his mouth was set in a grim line and his eyes narrowed resolutely.

A somewhat muted early supper had followed, after which the temple had begun its preparations for nightfall. Just before Havo's Evening Invocation, Kemal and Yashar had escorted Brax and Spar to Kaptin Haldin's shrine past a double line of Cyan Company already armed for battle. As Kaptin Julide gave them an encouraging nod, Brax could almost feel the sense of greedy anticipation growing in the air.

Inside the shrine, however, the familiar, muted silence had settled around him like a comforting balm. Crossing the room, he'd laid his sword across the altar while Yashar had taken first him and then Spar in his usual bear hug and Kemal'd lit the mangel in the far corner. Once it burned with a steady glow, the younger man had caught them up in his own hug before staring searchingly into Brax's eyes.

"This is the very heart of Her temple," he said, trying to mask the worry in his voice. "You'll be safe here. You've got food, drink, a pallet . . ."

"And a pot," Yashar interjected.

"And a pot," he agreed. "Yashar and I are just one level up in the Cyan Company's shrine. If you need anything . . ."

"Which you won't," Yashar interrupted again, giving Kemal a stern glance from under his bushy, black eyebrows. "You're safe, you're warm, and Jaq's here to guard your dreams, so get some sleep and we'll see you in the morning, yes?"

Brax nodded. Spar, his gaze already far away, just stroked one of the dog's silken ears with a disinterested expression.

"Good." Yashar turned toward the door. "Come on, Kem. Stop fretting like a mother hen, it's nearly time; we need to get into position or they'll start without us. Oh, and, Spar, here, I almost forgot." Reaching out, he pressed something into the younger boy's hand. "A game to pass the time with if you don't want to go to sleep right away."

Spar looked surprised for a moment, then his face lit up with such a wide and innocent smile of pleasure that Brax grew immediately suspicious, but before he could say anything, Yashar caught Kemal by the arm and drew him from the shrine. Their younger abayos gave them a last, worried glance and then the door was closed and they were alone.

Spar immediately climbed onto the pallet and, after scrunching down under the blankets, wrapped one arm around Jaq's neck and closed his eyes with every indication of going to sleep at once. Brax regarded him mistrustfully for a moment, but finally he, too, took up his usual position beside Kaptin Haldin's tomb, back against the altar, face raised to the great ebony statue of Estavia. The shrine was warm with the mangel burning, and slowly his head tipped back and he slept.

✦

Spar's eyes snapped open the moment the older boy's breathing deepened. Bringing his hand up from the covers, he stared down at Yashar's gift: a pair of wooden soldier's dice, the blue of his eyes fading before a thick, black mist. Closing his fingers around them once again, he began to shake them slowly back and forth, using the hypnotic movement to draw his mind away from the warm woolen blankets and quiet, familiar sound of Jaq's snoring, and down into the cool depths of prophecy. When he was ready, he opened his mind more fully than he ever had before.

✦

The dark place caught him up into its enveloping embrace, stretching out before him like a great, subterranean ocean, black and still and fathomless as time itself. Running his thoughts along its mirrored surface, he drew up the memory of each and every person whose lessons he might need, much as one might draw up a catch of fish in a silken net.

First the living: Elif and Liel, both of them powerful battle-seers used to scooping up their own cache of futures and making sense of their ever shifting patterns; Elif and Liel for clarity. Next Tanay and Ihsan, the gentle warmth of their words as comforting as the knowledge they contained; Tanay and Ihsan for stability and for learning. Then Kemal and Yashar, new and unexpectedly loving abayon standing together like a pair of twin towers, willing to protect them from any and all danger. Outmatched, perhaps, but willing. Kemal and Yashar for strength. And finally Brax himself, his kardos in all but blood; both jaded and naive, wise and reckless, heedless and heeding, standing before him and standing beside him, year after year, through prosperity and drought; danger and safety; Brax for loyalty and for unity.

A light splash across his consciousness made him blink in surprise as his memory of Paus rose up before him like a young dolphin. He didn't question it, merely added her to the whole with a practical expression devoid of cynicism for one brief instant; Paus for the certainty and purity of innocent belief.

With his living tutors now in place, Spar took a deep breath and reached down into the depths for the dead: Chian for patience, Cindar for rage, and Drove for caution.

These memories added a pale, wraithlike essence to his catch, and he considered them thoughtfully before bringing them into the whole. Then, squeezing Yashar's dice, he smiled coldly as he reached out, very gently, for two most darkly dangerous fish in his black ocean, fish who maneuvered as easily in this world as they did in their own: Graize more for the strength of their rivalry than for his visioning, and Illan for his cold, mercenary cunning so like Spar's own.

His catch now sparkling like a many-colored gemstone, his eyes returned to their natural blue as the warmth of the mangel drew him back into the present.

✦

Crouched on a rocky spit of land beneath the great bulk of Lazim-Hisar, a stone's throw away from the pulsating blue God-Wall, Graize lifted his head as the featherlight touch of Spar's thoughts passed across his mind. For a heartbeat he felt the warmth of a hearth fire, saw walls of white-and-golden marble rise up all around him, and then the scream of a gull swept it away once more.

Rubbing his badly damaged beetle between finger and thumb, he shrugged carelessly. He had time for neither random encounters nor meaningful messengers tonight. Maybe tomorrow when the rising sun had silenced the legion of spirits that filled his mind with their sibilant demands from far beyond Anavatan's shining defenses; but for now he had ears only for them as he'd promised.

Reaching up, he ran his fingers along the length of their leader, the Godling, wrapped, as usual, about his neck like a scarf. This close to Gol-Beyaz, It shimmered half in and half out of the world, its misting breath as silvery bright as Its opalescent eyes. It rumbled back at him in sleepy contentment, knowing that it was not yet time, and Graize turned his attention to his mortal companions crouched patiently on the rocks beside him, awaiting his signal.

✦

Despite their traditional mistrust of travel by water, he'd convinced his handpicked kazakin to take a small boat down the Halic-Salmanak that morning, Ozan and Kursk rowing quietly while Graize and Danjel wrapped their movement in mist and shadows and Rayne and Caleb stared into the gloom.

But they needn't have worried. This close to Havo's Dance, Anavatan was not interested in the north, only in the west. They'd come ashore an hour ago, drawing up the boat, and sharing a loaf of bread and a round of sheep's cheese washed down with a skin of kimiz before settling down to wait for nightfall. Now, Ozan played a quiet and melancholy tune on his kopuz while Kursk methodically tied a dozen loose knots into a braided piece of hemp; Rayne and Caleb lay sleeping, curled up together, wrapped in their aba's sheepskin coat, with their fur caps pulled tightly over their eyes, dreaming of riding and of fighting; Danjel sat, back pressed against the tower wall, apparently asleep as well, but Graize could feel the bi-gender wyrdin's mind racing across the Berbat-Dunya, gathering up their army of spirits for the attack that was to come.

Closing his eyes with a smile, Graize tossed a careless challenge toward Illan, before sending his own mind out to join Danjel's above the plains. For an instant the image of a tall, red tower wavered before his eyes, but with a wave of his stag beetle, he swept it away. They would be ready when all their enemies, both mortal and immortal, arose this Havo's Dance. Ready and happy to oblige them in battle.

✦

Far to the north, Illan Volinsk accepted the boy's challenge with a cold smile. Standing before his atlas table, he moved his small collection of Yuruk pieces to the mouth of the Bogazi-Isik beside Panos' new sea-green turtle, then ran one loving finger along the small, golden figurine already in place across the strait, before turning his attention to the bleakly gray sky beyond his window. As the cloud-obscured sun dropped below the waves, he raised a glass of mulled wine in salute toward Graize and Spar, then settled back into a thick brocaded chair to think of Panos and to wait for the drama to unfold.

✦

Beneath the shadow of Dovek-Hisar with her faithful mapmaker, Panos felt Illan's thoughts whisper through her mind like a love song in the distance. Taking her silver flask from her cloak, she downed the contents, allowing herself a wistful sigh that she wasn't back home standing naked beside the warm, sparkling waters of her own south Deniz-Hadi with Illan in her arms and with nothing more important to do than make love on the soft, musical sand of Amatus.

But there would be time enough for that later, she promised herself, when all this Godly nonsense was resolved and her duty to Memnos was concluded. Then she could deal with the pushy old oracle and set her own designs in motion, both hers and Illan's if they really matched as well as he'd promised her they would.

Trailing her fingers through the cold, power-filled waters of Gol-Beyaz, she sent a thread of loving, plum-colored passion toward her northern sorcerer before settling down to wait once more, her eyes as dark as Spar's.

✦

At Incasa-Sarayi, Freyiz was also waiting, although not nearly so patiently. The cold stone of the temple's High Seeking arzhane-chamber was making her joints ache, despite the heavy woolen carpet laid down especially for her, and the incense-saturated air was causing a thousand tiny visions to spin about her eyes like mayflies. One of the visions became the now familiar tower on the northern sea, and she glared at it in peevish displeasure. Banishing the vision with a brusque wave of one hand, she hunkered down into her nest of shawls and blankets, wishing once again that she'd never left her nice warm meditation room in Adasi-Koy. But it was too late for regrets now. For good or for ill, she had heeded the call of her God as she always had and returned to Anavatan to help Him mold the future to His own desire.

Deep within her mind, Incasa sent a mollifying trickle of cool power through her joints and she accepted it graciously as a mother might accept the apology of an errant child before turning her attention to the preparations going on all around her.

In the center of the arzhane half a dozen delinkon attended the First Oracle, some lighting the ring of incense braziers that surrounded him like so many tiny, iron towers while others arranged his robes and cushions in the manner laid down by Incasa Himself centuries before. He looked fretful and self-conscious and Freyiz remembered how stiflingly hot and restrictive it had all felt before the years of familiarity and the pressure of her increasingly powerful visions had pushed it all into the background of her awareness, proving that one could get used to anything in time. And proving that one could also miss even the most uncomfortable of routines after years of practice, she added with a cynical snort only slightly tinged with a kind of sad nostalgia. She had sat in that very same circle for nearly twenty-five years, as the most favored and beloved of Incasa's chosen, attended and revered for the intimacy of His prophetic touch. It was harder to give up than she'd thought.

For a moment, she considered alerting Bessic to the danger of the tower's presence, then dismissed the idea. The new First Oracle had enough to concern himself with right now without any perfectly reasonable advice that might come across as meddling. A High Seeking of this magnitude, coming as it did on another Deity's most powerful First Night, could burn out the mind of a stronger seer than Bessic in an instant; something he was obviously well aware of. His forehead was slick with sweat and his eyes, already misted over with a fine white veil, darted this way and that, unable to keep still. With a sigh, she quieted her own thoughts and sent a thin line of calming power his way. He blinked in surprise then, as his eyes met hers, he gave her a slightly rueful smile before returning his attention inward, noticeably more composed.

Accepting a cup of rize chai laced with raki from a junior priest, she returned to her own thoughts, willing to allow herself one moment of petty satisfaction at his inexperience while, around her, the rest of Incasa's temple-seers now took their places as the first note of Havo's Evening Invocation signaled the beginning of nightfall.

✦

Beneath Lazim-Hisar, Graize stood as the dusk fell about him like a shroud. The Godling awakened at once and, with a flick of his wrist, Graize sent It shooting out into the air to ride the wind of the coming storm before turning to rouse his kazakin.

And in Kaptin Haldin's shrine, Spar felt rather than heard the first note of Havo's priests echoing through his mind like a call to arms. Rising, he crossed the room, Jaq at his heels, to prod Brax with one sandaled toe.

"Come on. We're going."

Opening his eyes at once, Brax nodded.

The lower level corridors were dark and deserted, the click of Jaq's toenails as he followed obediently behind them the only sound to be heard.

"Everyone's in place," Brax said hoarsely and Spar could see the effort it took him not to turn toward the wide, marble stairwell that led up to the Infantry shrines. "I can feel it. Kemal and Yashar and the others. I can even feel Marshal Brayazi and Kaptin Liel waiting for Estavia to call them."

"We'll be in place long before that happens," the younger boy assured him. "This way."

He led him deeper into the temple proper, following one of the more narrow corridors he'd discovered that summer. It made its way due east, past a series of storerooms and wine cellars until it opened up into an octagonal atrium where the white, marble walls gave way to the hard, gray stone of the outer defenses. From there, he took a winding stairway that led up to a small, wooden door at the top. It was so like the one they'd entered a year ago that he froze suddenly, the memory of the terrible swarm of spirits that had attacked them on Liman-Caddesi causing the breath to catch in his throat. The overwhelming savagery of their hunger washed over him once again, but just before their icy, clawed fingers touched his flesh, Jaq shoved his nose into his palm, jerking him back to the present. With an angry gesture, he shoved the door open with more force than he'd intended. The wind caught it, sending it slamming against the wall, and Brax shot him an exasperated glance before he retrieved it, closing it carefully behind them. Spar paid it no heed, merely moved cautiously to the edge of the battlements before turning his whitewashed gaze to the western horizon.

Day had become dusk since they'd entered Kaptin Haldin's shrine, the air turned a dark, sickly-green and smelling of death. As the wind sent a scattering of fine rain mixed with ice pellets scoring across his face, he felt Brax crouch down, his back against the sentry box wall. Jaq began to whine gently, and he dropped his hand down to stroke the animal's great head as he stared past Estavia's statue and Her temple turrets to Anavatan, feeling the hungry anticipation of those spirits that had managed to worm their way through the cracks in the God-Wall, pooling in the shadowy crevices of the city like a liquid fungus.

He bared his teeth at them, his momentary lapse of resolve forgotten. Last year he'd been too young to do anything more than watch helplessly as they'd consumed everything in their path; this year he was no longer young and no longer helpless. The spirits would do well to realize that.

They seemed to understand his thoughts, hunkering down in their shadowy hiding places each time he turned his baleful regard on them, but that wouldn't last, he knew. Soon the God of Prophecy would make His move and they would boil out of their refuge like a plague of locusts.

Raising his face to the wind, Spar smiled suddenly. Incasa wasn't the only Deity poised to act this night and, although he knew the God of Prophecy had taken that into account, he also knew that Gods, like spirits and people, too, for that matter, were greedy and usually acted in their own self-interest if given half a chance. A good lifter knew how to exploit that to his own advantage.

"Greedy people are careless but they're also really ugly if they catch you lifting their shine, so you gotta be careful and you gotta be fast. Use the crowds; keep hidden."

Spar smiled. He was always careful and he was always hidden.

Sending his mind out on the wind, he felt the dusk pressing eagerly against the day. The Evening Invocations were nearly finished; at Havo-Sarayi the priests had turned to their revelry, knowing that the Seasonal God drew strength from their celebrations, Oristo's people stood by their hearths, and Usara's in their infirmaries, both continuing songs of power that could invoke their Gods at the slightest hint of danger. The Warriors of Estavia were still locked in the throes of their own God's violent embrace; Spar could tell that simply by glancing over to gauge the growing barge-poled expression on Brax's face. Ystazia's people would be next and finally Incasa's, and then it would begin. Returning his gaze to the dark waters below, he felt the God of Prophecy stir as His priests prepared to bring the power of their minds together as one.

✦

In the arzhane, Bessic stood when Ystazia's song finished. Raising his arms, he tipped his head back, and taking a deep breath, sounded the full bass note that began Incasa's High Seeking, rather than the traditional Evening Invocation. One by one, the God of Prophecy's seers added their voices to his from every rural and urban cami along the lakeshores.

And as they sounded the note that would release the night, the sun vanished below the horizon, the night rushed forward, and the surface of Gol-Beyaz exploded as the great green-and-brown-mottled God of the Seasons shot into the air. Hair writhing in the wind, Havo cut a great swath across the sky, then streaked down to land on the western walls of Anavatan with a sound like a thunderclap.

Below, a huge mass of spirits flung themselves at the God-Wall, hammering, squirming, and fighting to join those that had already begun to boil up from the cobblestone streets, urged on by Graize standing now and screaming in triumph at the feet of Lazim-Hisar.

The veins standing out in his neck like streaks of fire, the First Oracle sang out the bass note once again. Glutted with power, Incasa reared up from the waves like an icy sea serpent. As the spirits broke through the wall of power, the God of Prophecy hurled his dice into their midst.

The mass of spirits exploded over the city before suddenly being sucked into a narrow God-wrought channel leading straight to Estavia-Sarayi.

✦

On the battlements Brax threw his shield up instinctively as the force of the explosion flung him against the wall, but Spar, his face twisted into a mask of hate and rage, threw his arms into the air to welcome the storm's power. It broke over their heads with a ferocity matched only by the four remaining Gods who burst from Gol-Beyaz to defend Their city. As Estavia rose above Her temple in all Her feral glory, Brax swept his sword into the air, screaming out his oaths to Her. The Battle God's responding jolt of power shot down the blade and into his arm, outlining him in a spray of crimson light. As the spirits swarmed over the battlements toward Gol-Beyaz, he threw himself in front of them.

Once again, he stood before an army of sharp-clawed creatures of power and need, once again they came at him in twos and threes and tens and hundreds, and once again he slaughtered them all. Their ravaged potential rained down around him in a shower of blood-soaked silver ash, blinding him with its brilliance and filling him with a vitality so pure it threatened to tear him to pieces, but he never faltered. He was Estavia's Champion and he would not allow Her enemies to reach the lake of power. As gouts of red-and-golden fire began to stream from his mouth and nose, he screamed out his challenge to any who would oppose him.

But this time it was the Godling who accepted it. Streaking from the clouds above, It slammed into him with a force that nearly knocked him off the wall, sucking up the streams of power as fast as they emerged. Lightning cracked above them and, for a single heartbeat the half born God and half grown Champion hung suspended as if they were recorded in Ystazia's secret book already, but then, as the Godling made to drive its teeth into Brax's throat, Spar threw his great, black net between them, destroying the tableau.

"No! You won't take him," he shouted. "None of you will!"

The wind rose to a screaming crescendo as the Godling spun about, shrieking in fury, but Spar stood his ground, deliberately staring into Its blazing eyes, willing It to look deep into the dark place where he held dominion despite Gods and priests and oracles, willing It to see, to remember, the trap he'd once sprung on It before the black tower beyond Orzin-Hisar. The Godling froze, but as Brax swung his sword, Incasa turned to flick a single vision toward Graize with one fine-boned finger.

The world seemed to slow.

Beneath Lazim-Hisar, Graize was suddenly consumed by the vision of Brax and Spar destroying everything he'd spent the last year building. With a scream of rage, he summoned his army of spirits to him. They surrounded him like a swarm of locusts, catching up his arms and legs and flinging him into the air as they had so many months before on Liman-Caddesi. But this time they served under his command, hurling him up and over the battlements toward his most hated adversary.

Brax met him with a scream of his own.

Close to a full manifestation now, the Godling began to shimmer with a silvery-red glow as It slowly and almost painfully began to push Its way into the physical realm. Still latched onto Brax like a giant leech, It continued to suck greedily at the gouts of power that spewed from his chest. Spar leaped forward, but was suddenly thrown aside by Incasa Himself, rising up between them like a furious leviathan, His long, white hair writhing about his head like so many sea snakes. As Spar's head hit the wall of the sentry box with a crack, Freyiz's voice sounded in his mind.

"A child of great potential still unformed standing on the streets of Ana-vatan. The twin dogs of creation and destruction crouch at its feet. The child is ringed by silver swords and golden knives and its eyes are filled with fire. It draws strength from Anavatan's unsworn and will be born tonight under the cover of Havo's Dance."

And then a voice as cold as the deepest waters of Gol-Beyaz sounded in his head.

"THE GOD-WALL CANNOT HOLD FOREVER. EACH TIME IT FALLS, THE SPIRITS MUST BE BROUGHT INTO BEING AS A GOD AND THIS GOD MUST TAKE ITS PLACE IN GOL-BEYAZ TO SAVE THE FUTURE."

The words crashed over him, threatening to engulf his mind, but suddenly he found himself plunged deep into the past where the belea-guered Gol-Yearli prayed to their Gods for protection against their enemies. A priest of Ystazia crouched, bloody and dazed, on a corpse-littered battlefield recording the sight of Kaptin Haldin and Marshal Nurcan standing on the site that would some day become Ana-vatan, Incasa hovering like a great white bird above them, and a creature of unformed potential waiting to be born, a creature made of spirits surrounded by silver swords and golden knives, imprinted on a warrior who would one day command a temple, and brought into the world by the power of a Champion. A creature who would become Estavia, God of Battles.

"And, just as the God draws strength from the deeds we perform in life, so does She draw strength from our deaths. In this, She is the God of Death. It is Her domain."

Yashar's deep, comforting voice calmed him, but then he was standing on the bloodstained cobblestones of Liman-Caddesi, staring down at Drove's dead body as Incasa's voice rang in his ears once more.

"A FEW MUST ALWAYS BE SACRIFICED TO SAVE THE REST."

And once again, Spar watched as a swarm of spirits caught Drove up in a deadly enveloping shroud, flinging him about like a rag doll, leaping upon his back and neck and sucking greedily at his body like huge, misty lampreys, then flinging his corpse into the street. But just as they reached for him, the vision became the memory of the city guards dragging Cindar's body away, his staring eyes half concealed by a mat of shadowy gore-soaked hair, blood on their weapons and blood on the suddenly misty ground.

On the suddenly misty ground.

Then the battlements of Orzin-Hisar rose up before his mind's eye and Chian, already dying, drew Spar's mind up from the dark place as the Godling fled into the clouds, trailing a line of crimson blood.

Trailing Chian's blood. Trailing Chian's death.

Drove and Cindar and Chian.

"Sometimes when the God requires it, we gift Them strength in the form of pure power."

"The Gods only care about the Sworn."

"NO LITTLE SEER, THE GODS CARE FOR ALL THE PEOPLE. IT'S WHAT WE DO."

"Unwilling followers bring the Gods no strength."

Raiders from the north, Petchans from the south, Yuruk from the west, and the spirits of the wild lands attacking the people of the shining city and their villages year after year. And, as the people stood before the waters of Gol-Beyaz, their prayers formed the lake spirits into six beings of protection and power.

A child of unformed potential . . .

A child of unformed spirits, if left to fight and feed unchecked would overwhelm the wall and the people. A child who would take form by imprinting on Graize and be molded into a controllable form by the deaths of Drove and Cindar and Chian.

And now Brax.

Before him, the older boy's life began to falter and Spar struggled to his feet.

Not Brax.

Standing, Spar reached into the dark place and, pulling out another memory from Liman-Caddesi, hurled it into the wind with a strength he didn't know he possessed.

Brax's words took form, blazoning across the sky like a beacon.

"Save us, God of Battles, and I will pledge you my life, my worship, AND MY LAST DROP OF BLOOD, FOREVER!"

And the God of Battles responded as She had a year ago.

Swinging Her great swords in the air, Estavia leaped forward and dealt the Godling a blow that would have decapitated It had it been anything other than immortal. It went spinning off into the air, only to turn and hurl Itself back at them, misty claws outstretched like an enraged eagle's.

Spent now, Brax crumpled, his sword ringing against the stone, and Spar pushed himself up on one hand and flung his net toward their attacker. The black tendrils wrapped about the Godling like strands of sticky sea grass, but almost fully manifested, It shredded them with a single gesture, then streaked toward the two boys once again. But, standing guard over Her Champion's prone body, Estavia met It with an explosion of power that burst outward to impact against the armory tower. As bricks and stone rained down upon the courtyard below, Spar began to frantically rebuild his net of darkness into a heavy bow and arrow, strand by strand, working as quickly as his split focus would allow.

But Graize was also scrabbling to come to the Godling's aid. Leaping to the top of the battlement wall, he flung his mind outward.

"Swallow!" he screamed.

Below, Danjel's body snapped into a masculine form, his eyes rolling back in his head, as the power of his wild-land blood was suddenly absorbed into Graize's own.

"Nightingale and fox!"

Ozan began a screaming, discordant song of power, while Kursk sliced through his knots with his kinjal, sending a hurtling mass of spirits racing up the wall to merge with the Godling Itself.

"Marten!"

Claws and teeth and eyes glowing with a savage intelligence began to form on the Godling's features as Rayne sent her own budding power into the fray. The Godling rose up, blood-red eyes filled with strength and madness and, in a snarl of rage, Estavia called for Her own support.

In the Cyan Company shrine Kemal's head snapped back as the God of Battles sucked up the offered power of Her warriors in one breath and spewed it toward Her enemy in a gout of destructive power.

The Godling fell back before the onslaught, battered and frantic. It turned to flee, but Incasa brought His own people into the fray with a snap of His fingers. With the power of every seer behind Him, the God of Prophecy rose a thousand feet into the air, dwarfing temple, city, and Gods. Bending down, He caught up the Godling almost gently and then turned, and slammed It into Graize without warning. With one last unformed moment left before true manifestation, It caught him up in a smothering embrace for Its final imprinting and, his head tipped back in a parody of passion, Graize whispered one word.

"Mouse."

Caleb gave one piercing whistle that cut through the storm to dance across the sky and life flowed into the Godling's nearly physical form. But before It could rise, Spar stood, his eyes pooling with a mass of black flames, and shot a single shaft of darkness into the very center of Its forehead.

The impact sent Graize careening into Brax's arms as shards of power hurtled in every direction like a thousand wicked little knives. They shredded every remaining spirit for a hundred miles, and scored across the Gods, causing Ystazia and Usara to flee back into the cold depths of Gol-Beyaz. Havo exploded into the air, tearing through roofs and uprooting trees and Estavia pursued the maddened God of the Seasons, taking Them both down into the water as fires broke out across the city, heedless of the driving rain.

Meanwhile the Godling spun out of control, ricocheting from Graize's mind, to Danjel's, to Ozan's, Rayne's, and then to Caleb's. For a heartbeat the youngest of the kazakin was outlined in a blaze of burning glory until a piercing whistle jerked the Godling free and It was sucked into Kursk, tearing a savage hole through his mind. As blood sprayed from his kardos' mouth, Ozan screamed a single note of power into the air and the older man toppled into his arms, crushing his kopuz beneath him.

The Godling spun away to slam into Graize and Brax once more and Prophet, Champion, and Deity plunged into the water below. Incasa went spinning after them, but suddenly a break in the clouds caused a shaft of moonlight to fall upon Spar, standing on the wall, one hand raised high in the air to reveal Yashar's dice held almost negligently in his palm. As Incasa turned His snow-white gaze upon him, the boy stared back, the black tower in the dark place waiting behind his eyes.

"NOT BRAX," he grated.

For a heartbeat God and seer stared into each other's eyes, then Incasa raised His own pair of dice.

"FOR YOUR WORSHIP," He demanded.

Spar spat a curse back at Him. "GET STIFFED!"

"HE WILL DIE WITHOUT MY HELP."

"THE GODLING WON'T LIVE WITHOUT MINE."

Incasa's white eyes blazed, but then He tipped His great head in a veiled nod.

"YOU WILL NOT PUT MY CITY IN DANGER."

Spar's own eyes narrowed. "AND YOU WILL NOT PUT MY FAMILY IN DANGER."

"DONE."

Together they dropped their dice. They spun about like snowflakes in the wind. Then, just before they hit the churning waves below, Incasa's touched Oristo and the God who'd danced with Him across the vision-streets of Anavatan a year ago dove into the water. Spar's became a swirling vortex which sucked the Godling down into the dark place. The creature that exploded from the other side was like nothing the Gods of Gol-Beyaz had ever seen before.

"The best anyone can hope for is to die well."

As the shock waves tore through the streams, destroying and re-forming as many as they touched, Spar shook his head.

"No, the best anyone can hope for is to control death itself," he said quietly as the new God of Creation and Destruction rose above him like a dark tower wrapped in mist and shadow, then shot into the air and disappeared over the western plains. As Incasa streaked after It, Spar turned back to Gol-Beyaz.

"Nothing comes without a price, does it, Delon?"

Tanay's words flitted across his mind, and he smiled. "Not this time."

Jerking the bead from his hair, Spar dropped it over the wall, allowing himself a single hiss of indrawn breath as the power of his mind sent Jaq after it. As the dog hit the water, he swung his legs over the side and began his own swift but more controlled descent.

✦

A thousand stars exploded through Brax's mind as he hit the water, his armor dragging him down like a stone. As his breath froze in his lungs and his vision blurred, he suddenly smelled roses and lilies and saw a field of flowers the color of blood and gold strewn across a sunlit floor. Peering into the shining depths of Gol-Beyaz, he saw Estavia open Her ebony arms to him and felt the same peace and stillness he'd experienced during his first Morning Invocation. He reached out, but as he did so, his hand caught hold of Graize's sleeve and their future swept over him like the tide.

Once again he saw the enemies of Anavatan rise up. He saw himself a man, armed and armored, taking the field against them. He saw a figure on a white pony raise his hand in battle and knew it to be Graize, but Graize as he'd never seen him before, clear-eyed and armed with steel and stone. Together, they stood on a snowcapped mountain ridge overlooking a fleet of unfamiliar ships while a man in a red tower moved marble figurines on a board of mahogany and mist and a golden-haired woman danced in the surf.

Then the vision winked out, the cold of Gol-Beyaz rushed in, and the dark place rose up, promising the warmth and peace of Estavia's arms once more. But as he reached for Her again, a pulsing brown speck of power barred his way. He caught a fleeting glimpse of Spar, white-faced and angry, then both the bead about his neck and the four-legged stick figure ward upon his chest began to burn as a great, red body slammed into him. It drove the dark place away and he was struggling in the frigid waters of Gol-Beyaz once more.

This time, however, he was being propelled upward and, as his head broke the surface of the water, Spar's hand flew out to catch him by the hair and drag him up onto the rocky ground below the battlements. As Jaq scrambled up to lie exhausted beside them, Brax opened his eyes, staring past Spar's shoulder to the rising sun of Havo's First Morning.

✦

Brown eyes flashing in satisfaction, Oristo vanished into the waves.

Brax coughed weakly as the younger boy gathered him up in his arms almost gently.

"Is it over?" he asked.

Spar nodded.

"Did we do whatever it was you wanted us to?"

"Are you alive?"

"I think so."

"Then we did it."

"I . . . hurt everywhere."

"Beats the alternative."

"Does it?"

"Don't be an idiot."

Brax sighed. "Can we go back inside now?" he asked plaintively.

"We have to wait for Kemal and Yashar."

"Why?"

" 'Cause we can't fly," Spar answered, indicating Estavia-Sarayi's huge eastern wall behind them.

"Oh. Are they coming for us?"

His eyes the color of snow on the distant mountains of Brax's vision, Spar nodded. "They are now."

"What about Graize?"

The younger boy's eyes darkened again almost imperceptibly. "What about him?" he demanded.

"Where is he?"

"I don't care." He tipped his head to one side. "Why? Do you?"

Shivering with a sudden chill, Brax nodded. "I didn't think I would . . ." He trailed off. "But I think . . . he's important."

With an explosive snort, Spar allowed a dark mist to pass across his eyes for an instant. "He's alive," he said tersely.

"Are you sure?"

"Well, he's not dead, so that only leaves one other possibility, doesn't it?"

"Says you."

"Yeah, says me. I'm the wise seer, you're the idiot champion, re-member."

"Point."

"Right, point, so shut up and try to sleep. It'll take our abayon a little while to find a boat."

"All right." Brax closed his eyes, then opened them again with a start. "Spar?"

"What?"

"I lost my sword."

"Good."

"Spar . . ."

"It'll turn up."

"Promise?"

"Sure."

"I need it."

"I know." As the twin images of a golden sun and a tall red tower wavered before his eyes, Spar leaned his back against Jaq's wet flank with a frown. "We all do."

✦

Across the strait, hidden by the dawn mist and the strength of her prophecy, Panos of Amatus held Graize in her arms while Hares rowed past Anavatan's great watchtowers. Graize lay unconscious under a thick woolen blanket, his broken mind staring out at a deep, dark place where Spar smiled out at him, daring him to enter. The ruins of all he'd struggled to rebuild since the spirits of the Berbat-Dunya had stolen his life away lay stretched out before him in a sea of ash and blood and emptiness, while behind the younger seer a woman who might have been his long dead abia beckoned him, promising peace and warmth. He almost gave in to it, but then the featherlight touch of his Godling stroked across his mind and he sank back with an almost painful sigh of relief. He wasn't alone. He could still win the game. Closing his eyes, he reached out for his own prophecy.

A hundred ships made their way north from the Deniz-Hadi and a hundred more south from the Deniz-Siyah. A dark-haired man stood beside him, while another stood against him, and a great black tower battled the Gods of Gol-Beyaz in a shower of blood and gold.

"Blood and gold feed the people," he whispered.

✦

Making their way up the Halic-Salmanak, the kazakin paused as the voice of their young wyrdin whispered through their minds.

"Have faith, stay strong, and look for me when five new lambing seasons have come and gone. Together we will ride the storm that finally destroys the power of Anavatan forever."

Glancing over the heads of Rayne and Caleb holding the body of their aba, Danjel caught Ozan's eye. For a moment the two, of them considered the possibility of refusal, then nodded. The Yuruk had fought the Gods for centuries, five more years made little difference.

✦

At Incasa-Sarayi, Freyiz wiped the blood from her First Oracle's face with an unreadable expression as she, too, felt the streams rejoin for a five-year span. She sent the image to Her God and Incasa agreed. Five years would be just enough time to plan.

Rising from the depths, the God of Chance hovered above the western docks, watching a small white cat playing in the water, a featherlight creature of dark power dancing just out of the reach of its swatting paw. Incasa showed His teeth at the comparison. The God of Creation and Destruction had been born, and although It was not yet under control, It soon would be.

Breathing in a trickle of power, Incasa reached into the future and drew out a single form, then spoke one word.

"HISAR."

✦

On the surface of the water, a God named for a tower turned Its icy, black eyes on Its most powerful abayos before shooting up into the air to rejoin Its kindred above the Berbat-Dunya. Incasa and the white cat shared a glance then, as the God of Prophecy returned to the depths, the cat returned its attention to a sand crab hiding in the surf.